Acclaim for Jenny B. Jones

"There are few things I love more than curling up with a Jenny B. Jones cast of characters. *Save the Date* was no exception . . ."

—KRISTIN BILLERBECK, AUTHOR OF *A BILLION REASONS WHY*

"I *loved Save the Date!* Jenny B. Jones infuses the story with her trademark wit and sass, and has written a brilliant book with so many layers, I savored each one. This novel stayed with me long after I read it, the highest compliment I can pay an author."

—KATHLEEN FULLER, BEST-SELLING AUTHOR OF *A MAN OF HIS WORD* AND *A HAND TO HOLD*

"At turns sweet and funny, poignant and gripping, *Save the Date* is a wonderful smile-inducing read lovingly stitched together with a message of God's tender grace. Readers should definitely save the date for this latest offering from Jenny B. Jones."

—TAMARA LEIGH, BEST-SELLING, AWARD-WINNING AUTHOR OF *SPLITTING HARRIET*

". . . If you love novels with real characters wrestling with life and faith while they find love, this is the book for you. Add in heaping doses of humor that will leave you laughing even after you've closed the book, and you have the perfect recipe for a Jenny B. Jones romance and a book you will think about long after the last page."

—CARA C. PUTMAN, AUTHOR OF *STARS IN THE NIGHT*

"NOOOOOO . . . the word I wanted to scream when I came to the end of *Save the Date* . . . *Save the Date* is lively, funny, kind, romantic, unbelievably charming with a few twists that delighted and surprised me . . ."

—TANDEM

"For sassy, romantic banter, you need look no further than the novels of Jenny B. Jones ... If you're a fan of Jones's young adult novels, you're in for a treat—her novels for adults are even better."

—TRISH PERRY, AUTHOR OF *THE PERFECT BLEND*

"I stayed up late and got up early to read this book. *Save the Date* has sass, spirit, laughter, tears—buy this book. You. Will. Love. It."

—KIMBERLY STUART, AUTHOR OF *OPERATION BONNET*, *STRETCH MARKS*, AND *ACT TWO*

"Jenny B. Jones has done it again! *Save the Date* is a delightful story featuring quirky characters and just the right mix of humor and romance. You will laugh, cry, and think more deeply about what's truly important in life. Readers who enjoyed *Just Between You and Me* will love this new story."

—CARRIE TURANSKY, AUTHOR OF *SEEKING HIS LOVE* AND *CHRISTMAS MAIL-ORDER BRIDES*

Save the
Date

Save the Date

JENNY B. JONES

Thomas Nelson
Since 1798

NASHVILLE   DALLAS   MEXICO CITY   RIO DE JANEIRO

Published in Nashville, Tennessee, by Thomas Nelson. Thomas Nelson is a registered trademark of Thomas Nelson, Inc.

Thomas Nelson, Inc., titles may be purchased in bulk for educational, business, fund-raising, or sales promotional use. For information, please e-mail SpecialMarkets@ThomasNelson.com.

Publisher's Note: This novel is a work of fiction. Names, characters, places, and incidents are either products of the author's imagination or used fictitiously. All characters are fictional, and any similarity to people living or dead is purely coincidental.

Scripture references are taken from the HOLMAN CHRISTIAN STANDARD BIBLE. Copyright © 1999, 2000, 2002, 2003 by Broadman and Holman Publishers, Nashville, Tennessee. All rights reserved.

Author photograph taken by Belinda Robbins.

Library of Congress Cataloging-in-Publication Data

Jones, Jenny B., 1975–
  Save the date / Jenny B. Jones.
    p. cm.
  ISBN 978-1-59554-539-8 (softcover)
  1. Weddings—Planning—Fiction. I. Title.
PS3610.O6257S28 2011
813'.6—dc22
                                      2010043888

Printed in the United States of America

11 12 13 14 15 RRD 6 5 4 3 2 1

Saving Grace, a home for young women who have graduated from the foster care system, is a real place. With real girls. With real hopes and dreams. This book is dedicated to them.

You are an inspiration. We are all so excited for your futures. I admire the women you are, as well as the women God is shaping you to be. Never give up. Never lose hope. Never stop dreaming. And never stop reminding the world that our work has only begun. You are worthy, you are beautiful, you are . . . amazing.

. . . But one thing I do: forgetting what is behind and reaching forward to what is ahead, I pursue as my goal the prize promised by God's heavenly call in Christ Jesus.

—Philippians 3:13, 14

Prologue

*I*t was a good night to get engaged.

The moon was full. The candles lit. And Lucy Wiltshire wore a new black sheath that would have made Audrey Hepburn jealous. Her friends might say it was just another old find from the secondhand shop, but Lucy had known from the moment she'd spied the dress that it had been something more. Found on a tightly crammed rack between an avocado peacoat and an acid-washed denim skirt that had seen one too many Bon Jovi concerts, the dress had just called out to her. *Buy me. I'm yours. We belong together.*

And buy it she did. Despite the fact that the bodice was a bit tight, and she'd had to let out the waist a few inches, the dress just felt right. It made Lucy want to twirl in her tiny kitchen, letting her kitten heels slide across the gray tile floor.

It was the perfect outfit to wear when getting proposed to. She had dreamed of this day since she was six and had thrown a wedding for Barbie. And now her own Ken doll was four feet away, acting nervous as a man with marriage on his mind and a solitaire in his pocket.

Matthew tugged his navy tie loose and sat down at the kitchen table.

"Good day?" Lucy asked, as she put some garlic bread in the oven, humming to herself.

"It was fine." His voice was distracted, his focus on the stack of mail she had yet to move. "What's this?" He held up a gold embellished card.

She glanced his way then quickly turned back to the oven. "It's nothing."

"It looks like a class reunion invitation. I thought you didn't graduate in Charleston."

Her childhood in South Carolina was the last thing she wanted to discuss tonight. Or ever. "Obviously it's a mistake on someone's part." Or a cruel joke. The daughter of a maid, Lucy had been on the very bottom of the social food chain at the elite Montrose Academy. Her mother had cleaned the homes of her classmates. And they had never let her forget Lucy wasn't one of them. But now, back in Charleston, life couldn't be sweeter.

"Or maybe they just want to see you."

Lucy sat down and stared at the man who had asked her out one year ago today. Matt's fingers drumming next to his plate seemed out of sync for someone who was normally as calm as a morning sunrise. She adored his predictability. His sandy-blond hair always parted to the left. His white shirts starched and perfectly creased in the sleeves.

The timer over the stove dinged, and Lucy jumped up to take out the bread. "I hope you're hungry. I made your favorites."

"I noticed."

Lucy threw the bread in a basket and placed it on the table. Grabbing his plate, she loaded it with her homemade noodles, her own secret-recipe marinara sauce, and a salad—easy on the dressing, just like he liked. Lucy could envision them sitting together thirty years from now, sharing a meal and talking about their day.

"Maybe you should go to the reunion." Matt neatly placed his napkin in his lap. "If you're wanting to start that girls' home, you're going to need to rub elbows with as many people in the community as you can."

Lucy watched him as she sat down. "I'll get the funding from somewhere else. That's what federal grants are for. And besides, it's the same night as your award ceremony."

Matt was going to be honored for his charity work with senior citizens. An accountant, he had donated countless hours helping the older folks in Charleston with their taxes and providing free financial counseling. Every day she gave God a big "thank you" for sending Matt her way. He was . . . perfect.

He called his mother twice a week. He led a Bible study and played on a baseball league at church. He read autobiographies and watched CNBC. The guy drove a Volvo. What more could she ask for?

"Lucy?" Matt's face was taut as he reached for her hand.

This was it. She was going to become Mrs. Matthew Campbell. She hoped her lip gloss was still on. And where had she put that camera? If any occasion called for a "extend arm and take your own photo," this was it.

He swallowed and folded his fingers over hers. "I have something I need to talk to you about."

Her vision blurred with unshed tears. They would have a boy and a girl. They'd name the girl Anna, after her mother. He could name the boy. It didn't really matter to her. As long as it wasn't Maynard. After that uncle he liked so much.

"Lucy, we've been together a while now."

"A year," she said. "Our first date was a year today." Which was all part of his thoughtful plan.

His grip loosened on her hand. "And it's been great. I've enjoyed our time together. And I think you are one incredible person."

Matt reached into his pocket.

The ring. He was going for the ring. Marquis, pear, princess, round—she didn't care.

"Matt"—Lucy sniffed—"I want you to know I'm so happy God put you in my life and—"

He opened his hand.

And placed a business card on the table.

Lucy's pink lips clamped tight. Those were not wedding bells pealing in her head right now.

"What is this?" She picked up the card. "Matthew Campbell, senior accountant, Digby, Wallace, and Hinds?"

His smile was hesitant. "I got a job offer."

"Offer?" She ran her finger over his embossed name. "Looks like you've already progressed beyond that. When were you going to tell me?"

"I've tried." He pushed his plate aside. "You've just been so busy with the shelter."

"Residential home," she corrected. "Saving Grace is a residential home."

"You've been so occupied with getting that started, I haven't been able to get your attention lately."

"You've got it now." Something was very wrong here. "What's going on? I've never heard of these people. Are they new?"

His green eyes focused on the candle in the center of the table. "No. They're quite old, in fact. Very prestigious."

"And *where* are they old and prestigious?" She couldn't relocate. He knew that. Not with mere months before Saving Grace opened. Was he going to move—without her?

"In Dallas."

Lucy's heart fell somewhere to the vicinity of her shoes. "When are you leaving?"

He closed his eyes. "I'm sorry, Lucy."

"You're going to have to do better than that."

"I think we've been moving too fast."

Lucy thought of the bridal magazines under her bed. "Then let's slow it down. I'm okay with that. I think if we just—"

"I'm leaving next week. This is an opportunity I can't pass up." He spoke low and patiently, as if talking to a child. "I think we need to take a break. My relocating is the perfect opportunity to give ourselves some space and see what happens."

The white-picket fence was collapsing before her. *Was it too much to ask, God? Was it too much to want a family of my own? To finally have that home?* For the first time in her life, she had let herself believe she could have it all.

Her laugh sounded pitiful and strained. "Can you believe"—tears clogged her throat—"that I thought you were going to propose tonight?"

Matt stood up, walked over to her, and kissed her forehead. "I think I should probably go."

She grabbed his hand as he leaned away. "Is it me?" Because wasn't it always her?

Reaching out, he pushed a stray curl behind her ear. "No. I know you're ready for a permanent commitment, but I have to put my career first now—whether I want to or not."

The smells in the room—the food, her life decaying—made her want to throw up. "I could wait, you know. We could do the long distance thing."

"I'm sorry." He grabbed his jacket from the back of the chair. "For what it's worth, I believe you're the right girl—it's just not the right time."

Two minutes later Lucy stood in her living room and watched Matt drive away.

No ring. No engagement.

No happily ever after.

She walked upstairs to her bedroom.

Sucked it in as she unzipped the Audrey Hepburn dress.

Peeled it off her body.

And threw it out the window.

Chapter One

Two years later

Outside the birds sang happy little tunes as they sat on magnolia limbs old enough to have shaded Robert E. Lee. The May sunshine hovered over treetops and steeples, sending the good people of Charleston away from their porches and inside to the cool. Saving Grace occupied an old home downtown, wedged in tight next to an Italian restaurant that put out more than its share of trash and basil-scented air. But inside the house, Lucy sat in her swivel chair and wondered how many times a world could fall apart.

"I'm sorry, I don't think I heard you correctly." She stared at the slender woman sitting in her office.

"Sinclair Hotels will be cutting our funding to Saving Grace by forty percent, effective immediately."

Lucy had barely had time to put down her morning cup of coffee before the PR representative from Sinclair was knocking on her office door. Loosening the garage-sale Hermes scarf at her throat, Lucy tried to recall if she had put on deodorant that morning. It was all a blur. Surely she had. But she needed all her wits about her. And her Dry Idea.

"Miss Pierson," Lucy said. "I was promised this amount six months ago."

"Unfortunately, tough economic times sometimes necessitate cutbacks. I'm sure you understand." Miss Pierson speared her with a snotty gaze she had probably perfected in junior high. Lucy immediately had a memory of walking through the halls of her high school. The stares. The ridicule. Her classmates doing everything they could to make the poor scholarship girl feel inferior at that ridiculous private school her mother had made her attend. "Marcus Sinclair and the board are grieved over these decisions as well, which is why I was sent to personally deliver the news."

"And I am very grateful," Lucy managed to say. "Sinclair has been very generous. But if I can't guarantee the funds you initially quoted, I'll lose my federal and state grants."

"As you've probably read, Sinclair Hotels has suffered setbacks these last three years under the previous CEO. So Mr. Sinclair has come out of retirement and returned to the helm."

Miss Pierson had to be a size double zero. What a shame Sinclair didn't pay this woman enough to feed herself. Meanwhile Lucy's own size-ten skirt was about to cut her waist in two.

"Isn't there anyone I could talk to?" *Lord, help me be calm. Claiming your peace here. I'm breathing in. Breathing out. Breathing—oh, seriously, her arms are no bigger than toothpicks.*

"It was a board decision."

"Maybe I could speak with Mr. Sinclair?"

"That will not be possible. He's very busy with his duties as CEO, as well as campaigning for his son."

Lucy didn't even let herself think about Alex Sinclair, heir to the family fortune. Not that he needed anyone else's money. He had made his own as a quarterback for the New York Warriors. And she had gone to school with him, though she had been a year behind him. If he was still treating people the way he'd treated her, it's a wonder someone hadn't smothered him with a jersey in his sleep.

"You are still invited to the gala Friday night." Miss Pierson's eyes flitted over the walls of Lucy's office. Decorated with black-and-white photos of past and present girls of Saving Grace, it wasn't exactly art. But to Lucy, the pictures were more precious than any Van Gogh.

Tomorrow was the annual event when she would normally receive her donation check, happily assured that Saving Grace would carry on another year. Girls getting their educations. Gaining employment skills. Having a roof over their heads. Now she didn't know how they would continue through the winter.

Miss Pierson stood, her body gracefully rising from the scarred wooden chair. "On behalf of Sinclair Hotels, we appreciate you letting us participate in serving our community." Offering her hand in a limp handshake, Miss Pierson gathered her purse and exited the small office.

Lucy's head dropped to her desk. "Why me?" There had to be something she could do. She couldn't just sit there and let Saving Grace die simply because of one donation, substantial though it was. *Lord, what am I going to do? I need some colossal help here.*

She returned to pounding her head and muttering.

"Is this a private mental breakdown or can anyone join?"

Lucy's blonde curls flounced as she sat at attention. "Hey." The sight of her best friend Morgan should've been a welcome comfort. But spotting a young woman standing behind Morgan, Lucy knew there would be no time for her to pour out her heart.

"I was just telling Marinell here what a calm, sane person you are." Morgan sat in the chair Miss Pierson had just vacated and motioned for the girl to take the other vacant seat. "But that's after you've had your coffee."

Lucy barely withheld a glare from her smiling friend. "I'm giving crazy a try today. And so far . . . I'm rather good at it." Lucy turned her attention to the girl who looked like a young Salma Hayek. "Hello, Marinell. I'm so glad you've decided to meet with me."

As the foster-care caseworker, Morgan had shared with Lucy the contents of Marinell's file. Age eighteen. Spent the last year and a half in four different foster homes, the last one being so difficult she had dissolved ties with the system and moved out on her own. Getting ready to repeat her senior year, Marinell was homeless and living who knew where on the streets.

"I told Ms. Morgan I would hear you out, but I don't plan on moving in," Marinell said. "I'm fine right where I'm at."

"And where is that again?" Lucy asked.

"With a relative."

Most of the girls they saw were so beaten down by their circumstances, they were almost afraid to hope there was something better. Lucy knew Marinell had no family in Charleston but her mom, whose parental rights had been dissolved. Her younger brother had yet to be placed and stayed in a boys' home. "A relative, huh?"

She shrugged. "A friend."

"Then I guess it's my job to convince you to stay." Which would be fine except for the small detail of Saving Grace closing down if Lucy didn't find some financial support. "Morgan went over the expectations, right?" Marinell just stared in response. "We're a faith-based operation here. You simply have to go to school, work hard, and follow our rules." There were curfews, Bible studies, life-skill classes, and responsibilities in the house that the girls had to adhere to. Between Lucy and the two resident assistants, a supervising adult was always at Saving Grace, making sure the rules were followed.

She and Morgan worked closely together. As a caseworker for the county, Morgan had contact with girls who had aged out of the foster-care system. Once they were eighteen and out of school, the state considered them adults. Saving Grace provided transitional housing for those with nowhere to go. While the state provided some assistance until they turned twenty-one, few young adults took advantage of it and simply struck out on their own. And with foster kids far outnumbering willing homes, the chances for a kid to be out on the streets was shockingly high. It was a national epidemic that the average citizen knew nothing about, and the injustice never failed to light the fuse of Lucy's temper.

Morgan would expect Lucy to give the girl the selling points. "Why don't we take a tour?"

"I guess."

Leaving Morgan behind in the office, Lucy and Marinell started down the hall. Lucy brought her to the spacious living room first. "We had a large church group help out with the décor. This is where all the girls hang out and watch movies or do homework. We have a Bible study here every Wednesday night." From the hardwood floor to the teal lamps, the room was like something out of a Pottery Barn catalog. Lucy forced away the thoughts of losing it all. Too much work had gone into making this space a home.

"It's nice."

Lucy saw her eyeing the flat-screen TV over the fireplace. "The girls just got a Wii donated, so we've been having some serious bowling competitions this week." Pleased she got at least a faint smile out of Marinell, Lucy moved on. "We have two halls of bedrooms. Each one has been adopted by a community member and professionally decorated. No two rooms are the same."

Lucy flipped the light of one bedroom and walked inside.

Marinell couldn't hide the surprise on her face. "I never seen anything like it."

"It's cool, huh? This is our last room left."

Marinell ran her hand over the cream-colored duvet, then the printed green pillows.

"So tell me about your family." Every girl that came through Lucy's doors had a story.

Marinell studied an M. C. Escher print on the wall. "My mom moved here a few years ago. My brother got sick and she lost her job. When one of my teachers found out we didn't have a place to live, the state took us."

"And where's your father?"

"Gone." Marinell shrugged as if it were no big deal. "Do you feed us here?"

"Yes. And you get to learn how to cook." Thanks to a handful of community volunteers, the girls got trained in various life skills, like preparing a healthy dinner and balancing a checkbook.

Walking back down the hall, Lucy could hardly make the necessary small talk for her racing mind. She needed time. There were people to call, companies to contact. She had to find new donors. And quickly.

Lucy guided her back into the office, but Marinell stopped just inside. "What's that?" Marinell pointed to a series of worn indentions in the sun-bleached wooden floor.

"Saving Grace was a convent until about five years ago." The thought always made her heart warm. "This is where the nuns prayed. Those dents there? That's from many hours on their knees."

"You serious?"

Lucy nodded. "I'd like to think the sisters would be proud of what we do here. Those marks in the floor remind me that I can't solve anything without putting my own time in on my knees."

"My mom and dad are Catholic. Um, I mean my mom is."

"But you're not?" Lucy asked.

Marinell looked away from the floor. "I'm not anything."

Lucy exchanged a look with Morgan before handing Marinell her card. "This is how you can reach me. If you need anything, give me a call—night or day." Pressing it in Marinell's hand, Lucy felt the warmth of the girl's skin, the life that pulsed beneath it. *God, help me save this one.* "We'd like Saving Grace to be your home, Marinell." She smiled into the girl's weary eyes. "And we'd like to be your family."

"Do you know how many people have said that to me?" Marinell's chin lifted in challenge. "I need someone who's gonna come through for once. I don't want this to be just another place that lets me down."

Morgan smiled. "Then I've brought you to the right place." Lucy listened to her best friend's words and willed herself not to burst into tears. "I promise, Lucy won't let you down."

Chapter Two

Y ou really shouldn't go to this gala, Lucy." Morgan stuck her head into the bathroom for the fifth time. Lucy's apartment was slowly filling up with friends who were there for a Dr. Who marathon. Though Morgan was hosting, the Hobbits always met at their home base—Lucy's apartment. Officially the Hobbits gathered twice a month to discuss the latest books, movies, and anything else remotely resembling fantasy or science fiction. Unofficially, they hung out all the time.

"She's right." Chuck, Morgan's fiancé, ambled in from the crowded living room and leaned into the bathroom. "There's a fine line between nagging and stalking."

Lucy closed her compact with a snap and regarded them both. "I'm not going to hide in anyone's backseat. I just want to have a calm discussion with a few of the Sinclair board members."

They were an odd bunch—Morgan, Chuck, and the group eating pizza rolls in the living room. It was Morgan who had been her first friend after Lucy had returned to South Carolina three years ago. And when Morgan had introduced Lucy to the Hobbits, Lucy had felt like she belonged for the first time in her life.

After graduating from college in Florida, Lucy had remained in the state working for the Department of Human Services. Three years on the job, and a routine visit had taken her to a home like Saving

Grace. She had walked inside a caseworker, but walked out a woman with a purpose and an unmistakable call on her life. And even though she hadn't planned to return to Charleston, God had lined everything up and all but shoved her on the plane.

Glancing at her phone, Lucy checked the time. "I need to get going." She edged past her friends and into her small living room.

"Lucy, you're looking ravishing tonight." Sanjay, a fellow Hobbit, stood a little too close to her and visibly sniffed near her perfumed neck. By day, Sanjay worked in IT. But at least twice a month he put in overtime as Lucy's own harmless stalker.

"I can't stay." She smiled at the small assembly of friends around her. "I have . . . a thing."

"I make a great date for"—Sanjay slowly lifted one dark brow—"things."

"Please reconsider, Lucy. Or at least let us go with you," Morgan said, elbowing Chuck.

"Uh, yeah." He sounded about as interested as Lucy would be in sports. "We'd love to go to your swanky party."

"No offense, guys, but you'll just get in my way." She tugged at the waist of her dress. It seemed to have shrunk since she last tried it on. "I have a strategy for tonight. I owe it to the girls to give this one last try, and for that I need to stay focused."

Sanjay was not the most energetic of suitors. "And my nearby hotness would be a distraction."

She stifled an eye roll and sidestepped him toward the door.

Morgan followed Lucy to the door. "Have you at least rehearsed what you're going to say?"

"Something along the lines of 'twelve young women will be homeless because of your decisions.'" Lucy tapped her phone. "I also thought I'd show them some pictures. Let them see the girls they're kicking to the streets."

Chuck nodded solemnly. "This moment totally calls for light sabers."

"You should've updated me on the donation situation *before* I all but told Marinell you had a bedroom waiting for her," Morgan said.

She couldn't think about that now. Tonight was about a solution.

It was times like these Lucy wished she could pick up the phone and call her mother. Lucy had been eighteen when she'd died, leaving a gaping hole in her heart. Sometimes she even let herself wonder what her life would be like if her father was still alive. Lucy had never even met him. She only had two photos of him, but she imagined he would've loved her. Provided them with a happy home. If he were alive right now, he'd probably invite her over for grilled steaks and give her loving advice over the smoke from his Weber grill.

"Let me pray for you—in case you don't make it back alive." Chuck threw an arm around her as he cleared his throat and found his youth-pastor voice. "Lord, we ask that you protect Lucy as she speaks with the board members. We ask for you to change their minds. And if that's not possible, we pray that you'd open a door for the home that only you can open. Oh, and that Lucy would stay calm. And not get arrested. Amen."

Lucy lifted her head. "I promise if I need any backup, I'll call."

"Go get 'em, girl." With his Big Mac body, Chuck wrapped all three of them in a group hug. "And may the force be with you."

∽

Lucy's hands shook as she smoothed them over her little black dress, a taffeta number with beaded straps she'd found at a new resale shop near the mall. The classic A-line had a slenderizing effect and didn't seem to scream, "I'm allergic to working out!"

Okay, Lucy. Get your game face on. There is work to be done. A girls' home to save. Board members to harass. Lord, I seriously need some help here.

As she looked around the ballroom at the crème de la crème of South Carolina, she struggled to draw a deep breath. She was a cubic zirconium in a sea of diamonds.

Lucy wove through the crush of people, her mind spinning with thoughts of her girls, her money woes, and the latest *Star Wars* novel that patiently waited for her on her bedside table.

"Lucy Wiltshire."

She turned at the nasally voice.

Ugh, not now. She didn't have time for this. "Hey, Bianca."

Bianca Drummond sashayed toward Lucy, her designer dress sparkling under the ballroom lights. A staple at all Charleston society events, Bianca could trace her wealthy family back to the Mayflower. And she made sure everyone knew it.

"How are you?" Her mouth moved into a pout as she flicked her long platinum hair away from her perfectly rounded chest. "I heard through the grapevine that donations are considerably smaller this year. I sure hate that. I know your little nonprof will be just devastated. I wanted to deliver my donation to you personally."

"Oh. Well. Thank you. We appreciate the help."

"I don't want to help." Bianca handed over a folded check. "That's to cover some packing expenses. Your home is sitting on land that's prime for a new parking garage. My daddy's on the city council, of course, and it's just a matter of time before that building is dozed to the ground." She pursed her pouty pink lips. "You hadn't heard?"

Some sorority girls just never grew up. "I have an extended lease-to-own contract, so I'm pretty sure you misunderstood."

Bianca laughed. "What the city wants, the city gets. Especially when a tenant's future is so unstable. The building's owners have been very cooperative with the council." Her head bounced up as she caught a glimpse of someone across the room. "Must go chat with the mayor's son. Make sure you send me a receipt." With a look that dismissed Lucy from her black heels to the top of her blonde head, Bianca walked away.

A wave of panic threatened to knock Lucy off her heels. Like she needed more bad news. So now not only did she have to find a couple hundred thousand, but if snotty Bianca's information was correct, she'd be finding a new location soon as well.

How much worse could this possibly get?

⮾

Alex Sinclair glanced at his TAG Heur watch, though it was a wasted effort. This year he couldn't make an appearance and leave. Because he didn't just represent Sinclair Hotels. Tonight he was a man asking for the votes of the First Congressional District of South Carolina. The room buzzed like a hive, filled with dignitaries and connections he desperately needed. The election was in less than three months. He felt the pressure of time slipping away from him like a noose around his neck.

"I saw your ad on TV last night." Mayor Blackwell rested his hand on Alex's shoulder. "Great work. But too bad about that article in last week's *Gazette*."

"My team is working hard to find the leak. I'm not sure how our information is getting out." The paper had revealed the records of private donations from very powerful people. Influential citizens who had preferred to keep their party affiliations neutral. Citizens who were now very unhappy with Alex's camp. Another devastating blow to what was turning out to be a lackluster campaign.

When Congressman Patton had died unexpectedly of a heart attack, no one had expected Alex to throw in his hat for the rushed special election. A blown knee had forced Alex to retire from football at thirty-two. And while the campaign was proving harder than any championship game, it was one fight he wouldn't limp away from.

His father joined them. "My son's the best thing on the ticket. With his ideas for health care, reducing state spending, and cutting taxes for middle and lower classes, the good folks of South Carolina would be crazy not to vote for him."

Alex gave a reluctant laugh. "I'm thinking of firing my campaign managers and hiring my parents."

Though the media was having a field day with his life at the moment, Alex wasn't about to give up. It was a foreign feeling—this losing. He was a conqueror. Just like on the field, he should be able to size up his opponent, zero in on his weakness, and go for the kill. But it wasn't working. Each day held another setback. Just last week *People* magazine had run a scathing exposé on every alleged bitter girlfriend Alex had ever had. Their group photo had taken two whole pages. Only part of it had been true—the rest lies and toxic slams on his character.

Yet, to sue a handful of women wouldn't get him any points with the voters either. Today's *Gazette* had a full-page spread on allegations that Alex had bet against his own team in his last Super Bowl. How could he prove to the voters that he wasn't the same man they thought he was? He had once reveled in his reputation of being the lady's man, the party-going celebrity athlete. His antics on the field and off had earned him the nickname the Playboy. But things had changed. He had changed. Losing a brother could do that to a guy.

He felt powerless to stop his descent in the voter approval ratings. He had won the primary, but the general election was a whole other matter. The August eighth election was approaching fast, and his numbers were in the basement. Desperation was not a familiar emotion, and he needed a solution. Quick. He'd even found himself praying again, something he'd returned to the day his brother had disappeared.

Looking up from his conversation with the mayor and three local businessmen, Alex saw a woman glaring his way. If looks could kill, he'd be shot, stuffed, and hanging over her mantel.

He nudged his father and pointed. "Who is that?"

His father squinted to get a better look. "Ah, Lucy Wiltshire. Runs one of the charities we're donating to tonight. Bright girl. Doing some great things. It's a shame we had to cut her funding."

Lucy Wiltshire. That name sounded vaguely familiar.

Her Goldilocks hair fell over delicate cheekbones leading to one indignant chin. Her dress reminded him of a modern June Cleaver as it hugged her subtle curves, the black material a stark contrast to her china doll skin. Her hands made sweeping gestures as she talked to Ruth Ellington, one of Sinclair's board members. He saw Ruth shake her head, then walk away.

"It looks like she's harassing your board members," Alex said as he watched her zero in on another one. "You might want to take care of that."

"Yes, I—" His father checked his phone and grimaced. "I have to take a call. Can you run interference for Ms. Wiltshire? Get her away from the board."

Alex refrained from sighing until his father was gone. The man had aged ten years in the last twelve months, and right now there was nothing Alex would refuse him.

"Excuse me, gentlemen." Alex traded pleasantries with the attendees as he worked his way to Lucy's table. "Mrs. Rindquist, you're looking lovely tonight. Mr. Ruiz, don't forget that golf game next Saturday."

He saw Lucy's blue eyes go wide as he approached. Then the fire returned, and she lifted that pert nose and let him know she wasn't going anywhere.

Alex stepped closer, feeling his first smile of the night. He didn't know exactly what Lucy Wiltshire was up to, but he still had a little Warrior left in him.

And there was more than one way to tackle an opponent.

Chapter Three

*T*he Playboy was coming her way.

The last thing Lucy wanted to do was make chitchat with a spoiled athlete who breathed in fawning and adoration like oxygen. He had been like that in school too. The jerk probably didn't even remember her.

His thick, dark hair had just enough muss to let the world know he mixed pleasure with his business. A designer tuxedo covered his athlete's body, but Lucy knew what was beneath it. The whole world did. At the height of Alex's career as quarterback for the New York Warriors, you could find him sprawled in his BVDs from small-town billboards to Times Square. If one put in a small amount of effort, the ads could still be found. Not that Lucy ever looked.

She tried to focus on Mr. and Mrs. Carter, the most recent addition to the Sinclair board, but she could hardly talk for watching Alex. He should move with all the bulk of a rhino with those ridiculous muscles. Instead he handled himself with the grace of a panther. Lithe. Predatory. And headed right for her.

"Good evening," Alex said as he approached. "Nice to see you all tonight." His eyes seared through her, but Lucy wouldn't give him the satisfaction of showing even an ounce of nerves. He'd been sent to sidetrack her, but she could talk to whomever she wanted.

"It's a lovely gala," Mr. Carter said. "Glad to be a part of it this year."

"I was just telling them about Saving Grace." Her tone sounded extra surly, even to her. The Sinclair family had been beyond generous for the last two years. But fear made her words clipped, and her patience on the verge of snapping like a fragile twig. And this man—this jock—thinking he could charm his way into politics! He hadn't grown up a bit since they were kids—he still thought he was entitled to the world.

Alex stood a head taller than Lucy, and his eyes held a warning. "We're all disappointed Sinclair had to decrease the usual contribution, but the company is still happy to support you."

"It's been a tough year." Mr. Carter scanned the perimeter and held his empty wine glass toward a nearby waiter.

"Perhaps you'll have more to celebrate next time," Alex said.

"I'm afraid there won't be a next time for us," Lucy said. "Unless we receive additional funding from another source, we'll have to shut down by the end of fall."

At Mrs. Carter's look of sympathy, Lucy stepped closer, only to have Alex move between them. "Ms. Wiltshire, why don't you and I discuss this somewhere else and let the Carters enjoy their evening?"

Mrs. Carter patted Alex's shoulder, her eyes alight with unfiltered awe. "I'm sure Alex has some connections, dear."

"Fellow underwear models?"

Those full lips curved as Alex smiled at Lucy. "I don't believe I like your tone. On behalf of undergarment ambassadors everywhere—"

"Alex! Oh, there you are." One more board member joined their group.

The one Lucy had purposely avoided.

Clare Deveraux, the former first lady of South Carolina, shimmered in her long gown and matching jacket. Though the state still revered her as the Queen Elizabeth of the South for her stoic ways and upper-crust decorum, Lucy thought the woman was about as low-class as you could get. One summer long ago, she had single-handedly insured that Lucy's mother would never get a cleaning job in Charleston by blacklisting Anna Wiltshire. Who would ruin a poor, working single mom like that?

Lucy had been around Mrs. Deveraux a few times at these events, and the woman usually did nothing more than offer Lucy a mute stare. Maybe Clare Deveraux reserved conversation only for those whose blood ran blue.

"Clare, you look beautiful tonight." Alex took both of Clare's hands in his and kissed her unnaturally smooth cheek. "Are you holding up okay?"

"It's hard to believe Steven's been gone three months." Clare looked into the crowd. "My son would have enjoyed tonight very much. I'm glad I have my work on the board to keep me busy."

Lucy opened her mouth to speak, but Alex's hand came to rest on her shoulder, his fingers giving a light squeeze of warning. That man needed to keep his bossy ways *and* his hands to himself.

"My sympathies to you."

Lucy had read in the paper of Steven Deveraux's passing. Cancer at the age of fifty-four.

"I'm sorry as well," Lucy said as her manners kicked in.

Clare narrowed her eagle eyes and let them roam over Lucy's dress. "Black is not your color."

And politeness was not Clare's forte. "I'm actually glad to run into you, Mrs. Deveraux. I feel like we might've gotten off on the wrong foot somehow." Though Lucy had probably exchanged ten words total with her. "If I've done something to offend you, or if there's something you don't understand about our mission at Saving Grace—"

"I understand all I need to know," she said evenly.

"I would love a chance to talk about whatever it is that seems to be between us." Had Clare voted against Lucy because of her mother? "My girls are the ones enduring the consequences. Would you like to step over—"

The pressure on her shoulder increased. "Lucy, you mentioned earlier you wanted to dance."

"Maybe if you saw what we did at the home, how we—"

"Not necessary," Clare snipped.

"Listen, Lucy." Alex tilted his head. "They're playing your favorite song."

"What do you have against me?" Lucy asked. "First you tried to sabotage my mother and then—"

"Okay, you talked me into it. But just a few turns around the floor." With a yank, Alex pulled her to him. "You know how sensitive my insteps are."

"No. I need to—"

"Dance. Now." He took Lucy by the hand, his fingers a pressure against her wrist as he guided her through the crowd, past Clare and the wide-eyed Carters.

"What are you doing?" she said as he stopped in the middle of the dance floor.

"Avoidance." He set one of his hands on her hip and put them into motion. "A tactic I use with you women on a regular basis."

"I was about to get some answers."

"You were about to get a face full of her chardonnay."

"Mrs. Deveraux practically ruined my mother. That woman is toxic, and I would think your father would require his board members to possess at least a modicum of decency."

"Would you quit leading?" He adjusted his hold on her, his fingers splayed on her back. "You can't go charging through this ballroom. If you're going to be here, then calm down and pretend to have a good time. No one is going to negotiate with you tonight."

The band played a jazz version of a Sinatra song, but all Lucy could hear was the blood rushing through her head. Despite being an oversized athlete, Alex didn't miss a step. He spun her out with a flick of his wrist, then slowly reeled her back in. "I'm Alex Sinclair, by the way."

Oh, if she could wipe the arrogance off that face. "We went to the same school for at least ten years. I know who you are." Not to mention his rake's grin was plastered on every cover on the magazine rack.

Alex lifted a dark brow. "I think I would've remembered you."

"Oh, really? Do you remember the time you and your friends used my gym bag as a football, passing it in the hall until it burst open and my sports bra flew out and tripped a girl on crutches?"

"No. I don't recall that." He was smart enough to look uncomfortable.

"Remember when you finally gave me an invitation to your summer pool party, only to ask me to serve you and your guests like I was your personal waitress?"

He looked away, over her head. "I'm afraid I was a rotten kid, Lucy. It was my brother who was the saint."

Lucy knew that Will Sinclair had not just been working as a reporter in Durnama, but had been opening one of his schools there. How he and Alex could be related was beyond her. Though twins, the brothers were nothing alike. One fair and gentle, one dark and a notorious rogue. She didn't remember much about Will from school, but she did recall he had never been part of Alex's clique of spoiled snobs. That alone made him admirable in Lucy's estimation.

"So what have you done to receive the cold shoulder from Clare?" His simmering smile returned.

"Just breathing, apparently," Lucy said. "My mom worked for her a long time ago. It didn't go well."

The song ended, but he only tightened his hold. "Just keep dancing. Don't even think about leaving this floor."

She barely came to his chin and had to lean back to look at him. "If you were this bossy with all your cheerleader girlfriends, it's no wonder they've all banded together in mutual hatred." She flexed her fingers against the smoothness of his dark tuxedo.

"They're just angry because they can't *all* have me."

But Lucy knew those articles had done nothing but hurt his campaign. Was it wrong that it gave her a wicked sense of satisfaction that Alex Sinclair had finally found something he couldn't buy or charm his way into? While playing for the Warriors, he had won the loyalty of every American man with an eye for the game, and the heart of every woman with a pulse. But the people of South Carolina were obviously intelligent enough to recognize that didn't qualify Alex for a seat in government.

"Does your mother still live in Charleston?" he asked as the music changed into a slower tune.

"No. She's . . . gone." The hurt that had once been a scream inside her was now quieter, hushed to a whisper by the passing years. "I moved to Florida the summer before my senior year." Her mother had met and fallen in love with a man in Tallahassee, and Lucy had finally gotten her young heart's wish to leave Charleston. "It was a car wreck." Lucy shook off the melancholy mood that had just enveloped her. "It was a long time ago. Tonight is what matters. And I need to talk to the board members. I've got to change their minds about this drastic cut."

"Won't do any good," he said. "Our previous CEO almost donated Sinclair Hotels into an early grave. My uncle Phillip was generous to a fault."

"I've always respected that quality about him."

"You need to let this go. I'm sure what you do is important, but if Sinclair Hotels' donation matters that much, then you need to do some restructuring."

"Do you even know what we do at Saving Grace?" And did he have any idea how hard it was to ask for money from the same town that had rejected her years ago? And here she was again. A poor girl holding out her hands for charity from her betters. It was like Dickens meets Lifetime. "Did you know in our country, wards of the state are considered adults at eighteen? As soon as they graduate high school, many of them are forced to leave the system. They become instantly homeless. With little help, no life skills. They have a thirty-five percent greater chance of winding up in jail. Only two percent will go on to college—"

"That's enough." He swirled her around.

"Maybe you could sway the board. If you wanted to stop by and see what we do—" If only she could get one person on her side. "And now apparently the city has its eye on our building for a new parking garage. Are you aware these kids—"

"Are you aware that you're standing an entire state away from me?" He drew her closer, pulling her tight against the hard planes of his chest. "I'd heard some talk about it. You can find another location."

She was losing. She could feel it. "But that's our home. It's become a safe place. The girls have their own bedrooms. And watch your hands."

His brown eyes held hers. "You are the most uptight woman I have ever met."

"You're the most arrogant man I've ever—"

"Not to mention, you're delusional—like I'd try to cop a feel with you on a dance floor in front of hundreds of people."

"Well, sport, according to the *People* article, the Dallas Cowboy cheerleaders are done with you, so maybe you're reduced to lowly non-profit workers such as myself."

His smile was a slow, small lift of the lips. "Maybe in your wildest dreams where—"

"I would do anything for those girls, Alex." She bravely met his Hollywood eyes. "Absolutely anything."

"Anything?" She heard the laughter in his voice.

"I'm desperate."

His eyebrow raised as he studied her, weighing her words. "Interesting."

"This is life or death for those young ladies."

Behind them, someone cleared his throat. "May I cut in?"

And Lucy's world shifted one more time.

Because she knew that voice. Still heard it in her dreams.

Turning around, Lucy stared at the man who had once held her future. And had handed it right back to her. "Matt?" The words barely formed on her lips. "What are you doing here?"

"Hello, Lucy." He gave a brief nod to Alex, then turned those green eyes on her. "I came here for you."

Chapter Four

*T*he disco ball could've dropped on Lucy and she wouldn't have even noticed.

"May I?" Matt asked. He moved toward her, a vision in a tux. No. She could be strong. She could be indifferent. Oh, he was wearing her favorite cologne.

"She's all yours." Alex's eyes sliced back to Lucy. "I'll just be talking to the mayor over there. Lucy, I trust you'll have a pleasant evening."

The message was not lost on her. *If you hunt down another board member, I will come after you.*

Her whole body numb, Lucy let herself be folded into Matt's loose embrace.

"How have you been?" His breath fanned over her ear.

Alone. Sad. Overwhelmed. "Fine. And you?"

"Would you believe me if I said I've missed you?"

She lifted her head and stared into those eyes that she knew so well. "Why are you here?"

"I took a job with Sinclair Hotels as a senior accountant. I started this week."

Just like that. He was back. Easy to leave and just as easy to return.

"I want to see you, Lucy." He pulled her closer as they navigated between two couples. My team and I have to leave in an hour for a business trip, but I'll be back next week."

"I don't think that's such a good idea." She had built all her dreams on this one man, convinced he was the one.

"I know I screwed up. I ended things horribly."

"You took two bites of spaghetti and said we were through." She'd had more meaningful breakups with hairdressers.

He pressed his forehead to hers. "I was wrong, but I'm finally right where I want to be. I've thought about you every day for two years. That job in Dallas was nothing without you there. That's why I'm back." He ran his hand over a curl at her temple. "*You're* why I'm back."

So this was what it was like to have a man look at you like *that*. She wanted to believe every beautiful word, wanted to believe that intensity in his eyes was just for her.

"Just give me a chance to explain myself," he said. "That's all I'm asking."

"Okay." Lucy nodded as hope warred with reluctance. "When you get back, we can—" Her focus shifted as a familiar bald man waltzed by. "Mr. Zaminski!" Jerking from Matt's embrace, Lucy shrugged off his hands and charged toward the elderly board member and his newest wife. Number five, if she remembered correctly. And younger than the last.

Couples swirled around her, and Lucy had to weave among them. Mr. Zaminski had some speed for a seventy-five-year-old man.

"Mr. Zaminski!" She finally caught up and walked in step with the twosome. "Sir, I'm Lucy Wiltshire. I was wondering if we could talk for a moment?" Lucy swayed beside them like a one-woman dance show. "Maybe off the floor?"

The man squinted behind small glasses and kept up his waltz. "Do I know you?"

She raced around to his other side as he turned. "I think you might've voted a few days ago to cut the funding for my nonprofit."

"I don't concern myself with Sinclair community projects. Just the hotels." He turned his wrinkled face to his wife. "Now go away. You're bothering me."

"But, sir." Lucy did a skip-step before she lost them. "If you could just let me explain." The man made an abrupt twirl away, and Lucy reached out her hand to stop him. "Mr. Zaminski, I—"

She gasped as her arm made contact with something hard. Out of the corner of her eye, Lucy caught sight of the waiter beside her, then his tray as it went airborne. She reached out in a blind grab, only to have her beaded shoulder-strap give up its weak hold. Black beads tumbled to the floor, and goblets of shrimp cocktail crashed around them.

Lucy clutched at her sagging top. "I'm so sorry. I didn't see you and—" Time moved in slow motion as she watched Mr. Zaminski fox-trot right over the mess. His foot descended into the slippery spill. "Mr. Zaminski!"

But it was too late. His shiny black shoes made contact with one blob of shrimp, and it was over. His mouth went wide, his arms reached for the air. And down he went. The crowd parted in two as if commanded by Moses himself.

Lucy raced to Mr. Zaminski's side. "Sir, are you okay?" Lucy's top gaped in pitiful defeat as she bent low and reached for his hand.

Mr. Zaminski blinked a few times before his eyes focused on his wife on his left, then Lucy at his right. "You," he hissed.

"I'm truly sorry." Her cheeks were flames of heat. Half the ball-room gathered around them. "I simply wanted to tell you about—"

"Get this woman out of my face!"

Lucy barely dodged a shrimp as Mr. Zaminski lobbed a handful of spilled *hors d'oeuvres* her way. She had to get out of here. People were staring, some idiot had just taken a picture, and her shoes were covered in cocktail sauce.

Her dress gave a slight groan as she pivoted on her heel and came to her feet. She raced through the crowd and searched the room for the nearest exit. The old shame followed her and ushered her out. Thirty years old, and these people still held the power to reduce her to the klutz of her childhood. The girl who couldn't do anything right.

Speed walking down a hallway, Lucy spotted a set of double doors. Bursting through, she stepped into the night air and made her escape.

Alex had no idea why he was pursuing the woman. What did he care if she was upset? He had better things to be concerned with, that was for sure. It's not like it was his fault she was half crazy. No wonder she couldn't acquire funding from other sources. She was an erratic mess.

He saw a blur of a black dress round the corner ahead. He picked up his pace and followed her down the hall. Pushing doors wide open, he stepped outside. "Lucy!"

The lunatic woman looked over her shoulder, then promptly broke into a run. Like she was any match for him. Gaining on her, he reached out his arms, wrapped them around her, and lifted her body off the ground.

"Let go of me!" Her legs kicked out, her heels connecting with his shins. "Put me down, you oaf."

He loosened his grip as she squirmed but didn't let go. "Not until I feel certain you're not going to run into the freeway."

"I don't want you *feeling* any part of me."

"Now, that's no way to talk. Where's your Southern hospitality?"

"On the floor with the rest of my dress." Her body flailed and jerked. "Don't make me use my pepper spray."

"Pretty sure I have the advantage here." She stopped struggling, and he felt her uneven breaths beneath his grip. "Are you going to play nice?" Sniffing, she reached up a shaking hand and wiped her eyes.

"Yes," came her defeated answer. "Just put me down . . . please."

He lowered her until her feet touched the grass. "Do you know you're missing a shoe?"

She looked up. Her eyes swam. That bottom lip quivered.

No, not tears. He could handle anything but that. Before caution had time to whisper in his ear, he gathered her in his arms and gave her stiff back a brotherly pat. "Would it be rude to ask you not to get snot on my jacket?"

"This is the worst night of my life," Lucy said, her head buried in his shirt. "Even worse than the time James Allred stood me up for prom." She gave a shaky inhale. "Two years in a row."

He needed to say something to wrap this up. To calm. To comfort. "James was an idiot who sniffed glue for a hobby. Anyone with a brain knew that."

"I didn't know." He saw two tears fall as she stepped back and attempted to hold her dress together. "So now I not only attack innocent senior citizens, show half the ballroom my worn-out strapless bra, but I'm brainless too?"

Alex raised his eyes toward heaven. Where had his finesse gone? He used to have a Midas touch. Did everything he attempt lately have to wither in front of him like a leaky balloon?

He softened the edges of his appeal. "It's hot, Lucy. Why don't we go back inside?"

"I'm never facing those people again." She shrugged his arm away and began walking.

"Are you planning on walking home? Hitching a ride?"

"Just go away, rich boy."

"You're going to get arrested for indecent exposure out here."

"Don't worry. You won't be my one phone call."

His brother had always been the sensitive, people-caring one in the family. This would be one of those situations where Will would know exactly what to do.

Muttering, Alex caught up with her, slipped off his jacket, and draped it over her shoulders. "I don't want your incarceration on my list of sins. It's bad enough I terrorized you in high school."

She gripped the lapels of his coat together and turned to face him. "At least you can finally admit it."

No matter what the world thought of his cavalier ways, his mother had raised a gentleman. "Let me take you home."

"Does that cheap line seriously work for you?"

The sooner they resolved this, the sooner he could go inside and get the evening over with. He still had hours of work waiting for him back at his campaign office. "Want to tell me what you thought you were doing in there?"

"Before or after I gave Mr. Zaminski a concussion?" Lucy shook her head. "Just go away."

He didn't know what possessed him, but his hands seemed to move of their own volition. Bracketing her shoulders, he slowly pulled her toward him. Lucy dropped her head. Alex would not be deterred. With one finger he lifted her chin. "Talk to me."

"Why are you out here?"

"Because your shrewish wail was like a siren's call."

"I wasn't wailing." She blew out a long-suffering breath, setting the curls around her face in motion. "If you must know . . . I've had an abysmal week. An epic amount of awful. And I don't know how to fix any of it."

Her mascara trailed a black path down her cheeks, and her lips were liquid shine, either from gloss or tears, he didn't know.

"You know the board didn't cut your funds because of any personal reasons."

"Tell that to Clare Deveraux. Did you see the way she looked at me? I've never been one of you, and I never will be."

"You mean rich? Privileged?" His lips thinned. "No, you're probably better than us."

He watched the storm clouds pass again as she turned her eyes to his. "Do you have any idea what it's like to beg for money from the very people who made my life a living nightmare?"

"No. I don't."

"Of course you don't. Any problems you have can be fixed with money."

"Not every problem." Not the aching weight that had settled in his chest ever since his brother had disappeared. Or since Alex had blown out his knee. And walked away from a game he no longer cared about into a life he barely recognized.

The night breeze blew, ruffling her hair again. The spirals around her face rose and fell right back into disarray. As if compelled to touch, he reached out and captured a silky strand, resting it behind her ear.

A light flashed over his shoulder. Alex spun around. Two reporters stood twenty feet away, their cameras capturing his every move.

The media—it was an aspect of his life he loathed. And now that he had stepped into the race for Congress, it was even worse. He moved them a few steps back into the shadows. "I can make some calls. Talk to some people I know."

"Right." She looked at him like he had just promised to sprout another arm. "I'll fix it myself."

"Then I guess you don't want to save Saving Grace as badly as I thought."

Her mouth fell open in an outraged O. "You wouldn't know sacrifice if it hit you between the eyeballs. That place is all I've got. All those girls have."

"Then fight for it." The faint note of her perfume hit him. The light floral scent suited her. If he were to give it a name, it would be *exasperation.*

"What do you think I do every day of my life? Not all of us get to toss around a football and play games for a living."

Alex shrugged a shoulder. "Just born lucky, I guess." He watched the two reporters get a few more shots and then walk away.

"You don't know real problems. I have young women who come to me with no place to sleep—nothing to eat. Society just kicks them out on the streets with no resources to take care of themselves. Meanwhile any problem you have can be solved by writing a check with lots of zeroes."

He knew problems. And pain. Yet he didn't know what to do with either. "If you're gonna wallow in it, I'm going in." Alex could be reading passing stats for all the feeling in his voice. "I simply wanted to make sure you weren't making plans to climb to the top of the hotel and dive off."

"Only if you go first," she mumbled. "Promise I'll catch you."

He couldn't help but laugh. "You're all out of finesse tonight, aren't you?"

"I think I lost it somewhere between flying shrimp and a potential lawsuit from a board member."

The doors slammed open and his father's latest accountant came running out. If that was her boyfriend, he was a little late. The woman could've done a belly flop off the Sinclair Hotel by now.

"Lucy, are you okay?"

Alex watched as she softened at the sight of the man. She didn't walk into his open arms, but she did let the guy put his arm around her.

"I think she's fine." Alex stepped away from the pair. "Nothing a little hot tea and some dry cleaning won't fix. Do you have it from here?"

"I'll take her home," the boyfriend said.

"Make sure you keep her there." And with an eye on his perimeter, Alex stepped away, grateful he wouldn't have to see Lucy Wiltshire again for another year.

And that would still be way too soon.

❧

A fog swirled in Lucy's head as she watched Matt's hands grip her key and unlock her apartment door. Hands that had held her. Then let her go.

Inside, Lucy sat on the edge of the couch and finally found her voice. "How long have you been back?"

Keeping his eyes on hers, Matt eased into the chair across from her. "I've missed you." He ran a hand over his face. "Do you have any idea how much?"

She stared at a spot near his polished black shoes. "Your occasional e-mails the past few years didn't say."

And then he was sitting next to her, his hand reaching for hers. "Lucy, I've got to catch a late plane, and I hate that we can't take all the time we need. But you have to believe me, I want you back in my life. I've been lost without you."

"You knew I assumed you were proposing that night two years ago. I thought we were going to spend the rest of our lives together." The old hurt lodged in her throat and made her words hoarse. "I can't do this right now, Matt."

He reached for her as she stood. "When I get back next week, I'm going to prove to you that I can be that man you wanted."

"I don't know." Looking at Matt right now, she knew it would be so easy to just fall back into love with him again. But was that a good thing?

"Whatever it takes and however long it takes. Because I'm not going anywhere." He leaned toward her, pressing a kiss to her cheek. "Except for right now because that red-eye flight isn't going to wait on some accountant." His eyes were locked on hers as he opened the door. "I love you, Lucy. Believe that."

And then he was gone.

The last time he had left her apartment, he had taken her heart.

And Lucy just didn't know if she had another one left to give.

Chapter Five

*H*er life could be an Emmy-winning soap opera. Between the stress of Saving Grace's money woes, Friday night's fiasco, and Matt's return, Lucy had about all the drama she could take.

"Yes, this is Lucy Wiltshire. I'm calling for Mr. Greene. Again." Lucy tapped a pen on the laminate top of her desk. She needed to know the scope of how much trouble Saving Grace was in, and she couldn't even get the landlord to call her back. Maybe he *wasn't* selling out to the city. "Tell him I need him to return my call, please. It's urgent."

Her head weighed too much for her shoulders today, and her eyes burned with a lack of sleep. The Monday morning sun shone through the small windows of the room, but her mood was anything but bright. She hadn't slept the entire weekend. Every time she closed her eyes, she saw her past and future looming over her like the Grim Reaper coming to make his next collection.

She lifted a glass of water from the desk and sipped.

"I'd be drinking, too, if I'd had the weekend you apparently had."

Morgan breezed her way into the office, looking annoyingly fresh and beautiful. She had the dark, long hair of some exotic beauty and a tall, trim figure that belonged on the catwalk. It was a wonder Lucy let the woman be her friend. Chuck ambled in behind her, his ear pressed to his phone.

Morgan took a chair across from Lucy's desk. "Start talking."

The headache was now a pounding drum. "About what?"

"You can't text me something like 'Matt just left my house' and expect me to let it go. I called you all weekend."

Chuck put down his phone. "Cough up the details."

"Don't you two have to be at work?"

"Going in late so we can take Shayla out for breakfast." Every girl at Saving Grace was assigned three mentors. Morgan was partnered with a twenty-year-old who was struggling through her first semester at the community college. "Now talk."

Lucy gave her friends the quick play-by-play, right down to the last slippery shrimp detail.

"Well, obviously you need an umbrella," Morgan said. "Because, girl, it's raining men." She plopped a newspaper on the scarred surface of the desk.

"What?" Lucy took a drink and picked up the front page. Water spewed from her lips. "What the heck?" Wiping her mouth she pressed the paper closer to her face. "What is this? Some sort of joke?"

There, on page one of the *Charleston Post*, was a picture of Lucy wrapped in Alex's arms as they danced at the gala. She read the headline aloud. "The Prince and Cinderella?" She scanned the first paragraph, which reported that Alex Sinclair, millionaire football star, was dating Lucy Wiltshire, director of a struggling nonprofit. It read like a romance novel starring Prince William and a lowly commoner.

"This is ridiculous." She kept reading. "Total trash. Like I would date him." Like Alex would date *her*. How people must be laughing.

"There's more." Morgan handed her another paper. "Girls' home director snares South Carolina's favorite football hero. Will she show him how the home fires burn?"

"Okay, now it's not only inaccurate, but really horrible journalism. That reporter should be fired for the bad writing alone."

Lucy grabbed a paper from the stack. Her pulse tripled at the sight of the pictures. One of her in Alex's jacket, standing inches away from him. Staring into his eyes. She couldn't even bring herself to read the caption beneath it. The next photo was the worst. A close-up of Alex brushing a strand of hair from her cheek. Taken out of context, it looked ... intimate.

Chuck wiggled his eyebrows. "Something you want to tell us?"

Lucy dropped the paper to the desk. "Don't be crazy. I ... he ... we ..." There were no words.

"I'm a pastor." Chuck adjusted the bill of his USC baseball cap. "Confession is good for the soul, my child."

Morgan smiled. "You do look good together."

"*Hmph.*" Alex would make anyone look good. That dark hair, with the slightest of wave. Body chiseled by years on the field, hours in the gym, and possibly a handshake with the devil. A face that belonged in movies. And who was she? A girl who apparently didn't know how to buy a fully functioning little black dress.

"With all these options, we could have a double wedding." Morgan jerked her thumb toward Chuck, who had managed to duck out of all the preparations so far. "Though I'm not sure *this* guy is even going to show."

The groom-to-be managed to look suitably contrite. "Of course I'm going to show."

"Yeah, in your jeans and flip-flops." Morgan turned on him. "You haven't even finalized your part of the rehearsal dinner guest list, honey. How hard is it to get your ten closest family members to confirm?"

"I'm a busy man," Chuck said with his ever-present grin. "I save souls all day."

Morgan rolled her eyes. "Yesterday you were golfing with the deacons."

"I can honestly say there was a lot of prayer going on."

With months left before the wedding, it was a familiar argument of late, and Morgan switched to a different prickly topic. "Any progress on Saving Grace?"

Lucy was growing sick of that question. "If worry had any value, we'd have a new home South of Broad," Lucy said. "I've called every business and person of interest in the county. The same list we try every year. We got two more individual donors, but nothing that could touch next year's operation costs."

"Maybe we can get the church behind this."

"Chuck, a bake sale isn't going to save us," Lucy said. "We need a serious miracle."

"I happen to have connections." He held out both of his hands. Wiggled his fingers. "Let us now pray and ask for one ginormo miracle."

And so they did. With head bowed, Chuck sent up his holy request for a timely solution for Saving Grace. For each young woman in the home to be protected, secure. And for God to move swiftly and in a drastically creative way.

Lucy held on to her friends' hands, drawing strength from their friendship, and for their hearts for God. Every fiber of her being sang in agreement with Chuck's words. *Lord, be big. Be bold.*

And be quick.

"Thank you," Lucy said. "It means a lot to have your support."

"God loves those girls, too, Luce." Morgan gave Lucy's hand a final squeeze. "Whatever happens will become a cool part of the Saving Grace legacy." She uncrossed her legs and leaned forward. "So what are you going to tell Matt?"

"He and I are not a couple. Just because he waltzed back into town and said all sorts of completely wonderful, beautiful, and totally convincing things does not mean that we're getting back together." Yet.

Morgan shook her head. "That boy broke your heart two years ago. Don't forget how we nursed you back to life. How we stayed up late every weekend and watched *Star Wars*. How we fed you Blue Bell ice cream until you could face the world again."

Lucy still had the extra ten pounds to prove it. "He does seem more settled, though. Different."

Chuck sighed. "All those banana splits and the man *still* isn't out of your system."

"God has brought him back into my life for a reason." Matt was still everything she ever wanted—stable, handsome, kind.

Morgan sighed and eyed her friend. "Just promise me you won't do something crazy."

"Me? Do something crazy?" She picked up a paper and tapped Alex Sinclair's face. "Like romance an American football hero?"

Morgan laughed. "At least we don't ever have to worry about *that* one."

Chapter Six

*A*lex sat behind his desk with one ear to the phone, one ear to his campaign advisors, and both eyes on ESPN. He had a headache that pounded harder than a three-man tackle, and the tabloid in his hand only sharpened the edge of his mood.

Lauren Billings sat down and crossed her legs. "Your approval ratings continue to skyrocket."

He nodded vacantly and spoke into the phone. "I'll stop by for a visit as soon as I can, Dad, but I'm still out for family dinner night, so tell Mom to quit forcing people to harass me. If I get a call from Aunt Marge, I'll boycott Fourth of July as well." Alex scanned a report as his father talked. "Because I have too much to do. Campaigns don't stop for holidays. . . . Yes, I understand I'm breaking my mother's heart." He held up a finger to his waiting advisors. "Just tell Finley I'll take her out to lunch sometime soon." His guilt spiked at the mention of his seventeen-year-old sister. Alex had been fifteen when Finley had unexpectedly come along, yet he and his twin had fallen in love with her. He knew his sister was struggling this year. The whole family was. But Alex had a drowning campaign to save, and right now that came first.

"Have you seen your latest numbers?" David Spear pushed another report across Alex's desk as soon as the call was over.

Alex clicked off the TV and finally gave his full attention to the two in his office. When he'd set out to find the best political advisors and campaign managers, he hadn't settled for anything less than the best. David and Lauren had each worked on successful presidential campaigns. They were tireless and they were bulldogs. Two qualities Alex admired. And needed.

He scanned over the document in his hands. "This is . . . unexpected."

"It's phenomenal progress in a remarkably short amount of time," David said.

The leather of Alex's chair crunched as he leaned back. "Maybe it's those revamped TV ads."

"You know perfectly well what it is." Lauren stood up and grabbed the magazine. With a French manicured nail, she pointed at page twelve. "*In Touch* magazine says you and Lucy Wiltshire are serious. Do you know how many calls for interviews we've had since your gala pictures hit the press two weeks ago? People love the down-home feel of this relationship. It's exactly what we've been missing."

"Too bad. Find something else to sway voters." He stretched the tight muscles in his neck. They had been going strong since six a.m. on this Thursday morning. By the time he finished up here and squeezed in a workout, it would be too late to even eat dinner.

"Your current mode of operation is getting us nowhere but second place." Dave loosened the tie at his neck. The man didn't believe in dressing down, even on weekends. Alex didn't know if he admired that or resented it. "You're one of the most well-known people in the country. There's no point in pretending you don't live in a fishbowl. You can either show the public some of your life, or as we saw a few weeks ago in *People*, they'll just make it up to suit themselves. And frankly, your personal life has been a crucial problem here."

"I still want to do a few pieces on the loss of your brother," Lauren said. "I really think if you sat down with *Good Morning America* and finally spoke about—"

"No." Just the thought of it made him want to tear someone apart. Only yesterday his own investigative team had called with some leads about possible sightings of his brother. He was afraid to be hopeful. "That topic is off-limits." A year since his brother had been gone. It had both moved too quickly and not fast enough. Six months to the day Will went missing, Alex had walked away from football. Besides the blown-out knee, the game had lost it lure. The fast-paced life had burned him out, and he was ready for a change.

"All they're seeing is the celebrity side of you." David stood up and planted his hands on the desk. "If you want to eclipse your playboy jock reputation, it's going to take some sacrifice." He gestured to the open page. "And crazy as it is, your involvement with Ms. Wiltshire seems to speak to people. Shows them a side of you they've yet to see."

"There is no involvement with Lucy Wiltshire beyond—"

"We're your campaign managers," Lauren said. "If you can't be honest with us, who can you be honest with?"

"I'm running for office," he said with a wry grin. "I don't have to be honest."

"*Entertainment Tonight* has called twice since the first pictures ran," Lauren said. "They want a quote."

"There is no quote. There is no Lucy—"

"If you want to win this thing, it's time to get aggressive."

As Lauren interrupted him again, Alex watched her brush a strand of dark hair from her cheek. The woman was beautiful. Legs that a cheerleader would envy. A brain just as potent as her model's face. And part of him knew, from years of experience, that she wouldn't turn him down if he suggested a little dinner and candlelight in their off-hours.

Yet he wasn't interested. Not even a glimmer. Where was the old Alex? The last year had been tough. He'd lost his brother, his game, and possibly this race for Congress. The Playboy was tired. And wrung out like a sweaty gym towel. There had to be more than this, and he was determined to find out what it was. The women in his life the last few years had been after only one thing—fame. Alex was ready to get back to real. People he could count on not to run to OK! magazine for just the right price. But he had a new goal, and that didn't include a wife or children for a long time. He had things to accomplish first. He owed it to his brother's life to do that.

"You're going to have to let your voters in," Lauren said. "They need to see more of that." She pointed to the magazine. "That's our best counterattack for the smear campaign that's begun—whether it's reality or not. We need you to convey good American values. Family. Stability."

David nodded. "And we need you on board."

"Let's get one thing straight." Alex shoved the magazine away. "You two work for me. I pay you for guidance and suggestions—not demands. Are we clear?"

Alex caught the look Lauren passed her fellow advisor. He hadn't dominated the field by missing signals.

"Alex"—David cleared his throat and took one step back—"we secured the primary because your competition was weak, but this is a whole new ball game. The campaign is done unless we see some drastic action. If you want this as bad as you say you do, you have to fight for it. It's time to show a new dimension."

"The only thing that's going to save you is one heck of a Hail Mary." Lauren gathered her briefcase and stood. "So find us one."

⁓

"... word today that eye witnesses have come forward. They claim to have information about NBC reporter Ben Hayes and CNN's own Will Sinclair, brother of former Warriors quarterback Alex Sinclair."

Lucy dropped the pen in her lap as the TV caught her attention. Details of the breaking news filled her living room.

"One Durnama native told investigators he saw only one man pulled out alive from the school before being taken in an unmarked van. This is the same school Will Sinclair helped establish, bombed in a terror attack when insurgents stormed the village. And so the search now continues in what might be a hostage situation. Back to you, Anderson."

That poor Sinclair family. No matter how much they had left Lucy high and dry, she would never wish this kind of pain on them. Closing her eyes, Lucy said a prayer for the missing reporters. For the families who had lost children. And even for Alex Sinclair.

And for herself.

Because as her eyes opened and returned to the list on her laptop, she crossed off her last potential donor. At this point, Saving Grace had mere months left of funding.

Running a hand over her face, Lucy could feel the puffiness in her eyes. She had avoided the mirror all day, but she knew what she'd see there. Bloated eyeballs that made her look as if she had spent the entire evening chugging pints and searching for a lampshade to pull over her head. Her night had been far less glamorous. She had tossed and turned in her bed, until finally she had gotten up before the sun to spend a few hours facedown on her carpet, praying.

Where she had fallen asleep. And had the carpet imprints to prove it.

In front of her, a Bible sat open on the coffee table, the ribbon marker lying across a page of Romans.

We know that all things work together for the good of those who love God: those who are called according to His purpose.

Well, there were definitely *things* going on, but she sure couldn't see any good in them.

The knock on her door momentarily pulled her out of her misery. Checking the clock on the microwave, she managed a smile. Matt had arrived. Punctual as ever.

If there was any bright spot in her week, it was this man. He had been auditing hotels on the West Coast, but he had called her every day since the gala. And tonight they were finally going to have that talk. She knew he was waiting on a decision from her about picking up where they'd left off. Still, something in her held back. No doubt it was fear of being hurt again. But so far there were no signs she had anything to worry about with the new and improved Matt.

Reaching her fingers into her hair, she tousled the curls, hoping to give the limp locks a boost. *I really think I'm ready for this, God. Finally, a home of my own.*

Lucy opened the door. And smiled.

"Flower delivery."

And there he was, standing in her doorway, a bouquet of roses so big, she couldn't see his face. But she had his every feature memorized anyway. At one time had planned on seeing it for the rest of her life. And now that he was there on her front stoop, she was nervous as a sixteen-year-old on her first date.

"They're beautiful," Lucy said.

Matt held them out to her, then kissed her cheek. "So are you."

She quickly put the flowers in a vase in the kitchen and then joined him in the living room.

"You look tired." His face was etched with concern as he sat down on her couch.

Lucy sat next to him, twisting her hands in her lap. "Monday I have to tell my girls that we're moving at the end of September." The numbers just weren't there. And no amount of begging for donations had increased the bottom line nearly enough.

"Aw, Luce." Matt folded his hand over hers. "Don't give up yet."

"I have to be realistic." Though she had been praying for a miracle, a winning lottery ticket hadn't miraculously shown up in her mailbox. "I've been trying to contact my landlord all week. He doesn't even have the guts to return my calls. So today I've been working on alternative places for us to move—maybe even temporary housing for each girl." Being moved again was not what the girls needed. They needed stability, security.

"I'm sure you'll figure something out." His positivity grated on Lucy's tired nerves, but she pushed her irritation away as Matt's fingers caressed the top of her hand. "Have you given any more thought to ... us?"

Of course she had. And if she didn't quit thinking about it and her menagerie of other problems, she was going to be completely gray by spring. "I just don't know, Matt." She couldn't let herself get too caught up again. Though she couldn't deny the smallest flicker of hope. "You want to know my honest take on this?"

"I want us to always be honest."

A little honesty would've gone a long way two years ago, so the breakup wouldn't have hit her like a runaway train out of nowhere. "My guess is that the job in Dallas wasn't all that you thought it would be. You're a guy who likes routine—likes the familiar. So when the job didn't satisfy you and something came available in Charleston, you moved back. And since you apparently don't have someone in your life, you thought you'd see if you could reconnect with me." She sat back and crossed her arms. She had to make sure he knew she wasn't just going to fall into his arms with gratitude.

"That's a fair shot." A half-smile appeared on his face, a look so achingly familiar, she wished his scowl would return. "But you're wrong." His voice was a rough whisper as he leaned closer. "I made partner within six months of being at that firm. I had a house in Highland Park. Expense account. But I just went through the motions every day. Because you weren't there. And I knew you couldn't relocate. Lucy, it was nothing without you."

Her heart was a polar ice cap. And it was melting.

His eyes searched hers. "I left it all for you. I'm here because of you. My whole life . . . is you."

Forever.

I've waited forever for those words.

Matt's fingers slid up her jaw and cupped her face. "I love you, Lucy." She sighed as his lips hovered over hers. "And I want you to be my wife."

Chapter Seven

When Alex Sinclair wanted something, he let nothing stand in his way. And today was no exception.

Standing in the small foyer, Alex could hear music blasting down the hall. "I'm here to see Lucy Wiltshire," he said to the resident assistant, taking in the spa-like colors of Saving Grace.

"Uh-huh," came her breathy reply.

He patiently stood and waited for the awestruck female to reclaim her power of speech. He was, after all, a citizen of this town. When would people stop treating him like some Tinseltown star and begin acting like he was one of their own?

"Do you have an appointment?" she finally asked.

"Yes." It wasn't a total lie. Lucy had suggested Alex visit the home.

"Okay." The young woman dropped her car keys, then bobbed down to the pick them up. "Okay, um, we're headed out to the library, so, um . . ." More staring.

"Follow Etta James?"

The R.A. nodded, then stumbled over her feet before walking out the door.

After a burnt run to her apartment, Alex was glad to finally track Lucy down. Because last night he had slept a solid six hours for the first time in a year. Finally something in his life felt right. All he needed was her cooperation.

As Etta's smooth contralto got closer, Lucy's own voice got louder. Rounding a corner, he found her in a large dining room, belting out "At Last" and dusting a china cabinet.

He stood still for a moment, enjoying the scene. She swept her rag across the front of the cabinet with a flourish, swaying to the music. She was nowhere near on beat and singing at the top of her voice somewhere in the key of awful.

From the curls that were captured in a lime-green paisley scarf to the blouse that looked like it came from her mother's high-school senior portrait, Lucy was the antithesis of traditional glamour. She was unrefined. A fully loaded weapon, ready to shoot through decorum and convention.

And she was his Hail Mary.

Tilting his head at her attempt at a high note, he observed that Lucy didn't have the willowy figure of many of his recent dates. She didn't have a face that would sell the latest Parisian perfume. Nor did she possess that confident air that ladies in his world wore like a necessary undergarment. But if he peeled back her hostility and the years of her bratty youth, Lucy Wiltshire was still a traffic stopper.

The certainty finally clicked into place as Alex locked his sights on his target.

And let the ball fly.

"What a beautiful rendition."

Lucy spun on her black patent flats. And screamed like a banshee.

He found the sound system and turned the music off. "You clearly missed your calling."

She clutched her heart, her eyes wide, then mutinous. "What in the *world* do you think you're doing?"

"You look good with dust on your nose." Like an angry pixie.

A fury stared back at him. "I repeat, what are you doing here?"

"You invited me, remember?"

"Yes, as in a scheduled visit. Not when everyone is gone. Who let you in?"

"A young woman. Nice girl, though not much of a conversationalist."

Alex smiled. "Maybe she was just trying to soak up as much of your concert as she could before she left."

"I have a phone, you know. You could've called—instead of sneaking up on me like some sort of creep." She twisted the dust rag in her hands. "A musically critical creep."

"Actually I went to your apartment, but Mr. Jenkins said you'd be here. Pleasant guy." Alex dropped his voice a notch. "Though the wife's a little bit of a nag."

She had a giant dust bunny occupying a prominent place on her blouse, but he decided to be a gentleman and not tell her.

"If you were as good at politics as you are at stalking, I think you could make it all the way to the White House."

The words sliced, but he'd belt out some blues himself before he'd reveal that to her. "Funny you should mention politics—and thank you for the vote of support, by the way. I like a girl with vision."

"And I like a guy who knows when to leave when he's not wanted."

"You really should lock your doors." He shook his head as he counted the chairs at the table. It could seat half of Congress. "Anyone could walk in here."

"True." She didn't let her gaze waver. "There are pervs all over this town."

"Speaking of that, according to the papers and gossip rags, you and I are dating." His lips stretched into an easy smile. "I'm a little hurt you don't make me dinner more often, but other than that, you've been an exemplary girlfriend."

If she were a tiger, she'd be snarling and baring her claws. "Look, unless you have news about Sinclair's donation, we really don't have anything to say to one another."

"Oh, but I think we do." He advanced another step. "I have a proposition for you." He continued as she opened her mouth. "Hear me out before you decide to get offended."

"Talk quick. I have a lunch date."

"Cancel it."

"Go away."

"I said cancel it."

Lucy blinked. "Why?"

That look in her eyes. That uncertainty. Alex found he liked her unbalanced. "I'll make it worth your while."

"I realize after that *People* story half the female population is mad at you right now, but I'm not interested." She pursed her lips as if in thought. "I do have a fourth cousin in Savannah who'd probably be up for a date." She turned back to her cabinet. "She's eighty-five."

Alex inhaled deeply. Did everything in his life have to be so unbelievably complicated? "Normally when I ask a woman out I get a different reaction. Like tears of gratefulness."

"Is this before or after you hand them a free autographed football?"

Lucy was not a woman to be swayed by pretty words, so he got right to it. "I want to talk about a donation for your home. Now . . . break your date."

She lifted one brow. "So Sinclair Hotels *is* going to help us after all?"

"No."

"But you just said—"

"Sinclair won't be helping you any more this year. But *I* will." That look on her face was making this all worth it. This idea could be halfway enjoyable. A boon to his campaign *and* a cure for the boredom that had plagued him for months. "I don't like to talk business on an empty stomach, and I'm a man in need of pie. Plus I don't really want to discuss it here."

"I don't think so."

"I'm talking a large amount of money."

She watched him with guarded eyes. "And what do I have to do in return?"

"All you have to do"—his cheek dimpled with a wolf's grin—"is marry me."

⌒

"You want me to do *what*?"

"Be quiet, will you?" Alex smiled and nodded his head to a couple sitting two tables away from theirs in Jestine's, a popular spot for home cooking, and the last place Lucy would have expected him to choose.

Alex scanned the restaurant. "There are ears all over this place. *Voting* ears."

"Insane." Lucy stabbed a piece of fried chicken on her plate. Oh, the nerve of this man. The insanity. She knew he was arrogant, condescending, and egotistical. But crazy? She had not seen that one coming. "I know you've had a lot of hits to the head over the last decade, but I'm not going to marry you just to get a check. I'm not some"—she could hardly process the thought—"mail-order bride. Some . . . prostitute."

"Easy now. Despite that article in OK!, I don't associate with hookers." Alex pointed his fork in her direction. "It's business. Pure and simple."

She leaned low across the table. "There is *nothing* simple about this. Marry you for money? I happen to think better of myself than that." She could hardly enjoy her food, which was just a batter-fried piece of heaven.

"Hear me out for a moment. In the popularity polls this week, my numbers have been off the charts. And do you know why?"

"You sent them eight-by-ten glossies?"

"Because of those pictures from the gala. They're everywhere."

"You and I both know they mean nothing."

"But it doesn't look that way. And America likes what they're seeing." He speared a bite of chicken-fried steak and smiled. "I'm the number one search topic on Google."

Lucy rolled her eyes. "I bet the guy who won a Pulitzer is totally jealous."

"You're number three."

She paused with the glass to her lips. "Three?"

"Yep."

"Who's number two?" Lucy took a few swallows and put down the glass. "Never mind. I don't care about any of this. Just because the *Enquirer* thinks we're interesting doesn't mean we're marriage material. I mean, I'm flattered." Lucy adjusted her voice to a tone reserved for a young woman who needed some correction. "But let's get real—I can do better than you."

Watching her, Alex slid the fork between his lips and chewed. It was all she could do not to squirm under his blatant scrutiny.

"I don't want a real wife."

"You want a fake one?" He was insane. He'd be perfect for politics after all.

"Yes." He looked out the window at the line of people standing outside, waiting to get in. "And no."

"I bet you're just a whiz in campaign meetings."

"Allow me to explain our game plan." Alex checked over both shoulders before continuing in a whisper. "You simply pretend to be my girlfriend. We hang out, we do dinner, you occasionally smile at me and try not to drip your venom on my golf shirt. After we date a short period of time, I will ask you to marry me. In a public place. There will be cameras. The whole world will see it. You pretend to by my fiancée for the duration of the campaign. Two months after the election, we go our separate ways. I leave with my new state office and you leave with a big fat check."

Lucy pushed her potatoes around on the plate. Nothing made sense. She saw Alex's lips move. She heard the words come out. But they refused to translate into anything logical in her head. "Alex, this . . . is absolutely the dumbest thing I've ever heard. I mean, I know you football players aren't typically Mensa members, but even the village idiot would concede this is just wrong." She had been praying for a miracle, but she'd never dreamed it would be hand-delivered by the president of Club Sin and Depravity.

"I dominated on that football field. And I know I can do the same in Congress. I just need a chance to get there. My opponent is running a total smear campaign, and my image has taken a severe beating."

"Those mean ol' cheerleaders. Darn them for expecting a commitment out of you." She pressed a napkin to her lips. "All twelve of them."

"Now see, you're gonna have to stop those little remarks." He'd spent the last eight years in New York, but his voice was still as Southern as

Dixie. "My future wife is supportive. Doesn't believe everything she reads. Loves me with my faults. Probably even bakes me cookies from time to time."

"Your future wife must've had a lobotomy because nobody is going to go for that."

"Five months. That's all." Alex draped his arm over the back of his chair as he lounged back, lazy as you please. As if he were discussing the weather. Instead of a dishonest farce. "Think of it as a long-term acting job."

The moral ramifications charged through her head like a running of the bulls. She would be living a lie. It was making a mockery of the political system. Of marriage. Of her life. "I can't. I just can't do this." And there was Matt. He had just come back into her life.

"But you're tempted."

"Not even a little." The lies. They were reproducing like roaches. She was desperate for Saving Grace to go on. Those girls couldn't lose their home. It was so much more than a place to sleep for those women. But what Alex was suggesting . . . it was like something from a movie on cable. Starring Tori Spelling. Or one of those Olsen twins.

He pulled his chair closer. His hand brushed against hers. "Lucy, I talked to Roger at city council today. Your building sold."

The ground shifted beneath her. "But Mr. Greene—he said he would honor the rest of our lease. He promised."

"A promise. Are you really that naive? Your agreement becomes null and void with a sale—with or without a promise. You know the city isn't going to honor that lease. They need the property."

This was so unfair. Why was everything falling apart? "We'll find another place."

"Your time is running out. You said yourself you only had months. I'm offering you the golden ticket here." His brown eyes lingered on her face before focusing on her eyes. "Take it."

"This is just about winning to you, isn't it? Are you truly that warped? The political race—and certainly marriage—they're not just another game."

Alex unclenched his jaw. "I do want to win, make no mistake about that. But this is about a lot more than victory."

Lucy shook her head. She wasn't buying it for a second. "You can't stand to lose. Everyone knows that about you."

Alex spiked his fingers through his hair. "Lucy, I . . ." He closed his mouth and drummed a hand on the table, as if weighing a decision. "I want to win for personal reasons, okay? Can we just leave it at that?"

"Nuh-uh."

He gave a growl that had probably intimidated a few opponents, but she wasn't about to back down.

"Fine," he said after a moment. "I . . . I want to make a difference."

Lucy snort-laughed. "Oh, that's a good one." As if people like him cared about anyone but themselves. "That almost sounded believable. For a second there I—" Cold eyes stared back at her. And was he . . . blushing? Alex Sinclair? "Oh. You're serious."

"Of course I'm serious."

She didn't know where to go from here. So she just stared. And shrugged. "But still . . . your tactics—"

"No matter what the news says right now, there's a very good chance my brother is dead," he said evenly. "Will was the good one. Worked for everything he had and left an amazing legacy." Alex stared at his hands as he spoke. "We couldn't have been more different. He spent his life helping others—making a difference. He saved the world—I played sports. He was planning on coming back home in a few months after he got that last school built."

Lucy knew Will had stayed out of the family business, so she hadn't seen him in person in years, but he had been kindhearted. Gentle. Soft-spoken. The antithesis of his tornado of a brother, right down to their opposing looks. She had watched him go from a local reporter to a favorite CNN correspondent and humanitarian.

She licked her lips and carefully stepped back into the conversation. "So you want to make a difference for your brother?" Alex said nothing. "You want to fill the hole you think he left."

"Something like that."

"But you're not Will."

His eyes went hard. "You think I don't know that?"

"Why me? Of all the women you know, you pick me? The scuttle over that last *People* magazine article will wear off soon, and all those bimbos will stop giving you the cold shoulder. What you need is a good trophy fiancée." She couldn't believe the track of this conversation. She was helping the man find a fake bride. "Someone perky. Who poses well. Someone with a sweet disposition."

Alex straightened as a waitress paused at their table to gather the empty plates. "The numbers are there," he said when they were alone again. "People respond to you. They like you."

"Um, pretty sure it's you they like. You're the famous face." She lightly coughed. "And underwear."

"You bring the qualities I lack."

"Like a fully functioning brain?"

"Like a big heart, down-home charm, family values. You've dedicated your life to helping at-risk young women. You're not wealthy—people relate to that."

"You mean I'm poor."

"You value life over things. You're a self-made success."

"So are you."

"As long as there's a silver spoon in your background, no success is ever truly your own."

"Lucky for me and my poverty," she drolled.

"Think of it as a job. One that pays very, very well."

With the way he was looking at her, she could see why half the Warrior cheerleaders had fallen at his feet and declared their blind allegiance. That face could convince any woman to toss aside her morals for ten minutes of sin. And that voice. A man could take over the world with that deep, Southern drawl.

"You know I can't do this. I have . . . someone in my life."

"That stuffed shirt from the gala?"

She eyed her butter knife and had a vision of sticking it somewhere besides the margarine. "Matt is more of a man than you'll ever be."

Alex leaned his head back and laughed, a deep, throaty sound that would've made her smile under different circumstances. "Clearly you don't know what a man is. But luckily for you, I'm willing to teach—"

"No deal, Sinclair."

Alex's expression shifted like a storm cloud. "Lucy . . . have you ever done one reckless thing in your life?" He leaned so close she could feel his breath on her cheek. He smelled like shampoo and spice. "If my brother's dead, he went out giving it all he had. Aren't you tired of living safe?"

Yes, as a matter of fact she was. But that didn't mean she wanted to swim with sharks.

"I save your house, while you save your girls. And I get my ticket to Washington, where I can make a difference. And something tells me, you don't want this town to see you fail. All you have to do is go on a few dates and pretend you like me."

"You do know I *don't* like you, right? We're clear on that?"

"My pride is bleeding, but I can deal with that." His eyes sparkled in the candlelight. "What do you say?"

"I—" Lucy's phone buzzed in the purse at her feet. "I, um, better get that." Grateful for the interruption, she checked the display. "Hello? Yes, this is she." Dread soaked into her spine as she listened to the frantic voice on the other end. "Okay. Don't panic. I'll be at the police station as soon as I can." She punched a button and ended the call. "I have to go."

His forehead wrinkled in a frown. "What's the problem?"

"A new girl who visited Saving Grace. She's been picked up."

Alex stood up as Lucy came to her feet. "I'll drive you."

"No." She held out a halting hand. "Thank you."

He stepped in front of her, blocking her exit, moving into her personal space like it was just another thing he owned. "Think about what I said. Your girls need you."

She shook her head. "Not at this cost."

"Wait." Pulling out a folded check from his pocket, he opened her fingers and placed it in her palm.

"What's this?"

His warm hand closed over hers. His eyes seared. "That, my lady disdain, is your future."

Lucy's phone buzzed again. "I really have to go."

"Be careful driving." He turned back toward the table. "We have a wedding to plan."

Chapter Eight

*I*t was impossible. Unthinkable.

Alex Sinclair had to be out of his mind. A life of excess and too many quarterback sacks had robbed him of logical thought. A post-dated check for two million dollars? It was an unfathomable amount of money to her, but probably a small cut of Alex's argyle sock allowance. She couldn't wait to tell Morgan this one. Lucy, from the wrong side of the tracks, engaged to Alex Sinclair, professional football's Playboy.

Lucy walked through the Charleston police department. Never having been there, she simply stared wide-eyed until someone noticed her.

"Can I help you?"

A man in cuffs burst through the entrance, held up by two officers on either side, yelling obscenities. The uniformed woman in front of her didn't even blink.

"Don't worry. That's Abe McGillis." She rolled her eyes. "He gets drunk every few days, stands on the Exchange building steps, and preaches about the dangers of tattoos, the Internet, and red-headed women. Can I help you?"

Lucy tore her eyes away from the raving Abe. "Yes, I got a call from Marinell Hernandez."

"Are you her guardian? Because she says she doesn't have one."

"She doesn't. Eighteen. On her own." Lucy struggled to focus her spinning thoughts. "Where is she?"

"Come on back."

The woman led Lucy into an office in need of a few windows. Lit only by a weak fluorescent, it was a grim room to send a scared teenager into.

"I'm Detective Benningfield." A tall man with hair graying at the temples shook Lucy's hand. Beside his desk sat Marinell, looking defiant as she clutched a juice box.

"I wasn't doing anything wrong."

"We just brought her in here so we could talk," Benningfield said. "And to get her some food. I don't think she's eaten in days. Are you a family member?"

Marinell shot a glance at the fair-skinned Lucy. "Yeah, we're twins."

"I'm with Saving Grace." *God, let this be an easy fix tonight. Because I have no idea how I'm going to tell this girl I can't let her stay at Saving Grace now.* "And I'm her friend."

"My guys were on patrol about an hour ago. Been watching some suspicious activity at abandoned houses." The detective handed Marinell a napkin from his desk drawer. "Heard some yelling and screaming and they went to check it out. Seems your girl here made the mistake of setting up camp in a house some druggies had already claimed." He regarded Marinell over the rim of his glasses. "Unless she's working for them."

"I told you I don't do drugs. I don't sell drugs. And I never met those people in my life."

Tapping a pen to his desk, the detective continued. "Our pharmaceutical-loving friends were trying to forcibly remove her when my men came up on the scene. Things were about to get ugly."

"What were you doing there?" Lucy asked.

"I'm interested in architecture." Marinell studied the toe of her scuffed Nike. "It looked like a nice house, so I was just checking it out."

"It's a condemned hovel barely fit for rats," Benningfield said. "She had a sleeping bag with her. A bag of clothes. Backpack."

"And I want my backpack. If I lose my school books, I'm dead meat."

"If you hang out in drug houses, you won't have to worry about any book fines." Picking up his stained *Carbs Are My Friend* coffee mug, the detective took a slow drink, somehow managing to keep one intimidating eye on his captive.

"Why weren't you at school?" Lucy asked.

Marinell answered with a shrug.

Lucy had been shocked when Morgan told her Marinell had been an honor roll student until her fall semester. Many girls who came through Saving Grace struggled academically. How could you care about your GPA when you didn't even know where your next meal was coming from?

"Marinell says she's going home with you, Miss Wiltshire?"

"You told me to call if I needed anything," Marinell said. "I mean, I did have plans to stay at the Hilton. But I seem to have run off and left my American Express."

"Of course you can stay at Saving Grace," Lucy said. *You just can't live there.* "I *thought* you were staying with friends."

Head bent, Marinell flicked at her bendy straw. "I might've exaggerated just a bit."

"She's free to go now. We have no reason to keep her." The detective stood up, gathering some files. "But we also don't want to see her here again. Marinell, you were lucky this afternoon. Those guys could've hurt you if we hadn't come by when we did." He gave a curt nod and then left them alone.

The lights above hummed and flickered. It was a dismal place, and Lucy was ready to leave.

How many ways can you twist me in two, God? I can't bring her in just to kick her right back out in a few months.

"Marinell, you should probably know that the home has encountered a funding problem. We don't know how much longer—"

"Look, I won't be much trouble. You told me I could stay. If you don't want me there, just say it."

Behind the fear, there was strength in those dark brown eyes, something Lucy hadn't had at Marinell's age. Tomorrow would just have to take care of itself. Because today this girl needed help. "You're wanted, Marinell. You are very much wanted."

"Well, okay then. I guess I'll go." She held up an empty juice box. "But can we stop and get some more of these?"

Thirty minutes later Marinell stood in the center of her new room. "This is all mine?"

"Yep." For now. Come September Lucy might have thirteen girls camped out in her own spare bedroom.

In the quiet of the room came the unmistakable sound of a growling tummy.

"When's the last time you ate?" Lucy glanced at her watch. It was well after three.

"Last night I guess." Marinell sat on the bed and grinned. "I had one of those sixty-nine–cent burritos from Taco Hut. You know what, that is a really good value too. Who needs a dollar menu when Taco Hut only asks for sixty-nine cents?"

"Let's grab you something from the kitchen. We can make a sandwich and maybe even find some cookies." Lucy moved to the doorway.

"Miss Lucy?"

"Yes?"

"If it's okay with you, I just want to crawl in this bed and sit a while."

"Did those men hurt you?"

She shook her head, her gold hoop earrings swinging. "Nah. I just never had nothing to sleep on but an old couch. Is it okay with you if I hang out here a while?"

"Take your time." Feeling more uncertain by the second, Lucy managed a smile and walked away.

❧

Lucy pressed the phone closer to her ear as she stuck her hand in the jammed printer. "I don't think I heard you right. Say that one more time." Stupid paper wouldn't budge.

"You have twenty-four hours to clear out of the building, Lucy. I'm sorry."

"Mr. Greene, we had a lease. An agreement." Her panic accelerated. "You said I could exercise my lease-to-own option any time."

"Are you telling me you're ready to buy?"

She thought of the check in her pocket. "No, but I think if you gave me another six months—"

"It's not enough. I don't normally do business like this, but the city drives a hard bargain. They want that land, and they want it now."

"And they can have it. When we finish out our lease, which isn't up 'til September."

"They offered me a huge bonus to sell this week. I have two kids to put in college."

"And I have thirteen ladies who will be homeless. We had a contract. A binding, legal document. Do you really want me to contact a lawyer? Because I think it's pretty cut-and-dry."

"You're right. It is," he said. "But you know you can't afford to drag this thing out. And that's exactly what would happen. The city won't fight fair with this. You can't win."

"Just meet with me. We can talk about this."

"I can't do that. Look, I'm sorry."

Her throat tightened. "We have nowhere to go. And no way of getting our stuff out by tomorrow. Please, Mr. Greene. I have people depending on me to fix this, to keep them safe."

But the line was dead. Mr. Greene was done with her. Done with Saving Grace.

Her work. Her dream. And within days it would be a pile of ash and concrete.

How would she move all this furniture? Where would they even go? How could she possibly break this to her girls?

Numb. Drained. Defeated. Still clutching her phone, she went to the window in the office. Squatting down, her fingers slid across the floor, running over the deep indentions left by the sisters. Women who were probably more devoted than she. Women who probably wouldn't be ready to fall apart in a moment like this. Who would know what to do, how to pray.

Lucy knelt, her knees settling into the wood floor, her forehead touching the ground.

Yet no words would come.

Seconds passed. Then minutes.

Her fingers trembling, she finally pulled out her phone and punched in a number. Matt loved her. It was all she could've asked for in this world.

She thought it had been all that mattered.

Lucy made no move to get up from the floor as the phone rang.

A deep voice answered. "Alex Sinclair."

She closed her eyes.

"Hello?"

"It's . . . me." She cleared her tear-clogged throat. "It's Lucy."

"Hello, Lucy." His voice was cautious, and silence followed. "Did you have something you wanted to say?"

". . . Alex?"

"Yes?"

"I do."

Chapter Nine

*A*s the Charleston sky gave way to nightfall, Lucy sat on her overstuffed couch and drummed her knees to the Harry Connick, Jr. song playing in her head.

What had she gotten herself into? She was doomed. This afternoon she had signed on the dotted line, cashing in her principles and jumping right on the sin train bound for calamity and ruination.

From her front door came the sound of three sharp knocks.

Her dark angel had arrived.

She couldn't open that door. To do so would unleash a world of hurt, a Pandora's Box of trouble, a tsunami of moral devastation.

But what choice did she have? She didn't need a solution next month. She needed help today.

Alex Sinclair knocked again. Louder. On the other side of that door was a man not used to being kept waiting. One who *was* accustomed to getting his way.

Lucy remained seated, her body unmoving as if supernaturally frozen.

"I know you're in there," he called. "Open up. It's hot, and I don't like to perspire."

Whispering a prayer, she eased from her seat, smoothed clammy hands over her cropped pants, and slowly made her way to the door. Her shaking fingers twisted the knob.

And there he stood, bathed in the fading glow of the five o'clock sun. Leaning on the wall as relaxed as a man coming over to watch TV, instead of a man ready to plot a fake engagement for all the world to see. "You weren't going to answer that door."

"No."

"You're thinking of backing out, aren't you?"

"Yes. I mean no." Lucy shook her head. "No." His smug smile only fueled her erratic thoughts.

Without invitation, Alex walked past her into the living room. She watched him turn a half circle and assess the place. Looking at her own apartment, she saw it through his eyes. Clean, tidy. Yet the beige carpet was worn and nubby. The open kitchen was tiny, with barely enough room for her dining room table. Pictures of some of her girls hung on the fridge, held up by ladybug magnets. *Lord, I am not that inferior girl anymore. I am an accomplished woman.* She repeated it to herself three more times.

Alex walked to the couch, filling up the small living room with his big muscles and even bigger personality. She briefly wondered why he was settling for Congress. With his charisma, he could probably go straight to the White House. Except for the fact that he thought he needed a fiancée.

He sat down and rested his arms on his thighs, his eyes landing on the coffee table. "I see you like to read." From a stack of magazines, he pulled out the bottom one. "*Science Fiction Monthly?*" He flipped through the first few pages and read from the table of contents. "Lessons Learned from Luke Skywalker: What your choice of light saber says about you." Lucy's cheeks grew warm as he turned another page. "Computer Graphics: blight or bounty for modern-day cinema?" His full lips curled into a grin as he looked at Lucy. "Any centerfolds in here?"

She grabbed the magazine from his hands and held it behind her back. "Do you always prowl through people's things?"

"Just my future non-wife's." He sank back into the couch and put one arm across the back. "Besides, if we're going to be engaged, I think I should know everything about you. Don't you agree?"

"I'll send you a memo."

"No." He drew out the word like it was something to be savored. "We're going to have to get to know one another the old-fashioned way. Talking. Spending time together. Texting."

Lucy prayed her wobbly knees wouldn't buckle beneath her. Alex was the master at playing games. But who was she? Just a poor girl from the wrong side of town who knew nothing about manipulation and high drama. Nothing about dating a famous man, a rich man . . . a wickedly handsome man.

"Can you save my girls' home?" That was all she needed to know.

"Done."

She moved to the chair farthest away from him. "Just like that? Impossible."

His eyes seared into hers. "One of the first thing's my opponents would learn about me on the field—never underestimate me."

"Your money," she said. "You mean never underestimate *your money.*"

Something flicked in those eyes before he shrugged. "Whichever. I would think you'd be grateful for it. Money saved your house today."

"Saving Grace gets to stay?"

"The city found a new location for its parking garage just a half a block down the road. And your home has a new owner."

"What did you do, wave some cash and offer season tickets?"

"And a signed football for Mayor Billings's son." His fingers tapped the back of the couch. "Plus I had to make a sizable donation that would enable them to purchase the much more expensive property." He reached into the pocket of his jacket and extracted an envelope. "Per our discussion at lunch, I've drawn up our agreement." Alex lifted a dark brow and took a quick perusal of Lucy. "Are you seriously so afraid of me that you can't even sit on the same couch?"

Lucy brushed a wild curl out of her face. "I'm not scared of you."

"Then prove it." He patted the seat cushion beside him. "We have a contract to review before we go on our first outing as the town's new power couple." His eyes traveled down the length of her. "Nice outfit, by the way. I like my women fashionable."

"My cheerleader uniform is at the cleaners."

"I guess I'll have to use my imagination."

The soles of Lucy's flats scuffed across the carpet as she joined him on the couch. She grabbed a throw pillow and held it to her stomach. "Please continue."

"Are you going to be this uppity the entire time we're dating?" He leaned in a few inches. "You're going to have to learn to smile. Maybe even laugh from time to time." He moved closer until their noses were nearly touching. "It's important to my ego that you act like I'm irresistible. We wouldn't want my self-esteem to suffer."

His face was so close, Lucy could almost reach out and trace the tiny scar on his stubbly cheek. "I'll just pretend you're someone attractive—like Tom Brady."

With a smile just this side of legal, he thrust the contract into her hands. "Just to review, we pretend to date for approximately one month. This time in June I will propose to you somewhere public and slightly humiliating to us both." His voice was as expressionless as if discussing his preference in athletic socks. "In five months—a month before our wedding date—you and I will have a very amicable, very quiet separation. We will realize we both want different things and go our separate ways. This will be the story we'll feed the press. No variations."

"And who's going to buy that we got engaged after a month of dating?"

"Already handled. I have a good friend who is a genius at photo editing. This week some pictures will be leaked of the two of us. We've been secretly seeing each other for the past four months."

And what would Matt think when that hit the press?

"You can tell no one anything different," he said as if reading her thoughts.

"I have to tell my best friend."

"No."

"Think about it. She and I talk every day, so she'll see right through this."

He rubbed the back of his neck as he considered this. "Do you know how much this story would be worth to a tabloid?"

"You can trust Morgan."

He didn't look like he believed her. "I have a whole team of attorneys. So I'm going to leave it up to you to decide whether you want to tell your friend or not. But know that if word gets out, I will make you and Morgan both regret you've ever heard my name."

Lucy weakly bobbed her head in agreement. "I'll need to tell one more person." She would go to Matt. Explain it all. If she could wait two years, he could hold out for five months. Couldn't he?

"I said one person."

"No, you don't understand." Panic was an expanding pressure in her chest. "I can't get into all this right now, but my ex-boyfriend—"

"I've done my homework. You're not dating anyone."

Lucy pulled herself up straighter on the couch. "Of all the nosy—"

"The guy from the gala?" He shook his head. "No."

"My future depends on this."

"Yes." Alex had probably taken down entire teams with that mutinous glare. "It certainly does. You have a decision to make here. We either do this my way, or I walk. With the check and the deed."

She turned her head and brushed a tear away with her finger. She thought of Trina, the twenty-year-old who had just gotten her associate's degree and was on her way to the university in the fall. And Padma, who after a year at being at Saving Grace, was finally opening up about her brutal past. Then there was Marinell.

She would just pray that God would somehow speak truth to Matt's heart. *Lord, I love that man. And the future I could have with him. Let it somehow be there when this is all over.*

"Fine." Lucy slowly turned back to him. "Morgan will be the only one."

Alex stood up and paced. "There's no room for error here, Lucy." He turned from his inspection of a signed photo of Leonard Nimoy. "I've got too much on the line."

"I'm not going to screw this up." But even as she said the words, doubts whispered in her ear. *A home. Family. Children. All gone.*

"For five months you act like I'm the planet your Starship Enterprise revolves around. That starts tonight. I have dinner reservations for us, then tickets for the theater." That good-time grin was back. "I maintain your current salary and the funding you need. Then you'll have the deed to your building when we're done."

"Plus the check?"

"It's all yours."

"Just like that?" It was so ridiculously complicated . . . yet so simple. He handed her a pen. "Sign."

His silver Montblanc bobbled in her fingers. She found his imposing signature. Studied its curves and angles. It was strong as he was, and just as hard to read.

Her heart crumbling into a thousand pieces, Lucy gripped the pen, then signed her name in an ink more permanent than their engagement.

When she looked up, she found him staring at the contract. "Is there a problem?" she asked.

He blinked and shook his dark head. "Of course not." He offered her his arm. "Let's get this courtship started."

She slipped her arm through his and let him lead her to the door. "You should know I don't put out for fake engagements."

"You wait until the fake wedding?"

She sighed to herself. "A girl has to have her standards."

Chapter Ten

*L*ucy almost killed a man during dinner.

It was her nerves. They were shot. Completely gone. And when Lucy got nervous, she got fidgety. It was a curse she had been born with. In first grade during the final round of the spelling bee, Lucy was given the word *violin*. Anxiety dueled with her limited understanding of vowels and consonants, and so she panicked, knocking over the microphone and giving little Johnny Rodriguez a black eye. Then there had been the science fair in the eighth grade when she'd passed out in front of everyone and broken her nose. But had it been her fault that Rachel Akin had done an experiment involving fake blood *knowing* the very sight of it made Lucy light in the head? Lucy had earned a C on her project and a trip to the ER.

Throughout dinner at the Peninsula Grill, she had felt the same unease gnawing on her insides like rabid butterflies desperate for freedom. As Alex had casually made small talk and taken nice even bites of his filet mignon, the enormity of what she had agreed to played out in her head like a late-night movie. And the butterflies only flapped harder. In her defense, it wasn't Lucy's fault that the waiter reached for the breadbasket just as her knife slipped. Or that she knocked the water pitcher out of his hand in an attempt to help him. Or that he slipped on the ice and carried the whole tablecloth down with him.

Not her fault. Not her fault at all.

Lucy sat in the passenger seat of Alex's black Mercedes and tried not to give into the threatening tears. She had survived much worse than this. Such as . . . well, she couldn't recall anything more horrible right now, but surely there was something. She tried to focus on something else. Like the words she would give to Matt, cutting out his heart and forevermore ruining her future.

"The waiter will be fine." Alex's deep voice interrupted her self-pitying thoughts. "Didn't you hear the maître'd say the bleeding had stopped?"

"No. I didn't catch that."

"Must've been when you had your head between your knees."

"I don't deal well with blood."

"I wasn't sure who to take care of first—you or the bleeder."

She heard his laugh and turned to study his face in the dim lights of the car. "I'm sorry."

"I believe you've said that already."

"I just wanted to say it again."

"Fifty times was more than plenty, Lucy."

"I just . . . I have a lot to think about right now." She pressed her forehead to the slick surface of the window. *God, when I open my eyes, can it be tomorrow?*

Alex adjusted his stereo until he found a classic rock station. "This isn't easy for me either."

"It was nice of you to pray for us at dinner."

He made a quick glance in her direction. "You say that like you're surprised."

"I am," she admitted. "I thought the only person Alex Sinclair worshiped was himself."

There was no anger in the look he gave her. Only mild amusement. "I know who's in charge."

"I'm sure he's *real* proud of us right now." Alex had no response to that, so Lucy decided to change the topic. "Where are we going next?"

"Performing Arts Center. Some Russian ballet dancers are doing Swan Lake." He maneuvered a turn and kept his eyes on the road. "There are some important people in attendance tonight."

"The ballet?" She reached for his hand on the armrest. "Are you kidding me?"

"I wish I were. The Stingrays have a game, and I'd much rather be there. Do me a favor—only wake me up if I'm drooling. A light slumber is totally fine. But the whole mouth open, snoring thing is probably a bit much for tonight's audience."

"I'm not dressed for this sort of thing." Her fitted sweater and 1950s cigarette pants were fine for running about town, but not for an evening of ballet.

"You look fine."

Men. What did they know? "The Russian Ballet is a big deal."

"It's people in tutus. Men in tights twirling around."

"Oh yeah, because football is so much better."

"Don't make me pull this car over."

"A game where you've been the cold cut in many a man sandwich."

She heard his deep, slow intake of breath. He was probably counting the reasons he had chosen the wrong fake girlfriend.

"You have to pretend you like the sport," he finally said. "It's in our contract."

"Is that so?"

"Page seven. Item number four."

She was pulling that blasted document out when she got home.

"Do you even know anything about football?"

She wiggled her captive toes in her flats. "You toss a ball around and throw people to the ground. What else is there to know?"

She could almost hear those perfectly white teeth grinding. "Okay, then, what's a birdcage?"

Considering this, she tapped a finger to her lips. "The name of the bar where you met your last girlfriend?"

"A cut?"

"A fantasy I have involving your throat."

His tan hands tightened on the steering wheel. "A hot receiver?"

"Um . . . a mistake you made in college?"

He unclenched his jaw and slid her a look. "You are one bitter woman, Lucy Wiltshire. I hope your hostility doesn't rub off on our future fake children." He signaled and made a left turn. "Are you also aware you have to call me Mr. Amazing Hotness for all dates involving artsy crap?"

"I most certainly do not."

"Yep." He pulled into the arts center parking lot. "A minimum of five times. Out loud. With lots of sighing."

Though she tried not to, Lucy found herself smiling. She supposed laughing at his jokes didn't mean that she liked him any more or imply any sort of surrender on the old grudge.

Alex parked the car, and Lucy opened her door.

"Shut that," he commanded.

"Excuse me?"

He rolled those eyes that had no doubt caused many a female fan to swoon. "It's my job to open the car door for you. Haven't you ever dated a real man before?"

"Haven't even seen one in days."

He pulled his lithe form out of the car and reappeared at her door. "Take my hand like I'm the light of your life or our next date is at a sports bar with stale pretzels and ESPN."

She slid her fingers through his. The warm night air whipped around them as they walked toward the arts center, and she inhaled the scent of him as it floated on the breeze. He smelled as enticing as he looked. It was a good thing Alex was the farthest thing from her type. She could see how easily a girl could fall for his charms. But she knew the real Alex. He was just a spoiled overgrown kid. One who would stop at nothing to get what he wanted. And she would do well to remember that.

Lucy gasped as they entered the grand foyer. Little black dresses here, sequined formals there. She was surrounded by elegance. "You told me to dress nice," she hissed. "You didn't say this was a fancy event." It was like God had delivered her back to high school again.

He waved to a man across the room, but his voice was just for her. "You look fine. It's just a ballet."

Lucy read a nearby sign. "The United Way benefit? You brought me to a rich person's event?"

He smiled and spoke through gritted teeth. "Wipe the frown off your face, *sweetheart*. We've got people watching." He wrapped an arm around her and pulled her close. "Governor," his voice boomed. "Good to see you." Lucy stood in mute silence as introductions were made. As she eyed the first lady's sapphire-blue cocktail dress, she realized the scene at the restaurant hadn't been all that bad. Things could always be worse. Like now. When she got Alex alone, she was going to strangle him.

"It's lovely to meet you, Ms. Wiltshire," Governor Trenton said. "We're so glad to have our favorite football player back in this great state full time."

Alex's grip on her waist tightened. "Yes," Lucy blurted. "No one is more pleased than I am that he's making his full-time home here once again." It was so hard to carry on charming sweet talk when all she wanted to do was call Matt and beg him to understand. All afternoon she had rehearsed what she would say to him. She had to speak to him before the media ran the first photo of her on Alex's arm.

"Lucy runs Saving Grace right here in Charleston." Alex gazed down at her with something that resembled adoring pride. "You might've heard of it, Governor Trenton. She's done incredible things to help girls who've aged out of the foster-care system."

The governor's wife entered the conversation, describing her own initiatives for teenagers. As Lucy told them about her program, she caught Alex's eye. He gave her a slow wink and ran a caressing hand down her shoulder.

Oh, he was good.

As Alex led her by the hand to their seats, Lucy couldn't get over the stares and murmurs he caused. He created a ripple of awareness everywhere he went. Alex stopped, muttered something under his breath, then lifted his hand in greeting to a couple she recognized as his parents. Lucy swallowed back the old familiar pangs of bitterness as she met the curious faces of Donna and Marcus Sinclair. They were the Hiltons of the South and made money in their sleep. Minus the large yearly donation, these were exactly the type of people Lucy had spent her adult years staying away from.

Alex made quick introductions. "I thought you two were out of town."

"We had a little trouble with Finley," his mother said. "Your sister has gone from seventeen to twenty-five in one month. It's this new boyfriend. We had to cancel our weekend plans. And theirs."

"Did you get my e-mail?" Marcus Sinclair asked his son. "I have to go to Orlando to check on a hotel remodel. Come with me—we can hit the greens."

"Still not interested." Alex stared straight ahead, his hand still on Lucy's. "I need to work."

His father leaned over. "You're going to wake up one day and realize all you have is work."

"Marcus, not tonight," his wife admonished. "Alex, I'm setting a place for you for family dinner Sunday. You know you can't turn down my mashed potatoes and gravy."

"I'm sorry, Mom." Alex's face softened as he looked at the elegant woman. "I'm in campaign meetings all day. Except for lunch with Lucy." Alex moved their joined hands to his thigh. "My schedule's jam-packed, but she talked me into it." He sent her a look that could melt the caramel off a Twix.

Donna Sinclair leaned across her husband and thwacked her son's knee. "If you want my vote, Congressman, you better show up at my dinner table. Don't make me throw around my influence."

Marcus nodded. "Her garden club can be vicious."

"You have to eat," Donna said. "I'll bet your competition spends time with his family." Donna looked at Lucy. "We'd love to have you join us." Lucy was caught off guard by the kind eyes looking back at her. "Maybe you could get Alex to spare some time for the family?"

Marcus glowered at his son. "Your mother cries in her sleep."

Donna leaned over again, her expression serious. "You're my son," she said quietly. "And I miss you. This is a time for our family to draw together, *not* drift apart."

Though Alex's face was its usual picture of devil-may-care, Lucy could almost touch the grief swirling around him. "We'll discuss this later," he said.

"Your sister needs to see you too." Marcus lowered his voice. "And we have to make some decisions about your brother's apartment in Atlanta. Some of his assets."

"No." Alex snapped open his playbill. "Handle it without me. I'm sure whatever you choose to do will be fine."

The lights dimmed three times before plunging the auditorium into complete darkness.

Lucy felt Alex's breath on her cheek. "Keep your hands to yourself tonight," he said. "I don't want my parents to think you're one of *those* girls."

She turned to meet his hooded stare. "And by *those*, you mean every other girl you've ever dated?"

"Don't tell me you read those trash magazines too?"

"You say trashy. I say enlightening."

"Remind me to get you a new subscription to something more mind-enriching." Alex shifted in the seat, wrapping an arm around her shoulders. "Like *Sports Illustrated*."

Chapter Eleven

By the time intermission came, Lucy had decided ballet would be better if more full-sized women were allowed to participate. An entire stage full of perfectly shaped dancers was more than any woman should have to look at. Especially while sitting next to a man who had models on speed dial.

The theater came alive with the sounds of swishing dresses and rustling jackets as the house lights came up.

"Alex, I want to talk to you about the Fourth of July." His mother blinked twice as she adjusted to the lights. "It's important that we have a big celebration as usual—for Finley's sake. Your sister needs things to be as normal and festive as possible."

"I'm traveling on that day," he said. "I'll get back with you."

"But it's your birthday—"

"Lucy wants something to drink." With a look she couldn't decipher, Alex reached for Lucy's hand and gave her a nudge. "We'll be back."

As he led her through the lobby, she wanted to stop him. To ask him about his brother. About the hurt his mother wore beneath her smile. About Alex's own pain. She settled for a safer topic instead. "Aren't you going to let your family in on our little game?"

"Of course not. Just don't get too cozy with them and things will be fine."

"I'll try to put away my dreams of a country club lunch with your mother."

"You'd probably bore her with your Trekkie talk."

He got her a bottled water and himself a seltzer. "I'm going to go remind some people why they love me," Alex said dryly. "Can I leave you alone for fifteen minutes?"

She tried to ignore the way his hand lightly rested at the small of her back. "Of course. I'll just stand here and try to make up some good things to tell them about you."

"Guess I better give you more than fifteen minutes." His eyes lingered on hers. "It's gonna take you a while to list my many fine qualities."

"Like humility?"

His eyes lit with one of those looks that made a woman think of backseats, hurried hands, and foggy windows.

"Behave while I'm gone." Leaning toward her, he slowly pressed his lips to her cheek.

She squirmed from his touch. "I'll count the seconds you're away."

The low rumble of his laughter followed him as he went to join a group of men across the lobby.

Lucy reached into her purse and fished out her phone. She had to talk to Matt. By tomorrow morning, pictures of her with Alex would be all over the Internet.

The phone rang twice. "Hi, you've reached Matt Campbell. Leave a message . . ." Stifling her frustration, she tried two more times. No response.

"That's some man you have on your arm tonight."

Lucy turned to find a woman beside her. She knew they had been introduced earlier, and Lucy struggled to remember her name. "Yes, he's . . . something else."

"I was really intrigued by Alex's health care ideas in the *Gazette's* interview last week." Large diamonds swung from her ears. She looked to be about Donna Sinclair's age. "What do you think of Robertson's counterattack?"

Lucy checked her front teeth for lipstick with her tongue. "Um . . ."

It sure was warm in this place. And so many people. So sparkly. "I must've missed that, um, attack. I've been so occupied with my own work lately."

Heavily lined lids went wide. "But everyone's talking about it."

"Right." How much longer until the ballet? Or a good fire alarm. "*That* counterattack. Well, clearly he's no match for Alex's ideas on health care." Whatever those were. Lucy had been too busy keeping her girls off the streets to keep up with any politics.

"He has some very edgy ideas about insurance," another woman said as she joined them. "As a doctor with my own clinic, I'm very interested in how that's going to play out." She turned to Lucy. "What do you think?"

"Well . . ." Was it rude to fake unconsciousness and fall to the floor? "I am really proud of his ideas on health care for children." Yes. That sounded perfectly safe.

The doctor lifted a hand to her short bob. "He hasn't outlined any measures for children."

"Oh." Lucy swallowed. "Then I guess I can't talk about those right now. But children"—she nodded lamely—"he likes them. Them and their health care." *Shoot me now. Someone just put me out of my misery.*

"Nice to chat with you," the doctor said. She and the other woman walked away. Whispering.

Lucy pinched the bridge of her nose and took five deep breaths. If she was going to be Alex's fiancée, she had some homework to do. She did know he didn't represent anything she was spiritually or ethically against. Except looking like total man-dessert in that suit. Why couldn't he be homely? Or at least average? She was *not* going to fall under his spell like every woman in America. And probably a few misguided men.

"Lucy Wiltshire." The governor's wife waved from her post next to a framed oil painting. "Join us."

Great. The woman was standing in a sea of social piranhas. Beside her stood their leader—Clare Deveraux.

First Lady Trenton patted Lucy's shoulder. "Ladies, I'd like to introduce you to Alex Sinclair's friend. This is—"

"I hear someone bought you a present," Clare said, watching Lucy a little too intensely. "Your home is saved after all."

This was public knowledge already? Could the man even blow his nose without the whole town knowing? "Yes." She made her eyes go dreamy as she smiled. "It's the best gift I've ever received. Alex is so thoughtful like that." Lucy was about to dry heave on her fake Pradas.

"Wiltshire." The gentleman to Clare's right stared at Lucy thoughtfully. She recognized him as the lieutenant governor. Finally, a face she could remember. His wife stood beside him. "I went to Yale with a man by that name," he said. "Are you Cecil Wiltshire's daughter?"

"No." In this town, in certain circles, a name still meant everything.

He frowned. "Then what Wiltshire are you?"

The kind that vacuumed after your kind. "I have no family here," she said, letting her gaze pan the vast room. Where was Alex?

"You're not the shipping Wiltshires?" The man wasn't going to let it go.

"No, my mother was a maid. In fact, she once cleaned Mrs. Deveraux's Charleston home." How was it possible for the bitterness to creep in after all these years? But there it was, punctuating Lucy's every word. "She was the best at what she did and always in high demand."

A woman who reeked of Chanel arched a pencil-thin brow. "And now you're dating Alex Sinclair." Her red lips sneered. "My, how you've come up in the world."

"There is no shame in hard work." Clare finally spoke, her voice as uppity as an antebellum mansion.

Seconds ticked by in weighty silence before the governor's wife spoke. "I see Hillary Davidson is here."

"Going strapless again. She's been doing that since I was first lady thirty years ago." Clare chuckled. "Like she's not seventy-one. And there's Mimsy Taylor."

The first lady shared a laugh with Clare. "Hose and open-toe shoes. When *will* she learn?" She then pointed to a woman across the way. "Lucy, look at that woman."

"Wow." She fixed her eyes on the lady's skyscraper hair. "Hello, eighties, huh?"

"That's my sister," said the governor's wife.

"Oh." Lucy wanted to just sink to the floor and wave a white flag. *Lord, who am I to rub elbows with these people?*

Mrs. Trenton's lips thinned. "I was going to suggest you introduce yourself to her. She works for South Carolina Department of Social Services."

"If . . . if you'll excuse me, I need to find Alex." *And flush myself down the toilet.* "It was a pleasure chatting with you."

Clare's hand stopped her. "Young lady, if you're going to be dating Alex Sinclair," she said in a low voice, "you might want to brush up on the who's who of our state." The woman only spared Lucy the smallest of glances. "I'd hate for you to mess things up."

"Right." Lucy quickly turned to leave, only to find her face colliding into the chest of a man. "Oomph. I'm sorry." She reached out to steady herself.

Cold hands went to her shoulders. "Lucy Wiltshire?"

She looked at the man who was eye level to her and immediately stepped away. "Yes?"

"Garrett Lewis of the *Gazette*."

She rubbed her wounded nose. Not more health care questions. Not tonight.

"I was wondering if I could talk to you for a moment?" A high forehead gave way to slicked-back hair a shade somewhere between raven black and dead crow.

"I really need to go. Someone is looking for me." The Jekyll-like nerves were taking over her body. Disaster was sure to follow if she didn't get herself under control.

"It'll just take a moment."

"I'd rather not."

"Would you like to set the record straight about your relationship with Alex Sinclair? There's so much public speculation. What about an exclusive?"

"I'm not here to talk about my personal life. Or Alex's."

Beady eyes stared back at her. "With his seemingly bottomless bank account, do you think he's buying his Congressional seat?"

No. Just a fiancée. "I think he's passionate about his values and making this state the best it can be."

"He's openly spoken against proposed amendment seven. Not everyone agrees with that. What do you think?"

Amendment seven? She had much Googling to do when she got home, and she couldn't get there quick enough. "I completely stand by and support Alex."

Garrett Lewis's face turned smug. "Tell the people in your own words how you would define the amendment."

Lucy's steak dinner was staging a full-arsenal attack in her stomach. "I have to go."

His sweaty hands latched on to her arms. "Just a moment more."

"We're done here." She shrugged out of his grip and moved to put some much-needed distance between them. She had to find Alex. And get out of there.

"Miss Wiltshire!" One quick look back told Lucy the creep was still on her heels.

"Excuse me." She maneuvered through a group of people wedged together.

"Miss Wiltshire!"

This was all too much. She hadn't planned on being quizzed. On being openly judged. Being expected to comment on amendments. And *not* on hairdo violations.

She squeezed past the patrons standing in the middle of the walkway. "Pardon me." They wouldn't move. Didn't even hear her.

"Lucy!" Garrett Lewis was getting closer.

She tried to force her way through the wall and a trio of men. Pushing a little harder, she was desperate to get away.

A giant of a man turned around, and his right side knocked into Lucy, sending her into the wall. "Sorry," he mumbled. "Hey, watch out for the—"

But it was too late. Lucy's head made contact with a hanging painting. Her hands flailed. And as she came straight down to the floor, *Flowers in the Summertime* came with her. The gilded frame broke into pieces.

Lucy looked at the chaos around her. At the lobby full of rich people staring at her. And did the only mature thing she could do.

She ran.

❧

He found her in the parking lot.

Standing between a Mercedes and an Escalade, Lucy was bent at the waist, gasping for air.

"Lucy?" He strolled over beside her. She ignored him. "Are you hyperventilating?"

Her yellow-gold curls bobbed as she nodded and breathed. Nodded and breathed. "Is this going to become a habit?"

She reared up, her eyes glimmering with fire and water. "Pick someone else."

"Tell me what's wrong." Lucy Wiltshire just shook her head.

He had been trying to make his way to her in the cavernous lobby. The crowd seemed to have multiplied by the time intermission began, and he couldn't get to her. He'd watched that slime-bag reporter lay his hands on her. Watched Lucy's face go white. Alex had shoved his way past a senator and junior congressman at that point. He had wanted to rip that man's arm from the socket no matter who saw. Fake girlfriend or not, nobody would be touching Lucy. But him.

Alex reached out and pulled her to him. She stiffened in response. "I'm sorry I dragged you here with me tonight. Maybe you're not ready for all this yet." But he didn't have time to wait for her to catch up.

With her arms straight at her sides, she spoke into his shirt. "I just get so clumsy when I get nervous. And I couldn't move. Or breathe." Her voice hitched, and he rubbed her back, making circles with his fingers. "And then that reporter wouldn't leave me alone. And I couldn't squeeze through because that other man was as big as a building and wouldn't let me by. I hit the wall." She sniffed. "And the painting."

"It's gonna look great over your mantel."

She lifted teary eyes to his. "And I don't know what amendment seven is. I barely know the preamble to the Constitution. And some woman had eighties hair, but I shouldn't have said anything, but I did because clearly anyone with an AquaNet dependence is just asking for it."

He wondered if she knew she had not only wrapped her arms around his waist, but was snuggling to the point of burrowing into his chest.

"Listen to me—"

"And Clare Deveraux is a viper with a staring problem. And I can't remember all these names of all these important people."

The tropical storm in his arms was about to turn into a category 4 hurricane. "Lucy—"

"Important rich people who dress properly for an event, unlike *your* date tonight because *you* didn't tell her it was fancy!"

"I'm sorry. It was a last-minute invitation, and I didn't have all the particulars."

She stared at him with a disdain reserved for murderers and men who kick puppies. "I don't have one single sparkle on."

He took her face in his hands. "I think you look beautiful tonight."

She rolled her eyes. "You think anything with boobs is beautiful."

"That's not true. I don't think Governor Trenton is especially attractive." A weak smile appeared on Alex's cheeks, turned pink by the evening humidity. "I need you right now. In this campaign with me. By my side." He knew she was on the edge, and he felt a small measure of panic at the thought of her backing out now. "You're the one I chose, Lucy." He rubbed his thumb over her cheek. Told himself to take his eyes off her parted lips. "I'll get you up to speed, I promise."

"I don't know if I can do this," she whispered.

"You can." He gently rested his forehead on hers. He would have to get a game plan where she was concerned. She needed the type of help he couldn't provide. A woman's touch. A mentor. "Obviously you ended up back in Charleston for a reason, so it's time to show this town who Lucy Wiltshire really is." If Alex had learned anything on the field, it was how to target your opponent's weak spot. "Think of your girls."

She swiped the stray mascara beneath her eyes. "You're right. I have to do this."

He let out the breath he'd been holding. "That's my girl." Pulling her to him in a hug, he told himself he was only blocking her from lurking paparazzi. "Now let's go."

"I can't go back in there. Please—I just want to go home." Her face was a desperate plea.

Alex sighed, then nodded. "I'll take you now."

Had he done the right thing? This woman was a walking disaster. If they were going to pull this off, Lucy needed some serious help.

Unfortunately, he knew just the person for the job.

Chapter Twelve

Whoever was at her door was going to pay.

Lucy's heart hammered beneath her Lord of the Rings T-shirt as she listened to the pounding on her apartment door. She stared around the sun-filled room to get her bearings. It was eight o'clock. The latest she'd slept in years. But after last night, she wanted nothing more than to pull the covers over her head and go back to sleep.

The incessant knocking continued.

Lucy threw her legs over the side of the bed, slipped on a robe, and trudged to the living room. She pressed one bleary eye to the peephole. And sucked in a breath.

Clare Deveraux stood on the other side of the door. "What do you want?" Lucy called. She was too tired to bother with nice.

"Open up. It's an oven out here," came Clare Deveraux's uppity voice. "I bet your house has a nice air conditioner."

"I must speak with you."

Lucy opened the door, holding out a hand to block the sun. "I'm not really prepared for company at the moment." Besides the fact that her hair was standing on end, Lucy had nothing to say to the woman who had voted to shut down Saving Grace and sabotaged her mother's job. She was about to close the door when she realized that Clare was not alone. Beside her stood a yawning man in outrageous lavender pants.

"If you came to show off your boyfriend, you could've at least waited until a proper hour."

Clare waved a gloved hand. "Don't be ridiculous. Julian is twenty years younger than me."

The slender man shot her a withering look. "Try forty."

"Whatever." Clutching Lucy's newspaper, Clare elbowed past her and entered the living room. "Lucy Wiltshire, I have a proposition for you."

"Oh, no." Lucy couldn't handle one more proposition in her life. "Whatever you've concocted, you can just forget it. You and your boyfriend need to leave."

Clare plopped herself on the couch. She patted the cushion beside her. With an apologetic look to Lucy, Clare's companion walked across the Berber carpet and sat down.

Wishing she had taken the time to get her slippers, Lucy eased herself into a chair and pulled her short robe tighter around her. "What do you need?"

"Let's have breakfast, shall we?" Clare clasped her hands together. "We can talk and eat."

Lucy blinked. "You want to bond over a bowl of Wheaties? Because that's all I've got."

The older woman sniffed. "Of course not." She snapped her fingers at the man. "Julian can whip up something grand from whatever is in your kitchen."

"A rotten banana and some protein powder." Lucy rubbed a hand over her face. "Maybe you two could go out for some waffles and then call me later."

"I want to talk about last night," Clare said.

"Well, I don't." Just the mention of it brought the awful memories shrieking back.

"You need some assistance, and I've decided I'm going to give it to you."

"No, thanks."

"But first we share breakfast. I'm old and weak and need to eat now." Clare slapped the armrest. "Do you know what it's like to be old? And so feeble you need a personal assistant?"

"You're about as feeble as a Rockette," her friend said from the couch.

Clare ignored him and continued. "Of course you don't know what it's like. I roam my house with nothing to do. But as of this morning, that changes. You are my new mission, Lucy Wiltshire." She stopped talking long enough to let her eyes travel over the apartment. "Yes, I can see I have my work cut out for me." She patted the blond man's knee. "I hope you're not having flashbacks, dear." Her attention returned to Lucy. "I saved Julian from the mean streets. I don't want him to go back there."

Julian rolled his eyes. "I was in the chorus in *The Lion King.* You didn't save me from the streets, you old battle-ax. You saved me from my addiction to stage makeup and a nasty allergy to glue and whiskers."

This was too weird. "I really want to go back to bed now, so if you two could take your variety show somewhere else—"

"They let men be secretaries now, did you know that?" Clare smiled at her friend. "He can update my Tweeter thing while singing 'Seventy-Six Trombones.' Now, where was I? Oh, yes." Clare focused those Medusa eyes on Lucy. "I was saying without my help you are going to single-handedly destroy what little chance Alex has for securing his seat in Congress."

Lucy closed her eyes and imagined herself taking a flying leap at the woman, clotheslining her WWE-style. Yet rude as she was, Clare was telling the truth. Who was Lucy to be running in Alex Sinclair's circles? Just because she wasn't seventeen anymore didn't mean she was any more qualified to be hanging out with the monied elite than she had been in her Clearasil and hand-me-down days.

"Just hear what I have to say before you kick me out," Clare said in her sophisticated Southern lilt.

Julian stood up. "I'll just find the kitchen and get something going."

Clare trailed after him, and Lucy had no choice but to follow.

"You were right." The cabinets rattled as Julian rifled through them. "Slim pickin's."

"I haven't had time to shop lately." *I've been too busy selling my soul.*

Clare sat at the table and unfolded the morning paper. She read for a moment as Lucy stood useless in the kitchen like a guest in her own home.

Finally pulling her attention from the front page, Clare studied Lucy. "That hair of yours. It's a tad unruly." Her eyes went back to the news. "My son's was curly like that when he was a toddler. I let it go long and natural, though my husband hated it. Said it made him look prissy."

Julian poured juice into a wine glass. "Nothing wrong with getting in touch with your feminine side."

It was like a bad Fox sitcom, this cozy tableau. Here was the woman who had been snippy and snooty to Lucy as long as she had known her. And now Clare was sitting in her kitchen sharing breakfast, reading *her* paper, and discussing hairdos.

"Who wants pancakes? I'll have to make a few substitutions, but I think I've got all I need," Julian said.

Clare turned another page. "He went to Cordon Bleu."

Lucy counted to ten in Klingon before she was able to think of something civil to say. "Maybe we could eat something . . . quicker?"

"Oh, look at this blind item in the society section. It says Lady R, a certain socialite, attended Mrs. M's tea party and left with the family silver." She lifted her brows toward Julian. "If that isn't Roxie Stinson, I'll give up Botox and foot scrubs."

"Sticky Fingers strikes again." Julian poured the batter onto a skillet. "Remember when she tried to make off with your pearls?"

Clare scanned the rest of the article. "Just shows money cannot buy good manners." She laid down the paper with a thud of her hands and turned those predatory eyes on Lucy. "Speaking of that, I'm here to offer you my show of support."

"Thanks." *Now please leave.*

"Alex contacted me this morning about mentoring you. I am a former first lady." She fluttered a hand to her chest and let the silence hang as heavy as wet laundry. "And I've decided it's time."

"Time for what?" Lucy asked, unable to look away from the woman's intensity.

Clare opened her mouth. Closed it. Shared a look with Julian. "Time to share what I know with the younger generation. I have a great many things I could teach you. And that's exactly what Alex has asked me to do."

Why were the words like a slap? It was one thing for Lucy to know she was an ugly duckling in his world of swans. But that Alex thought she was just as graceless and awkward as she felt—it hurt. "So he asked you to *tutor* me."

"Yes." Clare couldn't hide the curiosity in her voice. "But it's because he . . . seems to care about you."

"Right."

"The interesting thing is when I went home last night, I had already decided I would offer my assistance. Didn't I say just that, Julian?"

"Just that." He flipped a pancake. "Okay, who's ready for some food?" He found plates and set the table as Lucy sat there, unmoving, watching it all from a distance. She had never been good enough to hang out with the Charleston aristocracy, and now they wouldn't leave her alone.

Julian served both women and took a chair. "Let us pray, shall we?" He patted Clare's hand. "Muffin, I believe it's your turn."

"Yes, so it is." She caught Lucy's watchful eye. "What? Bow your head. Don't you understand prayer etiquette? The prayers won't work if you don't bow your head."

"We're kind of new to this," Julian said.

Biting back a retort, Lucy did as she was told.

"Lord, we thank you for this fine breakfast. Even if someone isn't grateful for it right now. And even if getting out in the sweltering heat has fired up my arthritis."

"Yes, Lord," called Julian.

"And we ask that you prepare Lucy's heart for what is about to come. It's going to be hard. It's going to be trying. And that's just my part."

"Yes, Jesus."

"Please comfort Lucy as she endures her training. And . . . as she discovers a side of herself she didn't know existed. Because I have much to teach her. But I'm determined to bring her into the inner circle. And I can do that through the help of our precious Father. Even though Julian and I are new to your flock. But already membership has its privileges."

"Like a gold card, Lord."

"Okay." Lucy jerked her head up. "Amen." She picked up her fork and cut into a pancake.

"So we will begin our lessons tomorrow night," Clare continued. "You will come to my house. I'll send Julian with the car for you."

"I have church."

Clare took a dainty bite. "Remove your elbows from the table."

Bossed around in her own house. "Don't take this the wrong way, Mrs. Deveraux, but I'd rather get help from someone else."

"From whom, dear?" Clare's expression dared Lucy to come up with one single name.

She sipped her juice. "My friend Amy was Miss Magnolia Blossom." In the third grade.

"Young lady, this is more than just poise and primping. Do you know the names of the current governor's grandchildren?"

"No."

"Rachelle and Michael." Julian pressed a napkin to his lips. "Total heathens in need of a good time-out. Eh, Clare?"

"I'm sure you can tell me what group Alex's opponent is going after in his latest campaign, correct?"

The pancake was a wad of glue in her mouth. "No."

"Do you know where Alex stands on education?"

Her head was pounding. "I'm pretty sure he likes it."

Clare huffed and put down her fork. "Leave us, Julian."

He stood and bowed. "Yes, madam. I'll just go in the living room and pretend I'm not listening to your every heavy-handed word." And with a friendly wink he was gone.

"Mrs. Deveraux—"

"You may call me Clare."

Lucy wanted to call her *gone.* "Clare, I realize I can be a disaster in social situations. And I have a lot of reading to do to get familiar with Alex's politics. But these are quick fixes. I don't require lessons." *Especially from you.*

"My dear." Clare's face had gone intense again. "I have more than my years of experience to offer. I'm about to share with you something that can't be learned from a book. Something only I can impart. Today I bring to you a gift that will give you credibility."

"A decent pair of heels?"

Clare didn't crack a smile. She reached out and laid her hand on Lucy's. "I'm giving you my name."

Okay, weird. Just weird.

"My dear girl." Clare curled her fingers around Lucy's hand. "I know who your father is."

A million thoughts slammed through Lucy's brain. "So do I. His name is Thomas Miller. He was a fighter pilot in the navy." Chill bumps raced up her arms.

"That's not possible."

Lucy struggled to catch her breath. "Why not?"

Blue eyes locked on to blue. "Because your father . . . was my son."

Chapter Thirteen

*A*lex found her speed-walking down Pecan Street in a knee-length robe and snow boots.

"Look at that crazy woman," his sister said from the passenger side.

His Mercedes slowed to a crawl as he pulled alongside Lucy and rolled down his window.

Finley double-checked the locks.

"Nice morning for a walk." His dashboard read eighty-six degrees.

Finley leaned over to get a better look. "You're not gonna give her a ride, are you?"

"Nah." Alex kept up Lucy's pace. "Just gonna marry her."

Finally his angel of morning hair and bad shoe choices spoke. "Any moment I'm going to wake up. I'm going to wake up and this will all have been a bad dream." She marched right on, like a solider heading to the battlefield. "My girls' home," she huffed. "Clare Deveraux. My father." Her next words came out in a hiss. "And *you*."

"PMS." He shot Finley a look. "Hits her hard every time."

"I hear that."

He watched as his soon-to-be intended stepped right over a dead, bloated possum without so much as slowing down. "Babe, you want to tell me what's going on?"

"Go drive off a cliff."

He gave his sister a smile. "Loves me so much she sometimes has a hard time expressing it." He maneuvered past a pothole as three vehicles went by. All staring. "Do you want to get in the car?"

He could see her lip curl from here. "Does it look like I want to get in the car?"

"It looks like you're on your way to strangle someone at a slumber party." He tried to pull up a little ahead of her so he could get a better look at her face. "But I've never been one to judge by appearances."

Alex smiled when he heard her predictable snort.

"My sister Finley and I were on our way to breakfast. I thought you might like to meet her and go with us."

Lucy dipped her head and peered inside the car. "Nice to make your acquaintance." She pulled her attention back to her path. "I've already eaten, though. With my grandma."

If a man kept things shallow and casual, he didn't have to deal with this sort of thing. Something told him Lucy's problem couldn't be solved with a pretty trinket or a weekend getaway. He was fairly good at reading the signs. Like how her robe was tucked into the back of her boxers. They weren't even his brand. *Lord, I need some help with this one.*

"You want to talk about this?" He watched the cars begin to pile up behind him.

"No."

"I can't follow you forever," he said. "I might run out of gas and what would it do to my image for the public to see two women pushing me in my car?"

Lucy swiped at her eyes with the back of her hand. She sure did cry a lot. He was really hoping this wasn't the norm because he didn't deal well with criers. Finley knew from infancy if she wanted anything, all she had to do was turn on the waterworks, and he and Will would move heaven and earth to get it.

Alex tried again. "Can we take you somewhere?"

His sister cranked up the air. "Like a mental ward?"

"Um, Luce." He waved two cars on. "Isn't that outfit kind of drafty?"

And then she stopped. Right there on Pecan Street, Lucy sat down, leaned her elbows on her legs, and dropped her head. *Uh-oh.*

Alex pulled over. Got out. Stuck his head back in the window. "Drive around the block a few times."

Finley jumped over the console. "Sweet."

"No scratches this time."

With screeching tires, she was gone.

Alex studied the wild arrangement of Lucy's morning hair before dropping to his knees beside her. The dewy grass soaked right through his jeans. "I can't help you unless you talk to me."

"Nobody can help me." Her head shot up, and crazy eyes stared back at him. "I'm trapped in some psychotic soap opera, and I just want my life back." She sniffed her red nose. "And you"—she punched her finger to his chest—"how could you ask Clare Deveraux to tutor me?"

"*Mentor* you. Give you some advice." Lucy had herself some nice legs beneath that robe. "Is that what this is about?"

"Yes." She rubbed her sleeve across her nose. "No. Maybe."

"Have you been drinking?"

Lucy pulled her hands inside her sleeves. "She says she's my grandmother."

"Who?"

"Haven't you been listening to any of this? Clare Deveraux says her son, Steven, was my father. Can you imagine?"

"No." Alex couldn't imagine a useless fool like Steven Deveraux fathering someone like Lucy. Steven had been a cold-blooded snake whose only care had been getting his face in the society pages. "Tell me everything she said." He was going to wring Clare's wrinkle-free neck when he saw her. He'd asked her to befriend Lucy. To invite her to lunch. To share some advice and wisdom. Not scare her by claiming they shared DNA.

"She offered to *tutor* me." Lucy shot him a look of misery. "I know last night went badly. But I can do better than that, really. I just need to focus and get used to all this." She sniffed. "And watch some C-SPAN."

He rested his hand on her knee. "You're doing fine. Last night was just a little hiccup." More like a disaster of epic proportions. And one he couldn't afford to have again. "What else?"

"Then she said, 'My son is your father.' Just like that." Her face dropped to her hands again. "I totally know how Luke Skywalker felt."

"Did she give you any proof?"

"She pulled out some pictures—some of Steven as a baby. Steven as a teenager. But what do baby pictures prove, right? I mean, we all look the same as babies." The humid breeze blew the palmetto tree beside them and picked up Lucy's tangled hair. "I mean, sure, he and I were both white-headed. And his hair stood straight up like he'd been hit by lightning on the way through the birth canal—like mine. But it means nothing."

Alex's phone buzzed at his hip. He checked the display and inwardly winced. He needed to take the call but couldn't leave Lucy like this. "And what did you say when you told her the photos weren't confirmation of paternity?"

"I don't know." Lucy pulled at a tuft of grass. "I ran out. I just left her and her man friend alone in my apartment."

"Because walking down the road in your robe and snow boots made sense?"

Lucy's eyebrows slammed together. "Like all of your ideas are brilliant. I read in the *Enquirer* last year you had two girlfriends show up at your Malibu beach house. Two girls who didn't know about each other."

"I'm sorry, but two chicks and one me? You don't call that brilliant?" One look at Lucy's face, and Alex knew he should've taken that call. "You can't believe everything you read. Just look at all those stories about us. So tell me again what you know about your father."

Lucy pressed against her temple as she rattled off her list. "My father was in the Air Force. Fighter pilot. Died in a practice run. Never married my mother, but they had planned on it. He was an orphan. I never met him, but I have pictures."

"And do you look like him?"

"I don't know. I guess. Maybe." She shrugged. "Mostly I just look like my mom."

"There's one way to find out if Steven is your father."

"Clare said she had irrefutable proof at her house."

Alex started to rise. "Then let's go get it."

"No!" Lucy grabbed on to his hand. "I can't right now." She licked her lips, and Alex watched her as if in slow motion. Even with bed-hair, Lucy was something to look at. "I don't want to see her. I just want to go home. I want my old life back. And I want that woman out of my apartment. And—"

"You want to make better shoe choices?"

Lucy glanced down at her Sherpa stuffed snow boots. "They were all I had in my coat closet. I grabbed them on my way out the door." And then the tears started again.

Alex rubbed a hand over his face. He had to get Finley fed and himself back to the campaign office, but he couldn't just leave Lucy sobbing in her boxers on the side of the road.

"Lucy, you leave me no choice." He wondered if she realized she was still holding his hand. "It's time to show you the campaign head-quarters. Introduce you to my team. Give you some insight on my platform." He reached out and brushed his knuckles over her cheek. "Teach you how to put campaign signs in yards after dark."

She sniffed. "I'm a mess."

He swept his eyes over her nightwear. "Nothing a little lip gloss won't fix."

Having Lucy at the office would help in keeping Finley occupied as well.

His parents had been having a small battle with her lately, and he knew when they suggested a brother-sister outing this morning, they just wanted a few hours of peace.

Eyes as blue as a perfect summer sky looked up at him. "Do you think I'm a disaster?"

"No." Only he and Jesus would know he was lying. "I think you're overwhelmed. That's the only reason I asked Clare to contact you. Had I known she was going to drop an atomic bomb in your lap, I would never have suggested she offer her assistance."

Lucy turned as a red Camaro blared its horn. "Matt was going to ask me to marry him."

Guilt punched Alex straight in the gut. "Ah, Luce. I'm sorry." Great. Now he wasn't only living the biggest lie since Watergate, but he was ruining Lucy's future. "But how good could this guy be if he walked away from you once?"

She set that jaw and lifted her chin. "You don't even know him."

No, he didn't. But something about Matt Campbell didn't sit right with him. The accountant looked about as exciting as a tax code manual. He knew enough of Lucy by now to understand she'd be bored with a guy like Campbell in minutes.

He had to get her mind off this. "Did I mention we're throwing a big party next month? You like party planning, don't you?" Didn't every woman?

"Have you met me?" Lucy jerked her hand from his and stood. "I *stink* at this! Alex, maybe we need to cut our losses now. You find yourself some trophy lady, and I—"

"You'll what?" Alex pulled himself to his full height and towered over her. "Don't bail on me now. You need my money, and I need—"

"My ability to stab waiters? My impressive knack for destroying priceless art?"

She stomped away, but he caught her in two strides and hauled her to him. Anger sparked in those eyes she had trained on him like crossbows. "Don't bail on me. Not now. I have way too much at stake." It was everything to him.

Lucy stared at his hands, then back at his face. She smelled like pancakes and looked like a displaced nursery rhyme character. "How many people are we talking at this party?"

"Hundreds."

"Am I going to hate it?"

He dragged his eyes away from her pink lips. "Most assuredly."

Lucy nodded once, coming to some decision in her head. "If I don't get Matt back when this is over, I will never forgive myself."

"Understood."

"And I will relentlessly harass you and make you miserable for the rest of your life."

Alex reached for her hand as his car came into view. "Lucy Wiltshire, I do believe you're sounding like my wife already."

Chapter Fourteen

Sometimes the sight of a church could bring immediate peace and contentment, as if to say, *God is going to meet you here.*

Today was not one of those days.

As Lucy got out of her car, the red brick building looked imposing, mad. She felt like a hypocrite for even following the sidewalk that pointed to the sanctuary doors. *Hey, I'm lying to the world. Praise the Lord.*

Steeples poked through the clouds in the Charleston skyline like arrows to heaven. A church could be found on nearly every corner, which meant Lucy couldn't drive a block without seeing Guilt in her faded passenger seat. She had always been the good girl. The one to toe the line and do the right thing. And now look at her. She was walking the tightrope of depravity and about to fall right over. But every time she thought of backing out, she saw the faces of her girls from Saving Grace.

She did her third double take as she walked away from the dusty car. As she had navigated the highway, she'd thought for a moment a red sedan was following her. To be with Alex meant paparazzi everywhere, and paranoia was quickly becoming her new best friend—right after lipstick, which she was constantly applying. Photos could be so brutal. Like in this morning's Sunday paper. A big unflattering picture of her at the art center, caught just as she had brought down the expensive painting. And of course it had been accompanied by an article about her humble background. Obviously it had been a slow week if a reporter had to resort to that. But it stung. And Lucy hadn't even finished her oatmeal before she knew it was time for drastic action—no matter the cost.

Chuck greeted her at the door. "Welcome, sister. Glad you're here."

She laughed. "No jeans today?"

He tugged at the tie below his lopsided collar as Morgan came to stand beside him. "Pastor's sick. I'm filling in."

"Nervous?" Lucy asked.

He wiped his sweating brow. "It's quite possible I peed my pants thirty minutes ago."

"He's going to do great," Morgan said, patting Chuck's arm.

"Yeah, I hope I remember how to preach to a crowd older than sixteen." He waved to another friend. "It's okay to use the word 'dude' in prayer, right?"

Lucy smiled. Chuck was so good at what he did, but his confidence had yet to catch up to his ability. "Hey, do you guys want to grab lunch afterward? Hang out—talk?" She had yet to process Clare Deveraux's revelation. She wanted to share it with her friends and get their insight. And sympathy.

"We can't," Morgan said. "I've finally talked him into registering at the mall."

Chuck greeted a passing couple. "Is it bad etiquette to ask for a new Guitar Hero?"

"Okay. Maybe later." Talking would have to wait. "Good luck in there."

"Oh, I almost forgot." Morgan tilted her head and gave Lucy a questioning stare. "There's someone waiting for you."

Lucy looked beyond Chuck into the sanctuary. There on the tenth row sat Alex Sinclair. "Huh."

"Yeah, I said the same thing." Morgan frowned. "Lucy, what is going on with you two?"

Lucy shrugged. "Pretty much what it looks like." Minus a few glaring details.

"So you're serious? I mean, I know we haven't gotten to hang out much lately, but *him*? And *you*?"

"Yes." Lucy's voice was a dry monotone. "He's everything I could want and more."

Morgan wasn't buying it. "And you couldn't tell me the two of you have been dating?"

"Look," Chuck said, "we think you're worthy of the best man on the planet—you know that. But Alex Sinclair—the Playboy? Are you sure you know what you're doing?" He spoke in a whispered hush. "I might be a pastor, but if he messes with you, I will run my light saber right through his black heart, you got that?"

"I care about him. He's actually not a bad guy once you get to know him."

"What about Matt?" Morgan asked.

He had yet to return Lucy's phone calls, and that only added to the yarn ball of stress in her stomach. "Let's just discuss this later."

Morgan shook her dark head and leaned closer to Lucy. "I don't know what's going on, but I want the truth. So as soon as I wrap up some of these wedding details, you and I are going to have a nice long chat."

"I'd better go. Alex is waiting for me."

She walked down the aisle, slipped past Alex and into the empty seat beside him.

"Saving this?" she asked.

"Yes. For my girlfriend." He smiled, revealing a dimple in his cheek. "You can sit there until she arrives, but don't be surprised if I get handsy during 'I Surrender All.'" His arm curved over the back of her chair. "That song does something to me every time."

"So what are you doing?" she asked.

"Going to church."

"Why?"

"Because it's Sunday."

"Is this about your image?"

Something in those dark chocolate eyes shifted. "Believe what you want."

She watched him for a moment, not sure what to make of his appearance. "Well, I'm not sharing my Bible."

The frat boy grin returned. "I have my own."

"Precious Moments?"

He smiled at the couple taking seats in front of them. "I hope you get your man-hating issues taken care of before our wedding. I can't live with this abuse for fifty years." He leaned closer, and she had to remind herself to breathe. The laughter left his eyes as he studied her. "How are you this morning? Have you had any more communication with Clare?"

She didn't know what to do with the concern she saw in his face. Sarcasm and animosity she was comfortable with. But this fledgling friendship they were building? Terrifying. "She's called a few times. But I haven't picked up. I'll get cotillion lessons from someone else."

"I meant about your dad."

"I can't even think about that now." Lucy watched Chuck take the pulpit. "But I am strangely glad you're here. I just hope lightning doesn't strike our row or anything."

"For your information, I was raised in a church. I took first place in Bible drills in the fifth grade."

Her lips shifted into an easy smile. "Really?"

He nodded. "I got a medal and everything."

"I'm impressed."

"Don't be," he said. "I got caught kissing Emily Fletcher behind the oak tree of Trinity Methodist, and Pastor Hamby took back my award."

"You were totally robbed."

Alex tugged on one of her curls. "Anything for a girl."

She had to turn away from the warmth in that million-dollar smile. The guy was getting under her skin.

Yesterday had been quite an eye-opener. Watching him in his office fielding phone calls, holding a staff meeting, planning next week's commercial shoots. She had expected to find Alex just going through the motions of the campaign—letting others do the heavy lifting. But the only thing he hadn't weighed in on was lunch. That had been his sister Finley's job. He was quite the big brother to her. How many times had

Lucy caught him sharing a joke with his sister or praising Finley for helping make phone calls? And in the midst of it all, he had shown Lucy around, taken the time to introduce her to everyone on his staff. Like she was a part of his team. A member of Alex Sinclair's inner circle.

And now he was leaning into her side like any boyfriend would. One who wasn't a hoax for political gains. One who wasn't paying her to date him. But if she closed her eyes, it was almost real. She could imagine her heart wasn't breaking over Matt. It was too easy to step into this fantasy they were creating—that Alex was someone who cared about her. Who could comfort her in this confusing time of paternity bombshells and social suicide.

Chuck's voice permeated her wandering thoughts. "In First Peter God says it's time to be on alert. The devil prowls around, looking for our weakness. Do you know when we are at our weakest?"

At rich people parties, Lucy thought.

"We are such easy prey when we're broken down like an old truck on the side of the road," Chuck said. "When life has knocked you to your knees, and you have no idea how you're going to fix it. When your brain is consumed with hurt . . . and all the solutions you've come up with are filling up your head."

Beside her Alex scribbled notes on the back of the church bulletin. His hand covered up the page, and she couldn't make out what he had written. Probably another one of his endless agendas.

"God tells us to get humble. To run to him and just say, 'Take care of me. Take the decision-making out of my hands.'" The pinstriped shirt stretched taut across Chuck's ample belly as he held up his Bible. "He promises to lift us up in due time. He says, 'After you've suffered for a while, I'm gonna pull you right out, and you're going to be stronger than ever.'"

If the Lord let Lucy dawdle in her misery any longer, she was going to be strong enough to lift a house. She was that misfit teenager again. It was a fine time for God to point out she wasn't any more delivered from the old securities at thirty than she had been at sixteen.

"Guys"—Chuck let his eyes fall on everyone in the worship

center—"we gotta stay tough. We have to stay in the Word and on our knees in prayer. Are you going through something?"

Yes, a fake engagement. Anyone else?

"Now is not the time to shrink back. Satan wants you to quit and run away. But the Lord tells us to face our problems bravely, because just like a young David facing his Goliath, we've got God on our side. He is our defense and our refuge. Does life seem unfair right now? Well, just hang on," Chuck said. "Because your breakthrough is coming—for those who are courageous enough to wait it out."

With the swishing lull of the ceiling fans overhead, Lucy's mind wandered over her years in Charleston. It was like a play with two distinct acts. There was her miserable growing-up years, forced to attend that stupid private school. Her mother passing away. Then there was Lucy's return three summers ago when she had been bent on coming back and proving to herself she could be someone in this town. Yet all she had proven to anyone watching was that she couldn't adequately run a nonprofit.

And now these new developments. If Clare was telling the truth, her mother had lied to her. With no intentions of ever telling her about her real father. Clare's belief that Steven Deveraux was her dad was preposterous, but yet there were holes in her mother's stories about the man Lucy had presumed to be her father. Lucy had been raised on lies, and her mother had taken the truth with her.

"What is it that's defeating you today? That keeps you up at night and makes you want to give up?" Chuck paced the length of the altar. "Are you ready to let God be your champion? Give him all your confusion, your worry, your past. And just let it go. Do not go one more day living in fear of defeat. We are *more* than conquerors." Not even the toddler two rows up made a peep as Chuck surveyed the room. "Let's pray."

As Lucy lowered her head, she caught sight of the bulletin in Alex's lap. His brother's name was in blue ink at the top. Beneath it indecipherable fragments that clearly meant something to Alex in regard to Will. In an adjacent column, a list of points from Chuck's sermon.

Lord, I lift up Alex to you. Help him in his grief with his brother and with the campaign. *And father, give me answers. I need to know if every-thing I believed about my birth has been a lie. I'm not exactly deserving in the truth department at the moment, but I'm asking anyway. I have to get this settled. And yes, God, I'm going to go ahead and be bold and ask for the strength to do what needs to be done to be the best fake fiancée Alex could have. I'm through being the weakling.*

At least for today.

At Chuck's amen, the choir took over and sang everyone out. Alex slid his warm hand to the base of Lucy's neck as they walked outside.

"Good service." He shook Chuck's hand.

"Thanks, man. Come back anytime." Chuck dropped his preacher voice. "But if you hurt Lucy, I will be honor-bound to break both your kneecaps."

Alex had more muscle in his right tricep than Chuck had in his entire body, yet he nodded solemnly anyway. "I wouldn't expect anything less."

"Alex, can I have your autograph?" Mrs. Baker's ten-year-old son stood holding a pen and notebook. Five of his friends stood behind him, looking as if they beheld a king.

"Sure, guys." Sending a sheepish grin to Lucy, Alex signed two bulletins, one hat, two notebooks, and a gum wrapper.

He didn't just hurriedly scribble his name, though. He looked at each boy, asked questions, chatted. Made them all feel important. Like they were the stars instead of him. She found herself smiling.

He wasn't supposed to be charming. He wasn't supposed to be intelligent and funny and kind to little boys. *Say something arrogant. Refuse to take a picture.* Lucy was seeing more and more of the workings of Alex's heart. And it left her unsettled. No, she would not be taken in by this man. Not today and not ever. The last two days she had enjoyed her time with him. And that just couldn't happen.

"Lucy, I see a couple of people I'd like to talk to," Alex said. "Can you give me ten minutes, then I'll take you to lunch?"

She knew she was supposed to smile and agree. Play the role of dutiful girlfriend. But Chuck was right. It was time to take care of some of her own baggage, and if she didn't do it now, she might never have the nerve to face it again.

"I can't." She barely got the words out. "I . . . I have to go home and"— her mind was as empty as her bank account—"check on some things."

"Things?"

"Yes. Important ones." She couldn't tell from his face whether he bought her lame excuse or not. She didn't care. "I'll see you later." Lucy leaned up on tiptoes to press her lips to his cheek.

"You okay?"

"Yes."

"You just kissed me." He tapped a lean finger against his cheek. "Voluntarily."

"I couldn't bank my fiery passion."

His smile was steamier than a summer rain. "It happens."

She dug into her purse and pulled out her keys. "I'll call you later."

Leaving him staring after her, Lucy peeled open her creaky car door. Cranking up the radio, she drove away from the church, desperate to drown out the clattering, clashing thoughts in her head. She had to silence at least one source of the noise.

Twenty minutes later she cruised by the Battery downtown, past homes that had withstood the Civil War, hurricanes, and the heavy hand of the sea. The live oaks hung over a narrow driveway, making a canopy over Lucy's car as she pulled in. Getting out, she approached one of the only brick homes on the street. With trembling fingers, she pushed a red call button. A small camera above her head captured her every move.

"Yes?" A male voice said.

"Julian?"

"Yes?"

"It's—"

"Please say it's Madonna."

"Um, no." A red bird landed on a perfectly shaped shrub. "It's Lucy. Lucy Wiltshire."

"Shoot." And then a sigh. "I guess you'll do." The gates creaked as they began to move. "Come on in, honey. We've been waiting for you."

Chapter Fifteen

*L*ucy." Julian pulled her into a light embrace and air-kissed both cheeks. "I'm so glad you came. It's been dreadfully dull around this neighborhood since Tizzy Washington went to rehab and quit dancing on the lawn in nothing but her girdle and Dr. Scholl's." He pulled her into the entryway. "You're just in time for Sunday lunch."

Lucy stared at the wealth around her. Hardwood floors. A formal sitting room bigger than her apartment. Silk draperies. Fresh-cut flowers. Fine art perfectly centered on the walls.

"I know," Julian said. "It's a bit much. I'm more of a Pottery Barn fellow myself, but I cannot get Clare to go with the slip-covered look to save her Cole Haans."

Looking down at her reflection in the shiny varnish of the floor, Lucy stood on the threshold of desperation and pride. How much time had Steven spent here? She had passed this neighborhood all her life. Had he and Clare known about her all along? Known she and her mother had lived from one meager paycheck to another? On secondhand clothes and borrowed credit?

"Um . . ." She needed cue cards. A script for this awkward moment. "I wondered if I might have a word with Mrs. Deveraux."

"You got it. Let me page her." He reached into his pocket and pulled out a small walkie-talkie. "Sugar Lips, you have a guest in the fourth dimension. I repeat, you have a guest in the fourth dimension. This is Tijuana Daddy, over and out." With a smile he turned his attention back to Lucy, holding out a hand toward a brocade sofa. "She'll be along shortly. Do make yourself at home."

Lucy sat on the edge of the fuchsia couch, her posture as straight and proper as the room seemed to demand.

What was she doing? This was madness. But yet she needed answers. And she needed Clare's expertise and wisdom. She was determined not to be a weak link in Alex's campaign. She *would* succeed at this. She would show all those who thought she'd never amount to anything. Those who, for years, looked down their Southern belle noses and made her life miserable. Yeah, well, now she was going to be a congressman's fiancée.

Sort of.

Lucy's entire body tightened as she heard the unmistakable sound of a snotty woman in overpriced heels.

"Julian, how many times have I asked you not to use those ridiculous names and—" Clare stopped at the sight of Lucy on her couch. "Oh. It's you."

Her assistant planted a hand on his chino-covered hip. "I told you you had a guest."

Clare pressed her lips together as she stared. "I didn't expect Lucy."

Julian rolled his eyes. "It is high past time you gave up on this little fantasy of George Clooney stopping by. Just because you're friends on Facebook doesn't mean a thing."

Lucy twirled her earring. She wanted this over. And quick. "I'm here for two reasons, Mrs. Deveraux."

"Please." Clare sat opposite her in a chair that complemented the pattern in the drapes. "Call me Clare."

Lucy swallowed and said a short haiku of a prayer. "I came here to tell you I don't believe you about my father. But most importantly, I wanted to . . ." Oh, it was so hard. Why this woman? "I mean, that is, I have realized that I do need some . . . help. Despite the fact that your family hasn't exactly been kind to mine, I know there is no better expert on the political and social aspects of South Carolina than you. And I don't want to be the bullet that wipes out Alex's campaign. So whatever it takes, I want to succeed at this."

Clare slowly blinked. "Julian, I do believe you were making us root beer floats. You may return to the kitchen, if you please. And add one to the order." In her black pencil skirt, she crossed her slender legs. "Every week I'm trying a new thing. It was Julian's idea, wasn't it?"

"Yes, my little toadstool." He left the room, muttering under his breath.

"I've lived a very genteel life. Always doing what others told me." She drummed her red nails on the armrest. "I was raised old money, you know."

Lucy glanced at her watch. "That's something I never tire of hearing."

"Yes, I know what you're thinking. I've lived a wonderful life, but mistakes have been made. You were one of those extreme errors in judgment, Lucy."

"Excuse me?"

Clare held up a hand. "I mean my treatment of your mother. Dismissing you both from our lives." She paused for an unbearable length of time. "I have much to tell you."

"I don't want to know." Now that she was here, she just couldn't.

"Yes, you do." She leaned forward. "I can see it in your eyes. I've watched you all these years. You're proud. You hold that head up so high, but it's just a façade. An act. You can't stand me, can you? Me—or what I represent."

Lucy could feel her skin warming. Her pulse accelerating. "You had my mother fired. You fabricated some ridiculous story and got her blacklisted as a housekeeper in Charleston."

Clare nodded. "It's true. I did that."

Her voice rose. "And then my mother had to drive over an hour out of town to get cleaning jobs. And because she was no longer working for you and your elitist friends, she had to take on a waitressing job in addition to everything else she did. So if you're wondering how it makes me feel to have to sit here in your fancy living room and ask you for the keys to Alex's world, I probably couldn't say, at least not without dropping a few words your newly churched ears wouldn't want to hear." As soon as the words were out, Lucy regretted them. But she wouldn't take them back. What did a woman like Clare know of Christ and love? Of grace and mercy? Where had her mercy been all those years ago when her mother had worked herself to the bone?

"I deserved that." Clare inhaled through thin nostrils. "And I won't ask for forgiveness. At least not until you hear the whole truth."

"Thomas Miller is my father." Lucy ripped open her purse. She rifled through until she found the photos. "Here." She slapped the pictures down on the maple coffee table. Slid them toward Clare. "This is my dad."

Clare looked.

Frowned.

"It's him," Lucy said. "He was my mom's old boyfriend."

Clare slipped on her bifocals. "I highly doubt it." She held up the one of her dad on the beach. He wore shorts and waved to the camera. "This is Randy Pollack. He graduated with my son."

"But . . . that's my dad." She could hear the desperation in her own voice. "I have more pictures."

Clare picked up the other photo. "I'm telling you, the person in this photo could not be your father."

"And you know this because?"

"Because Randy now lives as *Rhonda* Pollack in Reno. She sells Mary Kay, has a cabaret act at the Lucky Horseshoe, and makes her Presbyterian mother cry on a regular basis."

Lucy sat back against the couch. "Oh."

Lies. All of it lies. How could her mother have raised her on such fables and myths? Where in the world did she come from? *Lord, I don't want Steven Deveraux to have so much as dipped his toe in my gene pool. Anyone but him. Anything but this family. Why couldn't I be related to a nice, wealthy Southerner? Like Paula Deen.*

"Are you ready to hear your story?"

Lucy closed her eyes. Squeezed them tight.

But when she opened them again, she was still there. Sitting in Clare Deveraux's living room. And her life was still unraveling.

"Yes."

Clare nodded solemnly. "Then we'll talk. *And* eat."

Lucy pushed off from the armrest and came to her feet.

"Oh, no, no." Clare wagged a finger. "A lady does not schlump from her seat. She rises as if lifted by air. Watch me."

"Kind of not in the mood for this right now." Lucy was just grateful her spine was still holding her up.

With flawless posture and weightless grace, Clare stood. "See?"

"Hey." Julian stalked into the room. "You two gonna practice sitting all day, or will you be joining me for pot roast?"

"On our way," Clare said. "Lucy, you may follow me so you can study my stroll."

Clare went first. Followed by Julian, who, with a wink, walked in a perfect imitation.

The dining room was a large, sunny space. A silver chandelier hung from the center of the floral-carved ceiling. Matching antique buffets flanked either side.

Lucy sat down and rested her napkin in her lap. Clare shook her head. Was there anything she did that was correct? Did she really think there was a proper way to unfold a napkin?

Julian set the final platter down. "Okay, let's eat."

Lucy pulled herself from her fog long enough to take in the spread before her. "Roast, french fries, Kraft Mac & Cheese, root beer floats, and pudding?" And this woman had just corrected her napkin usage?

Clare shrugged. "As I was saying earlier, I have denied myself many common things that others take for granted. But those days are over. Julian has convinced me I need to branch out. Live a little."

Julian nodded, then folded his hands, ready to pray. "We made a bucket list. She's already done all the big things—seen the world from the Eiffel Tower, toured the Holy Lands, sipped tea with the Dali

Lama. What she needed to do was experience some of the smaller, simpler joys in life."

Clare wrapped her lips around her straw and took a drink. "Last week I went to a garage sale." She shuddered. "Horrible thing."

"Oh, whatever." Julian clearly wasn't the least bit intimidated by the woman. "You came home with a Christmas sweatshirt and a toilet paper cozy."

"Just stop your insolence and bless our food." Clare's cheeks sunk in as she took another drink. "This is quite good. You may make these again."

"You're lucky I didn't lace yours with cyanide, you old bat."

She harrumphed. "All I'm leaving you in my will is my best pair of Gucci heels, so I'm pretty certain I'll sleep well tonight."

Lucy couldn't even focus on Julian's short prayer for the questions dueling in her head. By the time she left, she would know if Steven Deveraux was her father, why her mother lied, and which fork to use for dessert.

Taking the platter of meat from Julian, Lucy put a small helping on her plate. She knew it was more than she'd be able to choke down. "Start from the beginning," she said. "I have to know everything."

Clare shot Julian a pointed look. He reached for Lucy's knife and pulled it out of reach.

"As you know, many years ago your mother cleaned our home. We lived in the governor's mansion in Columbia, but this was our *home* and Steven and I stayed here often."

At the mere mention of her mother, the wound on Lucy's heart peeled open again.

"She was good at what she did. Your mother found a lot of work in this area. I recommended her to all my friends who didn't have full-time staff." Clare took a bite of macaroni and cheese and smiled like she was inhaling a fine wine. "That's very nice, Julian. I like that a lot. Let's have that tomorrow night."

"Yes, madam."

"My son was a senior in college," Clare continued. "His father was in office at the time, and Steven was being groomed for politics. Everyone likened him to John F. Kennedy. When we looked at our son, we thought we were looking at the future president of the United States."

But clearly something had gone wrong. Because Steven never went into politics. Lucy knew he had had a few failed businesses. And besides owning some shares in Sinclair, she thought he'd just lived off his trust fund.

"The day my son came home from school for spring break, I knew there would be trouble. He took one look at your mother and he was a goner. Steven had quite the reputation as a ladies' man."

Julian buttered a roll. "Happens to the best of us."

"And we'd had to get him out of a few situations before. But this time," Clare said, "I could see things were going on we couldn't stop. When Steven talked to your mother, she looked at him like he was a god. I forbid him to see her. She was a maid, after all. My son was a future leader—a Deveraux."

"My mom was better than your son on his finest day," Lucy said, her food a weighted mass at the pit of her stomach. "She was kind and good. She didn't judge people by their bank accounts or by which Civil War general they were related to."

"I was always a fan of Van Dorn myself," Julian remarked.

Clare dipped two fries in ketchup and continued. "My son was my world. At that time I thought I was protecting him. Looking back, I know how wrong I was. How horrible I was to your mother." She pushed her plate away and focused her blue eyes on Lucy. "A few months after spring break, Steven came to me. Told me Anna was pregnant. He was inconsolable. Begged me not to tell his father. Of course, I didn't. It would've killed my husband. And in those days, could've killed his career. Definitely would've ruined my son's future. I couldn't have him marrying the cleaning lady."

Lucy wanted to throw up as the truth bounced on her gag reflexes. How had her mother kept this from her?

"Steven was still young, a fraternity boy. By this time he was already through with your mother and dating a woman who would've made an ideal wife. He begged me to help him. And hadn't I always taken care of everything?" Clare stared at a spot beyond Lucy's shoulder, her eyes distant and unfocused. "So I went to see Anna. Offered her some money to leave town. She refused. Said her home was in Charleston, and that's where she would stay."

"Her parents' graves are here," Lucy said, her voice a dead monotone. "It was all she had left of her family."

"She refused to leave. So I set her straight about my son not wanting anything to do with her. She knew it herself by that time anyway. I upped the price for her silence, and she finally took it. But she still wouldn't get out of town." Clare nudged her head toward one of the buffets.

Julian got up, grabbed an envelope, and handed it to Clare.

"This is the check I wrote her." She flipped it over. Her mother's signature was still strong and black on the back. "And this is the legal contract I made her sign." She slid it toward Lucy. "In exchange for a large sum of cash, your mother agreed to never speak of my son, never be in his presence again, and certainly to never claim he was your father."

Lucy's fingers shook as she took the check. So this was how much she had been worth. All this time, and her mother had never said a word. Why hadn't she told her the truth? Had she been afraid Lucy would judge her?

That hideous private school. Bought with Clare's blood money. And her mother's dignity.

More pieces locked into place. "So since my mom wouldn't leave town, you made it impossible for her to work in Charleston."

"At the time I thought she was just a gold digger after my son. An opportunist. Yes, I wanted her out of my sight and away from Steven." Clare clutched her napkin. "Lucy, I was wrong. I know that now. The guilt keeps me up at night."

"It's true," Julian said. "She watches a lot of infomercials. Last month she ordered a blender the size of a pencil."

"Please say you forgive me."

Lucy's tongue could barely utter a coherent sentence. "So you're telling me that you've known who I was this entire time?"

"Yes."

"And the man you claim to be my father knew who I was?"

"Also true."

"And he never had anything to say to me?" Her volume began to climb. "And the only energy you've wasted on me was to vote against my Sinclair funding."

"I voted for you. It's important you know that. My life is completely different now." The distinguished woman took a slurping bite of pudding. "See?"

"I can't deal with this." Lucy stood up, tears clouding her vision. "I have to go."

"Lucy, wait—"

She turned back to the table. "My whole life you've denied me. Rejected me. And so has my *father*. And you expect me to just open my arms and forgive you? Is that seriously what you thought would happen here? Do you have any idea what I've been through?"

Clare's eyebrows defied Botox and came together. "You asked for the truth. And I will remind you that you need me right now. I couldn't work with you day in and day out and have that lie between us." Clare stood and went to her side. "If I could go back and change it, I would."

"It's too late." Lucy reached for her purse. "It's just too late." She stepped around Clare and sailed out of the dining room and out the door.

Chapter Sixteen

*M*oving boxes stood in neat stacks against the wall of Matt's open garage. Lucy didn't know whether to knock on the front door or the garage entrance, so she just stood in his driveway for a few moments waiting for enlightenment.

Maybe she should leave. Try this another day. Sunday was a day of rest, after all. And telling the man you had once hoped to marry that you had the hots for a quarterback just sounded like work. She pivoted on her shiny red heel and made a step toward the car.

"Lucy?"

As she froze, she briefly wondered about the possibility of starting this day over.

"Hello, Matt." The distance to where Matt stood at his front door stretched out like the last mile of a marathon. Her energy depleted, her mind the consistency of mush, Lucy walked toward him.

"It's still a mess, but come inside." He made no move to touch her but held open the door as she squeezed by him.

His home was a modernized ranch-style. New beige carpet covered the floors. His brown leather couch sat adjacent to his matching loveseat. A large-screen TV hung over a fireplace she knew he would never light. He wouldn't like the mess. White walls framed every room she could see, reminding her of the walls in his old apartment. She had surprised him one weekend, getting his key and painting his kitchen a beautiful spun gold. His appreciation had been kind and gracious. But by the next week, the cotton white walls had returned. Change made Matt uncomfortable, and while it was occasionally annoying, Lucy had admired his stability.

"Take a seat." Dressed in khaki pants and a three-button polo, Matt gestured toward the couch.

Inhaling the scent of new carpet, Lucy sat down. And saw the paper on the coffee table.

There on the front page of the society section was a color photo of her and Alex at the ballet. With his arm anchored around her, Alex looked like a man staking his claim, letting the world know that Lucy Wiltshire was spoken for.

Matt cleared his throat. "When I saw the first pictures of you two, I laughed it off. I knew you would never date a guy like Sinclair."

Right. Because who would ever imagine the maid's daughter growing up to fall for Prince Charming?

"Matt, I—"

"But it is true." He walked to the table and picked up the paper. "Isn't it?"

Her tongue was a foreign object in her mouth. "I . . . we . . ."

"Are you seeing this guy?"

Swallowing past the lump in her throat, Lucy could only nod.

"And you couldn't tell me?"

"I wanted to, but—"

"What about that night at the gala—when I saw you two outside the hotel? Were you together then?"

Nothing like lying on the Lord's day. "Yes."

"And you let me take you home?"

"Alex and I were . . . fighting." Technically it was sort of true.

"It didn't look like it to me."

"Yes, fighting." She dragged her eyes away from the paper. "About football. He . . . um, watches it all the time. I'm trying to get him to go to an . . . ESPN recovery group." It was like God was holding the pause button on her brain. Not a single coherent thought would form. "I'm sorry."

In three strides he was in front of her, looming, his voice sharp with hurt. "I don't believe you, Lucy."

"But I *am* sorry. I—"

"I don't believe you're seeing this guy."

The tears pushed at her eyes, and she blinked them away. "Because he's better than me?" Later she would think about how this bothered her more than having to tell Matt good-bye. But for now, Lucy was that girl at Montrose Academy again. Doing the walk of shame down the hall in her worn uniform and garage-sale shoes.

Matt went to his knees and reached for Lucy's hands. "He doesn't hold a candle to you. Don't you get that? What are you doing with a guy like him? He's arrogant, conceited, cares nothing about anyone but himself."

"That's not true. He's surprisingly kind. Polite. He can't help it how the media has portrayed him. How would you like it if cameras followed your every step? How perfect would your life look then?" Lucy closed her eyes on an indrawn breath. Had she just taken up for Alex? It was like something had invaded her body. She didn't even know who she was anymore. Steven Deveraux's daughter. Clare's grandchild. And now Alex's champion? Next she'd be spitting tobacco, quoting stats, and scratching in indecent places.

"I love you, Lucy. I want us to build a life together."

She blinked back the tears. "It's . . . it's too late." It was too late for her dream of a home. A family of her own, gathered around the kitchen table on Friday nights playing Monopoly and eating popcorn. Gone. She had traded it all in for Saving Grace.

Sniffing once, Lucy looked at the man who could've been her world. "You are a good guy, Matt. And it would've been an honor to have married you."

"You still can." His grip was strong on her hands. "I know you still care."

She couldn't deny that. It would be too much, even for her. "But my place is with Alex now."

"We're good together. No one knows me like you." His voice dipped. "Do you love him?"

It was like twisting a rusty knife into her own heart. "I'm going to marry him."

Matt rose to his feet and put some space between them. "We talked the other night. You said nothing about any of this. I *know* you were going to come back to me."

She shook her head. "I was confused."

"Because you know being with Alex is a lie."

Oh, he had no idea. "I have to go," she whispered. "I'm sorry. You will never know how truly sorry I am." She wanted to throw herself at him and beg him to wait for her.

"I'm not giving up on us. I threw it away once, but I won't do it again."

It was like he had a script—saying all the right things.

"Alex Sinclair can't make you happy. You once told me I was everything you wanted in a man." His eyes searched hers. "He'll never be able to give you what you need."

"That's where you're wrong." On shaking legs, Lucy stood up and forced herself to meet his hard stare. "Because he's given me exactly what I need."

"I won't let you go, Lucy."

She pulled her purse to her and gave a weak smile. "If only you had said that two years ago."

"It's not too late," he said.

Her mind turned to the girls, the home, and where she would be six months from now.

And she hoped Matt was right.

❧

Restless as a fly on hot pavement, Lucy aimed her car straight for Saving Grace. Not only did she need to take her mind off her imploding life, she needed to see the place. To check in and reconnect with the girls she had sacrificed everything for. Because Saving Grace really wasn't about the building. It was about the thirteen young women who were rebuilding their lives and breaking the destructive cycles that had trapped those who had come before them.

"Girl, you look rough."

Lucy closed the door and stepped into the living room where Tyneisha Hollister sat in front of the TV, painting her toes fuchsia with one hand and pointing a remote with the other.

"I'm fine," Lucy said. "Just tired."

Tyneisha gave her another once-over and scrunched up her face as if she found Lucy's explanation lacking. "You know what you need?"

The list of possible responses was way too long. "No, tell me."

Patting her new Rihanna haircut, Tyneisha smiled. "You need you some cake. We had us a big birthday party last night for Deondra, and there's enough cake left in the kitchen to feed half of Charleston."

"Did you go to church today?"

"Girl, you know I did." Tyneisha fixed a smudge on her big toe. "I even joined the choir."

"Get out."

"I did!" Her belly chuckle brought a smile to Lucy's face. "For real. I walked up to that worship minister, and I said, 'My name is Tyneisha Monique Hollister, and I have decided you may borrow the use of my fine soprano.'"

The tears resurfaced again, and Lucy wrapped Tyneisha in a hug before she could see them. "I'm proud of you. I'm proud of every part of your life, Tyneisha."

Tyneisha hung on. "I love you, Miss Lucy."

"Right back at you."

Lucy wiped a hand over her leaky nose and willed herself to pull it together.

"Oh, your new girl's been sneaking out at night."

"Marinell?"

"Uh-huh." The self-appointed mama, Tyneisha watched the comings and goings in the house like an armed sentry. "She think she can sneak out the back door and nobody notice? Huh, I notice."

"Have you told Josie and Tracey?" Because if she had, the two on-site resident assistants had said nothing to Lucy.

"Naw, you know I don't like to stick my nose in other people's business. But last night she didn't come home, and I sat up late worrying."

Just what Lucy needed. If Marinell couldn't abide by the rules, then she couldn't stay. And where would that leave her?

On a mission, Lucy stormed down the hall. She would get to the bottom of this. Most of the bedrooms were empty today, as many of the girls usually went to Sunday lunch with their mentors. Today was no exception. But Marinell was definitely in.

She stopped at her door and knocked.

"It's open."

The lecture died on Lucy's lips as she took in the sight of the girl sitting on the bed. "What's wrong?"

Marinell turned the page of a literature book and jotted down some notes. "Nothing."

Without invitation, Lucy sat down next to her. "You look like you haven't slept in a week."

Flipping through a folder, Marinell pulled out a piece of paper. "I need you to sign this."

"What is it?"

"A field trip permission slip. Don't worry about reading all the boring stuff. It just says we're going to the aquarium Tuesday. Sign at the bottom."

The girls had initiated Lucy quickly on all the tricks a teenager could have up her sleeve. Lucy read every single line. "It's a note from your counselor." She reread a few significant lines. "It says here your grades have dropped in the last two weeks, and you haven't registered yet for summer school."

"I don't need summer school."

"You do if you want to catch up and graduate next year. You can't take off a whole semester and expect the school to just wave you on through."

"I can get my GED."

"No." Some of the girls had GEDs, and that was fine for them, but Lucy had seen Marinell's transcript before her fall semester backslide. The girl had three years of As and Bs, so a GED was not what she needed on her college applications. "You're gonna get that diploma so all of us can go to your graduation next year."

"Why, so you can make fun of me in that stupid hat?"

"Exactly," Lucy said. "Now start talking."

"'Bout what?"

"About the fact that you're apparently sleeping somewhere besides this bed and bailing on school."

"I got a boyfriend."

She didn't know why, but something told Lucy that Marinell was lying out her teeth. *Oh no. Lord, am I such an accomplished liar myself now that I can smell it on everyone else?* "Where have you been going, Marinell?"

"Just . . . out."

Lucy rubbed the sensitive skin over her right temple. "I've had a really cruddy day, and I'm fresh out of patience. So if you don't deal straight with me—"

"I went to see my brother at the hospital, okay?"

Lucy stilled. "I didn't know he was sick."

Marinell sniffed and finally lifted her head. Tortured eyes stared back at Lucy. "Relapse," she said. "Carlos has kidney problems, and he's back at the Children's Hospital. He didn't get placed with no family, so he's all alone."

Lucy's breath caught in her throat. "What about your mom?"

"She lost her job 'cause she visited the hospital so much. She sees him as often as she can, but she doesn't have a car."

"I can take you to see your brother any time."

"He's just eight, you know? He needs family. A group home isn't the same."

Lucy lifted Marinell's long brown hair away from her face. "No, it's not the same."

"I need to keep an eye on him. I promised my dad, I—"

"I thought your dad was dead."

"Dead? He's just . . . gone. Not around." Marinell picked a thread on her bedspread. "I can't talk about it."

"What does that mean?"

"Nothing, okay?" She stared back with doubt. "You'll really take me to see Carlos?"

"We'll go together," Lucy said. "But you have to do your school-work. You're not doing anyone any favors by flunking out."

"I just feel so . . ."

"Alone?"

Marinell's watery eyes closed. "Yeah."

"But you're not." Lucy took a risk and pulled the girl to her, wrapping her in her arms. "You are not alone. You have me. And you have Saving Grace." She held Marinell as the girl sniffled on her shoulder. "This might weird you out, but I'm going to pray for you. Okay?"

Marinell nodded against Lucy's shoulder.

"God, we come to you today and ask for comfort for Marinell. Give her strength and courage, and wrap your loving arms around her. We pray for healing for Carlos. Let him feel your holy touch. Let him know he is not alone and that he is loved. In Jesus' name, amen."

Marinell ran her finger across the edge of the pages. "I have some studying to do."

It was enough. For now. "I'll check in on you later." With a heart weighted down like a water buoy, Lucy made her way to her office.

Where Alex Sinclair was waiting.

"Where've you been?" He sat in her chair like the captain of a yacht. Seat reclined, elbows locked on the armrest. He filled that small office and had her taking a step back for space.

"What are you doing?" was all she could manage. Had she noticed earlier how the lime green of his shirt set off his tan?

He made no move to get out of her seat but watched her with a casual interest that belied the tightly bound energy rolling off him in waves. "I was worried about you after church. I've been calling."

Why was he looking at her like that? Like he could see straight through her. "I had some things to take care of."

And then his voice softened. "Want to talk about it?"

She was at that point where talking could only lead to tears. "Probably about as much as you want to talk about your brother."

And then Alex Sinclair, with his football player's body and Playboy smile, peeled himself from the chair, closed the distance between them, and met her where she stood in the doorway.

"Bad day?" he asked quietly.

Lucy nodded. "Just worried about one of my girls."

"Why don't you tell me about it." And he listened as she outlined Marinell's situation.

"You"—he tilted his head, studied her—"are a very good person."

"Minus a few lies here and there?"

He smiled. "Did you speak to Clare this afternoon?"

"Yes."

"Anyone else?"

She nodded again, expecting him to press. To pry. At the very least, she waited for the comfort of his familiar sarcasm.

"I'm sorry." Frowning, he brought his hand to her cheek, then slid his fingers to the back of her head. Pulling her close, he wrapped those steely arms around her and drew her tight.

He smelled of Ivory soap, expensive cologne, and the raw power that could only be derived from the golden branch of a family tree. Goose bumps broke out on her skin as a rogue frisson of electricity danced through her system. The air around them swirled with heat, saturating her senses. Confusing her even more.

Lucy broke away. "I have to . . . um, get some work done." It was a weak excuse. But she would not fall like every other woman who had encountered him.

His lips curved, dimpling his right cheek. "You have issues, Lucy Wiltshire."

"My allergic reaction to football players?" She nodded and gave a bored little sigh. "Every time you touch me, I do break out in a rash."

He laughed low and gave her a slow wink. "Let me know if you need help with that." And walked away.

Wilting into her desk chair, Lucy could still catch his scent. She didn't know what had just happened.

She only knew it couldn't happen again.

Chapter Seventeen

*T*wo weeks and twelve dates later, Morgan stood in Lucy's apartment, her finger pointed like a pistol ready to fire.

"Did you think I wouldn't read today's paper?"

Lucy pulled a Cool-Whip bowl from the kitchen cabinet and positioned it on her coffee table in the living room next to her sweating glass of tea. It was the third day of the apartment upstairs leaking, and despite her landlord's promises, it had yet to be fixed. As if split into a triplex against its wishes, the old house protested with fierce regularity.

Apparently the landlord didn't care that the leak had already ruined the cover of one Brian Jacques novel and the latest issue of *Vogue*, a magazine she had purchased for the sole purpose of adopting a new style for Alex. Never mind that she hadn't even opened it yet. She would've. Eventually. Because who didn't want to read about purses that cost more than her car the day she bought it or earrings that elongated the neck and overloaded the credit card?

"Lucy, I'm talking to you."

And then there was Morgan.

"Do you smell that?" Lucy sniffed the stale air in her living room. "It smells musty, doesn't it?"

"The only thing that stinks here is the fact that you've been keeping things from me." She held up the paper and regarded Lucy like she was about to hand over a red letter *A*. "This says you and Alex have been dating for almost five months. There are even photos to back it up." She pointed to one that had been artfully created on someone's computer. "Look, here you and Alex are at a ski lodge in Vail on January fifteenth."

"Uh-huh."

"I happen to know you weren't anywhere near the state of Colorado on that date because that was the night Chuck proposed to me, and you were planted in our carriage taking our pictures. Remember that?"

"I do vaguely recall being a little too close to a pair of mules at some point that night."

"I don't understand." Morgan pulled the magazine from Lucy's hands. "First you start dating Alex. You kick Matt to the curb, which really didn't bother me. But *now* I'm supposed to believe that your relationship goes all the way back to the beginning of the year?"

"Fine." She couldn't put it off any longer. "I'm a liar, Morgan. I'm the scum of society." Lucy blew an exasperated breath and flopped down on the couch, covering her face with her hands. "I've crossed over to the dark side and . . . I have become its mistress."

She thought she heard Morgan give a small laugh, but Lucy kept going. "I was going to tell you. But I couldn't seem to find the time to let you know that your best friend was daily walking in danger of God smiting her off the planet."

"Just tell me what's going on."

And Lucy did. Every last *Days of Our Lives* moment.

When she had finished her story and wrung out her heart like a soapy dishrag, Morgan just stared. Gob-smacked and silent.

"Morgan?"

Her friend got up. Went to the kitchen. Poured herself a Diet Coke, no ice. Tipped it back and downed it like discount liquor, then turned blazing eyes to Lucy. "Are you *insane*?"

"No, I just—"

"You should've come to me. You should've told me."

Lucy's temper kicked in. "So you could talk me out of it?"

"Yes!"

"What choice did I have?"

"Oh, I don't know." Morgan threw up her hands. "Maybe let God take care of it instead of charging in and faking an engagement with some self-indulgent skirt chaser?"

"He's really been misrepresented and I—"

"Lucy, open your eyes." Morgan crashed back onto the couch and pulled her long Angelina Jolie locks off her shoulder. "The man is dangerous. He's a user."

"So am I!" Lucy pointed to the paper. "I'm clearly a master manipulator, and we didn't even know it. Which is just further proof I *must* be Steven Deveraux's daughter."

"You have to end this thing with Alex. It's insanity."

"It saved my girls."

"Nothing is worth that cost."

"I have thirteen lives depending on me who prove otherwise."

"You didn't even let God move in this. You just jumped at the first crazy idea that came your way."

Lucy's cheeks burned with the accusation. "I was hours away from kicking my girls out on the streets. I couldn't do that to them because I—" Lucy stopped herself. Morgan would never understand. She couldn't possibly know what it was like to be homeless. To not have anyone to take care of you. To sleep with your belongings as your pillow and your meager cash stuffed in your bra.

"God often comes through in the midnight hour too," Morgan said. "Wasn't it just a few months ago we had a Bible study on that very thing for the girls?"

"Okay, yes. I know." Lucy got that she was supposed to totally depend on him and not merely give the Lord a few multiple-choice options to use to save her. "I'm not saying what I did was the right thing." She moistened her dry lips and prayed for words. "But God hadn't shown up, and I panicked. It's so easy to sit where you are and say what I should've done. But it doesn't change the fact that I'm in this thing. Saving Grace will be set for at least five years now. And we can help even more people." And Alex, in return, was now closing in on his opponent in the polls.

"And you lost everything . . . so your girls could gain it all."

"I had to save them. It's what I'm put on this planet to do."

"But not by your own power."

There was no arguing the truth.

"This is why you walked away from Matt, isn't it?" Morgan asked. "Not because you doubted him, but because you had already committed to Alex."

Matt had called her numerous times since that day at his house. She had let her voice mail pick up every time. She just couldn't deal with the life he was still offering her. That door was closed. For now.

Morgan reached for her friend's hand. "You should've told me. That's what best friends do."

Lucy took a drink of her iced tea, but her throat still felt like she had swallowed a cotton plant. "This has to stay between us, Morgan. Please just trust me to handle this."

Morgan shook her dark head. "This isn't like you at all." She gestured to the paper. "And neither are those pictures. In every one you're dressed up like you're on the red carpet but look like you're down to your last friend."

"You try having a camera trained on you everywhere you go."

"Lucy, you look miserable. What's wrong with dressing like yourself?"

It earned her the censorious looks from Clare Deveraux, for one. "I need to be more polished, at least for the formal events with Alex. You know, less . . . Doris Day."

"But everyone loves Doris Day. It's you. It's cute. This"—she pointed to a photo of Lucy in a black evening gown that had cost Lucy half of her last paycheck—"is for Miss America. And look at your shoulders, all slumped over."

"I'm sure I was just tired."

"What you are is beaten down—again. God's brought you a long way—don't go back to doubting who you are. Why let those people in your head? You're just as good as anyone Alex could possibly introduce you to. If you're going to play this game, at least don't let it devastate what's left of the confidence you've built."

"It's not. I'm fine." But Morgan was right. The upper crust of Charleston made Lucy feel like low-country trash. She was praying about it, but she just couldn't make herself believe that she had graduated from that tormented child. "I need your support on this," Lucy said. "It's important that you understand."

"I'm going to be there for you, but I don't think I'm ever going to understand."

"That's all I ask for."

Morgan shook her head. "First headline I see that says you're pregnant with his love-child triplets, and I'm punching Alex Sinclair in the throat."

"And that's why we're friends." Lucy hugged Morgan. "It will all be okay."

"For your sake," Morgan said. "I hope you're right."

Chapter Eighteen

*T*he next day Alex stood beside Lucy on the grounds of the beautiful Drayton Hall. Beside him a banner proclaimed the anniversary of the Siege of Charleston. More than two hundred and twenty-five years ago, the British had crossed the Ashley River in a bid to take over the town. Though the celebration usually took place in May, a severe storm front had swept through, and the accompanying hailstorm had cancelled the event. Charlestonians would not be denied their reenactment, however, and today's sunshine provided the perfect chance to try again—and it gave Alex an ideal opportunity for community outreach with the district's history-conscious citizens. Though well used during the Revolution and the centuries that followed, Drayton Hall still stood tall and proud on the lush green grounds. But you only had to look at the peeling paint and worn ceiling to see that nothing lasted forever. Not even a grand estate could outrun the brutal hand of time.

Time seemed to have Alex by the throat as well. There had been no word on his brother Will since the eyewitness had come forward with the news of a possible survivor. Alex was afraid to hope but couldn't make himself completely give up. Every night he went to sleep with a plea to God on his lips. As each day trickled into the next, the election drew closer and the likelihood of Will being alive drifted further away. He and his brother had never had that mystical twin connection and Alex had never wished for it. Until now.

He received updates from the search in pieces and fragments. Even the unreliable ones spurred him on. The call that had interrupted dinner last night had been nothing but a report on a dead end. Sitting next to him, Lucy had overheard, but he couldn't bring himself to answer her questions. He knew she was concerned. But she would be gone in a matter of months, and there was no point in letting his heart bleed all over her.

His campaign efforts had shown small gains, which almost made all the sixteen-hour days worth it. Between not knowing what to do with the whirling dervish that was Lucy Wiltshire and keeping his mind off Will, it had become easy to pour himself into the work. But as he massaged the stiffness in his neck and stifled a yawn, he knew it was catching up with him. His mother still called him daily, worried if he was getting enough rest and eating his vegetables. Knowing he was the cause of further stress only brought more guilt.

Bands of men in period uniforms marched across the field with plumed hats and imposing muskets. Beside him Lucy pointed to a large group meant to represent the Colonial troops. "You'd look dashing in feathers and tight breeches."

"Only if you'll wear a corset."

Under the shade of a live oak dripping with moss, Alex rested his hand at her hip. He had stopped by Saving Grace this morning and had breakfast with her and Marinell, lingering to help Marinell with history, which had been his college major. Lucy had made the home a welcoming place, and Alex stayed longer every time he visited. As Lucy had sat beside him, he noticed his hand seemed to move toward her as if magnetically pulled. He didn't even think about it anymore. If she was near, he reached for her.

There were hundreds of Charlestonians here today, and Alex watched his team mingle and pass out buttons and fans with his slogan on it. "A Return to Basics," had been David's idea. It was better, he guessed, than "I might be famous with little experience, but I really can do this job," which apparently wouldn't fit on a bumper sticker.

Alex had spent the first hour at the reenactment talking to every person on the property. Many wanted his autograph. Most days that was fine, but the closer he got to August, the more he was convinced signing a T-shirt wasn't going to turn into votes. What did it take to make them see more than a football player?

"Your blog post yesterday was really good," Lucy said, pulling him from his thoughts. Bringing her along had been a last-minute idea. He found he could relax more when she was at these campaign events. He had dropped by Saving Grace on a whim and, despite her protests, hadn't given her time to change. She wore skinny black pants that stopped just above her ankles and hot pink strappy sandals that matched her capped-sleeve blouse. Her shoes revealed glitter-painted toes that matched the same polish he'd spied on Marinell. A black flower decorated the headband that held back her raucous hair. He enjoyed seeing her this way—like herself. Occasionally she wore some outfits handpicked by Clare, but he didn't see how dressing like Laura Bush was helping her one bit. Last night during dinner with some city officials, she'd spilled her water twice and accidentally stuck her hand in John Peterson's lobster soufflé. Her two-piece business suit, buttoned clear up to her neck, had done nothing to keep her nerves in low gear.

Lucy nudged him in the side. "I liked what you said about helping out senior citizens. Your ideas on nursing homes were really clever. Mrs. Barnes from across the street read it and called to tell me you had her vote."

"Thanks." It was weird that Lucy's opinion meant so much. But it did.

"Though you really should have let me change my clothes."

"You take too long to get ready."

"Says the man with the bag of Clinique moisturizers."

"All for you, babe." Two weeks ago Lucy had been in a funk so deep, he'd worried she was on the edge of backing out of their deal again. He knew she had been to see that Matt guy. What was it about him anyway? He was black and white, while Lucy was vivid Technicolor.

Her phone buzzed in her purse, and Lucy checked the display. "My neighbor calling. I already told her I don't want to buy any Avon." She slipped it back in the compartment. "Unless you needed some more Skin So Soft."

"Keep it up, blondie, and I'll tell the press you have the entire Lord of the Rings trilogy memorized."

"There's no shame in that."

"If you're a fourteen-year-old boy."

"Is this your way of asking to borrow it?"

A leaf fluttered from the branch above, landing right in the tangle of her hair. With gentle fingers he pulled it loose, touching her smooth cheek in the process. Her cotton-candy lips opened as if to say something, but no words came out. He tore his gaze from that showgirl mouth and met her wide eyes. She was supposed to be his girlfriend. Would it hurt if he kissed her just once? After they were engaged, the public would expect it.

Today seemed like a good day for a little dry run.

"Lucy?" His hands moved to her shoulders.

"Yes?" She had yet to so much as blink.

Alex leaned closer until he could smell the exact spot she had sprayed her perfume. His eyes held hers captive. "I'm going to kiss you now."

Her eyes widened, but she made no attempt to step away. "I really don't think you should."

His lips curved into a grin. "We have to be convincing."

He saw her swallow. "We probably shouldn't."

"Afraid you won't be able to control yourself?"

That flustered her. "Because it's rude . . . to ignore the soldiers."

"You can kiss them when I'm done." And he lowered his head those last few inches, cupping her face in his hands. His lips brushed across hers. Just a hint of contact, the lightest of touches. He had thought to simply test the waters, but one taste would not be enough.

Her phone buzzed again, and Lucy jumped from his arms like someone had poked a bayonet in her backside. Her face pink as a flamingo, she grappled with her purse, dropping it on the ground.

Torn between amusement and frustration, Alex bent at the waist and picked up her bag. He would swear her hands were unsteady as she fumbled finding the Blackberry. He reached in the left compartment, his hand sliding over hers, and pulled out her phone. "Is there a problem?"

"Just my neighbor. Again." She lifted her face to his. "Are you going to tell me about your phone call from last night? I care about what's happening."

A cooler of Gatorade over his head couldn't have squelched the moment more.

"I was right *there*," she said. "You said Will's name."

"It's nothing."

She had that disappointed schoolmarm face. "It must be tough being bulletproof all the time."

His upper-hand advantage was slipping; it was time to show her who was in charge. "I'd be glad to discuss this after you've had the guts to talk to Clare Deveraux."

She gave a little gasp and narrowed those Caribbean ocean eyes. "That's totally different."

He ran his finger over the flower on her headband. "How convenient you think so."

"I *did* go talk to her."

"You taste-tested her pot roast and ran out of the house."

"Did she tell you that?" A horn was sounded and the troops began to march on the field. "Don't try to divert me. At least I tried with Clare. You can't even be in the same room with your parents without twitching like a—"

"Watch yourself."

"What are *you* afraid of, Alex? I know why I'm avoiding my supposed family. What about you?"

He would not be baited by a woman who dropped something every time someone stepped on her self-confidence.

"Alex." His campaign manager chose that moment to appear. "The superintendent of Charleston County schools wants to meet you." David looked at Lucy, then back to Alex. "Are you coming?"

"Be right there." Alex waited until David was a few steps away before he turned his attention back to Lucy.

"It's all about focus. And right now mine is on this election. When I feel there's something about my brother or family that's relevant to you, I'll let you know."

"Well." Those pink lips he had barely touched now formed a taut line. "There's the Alex I remember."

"Grow up, Lucy."

"Alex!" David called. "We need you over here."

Alex stared at the woman who looked like she was ready to light a cannon herself. "I'll call you later." He dutifully pressed a kiss to her stiff cheek.

"Don't bother," she said as the first rifle fired. "I'm taking the night off."

Chapter Nineteen

*H*e was incorrigible. Insulting. Aggravating. Arrogant.

Lucy slammed her car door and marched up her front walk like Sherman storming Atlanta. Did Alex really think all he had to do was bat those baby browns, pull some moves out of his old trick bag, and she would roll over like every other girl who had stepped foot on Planet Sinclair? How could the same man who had held her after her disastrous day with Matt and Clare be the same one who completely shut her down today?

Twisting the key in the lock, she bumped her hip against the front door and swung it open wide.

And felt her world crumble again.

Water. Everywhere.

The roof of her living room dripped like Noah had just docked in the apartment above her. Her shoes squished in the carpet as she made her way across the room, picking up items and assessing the damage. Her couch—soaked. Her books—limp and curling. Even the pictures along one wall sagged beneath their frames.

"There you are!" Mrs. Bortelli waddled into Lucy's living room and clucked her tongue. "Oh, such a mess. I *tried* to call you, but you didn't answer your phone."

Lucy held back every awful word she wanted to fling her neighbor's way. "Mrs. Bortelli, *what* happened?"

"A few pipes burst. Old rusty things, you know. There's been a slow leak upstairs, but we couldn't seem to locate it."

Lucy's eyes shot to her weeping ceiling. "I guess we found it."

"The landlord said he'll be by tomorrow to assess the damage."

"Tomorrow? Are you telling me you haven't called a plumber?"

Mrs. Bortelli laid a hand over the front of her Florida orange muumuu. "Fred and I are on a fixed income, you know. I mean, I guess we could call someone, but the damage is already done. My sweet man did turn the water off. Some gentleman with a big camera was sitting in your backyard and offered to help. Wasn't that nice?"

Lucy wanted to collapse into a chair, but a puddle sat in every one.

Mrs. Bortelli's eyes widened at Lucy's groan. "Oh. My. I guess Fred doesn't have to have his heart medicine right now." Her neighbor picked up a couch cushion and kindly wrung it out. "I suppose we could just wait a few days on his prescription and get someone to take care of the water damage until the landlord steps in."

Lord, was this how Job felt? "No." She would have to go to Morgan's. Or the Holiday Inn. "I'll just call the landlord again and see what I can do." Like yell and scream and tell his wife that he plays the ponies when she goes out of town to see her mother.

Mrs. Bortelli patted Lucy on the back. "I'm sorry about your stuff, dear. It all looks fixable though." The woman glanced at her silver Timex. "Noon already? Fred will be crowing if I don't get his bologna sandwich on the table. Plus Sammy's up to no good on my stories, so it's important I see what the little snipe's going to do today. Toodle-loo!"

Clemson Tiger flip-flops smacking her cracked feet, Mrs. Bortelli stepped over a *Dragons and Droids* magazine on the floor and scurried out before Lucy changed her mind and denied Fred his heart pills.

Lucy's hands shook as she tried to pick up what she could. How could a few pipes cause this much damage? Was the water line directly connected to the Atlantic Ocean?

She reached for that morning's tea glass, still covered in a sheen of condensation. A flash of movement caught her eye, and she turned to see two paparazzi in the bushes outside her living room window.

"Enough!" She jerked the cord on the blinds, only to have the blinds come crashing down, smashing her tea glass beneath it. "Great," she mumbled. "Just great."

Using a magazine, Lucy swept up what glass she could. Some how, some way—this was all Alex's fault.

Lucy sat down on the arm of the couch and the water immediately soaked into her pants, but she no longer cared.

She had to get out of this house before she started to mildew. There was plenty of work to be done at Saving Grace, like finalize their Fourth of July party and call Marinell's counselor. She'd even scrub some toilets with her own toothbrush just to stay away from home.

Her shoe crunched as she stepped away from the heap of blinds. Spying two more pieces of glass, Lucy bent down.

A telescopic lens pressed to the window, nearly jolting her out of her pink shoes. "Hey!"

A stinging pain registered, and Lucy looked down at her clutched hand. Opening her fingers, a piece of glass, no bigger than a bottle cap, dropped to the floor. Along with a few drops of blood.

"Uh-oh." The ache barely registered.

But the blood—that completely captured her attention.

Chills skittered across her skin. Beads of sweat bubbled on clammy arms. "This is bad," she heard herself say. "I gotta . . . I gotta sit down."

She held up her hand. Watched the blood trickle down her wrist in a rapid path of red. Felt the earth sway.

And promptly passed out.

❧

So maybe he had lost his temper. And there was a slight chance he had crossed a line with Lucy this morning. But he'd pledge his allegiance to the Cowboys before he'd turn into one of those men who drank soy lattés and talked about their feelings. Did she think it was mere coincidence that he had played for a team called the Warriors? Not a Colt.

Not a cute little Dolphin. He was a *warrior*. And right now he was an angry one. He'd been trying to call her the last hour and she had the nerve to ignore him. All he got was the chipper voice-mail message that reminded him of laughing eyes and blush-tinted lips.

First he noticed the short, bald photographer slinking near Lucy's magnolia tree. Then Alex caught sight of his partner digging through the trash can at the curb.

"I don't think you're going to find what you want in there." Alex's fists itched to speak for him as he stood behind the man sifting through coffee grounds and banana peels.

The prowler jerked upright, a gold anchor charm dangling off his shiny gold chain. "I—I was just, uh—"

"That trash can belongs to the elderly neighbors," Alex said through clenched teeth. "If you're that hard up for Depends and Super Polident, you're not charging enough for your work."

The loser didn't even bother to explain. His tattooed fingers dropped the lid and he took off in a run, his buddy already gone.

It was one thing to target a political candidate, Alex thought as his loafers sliced through Lucy's lawn, but it was another to go after her. Wasn't it enough their picture appeared somewhere nearly every day? And while he appreciated the publicity, he didn't want Lucy harmed in any way. He was used to living in the fishbowl. She, however, was not.

He pounded on the door. Waited. The resident assistant at Saving Grace had told Alex he'd find Lucy working at home, but there was no answer. The door handle turned easily in his hand, giving him his first niggle of concern. She always kept that door locked.

"Lucy?" He stepped inside, catching a whiff of the damp aroma.

Then he saw her.

Sitting up against her living room wall, her head lolled back with blood covering the side of her face.

"Lucy!" He dove to the floor beside her. "Where are you hurt?" *God, help me.* Rage warred with panic as he ran his hands over her body.

"My hand." Her words slurred like she had chugged a six-pack on her way home. "I hate blood." Lucy leaned forward until she was eye-to-eye. "Really grody."

"Okay." His heart slowed enough so that the logic could squeeze back in. She was all right. "Let's see that hand."

She turned her face and held it out. "First the floods came, then the sky fell." Her weak giggle was not amusing him. "Broke my favorite tea glass. Got it at a flea market. Vintage Pizza Hut. Princess Leia."

She tried to sit up, but Alex held her down with his other hand. "No way." He inspected the cut, then tugged his tie loose, yanking it off his neck, and wrapping it tightly around her hand. "Where else are you hurt?"

"Nowhere."

"You've got blood all over you."

She squeezed her eyes shut. "A gentleman would stop reminding me."

"Unfortunately there's not one here."

"I passed out for a bit." Her skin was pale as paste. "I guess my hand flopped on my face. The carpet." She glanced at the floor. "Not that it matters. Carpet's ruined anyway. Stupid neighbors. I'll *never* buy her Avon now."

She practically had Tweety birds flapping around her head. "I think we need to get you to the hospital."

"I'd rather not."

"Too bad."

Careful to avoid her hand, he scooped her into his arms. "You're really a mess."

"Don't let me stain your Hugo Boss."

"I hear that sarcasm." And for some reason it made him feel better.

The sun shone like a spotlight as he carried her to his car. He saw another camera sticking out of a shrub across the street, but he didn't have time to deal with it.

"I'm bleeding on your leather seat."

"I'll bill you." Alex reached across and buckled her in.

"This is ridiculous." She slapped at his too-close hands. "You probably use this ploy on all your cheerleaders."

"Just the dance team." He ran around to his side and climbed in. "Did you see some paps today?"

With her head pressed to the seat, she took an audible breath. "Saw one right at my window. That's when I cut my hand."

Alex wasn't sure exactly what that meant, but he did know it was past time to put an end to her easy accessibility. Any half-brained moron with a camera thought he was a member of the press these days. He could've gotten in her apartment. He didn't even want to think about the rest.

He couldn't erase the image of Lucy sprawled out on the floor. Visions of his brother wove their way in. Had he suffered? Had there been blood? Had Will cried out for help? "You need bodyguards," Alex said. "And a security system."

"Don't think just because you wrapped my hand in one very expensive Band-Aid you've earned the right to butt into my life. There will be no bodyguards *or* you telling me what I'm going to do."

"Pretend we have that kind of relationship."

"What kind?"

"The kind in which one of us makes smart decisions."

He could almost see the steam coming out of her ears. She wasn't as pearly white anymore. Wasn't shaking.

But he still was.

"I am an independent person, *Playboy*." The smart aleck had figured out he hated that moniker. "And I don't take orders from you or anyone else."

Not trusting himself to talk to her anymore, he picked up his phone and made a few calls. One to a doctor friend at the hospital to let him know they were on their way. A call to her friend Morgan, because he was tired of the woman looking at him like he was a serial killer every time she saw him. The last call was conducted in caveman grunts and simple yes–no answers, because if Lucy knew who was on the other end, she would smack him with that bleeding hand.

"This is stupid, Alex."

"We'll be at the hospital soon."

She was still doing some weird Lamaze breathing thing, and guilt gnawed his belly. Not because of the cut. He knew it probably looked worse than it was. But because her property, her safe haven, had been violated. All because she was connected to him.

He ran his hand down the side of her hair. It was as soft as his favorite shirt. Especially the part not sticky with blood. "You must've bumped your head on the floor. You have a knot above your eyebrow."

"Don't worry." Fatigue had her leaning against him. "I'll only tell one tabloid you put it there."

"Just make sure they give you top dollar for the exclusive."

Fifteen minutes later he pulled into the parking lot, squealing his tires like he was driving his first car.

"I am not going in there." She stared at the doors of the ER. "I've already dealt with one cranky politician, an obnoxious neighbor, and my apartment falling apart."

He sighed as he got out and went to her side of the car. She was beautiful when she was mad. Platonic was how he aimed to keep this relationship, but only a fool would miss those fiery blue eyes, that dusting of freckles dotting her nose, and those pink kiss-me lips. "Lucy, here's something you need to learn." He picked her up like she was delicate enough to break and pressed her head to his shoulder—more for privacy from cameras than comfort. "I'm the man in this relationship. And your bossy ways are getting a little bit grating." He smiled over her head, feeling a little better with each step. "If you don't want me to stray, you'd better start satisfying me with sweet words and tender sighs."

Princess Leia was full of honey. "Kiss it, Sinclair."

"And have you pass out again?" He walked through the entrance. "We'll take care of your outrageous demands later."

Yes, his Lucy was going to be just fine.

Chapter Twenty

*B*ack off—all of you." Lucy swung her feet over the hospital bed and started to rise. "Fainting at the sight of blood is no cause for a private room. And what are you all doing here anyway?"

"You're not going anywhere until the doctor dismisses you," Alex said from his stance beside her.

"Just sit still and show a modicum of patience." Clare ran her fingers over the brooch at her throat. "Though your father had a weak stomach when it came to blood as well."

And wasn't that just the last thing Lucy had wanted to hear? She had yet to figure out how Clare had gotten an invitation to this event, but she felt confident in blaming that one on Alex. Lucy looked to Morgan for support, but she just nodded in agreement with the other two.

"It was glass." Lucy lifted up her hand. "A few stitches."

"And a nasty lump on your head," Alex said. His mood had darkened, and she didn't know why. It wasn't like *he* was the one getting sewn up and stared at.

"And I really don't feel like company." She would be talking to Alex about this later. And it would probably involve some high-pitched yelling.

Clare pressed her lips and looked to Alex. "It was only a matter of time before the press started hounding her."

He only nodded, keeping his eyes leveled on Lucy.

A nurse stuck her head in the door. "Miss Wiltshire?" Lucy knew the second the young woman recognized Alex. It was an expression she was beginning to see with obnoxious regularity. "Um . . . oh. You look like Alex Sinclair. Er, I mean you are Alex Sinclair. That is to say . . ." She stared at Alex in a trance of celebrity adoration. "Paperwork. Almost done. Going home . . . soon."

"Thank you." Alex gave her the smile that dimpled his cheek and made girls like Nurse All-a-Flutter think of tight football uniforms and full-body tackles.

"Uh-huh." The woman couldn't seem to move.

"We appreciate all the help we've received here. Lucy's lucky to be in your able care." Alex held open the door and dismissed the woman using nothing but the brute strength of his charm.

He then turned to Lucy. Who sat with her arms crossed. "Women drooling over you—does it ever get old?"

"Now, babe." He swaggered back to her side. "Don't let a little local anesthetic go to your head." He sat down beside her on the bed, making her acutely aware of how fresh and clean he smelled. And she was a walking advertisement for disinfectant and latex gloves. "I have to endure all those men in your little Hobbits group, so you can put up with the occasional hot nurse or two." He picked up her good hand and ran his thumb across her skin. "But our love will see us through."

"There are five men in the group, and half of them live with their mothers."

He lifted one shoulder. "The jealousy still keeps me up at night."

Morgan cleared her throat. "So how about Lucy stays with me?"

"Thanks, but I'll be fine at home."

"No way." Alex dropped her hand and stood up. "Your place is a wreck and you're not going back home until we get you a security system."

"You can't go back to your apartment alone right now," Morgan said. "It's wet and nasty, and there're creepy men lurking around."

"You're coming to my house," Alex said.

"No," Lucy and Morgan said in perfect unison.

"It wouldn't look good." Clare raised a manicured brow. "Think of your image, Alex."

"This isn't 1950."

"No," she said to him. "But for a man whose campaign strategy file is labeled 'damage control,' why push it?" Clare turned calculating eyes to Lucy. "She can stay with me."

Lucy would rather sleep in her car. "I'll stay at Saving Grace."

"Are you going to kick one of the girls out?" Morgan asked. "Because Marinell took your last bedroom."

"We have a very nice couch there." Lucy did *not* want to be in Clare's house or hear any more excuses for Steven Deveraux.

"It's a good solution." Alex typed something in to his iPhone. "And it's temporary. Until I can get you a security system installed and some twenty-four-hour protection."

Morgan stood up and glanced at her watch. "So this is settled?"

"Oh, it's settled." Alex's face dared Lucy to argue.

Morgan gave her friend a light squeeze. "You sure you're okay? I would stay, but I've finally got an appointment for Chuck to try on tuxes."

"I'm fine. Go. Do your wedding planning." As Morgan eased out the door, Lucy felt panic slip inside the room in her place. She was alone with two people who wanted things from her that overwhelmed her conscience and addled her brain.

Alex turned to Clare. "She'll go home with you."

"I have friends I can stay with."

"Friends with a security detail in their carriage house?" Clare asked.

"No." Lucy took a drink of the water beside her. "Though Christina Meyer does have a schnauzer."

"This will give us a chance to get started on our homework." Clare was back to using that uppity voice. "And Julian can keep an eye on your injuries. He's good at that."

"But—" Lucy looked to Alex, but he was finishing up a text.

"I've got to make a quick call. You two settle this among yourselves." He disappeared, leaving her in Clare's clutches.

Clare's lips thinned as she took Alex's place beside Lucy on the bed. "Alex tells me you two are serious."

Seriously insane. "Does he?"

Clare watched her for a few uncomfortable, silent moments. Like she was telepathically scanning Lucy's brain for all her hidden secrets. Lucy shifted and looked away.

"You need help. It's time you accepted that," Clare finally said. "I've watched you at recent events. You're a wreck."

"My grandma for a matter of weeks and already you're spoiling me with compliments."

"But you have enormous potential. Given the fact that you need a large amount of assistance in a short period of time—basically a miracle —I'm your only option."

"Is this supposed to charm me into agreeing?"

Clare clasped her delicate fingers around Lucy's. "My dear, the election is two months away. As his girlfriend, you represent a wife-figure. Ring or not, you are important to his campaign."

Her head was beginning to throb worse than her hand. "Why are you doing this?"

"I would be lying if I said it was simply because you needed me— though you do." Clare stared at their joined hands, one still pink with lingering youth, and one lined and veined with age. "I need *you*, Lucy."

Lucy went on alert at the shift in Clare's tone.

"My recent dip into the Lord's wading pool has convinced me that I have a lot of amends to make," Clare continued. "Come and stay with me for a few days. I'll teach you everything I know about the political life, and when you're ready, you can ask me about your father. But I won't push. I shall be content just to have the opportunity to get to know you a little better."

Lucy chewed the inside of her jaw and prayed the Tylenol would kick in soon. Why was life getting so complicated? This was why she had lived an honest life up until now. Deceit was way too much drama.

"Put your bitterness aside for now," Clare said. "When this election is over, you can go back to hating me. I don't blame you. But you might be just the thing to turn the tide for Alex. We can make that happen. Together."

"Why do you care if he wins or not?"

"We're old family friends." Clare smiled wistfully. "And it's clear that he's ready for the world to see who he really is. That's something I relate to."

"I need some air. I'm going to go find Alex."

Lucy slipped off the bed and let her feet rest on the floor. Swinging open the door, she marched down the hospital hall in search of her fake boyfriend. She stopped to listen for girly shrieks or purring coos, but hearing neither, she just kept walking.

She finally found him in a waiting room, standing with his back to her, next to a faded blue couch somewhere in the color range of cornflower and ugly.

"Hey, Kat."

Lucy's flats halted on the peel-and-stick tile floor.

"It's good to hear your voice," he said. "I'm sorry I couldn't return your call right away. I hope I'm not interrupting, but I really needed to talk to you—"

Heat crawled up Lucy's neck. While she had been getting the guilt trip from Clare on the need to be Alex's perfect lady, he had been out here. Calling his girlfriend. Or one of them.

"Can we meet?" Alex nodded. "Perfect. Just the two of us." Like a cheetah aware of its prey, Alex pivoted. And locked his sights on Lucy.

There was no surprise on his face. Only barely concealed annoyance.

"Talk to you later." He hit a button and slipped the phone in his pocket. "Were you dismissed?"

Lucy advanced on him, trying to decide if he was worth tearing apart. "I have had the *worst* day. First, there's a water park in my house. Then some shutter-happy boys peek in my window." She took another step—close enough to smell the spice of his cologne. It probably cost more than her hospital bill. "Then *someone* drags me to the hospital for stitches when a butterfly bandage would have done just as well. *Then* I'm given the command that I'm not allowed to stay in my own apartment."

"Sounds like you've had a rough one." His voice was whiskey deep as his gaze dipped to her lips.

"And now," she hissed. "Now I come out here and find you on the phone with a member of your harem, plotting a little late-night meet-and-greet."

His mouth quirked. "Jealous?"

Lucy chalked it up to a miracle that she didn't spew dragon fire. "Jealous? Of her? Of you? Of you and her?" The nerve of this man. "I pity that woman, whoever she is. If you can't even stay faithful to a fake girlfriend, you sure as heck can't be loyal to a real one."

Alex glanced over her shoulder. "You should probably keep your voice down."

"I will not." The man wasn't even looking at her! "You can't just order me about. I don't want to stay with Clare, for your information. Besides, what good will it do for me to brush up on political trivia when my intended is shacked up with some bimbo at the nearest Motel 6?"

"You know I have better taste in motels than that."

He drew his eyes away from the hall until they locked on hers.

"Don't you have *anything* to say for yourself, Alex?"

"Yes." His gaze wandered to her mouth again.

Then his head lowered as he pulled her close, and his lips covered hers. "This."

❧

If Alex Sinclair played football as good as he kissed, Lucy knew he'd have an entire treasure chest of Super Bowl rings.

He pressed nearer, cupping her face in those strong hands.

Lucy murmured a protest against his lips, but it was useless.

"Close your eyes," came his muffled command.

She started to argue, but the day had sucked out all the energy from her body. She leaned into him, hating the way her heart raced in tempo. The way her skin all but sizzled beneath his touch. Sliding her arms around his back, Lucy allowed the most notorious player in the South to kiss her right in the middle of the hospital waiting room.

His hand journeyed across the slope of her neck as Roman candles took flight in her head. While his lips made a feather-light trail across her cheek, Lucy listed all the reasons she should be telling him to stop. And she was going to. Any second now.

This was a complication. This was wrong. This was . . . heaven.

"Okay, they're gone."

He stepped away. Brushed a piece of lint off his oxford shirt.

And yawned.

Lucy stood rooted in her spot, her eyes blinking in rapid succession. What had just happened?

He had just—

And then she had just—

She followed the direction of his stare and turned to see the retreating back of two men carrying cameras.

Paparazzi. Of course.

"Nothing like mauling a woman in the ER." Lucy was impressed at how positively bored her voice sounded.

"You didn't seem to mind."

She wanted to wipe that grin right off his face.

"You know, maybe I shouldn't be the only one getting a tutor here, Alex." She fluffed her hair, felt the remnants of dried blood and forced a smile. "Because that performance was a little underwhelming."

She saw the sparks ignite in his eyes before banking to a smolder. "Is that so?" He closed the gap between them and looked down that chiseled, arrogant nose. "Care to call the photographers back and try again?"

Chill bumps danced along the back of her spine. So this was what it was like to play with fire. "I guess your football performance isn't the only thing that's diminished in the last year." She patted his chest. "But don't worry. I won't tell anyone. Part of my job is to protect your reputation."

"I don't like to leave anyone unsatisfied." His hand slid back up her arm.

Unexpected, unwanted desire unfurled in her stomach. She had to get a grip. This was a game she wasn't prepared to play. She met those bedroom eyes and dropped her voice to a sultry whisper. "Alex?"

He said nothing. Just moved his face closer to hers. "Yes?"

Her lips hovered under his. "I'm not staying with Clare Deveraux."

He lifted his head and exhaled a long-suffering sigh. "You, Lucy Wiltshire, know how to ruin a perfectly good time."

"Oh." She blinked twice. "Is that what we were having?"

"Your only other option is to stay at my house." His eyebrows lifted in a challenge. "With me."

Chapter Twenty-one

*L*ucy walked down a second-story hall lined with oil paintings of generations of Deveraues. Just beyond a sixth bedroom, she found the image of her father as a young twentysomething. The age he would've been when he'd lured her mother into passion and ruin, only to discard her like a worn-out tennis racket.

"You look like him." Clare stepped out from the doorway behind Lucy, her eyes on the picture.

"Actually I favor my mother." A woman she didn't even know anymore.

Clare fingered the brooch at her neck. "Apparently you have Anna's kind heart. And that's a blessing." She wiggled her fingers. "Now come, come."

Lucy's bedroom could've been taken from the pages of *Traditional Home*. She was surrounded by chic, sophisticated white everywhere she looked. A four-poster bed sat as one focal point, covered in a white matelasse quilt and an abundance of fluffy pillows that made a girl just want to run and jump into them. Opposite the bed, a white fireplace stood, framed by a collection of antique mirrors over the mantel.

"It's . . . nice," Lucy said in the stilted silence.

"I know you don't want to be here. But I think it's a blessing."

"Clare, I don't know what to make of all this yet. My mother *lied* to me"—Lucy sighed—"about my father . . . about who I thought I was.

And the funny thing is, I've never missed her more. I just want the chance to talk to her—to ask her why she would accept money from you. Why she would allow herself to be bought off. She could've told me the truth."

Clare sat down in the matching chair beside her. "Initially, I'm sure your mother was scared to tell anyone. The agreement she signed was silence in exchange for cash."

"But I was her daughter. I deserved to know. And after a certain point, she had nothing to lose. She would've known you wouldn't have caused a scandal."

"Yes, I realize that." Clare ran her finger over the piping on the arm of the chair. "I think your mother wanted something better for you. My son floated from one scandal to another. Anna probably wanted you to think your father was a hero. A good man. There was little reason to want you connected to my family. No doubt she wanted to cut all ties with the Deverauxes."

"How could you just throw money at her like she was nothing? My mother was a hard-working, godly woman." Lucy watched the sun set in the evening sky. It was only six thirty, but she was exhausted and spent.

"It was a long time ago. I was different then—we all were. I had a family and a name to protect. I wasn't married to just any man—I was married to the governor." Clare stood up and went to an armoire. "You don't have to forgive me tonight. You don't even have to like me. But please at least pray about it."

Lucy had tried. But the words hadn't come. All she had been able to utter to the Holy Father was a profound *Are you kidding me?*

"Alex had a bag sent over while we were at the pharmacy." Clare opened the curving door of the cabinet. "He packed some things he thought you might need. I'll just leave you alone to get settled. And Lucy?" Clare stopped in the doorway, a queen of her manor.

"Yes?"

"No matter what you decide in terms of forgiving me, we shall begin your lessons tomorrow night. I hope you're mature enough to put aside your feelings for me in order to help Alex."

Lucy said nothing as Clare let herself out.

Reaching into the armoire, she pulled out a small suitcase and flung it on the bed. There was no telling what had been packed. Probably whatever his assistant could grab.

She unzipped the top and found a pair of jeans, her favorite red flats, and a white blouse. She pulled out her Wookiee sleep shirt and a note fluttered onto the quilt.

Lucy,

Searched for ten minutes for something lacy and hot. This is what I found. Ever heard of a place called Victoria's Secret? They sell nightwear. From this decade.

Sorry about your day—except when you kissed me. Twice.

I was embarrassed at your blatant displays of affection, but as I am a man for the people, I will do my duty.

Sleep well. Call you Wednesday morning.

Signed,

Your Han Solo

That man. He wasn't turning out to be what she had expected. What she had counted on him to be. And that thought made her head hurt even worse. She wondered again when he would wise up and trade her in for an upgrade—someone of his class and breeding.

Underneath the jeans she saw a Bible Alex must've found on her bookshelf. She ran her finger over her name on the peeling burgundy cover. He couldn't have known this wasn't the Bible she used now, but the one her mother had given her for her sixteenth birthday.

Flipping through the wispy pages, she paused as a highlighted passage caught her attention.

I WILL PRAISE YOU,

BECAUSE I HAVE BEEN REMARKABLY AND WONDERFULLY MADE.

Words Lucy had clung to as a teenager when everything in her said she wasn't good enough. And now? Her father was Steven Deveraux. She was sleeping in the former first lady's home. And her future fiancé was a legendary football hero.

Just like that sixteen-year-old girl, Lucy still felt the need to read the passage again. To whisper the words out loud.

And pray this time it would actually sink in.

Chapter Twenty-two

*H*e was a Greek Adonis in a waffle house.

"You gonna eat that?"

Alex reached across the table at the IHOP and plucked a piece of bacon from her plate.

He looked like he had walked right off a Ralph Lauren runway. Natural chestnut highlights shone in his dark hair, complementing his tan. His gray suit might have made him look sophisticated and serious, but it couldn't hide the athlete beneath it. While she, on the other hand, had slept a combined total of fifteen minutes. Between the nightmares about close-ups and long-angle lenses, thoughts of her family, and rolling on her sore hand, she was worn out. Lucy's eyes were so puffy she hadn't even bothered putting on makeup, and her hair was nothing more than a limp ponytail with stray curls staging spiral revolts. And he had the nerve to show up this morning at Clare's, whisk her off to breakfast, and look like Mr. GQ.

She sipped her tea and winced.

"Bitter?" Alex asked.

"It seems I am." She spooned in some sugar. "Did you put your bumper sticker on my car?"

He just smiled. "Probably raised the resale value."

"My car is a classic."

"Your car wants you to put it out of its misery." He chewed his piece of bacon. "Let it die with dignity."

"Yeah, remind me to pick myself up a Bentley next time we're out."

Alex gave her a heated wink and went back to his Rooty Tooty Fresh 'N Fruity. "Your grandma seemed happy this morning."

"Was that her happy face? It's hard to tell." The IHOP was full of people who chatted over steaming plates of short stacks and bottomless mugs of Folgers. With her resident assistants at the helm, Lucy had taken the day off so she could touch base with Marinell's school and talk to her insurance company about her shambles of an apartment.

"Are you still refusing to discuss your father with Clare?" he asked.

"I'm barely hanging on with her psycho tutorials. Listening to her justify her late son would just push me right over the edge to full-blown crazy."

"Funny," he said. "I had assumed you were already there."

She blew on her Earl Grey and studied the room over the rim of her cup. "Don't look now, but there are two guys sitting a couple booths over—I said don't look. I'm pretty sure they followed us here. They keep . . . watching us."

Alex frowned as he shot off a text. "That's Lou and Squid."

"Members of your boy band?"

"Nope. New friends of yours."

She glanced at the guys again. Large, hulking brutes. Pretending to eat breakfast. Faces only a mother on intravenous drugs could love. "Let me guess, my new bodyguards."

"Correct."

Lucy let her chin plunk into her hand. "Somebody following my every move. There are no words to thank you."

He pulled the rubber band from the newspaper and whistled low. "I'll be darned." He showed her the front page.

She choked on her tea. "That's us." Someone had caught a shot of Alex carrying Lucy out of her apartment. Her head rested on his chest, and he held her close, his face tight with concern. "You're a hero."

He pulled the paper back and scanned the article. "Looks that way."

"I guess that will be a boon for the campaign."

"I didn't want this hitting the media." His eyes were sharp on hers. "You were injured. Do you really think that's something I want to share with the world?"

"Oh, that's right. You don't do public pain." Sleep deprivation always made her cranky, and today was no exception. "Who are you texting there? Your girlfriend?" He had yet to tell her about his phone call at the hospital. But what right did she have to pry? She was just a prop.

"Why would I need a girlfriend when I have you?" He reached out a finger and flicked a crumb from her lip.

"Alex?" She tried to avoid staring at her two-member mafia across the way, but it was no use. "I'm sorry I pushed you about your brother yesterday." She had spent some of her time awake last night praying for Alex. And for Will.

"Uh-huh." He flipped to the sports section.

"But you know . . ." She was good at getting people to open up. It was her gift. One that worked all the time on her girls. "If you ever want to talk to me about it, you could."

He studied an article on the World Cup. "No thanks."

"What was he like?"

No response. And that was all she was going to take.

She grabbed his hand and pulled the offensive paper down. "I spent the night with Clare 'the Dragon' Deveraux—for you." Now she had his full attention. "Start talking."

The amber flecks in his eyes glimmered fire. But just for a moment. One single millisecond, she saw it. That flash of pain. She knew the look. And its disguises.

He sighed over his coffee. "What do you want to know?"

She could hear the countdown clock ticking and knew he wouldn't indulge her for long. "Were you close?" Lucy hadn't exactly studied their family dynamics when they'd been in school.

"Yes." He took a sip and stretched his arm across the back of the booth. "We were very close as kids." He would've stopped there, but

Lucy nodded and nudged him on. "But always very different. During eighth grade, he went on his first mission trip, and I went to football camp. Neither one of us came back the same." His fingers tightened on the mug. "It was like we spoke two different languages after that. He became the do-gooder who always made Mom and Dad proud, and I . . . just played sports."

"You did more than play sports. ESPN covered your University of Texas signing. You got drafted to the pros when you were, like, twelve." She knew exactly what year he'd been in college, but she wasn't going to let him know that. "Your life matters, Alex."

"This conversation is starting to get dull."

"I think we should pray for your brother."

"Maybe later."

"Or we could do it now." She lowered her head, keeping her eyes open until he did the same. He was not any too quick about it. "Lord, we ask that you be with Will Sinclair. That you would shelter him under your wing. Surround him with a hedge of holy protection. Open doors only you can open to get him safely back home."

Alex's hands slid across the table and clasped her hands.

She gave them a squeeze. He squeezed right back.

"Jesus, I pray for peace and comfort for his family." Her cheeks burned with her boldness, but she plunged on. "And I ask for you to wrap your love around Alex. Speak to his hurting heart."

At her amen, Alex kept his hands on hers. "Thank you." His voice was husky, rough.

"That's what fake fiancées are for."

Alex checked his phone and frowned. "We should go. I have back-to-back meetings today, plus a lunch at a senior center."

"Don't come back with any girlfriends."

He threw some cash on the table as he stood. "Only ones with teeth." His fingers meshed with hers as they walked to his Mercedes. "I really wish you would stay at Clare's a few more days."

"No way." It was bad enough she was going to have to visit for lessons.

As they pulled away, Lucy watched the rearview mirror. The bodyguards followed. "Lou and Squid aren't very subtle."

"They're not supposed to be."

Twenty minutes later she walked behind him as he carried her bag up the sidewalk to her apartment. It was such a minor thing—seeing him with her suitcase. Yet strangely intimate. Like they were a real couple.

Her heart sank as he opened her door and Lucy caught a glimpse at what was once her living room.

"Don't look." Alex made a little twirly motion with his finger. "Seriously, you don't want to see this."

But it was too late. She had just walked into a war zone.

Gaping holes covered her walls. Like someone had come through with a sledgehammer. Or a B-52.

"Lucy, it probably looks worse than it is." He picked up a picture frame, then shoved it behind his back at her approach.

"That idiot landlord started the repair work himself." She wanted to strangle someone. Anyone would do. "Just like when he tried to fix the roof, and half of it came off in the next rainstorm." Mr. Jenkins hadn't even bothered to take down her pictures. They lay in pieces on the floor, randomly scattered and broken as if the building had been shaken by an earthquake.

"This can be fixed," Alex said as if he were talking her off a ledge. "I'll take care of it."

"Let me see what you have behind your back."

"You can check out my rearview later."

"You're stalling, Sinclair."

"Luce, just out of curiosity, how much is that signed photo of Leonard Nimoy worth?"

"My mom gave it to me." Her throat tightened. "It's priceless."

His eyes briefly went to the ceiling, as if appealing to the heavens. "Take it from me, lives are what matter. Not material things."

The tears were back once more, and Lucy couldn't blink them away. Nor could she stand there and argue with a grieving man. "I loved Leonard," she whispered, turning away so he didn't have to witness yet another meltdown.

Lucy felt Alex behind her, his warmth pressing into her back. When his arms slipped around her, she could only lean into him. "We'll fix it." He pressed his lips to her temple.

"Rich people." She gave an indelicate sniff. "You guys just snap your fingers and spew fairy dust."

"Exactly what I used to get you to go out with me." His hold tightened. "Don't worry about this."

"This stuff is important to me—my books, my pictures . . . my Leonard." Tired of it all, her head lowered, giving her a bird's-eye view of a small pile shoved under the couch. The corner of a black antique frame stuck out just enough to reveal a familiar picture. She pushed away from Alex and crouched on the floor.

The black-and-white photo had been stepped on. Dripped on. And torn in two. It was Lucy's favorite—her mother enjoying a summer day on the boardwalk at Folly Beach. Her hair blowing in the breeze like a cover model, her smile wide in a moment of laughter, and her eyes staring into the distance as if she were waiting for something magical to wash up on shore. Lucy hadn't been born; her mother hadn't yet known Clare Deveraux's cold shoulder or Steven's cruel manipulation.

"She kept so much from me," Lucy said. "How many times did I walk by my own father in town, and she never said a word? She was my only family . . . and I didn't really even know her."

"Don't do this to yourself. She loved you and tried to do her best." Alex took the two pieces from her hands. "She's beautiful." His eyes lifted to hers. "She looks like you."

His kindness was about to break her. "I think I want to be alone."

He took her hand and pressed a kiss right on her white bandage. "I'm not leaving you here. You can stay at Clare's."

"No." Not there. Again.

He ran his hand up and down her arms. "I can't even put in a security system until they get this mess straightened out. I want you somewhere I know it's safe. You heard Clare say she has a security team in her carriage house."

"She probably keeps her cauldron out there too." Lucy thought of the sad balance in her checkbook and knew she couldn't do more than one a night at a hotel. "She's weird, Alex."

"See, you do have something in common." He smiled and tucked a stray curl behind her ear. "Can we just not argue about this? There's no way I'm leaving you alone, but if I don't get to these meetings, my campaign team is going to fire me."

He was so close she could smell his shampoo. See his eyes burn into hers. When he looked at her like that, she might promise him anything.

"Fine," she huffed. "Take me there."

Holding his hand, she paused at the door and wondered if her home wasn't the only thing deteriorating.

Like her willpower.

And her forcefield against hot, emotionally unavailable football stars.

She closed the door and said a prayer for her heart.

Because for the first time in her life, Lucy Wiltshire, being of sound mind and strong backbone, didn't feel quite so immune anymore.

In fact, what she felt . . . was a totally unwelcome kinship with *all* those cheerleaders.

Chapter Twenty-three

She had been at Clare's Den of Antiquities and Archaic Manners for almost a whole week now. When her landlord had told her that her apartment wouldn't be ready for weeks, Lucy had merely nodded, then gotten in her car and driven straight to Baskin-Robbins.

Clare's idea of tutoring resembled Lucy's idea of torture. Quizzes on Alex's campaign platform. Flash card reviews on state and county leaders. Even a history of former White House first ladies, with a special emphasis on Lady Bird Johnson and that "tragically slighted Pat Nixon." She was grateful to Julian, who played along and offered prizes at the end of the mind-numbing sessions, rewarding Lucy with homemade cobbler on Saturday and cream cheese strudel this morning. Lucy was learning a lot. Like the fact that she couldn't fit into any of her skirts anymore, giving Clare the perfect excuse to buy Lucy more clothing "better suited for a woman in politics."

The Monday afternoon heat gave way to rain showers, turning the clouds into puffs of gray as they fought to overtake the peeking sun. Lucy flicked on her windshield wipers and squinted as she struggled to stay within the white lines.

"Are windshield wipers supposed to squeak like that?" Marinell asked from her spot in the passenger seat.

"They're fine."

"Sounds like an angry pig to me."

"You've been hanging out with Alex too much." He had been stopping by Saving Grace the past few nights, helping Marinell with her summer school homework. Every time Lucy saw him, she was reminded of their kiss. But he hadn't so much as mentioned it. When your nickname was the Playboy, anything less than third base probably didn't even register.

"Tyneisha said you left the house last night after curfew." Lucy veered onto the exit that would take her to the Children's Hospital. "We discussed this. If you need to see your brother, you can call me—"

"I get it."

Lucy checked her rearview mirror and watched her bodyguards follow in the car behind her. "Marinell, we have rules. Third strike and you're out. I can't let you stay."

"Sometimes I just need to see my brother at night, okay?"

"So long as you're back before curfew. I don't think that's a lot to ask." Something wasn't right, but Lucy hoped Marinell would figure it out fast. She didn't want her to leave. "I know you're not sleeping well, and I can tell you've lost more weight."

"I'm going for the supermodel look." Marinell chewed on a ragged thumbnail. "I hear the waif thing pays major bucks."

"If you want to be there for your brother, you need to keep yourself healthy. And that includes eating—whether you feel like it or not." Some people lost their appetite when they got down, and Marinell appeared to fall into that category. Lucy wondered what that was like.

"So you and Alex seem to be pretty serious."

"Yes," Lucy said dryly. "He's the wind beneath my wings." She didn't want to talk about Alex today. The man consumed too much of her thoughts, and life was too short to think all day on a sexy, political-minded, emotionally void man. No matter how well he kissed.

"He says he's taking you to a fancy party Friday night." Marinell cracked a rare smile. "On a yacht. I mean, for real?"

Alex was having another one of his soirees, this time on a friend's swanky yacht. Lucy's threat to wear her one-piece and flippers had made Clare even more determined to help her shop for just the right dress.

She zipped into a parking spot and held a polka-dotted umbrella over Marinell's head as they ran inside the hospital lobby.

Squishing across the floor in wet flats, Lucy fumbled with the button on the umbrella. "C'mon, c'mon," she muttered, shaking and twisting the handle.

"Lucy?"

Pushing the hair out of her eyes, Lucy looked up. And her heart sank. "Matt."

There he stood, his dark-blond hair newly trimmed, a crisp white shirt unbuttoned at the collar, and charcoal slacks with a crease a four-star general would be proud of.

"How are you?" he asked.

"I'm going to go on up," Marinell said. "I'll meet you in the room."

Lucy could only nod as the girl walked away.

"It's good to see you." It sounded so trite to Lucy's ear. "How's work?" Did he miss her? Still love her? Pine for her and write dark anguished poetry during his midnight hours?

"Work is fine." The way he stared at her. Had he ever looked that hungry to see her?

"Do you know someone here?" Lucy asked.

"Hospital outreach for church."

He visited sick children on his lunch break. She would remind herself of this the next time Alex put the moves on her and robbed her of her ability to reason.

"I saw in the paper where you had an accident." Matt gestured to her hand.

"It was nothing."

"I always said those pipes were a disaster waiting to happen."

Was this small talk code for *I still love you and will wait the rest of my life to be your man?* "I've missed..." Lucy forced her errant thoughts back in line. "I've missed talking to you." And seeing his face. Hearing his voice. Imagining his perfectly starched clothes hanging in her closet.

A couple walked by hand in hand, and Matt stepped closer to Lucy to get out of the way.

"I think about you all the time." His eyes searched hers, asking questions Lucy couldn't answer. "I wish . . . I wish things had been different. I have so many regrets." Lucy could fill a book with her own. "I keep reminding myself that you're happy." He took another step closer. "You are happy, right? Because some of those photos I see—they make me wonder if—"

"I should find Marinell." Her heart gave a little tremor. Standing in this hall, everything she wanted was just a touch away. Everything except the security of saving her girls. "Take care of yourself." Her voice broke, and she knew she had to get away before she dissolved into a puddle and confessed it all.

"Lucy—"

"I have to go." She eluded his outreached hand and ran all the way to the elevator.

Just four more months. She could do this. It was a lot to ask, but Lucy repeated her prayer that Matt would still be there when it was all over.

Lucy found Carlos's room, rapped lightly on the door, then let herself in. Machines talked in beeps and clicks next to a small boy who sat up in bed, a Transformer in one hand and a crayon in the other.

"Hey, Carlos," Lucy said. She had taken Marinell to see her brother a handful of times, growing more attached to the boy with every visit.

Marinell stood near his pillow, her hand lightly combing through his black, wavy hair. A woman Lucy had never seen before sat in a chair nearby, her eyes downcast.

"Miss Lucy, this is my mother. Esther."

"Hello, there," Lucy said. Digging in her purse, Lucy pulled out the coloring book and markers she had bought for Carlos.

Esther Hernandez stood up. "You help my daughter," she said, struggling with the English. "Thank you."

"You're welcome. We'll take good care of her."

"Mom comes almost every morning when I can't be here," Marinell said. "But sometimes it's hard for her to get a ride."

Marinell spoke to her mother in rapid-fire Spanish, and Lucy used the time to sit with Carlos and show him how each marker smelled like fruit.

"I tell my mother that they started Carlos on the dialysis," Marinell said to Lucy. "Two days a week. It takes many hours, and he gets bored, so your coloring book will be something for him to do."

"I go now," Esther said, her worried eyes trained on Carlos. "You be brave and do what doctor tell you."

"No," Carlos whined. "You said you'd stay. Why won't you come back when Papi is here?"

The woman's eyes went wide, and she spoke to her son in fierce Spanish. The boy dropped his head, and a pitiful bottom lip pooched out.

Esther kissed the sad-faced Carlos. "Be back later."

Marinell nudged her brother. "Tell Mama good-bye."

Esther turned back twice before reluctantly letting herself out the door.

The sadness in the room was as palpable as humidity after a rain-storm. Carlos turned his head into his pillow and covered his face with his arm.

Marinell made shushing noises as she rubbed the shoulder of his dinosaur pajamas. "It's okay, *mi hermano*. She'll see you soon." She glanced at Lucy.

"And Papi? Will he be back again tonight?"

"Yes, Marinell," Lucy said. "Will your father be making an appearance tonight?"

❧

Lucy waited until she and Marinell were back in the car before starting her interrogation. "So do you want to tell me why you've been meeting your dad at the hospital at night?"

"I haven't. Carlos didn't mean his dad. He gets confused."

Confusion over your father's identity wasn't that far of a stretch for Lucy at the moment. "I've done this job a long time, Marinell, and I've heard it all." She reached for her hand. "You can trust me."

Marinell clutched her seatbelt and stared out the window. "It's complicated."

"The man I thought was my father is a cross-dressing lounge singer. Try me."

"My dad lives . . . somewhere else. He grew up in Mexico, got recruited into a gang early. He rose up in the ranks, but then he met my mom. The gang wouldn't let him out."

"Drug gang?"

"Yeah. Really horrible people. Before I came along, my parents emigrated to Texas. But the gang came after my dad. He's been running ever since."

"And so have you."

"We know they're still out there, and it's dangerous for him to be around us. The last few years have been the worst, and he can't contact us much. Can't send money. Can't see us. And my mom is doing the best she can, but we struggled when my brother got sick. That's when someone turned us in to child services. It's been a mess ever since."

"So he comes and sees your brother at night?"

"He's only been twice. Sometimes I go to the hospital just in case."

"What can I do to help you?"

Marinell turned in her seat, a teenager barely holding her world together. "Just don't let my little brother die."

❧

"Shopping." Julian clapped his hands together in the limo as the late afternoon sun finally reappeared, warming Charleston with a renewed vengeance. "This is going to be so much fun, isn't it?"

"The best," Lucy muttered. "Just pull over at the nearest Target," she called to the driver.

"Nonsense." Clare *tsked*. "Alex said to get you a fabulous gown for Friday night, and that's what we're going to do. My way."

"I still think my red dress would've done nicely," Lucy said.

"That is a dress for land," Clare snapped. "You need one for water."

"I sold them all at my garage sale last year."

"I hear your impertinence, but I know what I'm talking about. My dear, my job is to make you the best complement to Alex I can."

"If you put me in something nautical, I'm going to flush it down the toilet and go in my Mickey Mouse cover-up."

Clare's chandelier diamond earrings swayed as she shook her head. "I see we still need to work on your attitude. Julian, take note of that."

"Writing it down right now." Julian held out his hand and studied his nails.

"I like Charlaine's for evening dresses, don't you?" Clare asked, flipping through a fashion magazine as they all three sat in the back.

"Yes, her creations are divine." Julian patted Lucy on the leg. "You're so lucky."

"By the by, Lucy, I hear you ran into your old friend, a Mr. Campbell."

Lucy's hand froze on the armrest. She turned to stare at Clare. "How did you know I saw Matt?"

"My dear." Her voice held censure that could only be delivered by South of Broad royalty. "I have friends all over this town. And you'll do well to remember they're all watching—just waiting to see either you or Alex misstep. Given the special importance of this Friday's event, I would think you would want to stay away from the likes of Matthew Campbell and keep your pretty blue eyes focused on your handsome young man."

"What do you mean *special* importance?" The thought of shopping for yacht-wear wasn't the only thing putting Lucy on edge. "This is just another political event. Just another social gathering for the campaign." Lucy stared at Clare. "Right?"

"If that's what you want to call it."

"Then what do *you* call it?"

Clare pressed her hands together and gave one of her first genuine smiles. "A wonderful night to propose."

Chapter Twenty-four

*H*yperventilation. Fever. Dizziness. Rampant desires for carbs and calories.

And those were the fun aspects of a panic attack.

Lucy sat on the cold tile floor of Clare's guest bathroom and waited for the anxiety to roll out like the tide. Instead it pushed and shoved with the ferocity of a squall.

In thirty minutes Alex would arrive, dashing and confident, to whisk her away to some hoity-toity yacht, where she would smile at him like the arm candy she was. And where he would propose in front of hundreds of onlookers.

Lucy couldn't do it. They'd never pull it off.

In third grade she had auditioned for the class play. Lucy had memorized lines and practiced for weeks, because she'd known in her young soul that she had been born to play Sacajawea. But when the curtain rose, there she stood in the back of the stage, partially hidden by a curtain, in the role of Native American Number Thirteen. No lines. No action.

Because Lucy was not an actress. Her teacher had seen it then. And it was just as true today. And girls assigned the part of a mute Native American did not grow up to pull off a fake proposal.

"I do," Lucy whispered weakly. "I do." This time with a little more enthusiasm.

Lord, what if his friends laugh at me? What are the tabloids going to say? Alex Sinclair finds a bride and marries down?

"How's it coming, honey?" Julian asked from the other side.

"Awful." Hot tears spilled down her cheeks. Was it too late to cancel? Postpone the event? How hard could it be to call two hundred close friends and political connections and tell them to come back another time?

"Can you open the door?" Julian wiggled the handle.

"No, it's stuck." Her evening gown hung from a hook on the door with a mocking sway. "Guess I'll have to stay in here a while."

"Open the door, peaches."

"I can't do this. Tell Alex I've changed my mind. He'll understand." She fingered her hair and stifled a groan. In her attempt at chic, she had taken a straightening iron to her stubborn curls, only to produce something in between a wave and a disaster. Like a bad '80s crimp job—only worse. "I'm not going to the party. Tell Alex I'm sick."

"Don't be silly. The man will be here any moment."

"I'm not joking." She would not be the laughingstock of those Charleston highbrows. "I'm staying in tonight. I don't care how you get rid of him, but just do it."

"Baby, I know *show* business, not the miracle business. There is no getting rid of Alex. When he wants something, he gets it. And what he wants is you."

All because of a stupid contract. Alex didn't possess one ounce of real affection for her.

"Tell him I break up." Lucy's breath hitched. "Because I'm never coming out."

❧

At seven o'clock Alex pounded on the bathroom door.

"Lucy, open up." He used the voice of authority that his team had followed for years. No one contradicted him.

"Buzz off."

Leave it to Clare to take it upon herself to tell Lucy about tonight's proposal. He had wanted it to be a surprise, so Lucy wouldn't work herself into a panic. Like this one.

He jangled the knob. "Julian says you're not coming out."

"At least one man on the planet listens to me."

Alex lowered his voice until it was a calm drawl. "I know you're nervous about tonight. But you'll do fine. I'm going to be right there with you." He dug deep and threw her a lifeline. "I'm a little nervous, too, if it helps."

"It does not."

They were going to be late if he didn't get her out of that bathroom. And a man couldn't be late to his own party. "Lucy, I want you out of this bathroom on the count of three, you got it? One . . . two . . ." This was not looking good. Not good at all. "Two and a half. Two and three-quarters . . ."

No response.

He ran a rough hand over his face and leaned against the door. "Tell me what this is about."

"Don't you get it? I'm not Sacajawea."

Alex pressed his head against the door frame and closed his eyes.

"I can't do this anymore," she said pitifully. "Why did I think I could pull this off? That I was someone who could run in your circles? I can't even fix my own hair."

"Put it in a ponytail. Heck, wear a shower cap for all I care."

"This isn't a tennis match at the country club! Nobody else on that boat's gonna have a ponytail."

"I don't care about other women, Lucy. Just you. Just like you are."

He could hear her deep inhale. "That is . . . strangely hot."

"Let me in."

"No."

"You either open this door or I make like a defensive tackle and break it down."

"For your information, women are not attracted to brute force."

"I'll write you some sonnets later."

She kept him waiting a good minute. Sixty long seconds standing outside her bathroom door like a complete idiot, useless and inept. It was almost enough time to calm his own nerves.

Because the woman was going to send him to an early grave.

Tonight was big. It was major. The whole world would hear the news of their engagement, and it had to be just right. This was the final secret strategy of his campaign. If they messed it up, it was over. And then where would he be?

Alex shoved the negative thoughts from his mind. Tonight *would* go perfectly. And he *would* win this election. And then he'd get that peace he'd been chasing after so hard. He'd finish up what his brother didn't get to do, and he'd finally be able to close his eyes at night. He'd silence the voice that told him he was just a pretty face on a package of underwear.

Finally the lock clicked.

And the door opened.

And there Lucy stood. An angel with a halo of blonde frizz.

He stared at what they both knew was an absolute disaster and said the only thing he could. "I love it."

With a quivering lip, Lucy sank onto the floor, her pink Quiddich: The Sport of Real Men shirt hanging over her shorts.

He dropped down beside her. "I know you're nervous about tonight."

"I'm not nervous. I'm absolutely petrified, you insensitive Neanderthal."

Time was ticking. Now was the moment to pull out the big guns. "Think of your girls." He ran his hand down her cheek, skimming the softness beneath the pad of his thumb. "You're doing all of this for them. Do you have any idea how lucky those women are to have you?" Her confidence was as thin as parchment paper. "How lucky I am to have you?"

She leaned her cheek into his hand. "I don't want to ruin this for you."

"The only way that will happen is if you bail on me now." His lips found their way to her forehead, then lingered on her cheek, seeking reassurance. For her. And for himself. "I need you, Luce."

Three eternities passed before she ran a hand under her red nose and nodded. "Fine. I'll go."

Alex's lungs expanded as he let the air back in.

"But the first woman who makes a crack about my hair—"

"I'll punch her lights out." Alex pulled her to her feet.

"You're supposed to love me, so it needs to be more severe than that."

"I'll yank out her heart with ice tongs."

"Aw." Lucy patted his chest. "You would do that for me?"

He captured her hand, felt its warmth all the way through his shirt. "No amount of carnage is too much for my girl."

She reappeared fifteen minutes later, a vision in off-white, her hair pinned loosely on top of her head.

"Is that the dress you're wearing?"

It was the wrong thing to say. "What's wrong with it?"

A gossamer thing, it dipped low in the front, revealing not too much, but just enough to give a man a focal point. Tiny beads covered the bodice, like it had been iced in sugar crystals. A slit stopped halfway up the dress, showing off Lucy's long legs and shapely calves. She looked like something from the cover of *Vogue*. A Parisian runway. A Hollywood premiere.

"Take it off," he said.

She crossed her arms. "You and I should probably talk about the fake premarital sex we're not going to be having."

"The dress has got to go." She was not his Lucy. "I know you have something else you could wear."

"But Clare said—"

"I don't care what she said." Did Clare think he wanted Lucy to look like the runner-up to Miss Charleston? Lucy probably had Vaseline on her teeth and duct tape on her bra. "You have five minutes to find something else to wear," Alex said. "As long as you come out looking like you, I don't care what it is." His eyes went to her hair. "On second thought, I'll get Julian."

❧

Thirty minutes later Lucy walked out on four-inch heels and stood before him modeling a retro teal dress. It was like something out of an old black-and-white Katherine Hepburn movie. A scoop neck revealed creamy white shoulders that begged for a man to trace the curves. The narrow waist gave way to a full-bodied skirt that stopped right past her calves. Three-quarter-length sleeves accented the arms that had held broken young women and offered them a home.

He knew she was waiting for him to say something. The truth would probably have her locking herself in the bathroom again. He had been tackled by men twice his size and not been knocked this off-balance.

"You're beautiful." His voice came out rougher than he'd intended.

She gave a weak smile. "It's the hair."

With her hand in his, Alex escorted Lucy downstairs to parade her before Julian and Clare.

"It's our Goodwill find from last week." Julian twirled his finger for Lucy to spin. "Vintage Dolce never looked so grand."

Alex watched her cheeks blush as Lucy obliged, her skirt fanning around her. She was totally unaware how captivating she was. She didn't have the polished and glossed beauty of the models and actresses he'd dated. But what she had was something more. Somehow better. He felt more himself around her. His name didn't affect her, nor his money. He had to work harder to impress her, which, strangely enough, he found himself doing more and more lately. Just his competitive streak, he supposed.

Clare, dressed in a striking black floor-length gown, stood up and inspected her protégé. "*Hmph.* Not what I had envisioned for this evening, but not bad. I suppose it will have to do."

Alex lightly held Lucy's fingers in his. "She'll be the envy of every woman there."

Clare's razor-sharp gaze went from Lucy's red-painted toes peeping out of her heels to the top of her head. "The hair is an abomination, but you will hold your head up high," Clare said. "If anyone breathes a word of insult to you, I'll make sure it's the last party they ever attend in this town."

"Thank you." Lucy gave a small nod. "I think."

Ignoring the vibrating cell in his pocket, Alex held up Lucy's wrap and settled it over her shoulders. With his hand at her back, he guided her out the door and into the evening air.

It was time for the next phase of his campaign to begin. By the end of the night, Lucy Wiltshire was going to wear his ring.

And send him to Congress.

Chapter Twenty-five

The sun began its slow descent as the *Southern Mischief* slid across Charleston Harbor. The homes lining the Battery provided a pastel rainbow of colors meant to calm. But Lucy's stomach was tied in a perfect double knot, and her thoughts turned longingly to the *Dr. Who* DVD collection tucked in her suitcase at Clare's.

Alex was going to ask her to marry him. Tonight. He wouldn't tell her when or how, and that did nothing but agitate her frayed nerves. Last night she had dreamed that he had gone down on one knee, asked the necessary question, and the whole ship had erupted into laughter. People pointing. Staring. Alex had peered at Lucy as if seeing her for the first time. Then walked away.

"Son." Marcus Sinclair walked toward them and shook his son's hand as if they were business associates. "Good to see you. I guess you didn't get my call about golf yesterday?"

"I've been busy, Dad. I have this little election thing going on." Alex's voice was dry as toast.

"You also have a family," Marcus said.

Alex moved to kiss his mother's cheek, then his sister's. "Looking lovely tonight, ladies."

"We're just glad we got an invitation," his mother said with a wry grin. "Political functions are about the only time we see you anymore."

She reached out her hands to Lucy. "Fabulous dress. Somebody has good taste."

Lucy turned to find Finley staring at her hair. "You hardly look like the same crazy lady who was walking down the street in her pj's."

A fifteen-piece orchestra had set up nearby, and the faint strains of Beethoven matched the elegance of the yacht. But Lucy knew if it had been up to Alex, they'd be playing Aerosmith.

Donna rested her hand on her son's forearm, a gesture of comfort and familiarity. Lucy wondered what her own mother would've thought about tonight. She certainly couldn't have judged Lucy for her duplicity.

"We need to talk about Fourth of July arrangements, Alex," Donna Sinclair said. "You'll be joining us at the beach house, won't you?" She hastily explained to Lucy, "We have a family tradition of spending a few days together over the holiday." Her smile was wistful as she looked at her son. "And it's the boys' birthday, of course."

Tension swirled around Alex like morning fog on the bay. Lucy had no idea. Of course he would've just let it go by. "Yes, I've been counting the days until . . . Alex's birthday." As any future fiancée would. But how did a family celebrate the birthday of one son and the loss of another?

His mother sighed. "They were my Fourth of July babies."

Lucy found herself reeled in closer to the hard wall of Alex's chest. "Lucy and I might stop by for the day, but I can't afford to be gone for much more than that."

Donna's face fell. "Oh. Well. All right then."

"I see you've chosen yet another career to get in the way of your family." His father looked so much like Alex. A head full of dark hair, yet threaded with gray. Tall stature he wasn't afraid to use to intimidate. And eyes that missed nothing. "We need to be together as a family this year more than ever."

"Forget it." Finley checked a text on her phone. "It's not like he cares."

Alex stilled like a Roman statue. "I see some people I need to talk to. Enjoy yourselves tonight." He reached out and tweaked his sister's nose. "Stay out of trouble."

The snarl Finley sent him was nothing short of art. Lucy studied it with appreciation, hoping to remember it for future use. Reaching out an arm, she grabbed Alex by the sleeve, holding him in place. The least he could do was have a conversation with his family.

"Lucy, we want you to join us for the Fourth of July weekend, of course." The gracious smiled returned to Donna's face. "We'd love to spend some time with you."

Alex increased the pressure of his squeeze, but Lucy wasn't having any of it. "Thank you," she said. "I'll certainly see what I can do. And I agree—a person needs to spend time with family, right?"

Father stared at son. "Exactly."

Alex's hand snaked up her spine to massage the back of her neck. "We need to mingle."

"I mean, what's a holiday without the people you love?" Whatever rift was between Alex and his parents needed to be dealt with. He had pushed her toward Clare, so surely it was fine that she pushed back. Besides, the Sinclairs were unexpectedly nice. Lucy had thought they'd be snooty and perfectly awful, but they were so weirdly normal. Marcus had his arm around his daughter, and Donna couldn't take her worried eyes off Alex.

"You talk my son into coming." Donna smiled at her newest friend. "I put on a mean shrimp boil."

Lucy risked a peek at her soon-to-be fiancé. "He's been telling me how much he misses your cooking."

"Then you guys will come?" Finley tried not to look interested. "For real?"

"He'll be there. All weekend."

Lucy looked into Alex's face and knew the *Southern Mischief* was about to encounter choppy waters.

❧

He wasn't even married to Lucy, and she was already a meddling nuisance. With his strong hand at her back, Alex led his scheming girlfriend across the floor. "What was that all about?" he asked tightly.

"You were *such* a help in reuniting Clare and me, I just thought I would return the favor."

He nodded to a few friends. "My relationship with my family is just fine."

"You treat them like you can't stand to breathe the same air."

Alex made an abrupt stop and turned sharp eyes on Lucy. "You have no idea what you're talking about."

"You have a family who loves you." She looked up at him with pity, and he wanted to howl. He didn't deserve anyone's sympathy. "Keeping them at a distance isn't going to bring your brother back."

A muscle flexed in his stubborn jaw, and Lucy reached out a tentative hand. Her cool fingers touched his cheek, as if to stroke the tension away. He couldn't move, couldn't breathe.

Lucy's eyes widened, as if she'd caught herself by surprise. She lifted her hand as if it burned, but he grabbed it. And stared down into her questioning face. How could he explain his loss? His emptiness? There were no words for how his family's kindness ate at him like a pestilence.

"They need you, Alex."

He opened his mouth to argue, to say the words that would hurt her like he was hurting.

But not Lucy. The woman who saved homeless girls and bravely stood by his side night after night. He clamped his lips and turned his head toward the water. Inhaling the salty air, Alex stared at the fading sun and let the silence stretch. "There's nothing I can do for them," he finally said.

"You're not supposed to fix it for them." He wondered if she knew she no longer looked at him with that old resentment. "They're hurting, too, and they just want to be near you."

He shook his head, his expression as empty as his heart as he watched another ship pass by. "I can't do that right now."

Lucy stepped closer, and her light scent swept over him. "I don't know where your guilt comes from, but it's not from God. And it's undeserved and hurting the people you love."

Fire exploded behind his eyes. Who was *she* or anyone else to tell him to get rid of his guilt? Like it was that easy? He prayed to God every day to make it go away, along with the relentless fever that consumed him. He had to find his brother, and he had to win this election. Nothing else mattered.

He tore his eyes away from the sky and fastened them on Lucy. "Your job," he said, "is to just stick by my side tonight. That's all. I don't need your counseling nor do I need your prying."

"Right." He could tell she was considering how she might throw his body overboard. "Because I'm just a temporary companion."

She was becoming more than that. But he didn't know what and didn't have time to take it out and examine it tonight. "Are you up for this or not?"

"Don't worry." Her words dripped with venom. "I won't fail you." She took a step back, putting a mile of distance between them. "You may think you're just lying to the world, but the real tragedy here is you're lying to yourself."

"Hey, there you two are!"

Alex's blistering rebuttal died on his lips as Morgan and Chuck approached. Lucy's words played in his head like a taunt as she completely ignored him and chatted with her friends.

"Nice party." Morgan pulled Lucy into a hug. "Almost as good as the one we went to with the youth last weekend at Chuck E. Cheese's."

"Can't beat a night of skeeball," her fiancé said. Wearing a sleek black suit, Chuck looked more adult than Alex had ever seen him. And incredibly uncomfortable.

Lucy's friend Sanjay squeezed past a small group of women to join them. Snagging a shrimp puff from a passing waiter, he winked at a busty blonde. He was a fashion disaster in his powder-blue tuxedo, gray athletic socks, and yellow sneakers.

"We almost missed the ship," Sanjay said as some of the other Hobbits gathered. "I had a big fight with the lady."

"Girlfriend trouble?" Alex asked.

"Yeah, I told her I would take out the trash when I was good and ready. I'm the man of the house, and she isn't going to tell me what to do."

"Things will be fine when you get home." Chuck slapped a hand on Sanjay's bony shoulder. "Just give your mom some time to cool down."

"How are the wedding plans coming?" Alex asked Morgan.

"Busy, but good." Morgan's mama bear face melted as she took in her best friend. "Lucy, you look beautiful."

"Yes, she does." Alex reached for her. "I'm beyond blessed to be with the prettiest woman on the ship."

"Does anyone else smell dead fish?" Lucy tried to step away, but Alex held a firm grip.

"The Hobbits' meeting still on for Thursday?" Sanjay asked. "It's your night to make cookies, Lucy. Make them in the shape of Ewoks again."

"Actually, I'm not staying at my house right now." She cast a pointed glare at Alex. "I should be soon, though."

"Not too soon." He liked Lucy where he knew she was safe. And even though he didn't want to deal with his own family, it was just a matter of time before Lucy's soft heart let her grandmother in. "But I'm sure Clare wouldn't mind if you had your party there."

"We're not having a party." Sanjay pushed up the nose of his glasses. "It's an informational meeting for people with similar intellectual pursuits."

"It's a nerd social," Chuck said. "But we have good snacks."

Morgan pointed toward a table across the way. "The girls look stunning."

"The girls?" Lucy looked over her shoulder. All thirteen of her Saving Grace ladies waved in her direction. She turned a questioning eye to Alex.

He merely shrugged. "I thought they might enjoy a night out."

"That's just the half of it," Morgan said. "Today they got the works—a full day of shopping, spa, and hair."

Lucy's eyes widened in silent wonder.

"All his idea." Morgan gave him a reluctant smile.

"Alex, I . . . I don't know what to say."

From the playground to the pros, Alex had always been first draft pick. He'd had reps from Nike buy him cars. Agents hand him trips to exotic locales and box seats for the Lakers. Women offer things that would've made his mama cry. But nobody had ever looked at him with the kind of awe he saw in Lucy's face.

"It's nothing. I just thought the girls deserved a party too."

Then she was in his arms, hugging him like he had just given her access to his checking account. He settled one arm at her back and the other in the hair he couldn't quit touching. Just seconds ago Lucy had been ready to toss him to the sharks. And now he was her hero. He knew people were watching, but he didn't care. Pressing his lips to her temple, Alex just held on.

Chapter Twenty-six

*E*very party had a pooper. And this one was headed their way in a black Halston gown with coordinating clutch.

"Alex, Lucy." Clare's diamonds swung from her earlobes and circled her wrist. "You may conduct your displays of affection later. There are some people I'd like you to meet."

Reluctantly Lucy left her friends and stood by Alex's side as he worked the room. She tried to say as little as possible but kept her smile bright and cheery until she thought her lips would fall off. With Clare stuck to her like glue, Lucy felt her initial annoyance fade away. The former first lady was a genius at steering conversation. So much so that Lucy only had to contribute small bits of input when prompted. Yes, she did like Alex's new ideas for overhauling the foster care system. She loved that the state was seeing the heart behind the man. No, she didn't think his opponent had the public schools' best interest at heart. Had they seen all the research on Alex's website? Why, of course, she loved Gucci. They made the most fabulous shoes.

It was enough to wear a girl out. Didn't anyone want to talk about Britney Spears, the BOGO sale at Payless, or the delicious rumor that *Avatar* was going to be a trilogy?

But she held her own. And only slipped once—when she had referred to Senator Coolidge's current wife by his ex's name. Clare had discreetly coughed into her fist, and Lucy gracefully righted the error.

After making the rounds, Lucy and Alex found her girls and joined them. As Lucy chatted, Alex coaxed Marinell onto the small dance area, sending the girl into giggles, a sound that was music to Lucy's ears. Mesmerized, Lucy could hardly maintain a conversation as she watched him dance with each young lady brave enough to spin across the floor with an American icon. Tyneisha, the last to join him, could've been Beyoncé's twin in her hot-pink gown and matching heels. She struggled through Alex's patient instructions on a waltz, and Lucy had to laugh when Tyneisha maneuvered Alex into trying some hip-hop.

The music shifted from classics to a melody Lucy recognized as "The Way You Look Tonight." Music to fall in love to.

"I was wondering if you'd dance with me, Ms. Wiltshire."

With her chin in her palm, Lucy looked up to find Alex standing over her, hand extended. His earlier anger was gone, and in its place was a look that had her grateful for a good ocean breeze.

"I don't know." She placed her fingers in his palm. "You've danced with nearly every woman here."

"Just sad replacements for the one I really wanted."

She laughed as he swept her into his arms. "You're good, Sinclair."

He didn't bother with the formal style he had used on the girls. There was no holding each other at arm's length. He pressed her close, and she rested her head on his chest as they moved across the small space.

"The girls are having the time of their lives," she said.

His hand massaged the back of her neck, sending warm shivers across her skin. "I'm glad they're enjoying themselves."

"You're a nice man, Alex."

"I'm going to write that in my journal tonight."

She leaned back and looked into his face. "Do all your supermodel ex-girlfriends know you have a big heart?"

His lips curved slowly. "Only for you, Luce."

He leaned down and kissed her forehead.

It was all just a pretty façade, but it could still turn a woman's head.

Why couldn't he stay the arrogant stereotype? He was going off-script and she didn't know what to think.

She snuck another glance as they moved in time to the music. Alex looked both elegant and savage in his black tuxedo. It was a good thing someone like Matt was more her type. Stable. Calm. Predictable. Alex was none of those things. He was mercurial, intense, a man who defied all the rules.

Never mind that she fit so perfectly in his arms as they swayed under the stars. Or that her heart was beating an irregular cadence. It was merely a trick of moonlight and ocean magic.

Lucy watched some of her girls get up and mingle among the guests. "They're going to be okay, aren't they?"

He brushed his knuckles across her cheek. "How could they not?"

"Because they have everything in the world against them."

"But they've got you."

She turned her head until she was looking into his face. Brown eyes locked with blue. A tendril of heat slowly uncoiled as Alex watched her. She couldn't look away. Could only feel the pull that was Alex.

"You're really messing with my head," she whispered as she slid her hands up his chest.

His head dipped. His lips hovered. "Consider it payback."

He was going to kiss her. Was it real? Part of the charade? Did she even care?

She let her eyes flutter closed, felt the feather-light touch of his lips.

Only for him to lift his head and gaze over her. "We'll pick this up later."

Her brain shuddered as it struggled to process. He had been about to kiss her. She hadn't imagined that look in his eyes, that electric current passing between them, that—

Why were people leaving the dance floor? Where was everyone—

Looking over her shoulder, Lucy saw she and Alex had the space to themselves. She had been too wrapped up in him to even notice.

As the crowd circled around them, Lucy's knees turned to liquid.

She twisted back to Alex. And that's when she saw it in his eyes.

It was time.

"Oh my gosh," she muttered.

The orchestra began to play the theme to *Star Wars*.

Alex took Lucy's hand, pressed it tight as if to share some of his strength. "Are you ready for this?" He kissed her palm, never taking his eyes from her face.

"No," came her breathy reply.

"I find we have more in common every day." His slow wink sent heat dancing across her skin.

"Lucy Wiltshire." His voice was now loud enough for all to hear as he captured her other hand. "I knew you long ago. I was a young arrogant fool not to see what an amazing person you were. I passed by you then without so much as a glance." A crooked smile lifted his lips. "Luckily I got another opportunity. And I knew when I saw you that, this time, I wouldn't be passing by."

They were pretty thoughts. Elegant words, spinning around Lucy like pixie dust, drawing her heart to his.

"We haven't been together long, but it's been the best time of my life. You take me as I am, flaws and all." He quirked an eyebrow, and they shared a grin over his outrageous lie. "When we're together, I know you don't care about where I come from. You see me for myself—and the person I want to become—for you."

Lucy's breath constricted as Alex reached into his tuxedo jacket and extracted a box.

Oh, no. This was happening. Her head hurt. Her hands shook. Her stomach lurched.

With a small pop, the box snapped open, and there sat a ring fit for a princess.

He didn't go down on one knee. Somehow she'd known he wouldn't. Alex Sinclair bowed to no one. Maybe she should've been insulted, but it was one less thing to add to the mockery.

"Lucy, in front of all these people, including your friends and the ladies of Saving Grace, would you make me one happy man and agree to become my wife?"

Yes. The word stuck in her throat. It was her line—her one and only line.

His eyes narrowed a fraction. His grip tightened.

Lucy felt the boat sway and rock, and she wondered how she didn't topple over. She held the attention of a couple hundred people who had never cared about her before, and now they watched her with open curiosity. She knew what they were thinking. *Why* that *woman? What could he possibly see in her? He could do so much better.*

It was so wrong. They were lying to the world. To her friends. His family. To God. But she wanted it to be real. With someone she loved. More than anything, Lucy wanted someone on this planet to love her, to care for her. To adore her and look at her just as Alex was right now.

"Lucy?" His voice was a quiet plea.

And her undoing.

"Yes." The words were barely audible. She blinked, surprised at the silly tears in her eyes. "Yes, I will."

He paused only a moment—to read her face, to try and gauge what was in her mind—but she just shook her head, wiped her eyes, and let herself be crushed to him.

The audience erupted into applause. Their cheers rose to the sky.

He gave her one quick kiss, a mere brush of his lips. "Thank you."

Alex took the ring from the box as her girls squealed their approval. The ring slipped over her pink nail and stopped in a perfect fit at the end of her finger. Alex lifted her hand and pressed a warm kiss to her knuckles, sending lightning bolts all the way to her toes.

Then his hands cradled her face. His eyes seared into hers. The stirring swelled within her again, that magnetic pull that had her breath growing shallow and her heart doing crazy pirouettes.

She didn't know who moved first, but suddenly his mouth covered hers. His lips fit over her own, delicately, softly—as if she were the most fragile of possessions. Her hands moved up his back as he deepened the kiss, pulling her out of her role and into the moment. There was no pretense. No faking. Only feeling.

Until a familiar voice intruded.

"Ladies and gentlemen."

Lucy broke away first. Alex just stood there, his forehead pressed to hers, his breathing ragged. And a storm rolling into those chestnut eyes.

"I would like to be the first to congratulate the happy couple," Clare Deveraux said, her voice commanding attention. "To many years of wedded bliss—Alex Sinclair, this state's next Congressman. And Lucy Wiltshire"—Clare lifted up her glass in a toast—"my granddaughter."

Chapter Twenty-seven

So the old Spock could be in the same place as the young Spock?" Clare took a long swig of root beer. "Inconceivable."

Chuck laughed as he looked at Lucy. "Don't worry, Mrs. Deveraux. You'll catch on."

It was their bimonthly meeting of the Hobbits, and Lucy was still grounded to Clare's house. She went to work during the day and came back home to dinner and lessons at night. The phone had been ringing off the hook all week since Clare's big announcement just six chaotic days ago. The local and national papers had gone wild: South Carolina's dearly departed former governor had an illegitimate granddaughter. Even *Good Morning America* had called. The paparazzi had been bad before, but it was nothing compared to the past few days. For once Lucy was grateful for the bodyguards Alex had hired. No reporters got within fifteen feet of her. Clare said Lucy would eventually have to make a statement, but she just wasn't ready. She and her grandmother had barely spoken about it themselves. There were still so many questions, yet Lucy found her pride just wouldn't let her ask.

Julian nudged Clare and held up her phone. "It's that guy from the *Today Show*. Again."

"Can't you see I'm busy?" She glanced down at the agenda she had forced Lucy to make. "Besides, next we're talking about some zombie book I was supposed to have read." Clare shook her head, her white bob bouncing. "Face it, my lovelies, *Star Trek* is just a ridiculous story. Flying in space and being in two places at once? Absolutely silly."

"Ma'am, you go too far." Sanjay pointed a daring finger. "I'm going to have to ask you to take that back."

"No," she snapped. "I'm the guest at this meeting. I can say whatever I want." She held up her plate. "Julian, we need more Martian cucumber sandwiches. When they get a bite of these, the ladies at the DAR are going to go nuts."

"Most of them already are." He put down his own plate and started to get up.

"Keep your seat," Lucy said. "You can run interference for Clare." As soon as her group had seen the sci-fi–themed spread Julian had created, he had made ten instant friends. Larry, who sold computers at Best Buy, had already invited him to his company barbeque. And Monique, dressed in full *Battlestar Gallactica* wear tonight, had slipped him her phone number after her first taste of the Half-Blood punch.

Lucy got up from her seat in Clare's less-formal family room and made her way to the kitchen. She had just pulled the second tray of sandwiches from the fridge when Morgan and Chuck walked in.

"Hey," Lucy said. "Sanjay hasn't challenged Clare to a duel yet, has he?"

"No." Morgan picked up one of the petite sandwiches and took a bite. She could eat the whole platter and it would never show on her enviably thin frame. "But she did just ask him if he could show her how to use her iPad."

Lucy smiled as she leaned against the granite counter. If she were to be honest, Clare was growing on her.

"So Clare Deveraux is your grandmother." Chuck's eyes darted between Morgan and Lucy. "Anything else you two are keeping from me?"

Lucy tugged the plastic wrap off a tray. "Can't think of a thing."

"My mind's a total blank." Morgan's voice wasn't the least bit convincing.

"Well, the whole world certainly knows now," Chuck said.

Clare's announcement at the party had been a shock to Lucy and Alex too. When questioned, Clare had simply clammed up and said, "It was time." Time to bring on the legions of paparazzi? Time to cause a perfect storm of a media frenzy? But Alex's approval ratings had gone up. Again.

"And what about your relationship with Alex?" Chuck asked.

"What about it?"

"I knew it was serious, but marriage? Where did that come from?"

"Yes, where did that come from, Lucy?" Morgan asked sweetly.

"I know you," Chuck said. "And this isn't like you at all. You're Miss Cautious—you don't just jump into things." With years of leeching out the truth from teens, he turned those youth-minister eyes on Lucy. "I just think you're rushing things."

"Not everyone drags their feet like you, Chuck." Morgan said.

"I said I'd go get fitted for my tux, and I will."

Morgan turned on her fiancé. "You've already cancelled three times."

"I'll get to it. I promise." Chuck popped a sandwich in his mouth and changed the subject. "Is there a date set? I'd love to perform the ceremony."

"Um . . ." This whole conversation was a sinking ship. A Titanic. "October fifteenth."

"We'll save the date." Morgan didn't exactly look like she'd be writing it in ink on her calendar. "Alex does have good taste in engagement rings, though."

Lucy glanced at her sparkling rock of a ring for the millionth time. It wasn't Hollywood obnoxious, which she appreciated. The diamond was tasteful, yet large enough to make a bold statement. And though she didn't particularly like what it was saying, she couldn't stop looking at it either.

"We could start the premarital counseling. I'll be glad to do it."

Lucy didn't miss the air of challenge in her friend's voice. "I'll . . . talk to Alex." She'd rather step into oncoming traffic than sit through counseling sessions with Chuck. Ten minutes of relationship questions, and he'd see right through them.

"Well, I think it's really classy how you've forgiven Clare," he said. "It takes a strong woman to do that."

Forgiven her. Lucy hadn't quite gotten that far. "Clare sought me out. Apologized. It's still hard." She had paid off her mother. Put a price tag on her granddaughter. "But she's genuinely sorry. We're still not best friends or anything, but right now I need her help. Aside from my daily lessons on how to be one classy lady, we pretty much stay out of each other's way."

"And since when do you care what others think of you?" Morgan asked sharply. "Especially the people in this town?"

When had she not? "What's wrong with learning some new skills?"

"Like what heels to wear with what handbag? How to talk without really saying anything?" With a sigh that sounded like it came all the way from her leather sandals, Morgan nodded. "I really hope you know what you're doing."

That made two of them.

⁐

One good thing about staying at Clare's was an all-access pass to Julian's refrigerator. Lucy made her way down the stairs, surprised the lights were still on so close to midnight.

It wasn't until her foot touched the bottom step that she heard the voices.

"I just want to talk to her. I'm an old friend."

Lucy froze, her bare feet on the wood floor, her hands clutching the banister, as Matt tried to talk Julian into letting him inside. "It's really important I see her tonight."

"I don't think that's such a good idea, but I'll let her know you stopped by."

"Wait!" Lucy ran through the foyer and stepped onto the porch. Bathed in the overhead lights, Matt looked like a blond Romeo in search of his Juliet. "It's okay, Julian." She nodded at his worried look. "We'll just talk out here."

An indecisive Julian pursed his lips, then finally nodded. "I'll leave you two alone then."

"What are you doing here?" Lucy asked as Julian shut himself inside the house.

Matt stared at her ring as it sparkled in the dim lights. "I guess congratulations are in order."

"Thank you."

Lucy hadn't thought about Matt for days. And now that he was standing in front of her, his broken heart blazoned on his sleeve, the most horrible realization hit her.

She missed Alex.

"I know this is going to sound weird." Matt's hands cupped her shoulders. "But I can't shake this feeling that you're making a huge mistake by marrying Sinclair."

She missed Alex? How had this happened? She needed to lie down.

He had been going from morning to night this week, and she had seen him very little. She missed his laugh, the smell of his expensive shampoo, and the way his hand automatically reached for hers.

She steadied herself and gripped the porch rail as the thought struck her that she was no better than all those ladies before her who had fallen under Alex's spell. But surely there was still time to fight it. With level-headed thinking and a little self-control.

"Did you hear what I said?" Matt stepped closer. "I think you're operating out of hurt. I did this to you, Lucy, and now you're paying the price."

She forced her attention back to Matt. "No, I—"

He drew her to him, crushing Lucy against his chest. "He can't love you like I can."

"Campbell, you have two seconds to unhand my fiancée."

Lucy jumped at the voice behind her, her cheeks aflame.

Alex stepped from the shadows and onto the porch, his face lined with fatigue and anger.

Matt dropped his hands from Lucy and took a step back. "I was just—"

"Leaving," Alex supplied.

"I just don't want Lucy hurt," Matt said.

"I would never do that." Alex turned fierce eyes to Lucy, and her heart stuttered. "But I *would* hurt anyone who touched her, so you might want to walk away now before that last cup of coffee kicks in and I get my second wind."

Matt's shoulders collapsed as he gave Lucy one final appeal. "If you ever need me—"

"She won't."

Her heart was an azalea blossom, its petals falling to the ground and blowing away. "Good-bye, Matt."

"You know how to reach me." Afraid to get too close to Alex, Matt stepped around him and walked to his car.

It was so quiet Lucy could hear the stars blink. Alex remained in his spot at the edge of the porch, though he now reclined against a Georgian column, watching her fidget with her hands.

She lingered five long seconds under his weighty stare before she finally spoke. "It wasn't what it looked like."

He regarded her through heavy-lidded eyes. "It looked like that guy had his hands on you."

"It was nothing." The very idea that he could be jealous gave her a small, twisted thrill.

"Tell that to the neighbors. Probably half of them took pictures and sent it to the *Enquirer*."

Just like that, Lucy deflated like a leaky balloon. His concern was just for appearances. "I guess Matt and I do have . . . history." She was angry enough to punch that smug look right off Alex's beautiful face. "He is the man I had intended to marry."

Alex closed the distance in three long strides. "And I'm the man whose ring you're wearing." Without taking his eyes off of her, he lifted her left hand and pressed an angry kiss to the glittering finger. "Or had you forgotten?"

"No. I hadn't forgotten."

"I don't want to see Campbell again."

"If you hadn't gone skulking about in shrubbery, you wouldn't have."

"He's a fool, and I don't want you with him."

"Why are you here, Alex?"

He planted his hand against the wall over her head and sighed. "I have no idea."

She could hardly concentrate as his finger toyed with the silver necklace at her throat, his touch setting her skin on fire. "Do you want to come in?"

"I want to rip Campbell's head off."

She peeled a wilting curl from her cheek and forced herself to ignore the rush of joy at his words. "You look beat."

"Long week."

"I didn't think I'd see you until tomorrow."

He ran a hand over the light stubble on his face. "I wanted to see my adoring fiancée."

Lucy laughed. "You do this really well, you know?"

He tilted his head, then traced a finger along her cheek. "Who says I'm lying?"

Her heart thudded twice. There was only one way to distract a man with *that* look in his eye. "Want something to eat?"

In the kitchen, Lucy pulled out all the leftovers as Alex sat at the bar, his chin propped in his hand.

"You gonna tell me what Campbell was doing here?" Alex asked.

"He wants me back."

"You're mine 'til September." Weeks ago, those gruff words would've had her temper flaring like Roman candles. But tonight, something had shifted.

"What is this?" He took a bite of meatball in tomato sauce.

"Zombie guts."

"We should have these at our wedding." He patted the stool beside him.

Temptation was a six-foot-two man with a five o'clock shadow and an appreciation for monster-shaped snacks. The strongest of women couldn't resist, and her immunity to him diminished by the day.

She left her safe spot by the fridge and climbed up on the black leather stool. His knee brushed hers as he swiveled to face her. "Tell me about life with Clare this week."

"It's getting easier."

"The snob lessons or accepting that she's your grandmother?"

Lucy studied the auburn tints in his dark hair. "Both."

He inspected another appetizer, one Julian had fashioned in the shape of a space ship. When he looked up, his serious expression had returned. "I'm sorry, you know."

"For what?"

"How we all treated you back then. That the Deveraues denied you. Your life couldn't have been easy."

It was like water on a parched desert, words she hadn't even known she'd needed to hear. "I survived. I had a great mom." Though not an altogether honest one. There were so many things she wanted to ask her. But it was too late.

"You are who you are because of your life without Steven Deveraux." Alex bit into a carrot. "And I personally am grateful for that."

"Is that so?"

"Yeah," he said. "If I was engaged to a younger version of Clare, I'd have dumped you long before now."

She smiled and handed him another sandwich. "How were your meetings today?" He had toured the district, making strategic stops and talking one-on-one with people.

"Successful. It was a great time to hear the interests of the voters. They got to see that I'm more than just some overpaid jock. We have some great ideas for some TV spots. Got some good footage we can use." He spent the next half hour telling her about people he had met—a small business owner on the verge of bankruptcy. A single mom who just wanted insurance. A woman who had taught science for forty years and still couldn't afford to retire.

"I think you like this," Lucy said.

"You sound surprised."

At first, Lucy had assumed this was simply another diversion—

another game—for Alex. But she was learning he had more than just his money invested in this campaign.

Lucy rested a tentative hand on his. "Will would be proud."

She thought he would tense up, shut down. But instead he slowly nodded and clasped her fingers in his. "I hope so."

"So why did you stop by again?" Lucy asked.

"Because I knew you were missing me, and I couldn't deny you my studly manness any longer."

"I had a house full of men tonight."

"Cheap replacements."

Alex stood up and stretched his arms until his shirt pulled taut. "Well, unless you want to make out on the couch and pretend we're watching a movie, I've got to go."

"I would, but my lips are already tired from Sanjay and Larry." She stood and pushed in her stool.

He didn't smile, but instead studied Lucy as if weighing some heavy decision. He wrapped an arm around her, held tight, and kissed the top of her head. "You're not what I expected, Lucy Wiltshire."

"Next time you stop by, I'll have pom-poms." Her arms just naturally slipped around his waist.

His lips curved into a languid smile as he watched her. "Have lunch with me tomorrow." He ran his thumb across her bottom lip. "I promise I'll make it memorable."

"That's what all the boys say." Her voice was a sigh.

"Lucy?" His head lowered, his eyes searched.

"Yes?" To his question. To his kiss. To whatever he wanted.

"We should probably practice looking more engaged." He wasn't even trying to look sincere. "Just for the sake of believability, of course."

Electric currents of heat crackled between them until Lucy found herself somehow leaning against his chest. "Sounds grueling. Like two-a-days?"

"Two-a-days are for amateurs." Then his smile disappeared, and his lips descended.

Lucy closed her eyes, tilted her head and—

"Zombies!"

Clare burst through the kitchen, her slippers smacking the tile floor. Lucy stepped far from Alex's reach.

"I need a little bedtime munchie. Don't mind me." Wearing a new My Heart Belongs to Frodo T-shirt over her silk blouse, Clare went straight to the refrigerator and stuck her head right in. "Yes, thought I would grab a bite to eat, some of these zombie sandwiches. I'll probably be up for hours now." She straightened and pinned her hawk-eyes on Alex. "I wasn't interrupting anything, was I?"

"No, ma'am." Alex crossed his arms, looking innocent as an altar boy. "I was just telling Lucy about my campaign trip. A great time with the voters."

"Yes." Clare bit into a pastry, snapping its head off with her teeth. "It seems you're all about being *hands-on*." She grabbed two more sandwiches and wrapped them neatly in a napkin. "Well...I think I'll go on up to bed. Lucy, good night, dear." Clare reached out a hand and gave Lucy's shoulder an awkward pat. "Alex, good to see you, young man. We have a strict policy against sleepovers in this house, so don't get any ideas."

"I'll do everything in my power to resist Lucy's invitations."

Lucy felt her cheeks redden even more. "I'm exhausted too. I'm going to bed."

"Sweet dreams." Ever the doting fiancé, Alex pressed a chaste kiss to her cheek before letting his lips linger near her ear. "We'll continue training tomorrow."

Chapter Twenty-eight

A retirement home?

Lucy checked the address on her note again, then looked at the red brick building. Golden Meadows Retirement Village. This was her lunch date destination?

She hopped out of the Civic and walked up the curving sidewalk to the main entry. A peal of female giggles greeted her, and she knew she only had to follow the sound to locate Alex. He could charm the Depends off an octogenarian.

Today Lucy wore slacks and a fitted jacket from Macy's that Clare had picked out for her. After the engagement party, the protector of all things proper had insisted Lucy return to the more conservative look, to save her retro taste for the moments where no one would see her. Like when she was at home. With the blinds pulled. Lucy had felt some satisfaction in her one act of rebellion—her rainbow covered underwear. But unless she split her pants, Clare would never even know.

She found Alex in the cafeteria, surrounded by a handful of white-haired ladies and three men. His hair today was its usual mussed perfection—more respectable rock star than stodgy politician. It was young and hip, two adjectives she would never use to describe Matt.

As if sensing her near, Alex glanced up. Smiled. And as those molten chocolate eyes locked on hers, Lucy felt something break loose. Might've been her heart. Might've been her good sense.

She was *not* falling for him. In a matter of weeks, they were done. They would shake hands and walk away—he with his seat in Congress, and she with the deed for Saving Grace. This was just what every woman felt in the presence of Alex. The Sinclair allure was like a drug. Just a small taste and it fused into your system, humming through your blood and making you crave even more.

But she could resist him. She was a smart girl. She would not be ruled by her hormones.

Or that devastating smile.

"Lucy, come join us." Alex left his adoring groupies to meet Lucy halfway. Leaning down, he pressed his lips to hers in a quick kiss that went straight to Lucy's knees like a thunderbolt.

Must gain the upper hand here.

He smiled as his forehead furrowed. "You look like you just ate some bad sushi."

"Just processing that last kiss." She patted his bicep. "Were you *trying* to channel junior high?"

His smile was lethal. "Don't start something you can't finish."

They were standing in the middle of a retirement home. Lucy knew she was perfectly safe. "Maybe when your previous girlfriends said 'you got game,' they really *were* referring to your athletic abilities."

He took one menacing step closer until they were nose to nose. "You. Me. Tonight." Her skin broke into gooseflesh. "I'll pick you up at seven. No Clare. No Julian. Just the two of us, some candlelight, and dinner." His eyes dropped to her lips. "Then I'll show you game." With one final smoldering look, he turned on his heel and went back to chatting about social security benefits.

Lucy was left standing next to a table of cookies and watered-down punch, her brain locked in neutral. "Yeah," she finally managed to say. "Well, I've got game too. Lots of totally gamey things up my sleeves."

With none-too-steady hands, she reached for a Dixie cup and poured herself some fruit punch. She tossed it back like tequila, only to have another one handed to her.

"It's okay, dear," a woman said. A puff-paint rendition of Alex's face stared back at Lucy from a shirt tucked neatly into turquoise polyester pants. "I talk to myself sometimes too."

"Oh." Lucy clutched the cup and gave a wobbly smile. "I wasn't—"

"Nurse Hedley usually gives me a little purple pill afterward." She gave a knowing wink. "I would share, but Medicare doesn't cover them."

Lucy returned to Alex's side just as his campaign manager walked away.

"We have to do a craft before lunch." Alex held up a handful of pipe cleaners.

"That woman with the sun visor just offered me prescription meds, and I'm pretty sure the punch is spiked."

"It's just Metamucil." He checked his phone and shot off a quick text as he spoke. "Help me with this craft business, and I'll take you anywhere you want when we're done."

"*Aliens Take Over Thailand* just opened at the mall cinema."

"You have the worst taste."

"I know. You should hear who I'm engaged to." She watched him break out his phone again. "Alex, focus. These are not people who understand an obsession with a cell phone."

He frowned as he put it down on a table beside him. "I need three of me."

"To usher in Armageddon? The world couldn't handle that." She held out her hand. "Give me the phone."

"No way."

Mr. MVP wouldn't be able to turn down a challenge. "I don't think you can go through the next thirty minutes without it."

"Thirty? That's all?"

"You won't survive five."

He smiled for a pair of photographers there to capture the event. "Let's make it interesting, shall we?"

Heat was an unfurling bloom in her stomach. "What did you have in mind?"

"If I win, you spend Fourth of July with me and my family—you know, the event you volunteered me for."

"And when you lose?" Drawing from Clare's last lesson, Lucy composed her face into an expression a beauty queen would be proud of as the cameras clicked. Chin angled, eyes engaged.

"I'll take you to that stupid movie."

She held out her hand. "Done."

He took her hand, planted a warm kiss to her wrist. "Want to make out to seal the deal?"

She took his phone and forced a sigh she didn't feel. "I'd probably fall asleep." Lucy scanned the craft supplies on the table before them. She had taught enough Sunday school to know when she was looking at the makings of a bird feeder.

"Ladies and gentlemen, I think we're about to begin." Lucy couldn't believe this was her voice coming out. Loud, clear, confident. Her social skills might've needed work, but she was a rock star with a glue gun. "Alex and I are so glad you invited us for craft time. As he talks about his ideas for expanding senior citizen benefits, I'm going to walk you through the process of building a lovely birdhouse. So take your seats, load up on punch, and let's get to work."

Thirty minutes later Lucy glanced at her watch and saw her extended lunch break dwindling. She had dropped Marinell off at the children's hospital with a promise to pick her up when her date with Alex was done. Grabbing her purse, she gave Alex a quick kiss and slipped out through the crowd.

Driving down the highway, Lucy clenched the leather of the steering wheel. She had survived the retirement home, but her grip on her heart was another matter. *Lord, help me to stay focused. Who am I to have wishful thoughts about Alex?*

She pulled into the parking lot of the children's hospital and rode the elevator to the third floor. She was met in the hall by two nurses rushing out of the boy's room, and Marinell standing in the doorway, sobbing.

"What's happening?"

Marinell shook her head, the tears free-falling down her dark cheeks. "My brother . . . something's wrong. He got sick. And couldn't stay awake. All these nurses came and—"

"Slow down, Marinell." Lucy led her back into the empty room and into a chair. "What did the nurses say?"

"Something about an infection. One of the doctors mentioned surgery. I couldn't even understand all of it. My mom was moving today. She didn't know where she was staying tonight. I have to tell her." She sniffed and swiped at her nose. "His face . . . his color was bad." Marinell's shoulders shook as Lucy pulled her into a hug. "I'm so scared."

Lucy knew all about unfairness. About being responsible for more than you were ready for at eighteen.

"We'll find your mom."

And then Marinell said the words that ripped the lid off of Lucy's composure. "Would . . . would you say a prayer? Can you just . . . ask God to help my brother?"

Tears thickened Lucy's throat, and she took a few deep breaths until she could find her voice. "Of course." Keeping a firm hold on Marinell, Lucy prayed to the God of healing, of help, and miracles. She asked him to restore Carlos's kidney. To comfort his fears. To give strength to Marinell, and to help them find her mother.

"Amen," Lucy said, lifting her head. "Now let's go talk to a nurse so we'll know exactly what to tell your mom."

A flash from the TV overhead caught Lucy's eye. A familiar image of Will Sinclair dominated the screen, sending Lucy racing toward the bedside table to grab the remote.

An anchor's voice filled the room.

"—received word that Ben Hayes, one of the two reporters presumed dead in a school explosion in Afghanistan over a year ago, is now resting in a German hospital."

Lucy clicked the volume button again and moved closer to the television.

"According to Hayes, he and CNN correspondent Will Sinclair were in the school, but Hayes was pulled out immediately after the blast and *captured by insurgents. He is the only known survivor. We will pass on details as they emerge. More on the hour . . ."*

Alex. She had to call him.

"Marinell, go to the nurse's station. I'll be right there."

Lucy wasted no time, frantically digging through her purse for her phone. She punched the number that would connect her to Alex.

And then her purse rang.

She sucked in a breath as she reached for the other phone.

Alex's.

She had taken it at the retirement home and forgotten to give it back.

Checking his display, he had thirty-six missed calls. Half of them were from someone named Kat. A memory replayed of Alex on the phone the night he had taken her to the ER. Was he seeing this Kat? Had he been seeing her all along?

She pushed the thoughts to the back of her mind as the pressing reality intruded. Will Sinclair was dead.

Chapter Twenty-nine

*T*wo hours, four abandoned houses, and three homeless shelters later, Lucy found Esther Hernandez.

The faded sign on the door said CONDEMNED, but Marinell led Lucy around the back of the decaying duplex, jiggled off a screen, and lifted the window of what once was a living room.

"Are you coming?" Marinell asked from inside the house.

Lucy hoisted her leg over, feeling a give in her black slacks as the wooden splinters caught the material. That was what she got for listening to Clare and paying a hundred dollars for a pair of pants. Whoever said money was the only way to buy quality could just kiss her multi-colored underwear.

"Mami?" Marinell called.

The stench of rotten garbage hit Lucy's nostrils, and she tried not to gag. No windows were open, and the heat was enough to buckle the walls. The only air came from a hole in the roof over a collapsed fireplace.

"Mami?"

Rustling came from the front of the house. "*Mija?*"

Mrs. Hernandez peeked her head out from a plastic-covered doorway off the tiny hall. Marinell ran to her mother, collapsed against her, and told her about Carlos in between broken sobs. Lucy didn't remember much high school Spanish, but no translation was needed to see that Mrs. Hernandez was a mother barely surviving the weight of her breaking heart.

"*Mi hijo.*" Mrs. Hernandez held onto her daughter and shared in her tears. "*Mi hijo.*"

Lucy was an outsider, standing on the fringe of this family's pain, and for the millionth time she thought of Alex. She couldn't leave Marinell, but she had to get to him. If only she hadn't been so punch-drunk on his charm at lunch, she would've remembered to return his phone.

On the floor beside a dirty backpack sat an empty sandwich bag and a juice box. This would explain Marinell's lack of appetite. She was handing food off to her mother. That would have to stop—just as soon as they got Mrs. Hernandez out of this hovel.

"You can't stay here," Lucy said to Esther.

The woman wiped her face and shook her head. Marinell translated. "She has nowhere to go. She has no car and wants to stay close to the hospital so she can walk."

To let a family member stay at Saving Grace was against the rules. But the pressure on Lucy's conscience was so strong, God was practically writing Mrs. Hernandez an invitation himself. "Get your things," Lucy said. "We're all going back to Saving Grace." Esther could stay in Marinell's room. Somehow they would make it work, at least for now.

Mrs. Hernandez's hands flew as she spoke to her daughter.

"My mom just wants to see Carlos. She won't leave this house."

"Mrs. Hernandez, you're no good to your son sick. And that's exactly what's going to happen to you if you don't get out of this place." Lucy heard scratching overhead, and she was pretty sure it wasn't the Prize Patrol trying to make a surprise entrance. "You'll spend the night at Saving Grace, and I'll make sure you have transportation to the hospital whenever you want." Marinell repeated in Spanish as Lucy mentally sorted through her housing options for Esther.

"My mom says thank you." Beside Marinell, her mother nodded, tears flowing unchecked down her sallow cheeks.

Despite Mrs. Hernandez's matted hair and ripe smell, Lucy drew her into a hug. "It's going to be okay."

Though Lucy had no idea how.

~

The covered dishes were already arriving. Any good Southerner knew a life couldn't officially be over until the first green-bean casserole arrived.

Alex sat in Marcus Sinclair's home office. He could hear the front doorbell and signaled for his dad to shut the door.

Ben Hayes stared back from the computer screen on the desk, visibly weak but very much alive.

"You're sure it was him?" It was the third time Alex had asked. He couldn't let it go.

"I'm sorry," Hayes said into the laptop camera from his bed in Germany. "I know it's not the outcome you and your family hoped for."

It had taken Alex and his team a mere ten minutes to make the many calls to connect to Ben on Skype.

"*You* were pulled from the fire," Alex said. "Why do you assume no one else was?"

Ben's voice was faint and raspy. "The place burned to ashes." He paused for a moment to collect himself. "I was conscious when I was dragged away. I heard . . . I heard the screams." Alex closed his eyes as Ben continued. "I'm sorry, Mr. Sinclair. No one could've survived. It's just not possible."

The pain wasn't an ache. It was violent waves crashing until he thought he'd sink straight down. His brother. Gone.

Alex drove his fingers through his hair. He could hear his father sniffing behind him. "Where was my brother when the bomb hit?"

"If I remember correctly . . . he was telling a story and the children were acting it out."

That was so Will. Alex could see him surrounded by children, eager faces beaming as they waited for their cues.

His father scooted his chair closer to Alex. "What was my son's last day like?" He swiped at the tears falling down his cheeks. "Was Will happy?"

"There was a lot of laughter, Mr. Sinclair." Hayes was gaunt, but he smiled. "The children loved him. He told them stories, played games, gave each one gifts from the States. Your son died doing what he loved. He was making a difference—making the world a better place."

There were voices in the background on the other end. Ben nodded to someone off camera. "It's my therapy time. Gotta get up and walk the halls. We'll be in touch."

"Thank you." Alex's words sounded impotent and hollow. Just like his ravaged heart.

He shut down the connection on his dad's Mac. The room was silent and heavy. Until his father bent over and threw his head into his hands. His choking sobs sliced through Alex until he thought he would bleed from them. This was his father. Broken.

Alex clutched his own fist in his hand. He had no idea what to do. He had been able to fix everything in his life. Through hard work, some cash, there had been nothing he couldn't have. Until now. No amount of money could bring his brother back. No endorsement deal would fill this bottomless ache.

His father slowly lifted his head. "Son"—red-rimmed eyes looked straight into Alex's—"I want you to pray for us."

Him? Now? He was the guy who had pushed God aside until a year ago. Hadn't needed a savior. But after the news first hit of Will, he'd realized it had been a mirage, an illusion. His hands were useless. His bank account—worthless. *You have my attention now, God. Is that what you wanted?* Alex may have pushed God into the background, but he still knew who was in charge of miracles. And he had started begging for one the day of that fateful call.

Coughing past the lump in his throat, Alex reached out his hand and rested it on his father's shoulder. Marcus Sinclair latched on to Alex, drawing his son near as he bowed his head.

Alex opened his mouth and waited as a new wave of pain rolled through his system. His body ached like he had just climbed out of a three-man tackle. "God . . . we pray for peace for our family." *Are you listening? Do you hear me? Is this what I get for shutting you out until I had nowhere else to turn?* "Give us healing and comfort. Help us to—" He stopped. His mind searched for the right words, something to appeal to the God of his childhood, the God he had once believed in with all his heart before fame had become his answer. But Alex's well was dry. Not a single profound or inspiring word in him. "Just . . . pull us through."

His dad hugged him closer. "Amen." Marcus pulled a tissue from his desk and blew his red nose. "I better go check on your mother. You know how she gets around Uncle Bill."

Alex followed his dad down the long hallway into the main living room. Unlike the outside of the grand house, the inside wasn't formal. It was a family's home. Under this roof, three children had grown up. It had been the central hub for friends. This very living room was where his mom and dad hosted a weekly Bible study. For all their wealth, his parents were just normal people who loved their Jesus, their life, and their kids. Family was everything. But now one of them was gone. The home would never be the same.

Alex greeted two of his cousins who also lived in Charleston. He knew more were on the way. There was already talk of a memorial service, and the very thought made him want to run his fist through the wall.

His sister stood among a small group of friends, her head pressed to the shoulder of that boyfriend his parents were always complaining about. Aside from the grunge band hair draped in his eyes, the kid looked okay. Alex was glad Finley had people to turn to.

Across the room, his mother talked with her youngest sister and her best friend Marcy, the woman who had been her college roommate. His mom's eyes were swollen. He knew she'd held out hope, despite impossible odds, that Will had somehow survived. Now her heart was broken too.

A few more people trickled into the room, and he caught a flash of yellow-gold hair.

Lucy.

His lungs filled with his first deep breath as he took in the sight of her. Her wide eyes held that same compassion he'd seen her dole out to every one of her girls. There was a bronze button missing from her fitted jacket, and her pants were smudged with dust, but she still was a picture of grace.

He needed her.

Lucy said hello to a couple of people as she surveyed the room. Funny how they hadn't been together long, but he knew exactly what she was thinking. They could fit two of her apartments into this room. She would be horribly uncomfortable. The woman had an allergy to the finer things. She was so good, so decent. So many things he was not.

Alex dug his hands into his pockets, unsure of what to do with a female for the first time in his life. The women he had dated had always needed something from him. Never the other way around.

Her eyes scanned the perimeter until they finally lit on him. Then Lucy, his PDA-hating Lucy, pushed past an oxygen-tank–wearing neighbor to run straight to him. It was a sack worthy of a Warriors jersey.

Her arms held fiercely as they wrapped around him. His hands moved of their own volition, pressing her close. He breathed in all that was Lucy—her friendship, her heart, her strength.

"I'm sorry," she whispered against his neck. "I'm so sorry."

He couldn't speak. All he could do was hold her like she was his lifeline, as if he could absorb some of her comfort. Some of her faith.

When she finally pulled away, she held his face in her hands. "Tell me everything."

He shrugged. Shook his head. "He's gone."

"I saw it on TV." Her eyes glazed over with tears, and each one cut right through him. "I had your stupid phone and couldn't call."

And she had felt responsible. Because she was Lucy. And in her world people didn't have two other phones and an entourage of people around them. "We got the word before the story hit. About five minutes after you left the retirement home."

She pulled the phone out of her purse and handed it to him.

He took it and kept her hand in his. "I guess I won the bet after all."

Her smile was wobbly. "What can I do?"

Just don't stop being you. "Nothing."

"I prayed for you all the way here."

"I know you did." Then he kissed her. Because he was out of words, and he just wanted to feel—something. Anything besides the gripping despair.

Her body melted toward his, and her lips were a wispy touch. He didn't kiss her with a raging fire, but simply pressed his mouth to hers in the most basic of invitations. She gave back with her gentleness, her soft fingers threading through his hair. He couldn't close his eyes. Couldn't stop watching her.

Because she was watching him.

"Alex?"

He took her hand, held it to his heart. "I'm glad you're here." The words sounded like they came from a bumbling sixteen-year-old. But death put life through a new lens—at least for tonight—and he needed her to know. There had been so many things he hadn't said to his brother.

"My *Brides* magazine said I should support my fiancé." She cupped his cheek in her hand, her eyes full of something he couldn't quite read.

He had been about to speak with his grief-liberated tongue, but the phone in his pocket buzzed. Spared from saying something he'd probably later regret, he took the call. "Hey, David." He ran his hand down Lucy's arm. "Luce, I have to take this. Can you stay for a while?"

"I'm here," she said. "For as long as you need me."

Chapter Thirty

*A*nd that's why you can't just buy any aloe vera ointment. Mine is only $29.99 and the only brand that comes with zarkspur, a rare fruit extract from the floor of the South African rain forests."

Uncle Bill had Lucy cornered on the terrace as he finally wound up his sales pitch. She was about ready to hand over her wallet just to shut him up.

"And if you buy it tonight, I'll throw in a small tube of my special diaper ointment."

"I don't have children."

"Me neither." He scratched his large, bulbous nose. "But I've still found uses for it."

Behind them the patio door slid open. Alex. This damsel in distress was about to be saved. She and her checkbook were going to survive after all.

"I like cash, but I recently got acquainted with that PayPal thing and—"

"Uncle Bill, I think Finley wants to talk to you," Alex said, his eyes not straying from Lucy. "She was counting her birthday money."

Uncle Bill was gone before Lucy could say nice to meet you.

"You just threw your sister under the bus."

He traced the curve of a curl near her cheek. "Finley's antics have my dad on high blood pressure medicine. She can handle Uncle Bill."

Lucy could hardly form a coherent thought when he looked at her that way. Grief did strange things to a man. "How are you holding up?"

"I've had better days." His face was taut with worry and fatigue, and she just wanted to erase it all until he wore that cocky grin. "Let's talk about something besides bombs, funerals, and what Uncle Bill really does with that aloe stuff. Like why I see rainbows peeking out through a hole in your pants."

Lucy closed her eyes and sighed. "I just can't win."

He stole another glance. "They look like winners to me."

"Not that it compares, but it's been a wild day." She filled him in on Marinell. "And I caught my pants on the window."

Alex dropped his head and contemplated the floor for a moment before returning his gaze to Lucy. "You're telling me that you broke into a condemned house today?"

"I think 'broke' in is a really strong description. More like took a little tour," she said. "There weren't any photographers around. I checked."

"I don't care about that." His voice was a low growl. "What I care about is my *fiancée* being in a building that isn't safe for human habitation. Where a ceiling could fall in and crush you or a crazed vagrant could decide you're in his way. Do you want me to go on?"

"I think we're good."

"And where were Lou and Squid?"

"I might've talked one of the Saving Grace girls into providing a little distraction so we could get away." The bodyguards had arrived by the time Lucy had crawled back out of the window. And they hadn't been wearing smiles.

"Was it too much to call someone for help? If Marinell's mom was missing, why didn't you call the police?"

Lucy turned and contemplated the somber gray evening sky.

"All I got inside is more of Uncle Bill and his magic rash cream," Alex said from behind her. "I can stand here all day and wait this out."

"It's complicated."

"I'll try to follow along."

"Esther Hernandez kind of has to lie low. Her husband has some people looking for him."

"Like who?"

"Drug lords."

Alex stepped away from Lucy as if he didn't trust himself not to strangle her. It was not the encouragement she needed to tell all the parts of the tale she had previously left out, but she continued, watching Alex's anger notch with every detail.

"So Esther has been trying to keep the family together all by herself, never knowing if her husband is safe. Or even alive. When she gave up the kids, it was so Carlos could get the care he needed. And she can't work *and* sit by his bedside, so . . . she's homeless."

"And potentially in danger."

"Right."

"And you feel responsible."

Lucy walked to the edge of the balcony, resting her hands on the rail. She didn't expect him to understand. "The point is Marinell feels responsible, and she's been taking care of them all. I had to do something, Alex. She's too young to be carrying the world on her shoulders. She should be enjoying her summer, focusing on school, hanging out with her friends."

"Is that what your life was like at Marinell's age?"

Strong hands slid up her back and settled on her shoulders. Unable to stop herself, Lucy leaned into him, staring across the manicured backyard. This was where Alex had grown up. It was so far removed from the one-bedroom apartment she and her mom had shared.

"I don't know how to help them," Lucy said. "Mrs. Hernandez can't stay at Saving Grace more than a few days."

"We'll find her something."

Lucy turned in his arms to face him. "Really?"

He swept his thumb across the delicate skin over her cheekbone. "If you promise to let go of that guilt that's keeping you awake at night."

"I don't feel guilty, I just—"

"Yes, you do. You watch over those girls like a den mother, and then you're eaten up with guilt when something happens and you can't fix it."

"Like with a fake engagement? Is that what you mean?" Lucy was too keyed up to back down. "As long as we're on the subject, what about your guilt, *Playboy?*"

"Is this about that article in *OK!* magazine last week? Because I don't care what David Beckham says, I did not take Posh to dinner—"

"Somehow you've worked it out in your arrogant head that you're responsible for your brother's death—or I should say, the fact that you're still alive."

He jerked his gaze away from her. "You don't know what you're talking about."

"I could smell dysfunction on you within ten minutes of our first date."

Warm air breezed over them as Alex rubbed his hands over his face. "You wouldn't get it."

"We're not talking football here." She ran her finger across the scar over his eyebrow, then down his cheek. "I'll try to follow along."

Alex shoved away from the rail and began to pace the concrete floor in front of her. It was a full minute before he stopped. With eyes looking over her head into absolutely nothing, he began to talk. "Will was the good one. The saint. He had so much going for him. He was a godly guy. I mean, he lived it. Somebody who worked his butt off to make a difference . . . to bless others. He just gave off this energy that made you feel better about the world."

"So he was very charismatic—like you."

"He built schools and did exposés on child slavery." His laugh was hollow. "I played football, Lucy. My life has been so plastic, such a cartoon."

"That's not true."

His forehead wrinkled in a deep frown. "I was so into myself, I couldn't even make time to see him before he left that last day. It was just another one of his trips overseas. My last chance to see him, and I told him no."

"You had a career too."

"He said, 'One of these days life is going to catch up with you. And it's going to be too late.'" The wind tossed Alex's hair as he tipped his clenched jaw toward the sky. "And now it is too late."

Lucy slipped behind him, circled his waist with her arms, and pressed her cheek to his back. "You loved him. He knew that."

"I put it all aside—my family, my faith, even my own identity. I was too wrapped up in being a football star."

"Is that what this run for Congress is about? To be something—for him?"

"Maybe." Bitterness looked back at her as he turned. "At first. But I want it, Lucy. I want to make a difference and not waste any more time."

"Your brother is gone." Her voice caught. "But your family is still here. And they would die if they knew how you were punishing yourself."

He said nothing.

"The good Sinclair brother didn't die. Your parents raised two extraordinary men, and I'm staring at one of them." He tried to step away, but she wouldn't let him. "Will knew you loved him. Forgive yourself and quit listening to that bitter voice in your head. There's a family in there who wants you back."

The branch of a nearby magnolia tree bounced as a bird landed, then called into the sky. The tree had weathered decades of coastal storms and still stood, beautiful and proud. Lucy hoped the man she was holding in her arms now would be just as resilient. She wondered if she'd be with him when his healing came.

"We better get back in and mingle with the family." He gave a weary sigh as he turned and folded her in his strong embrace. "Unless you wanted to go fool around in the guesthouse?"

She smiled against his shirt. "No, thanks."

"I'm a grieving man, Lucy."

And one who was becoming a little too irresistible. "Then you're going to be even more upset when I tell you I ordered two cases of Uncle Bill's organic goo."

"Sounds like you have a problem."

She gave him a quick peck on the chin. "I put the order in your name."

Chapter Thirty-one

Whoever called shopping *retail therapy* had never gone to the mall with a former first lady.

"I missed my mid-morning tea." Clare handed Julian her purse to hold. "And the noise in here is absolutely deafening. Isn't there anywhere in the world a person can go to get a little peace and quiet?"

"I know a good nursing home." Julian tossed his Starbucks cup in the trash.

"I'm almost through with my shopping." Lucy couldn't contain her exasperation. She didn't know what had possessed her to allow Julian and Clare to tag along. Lucy still had to buy a few things for the Fourth of July trip to the Sinclairs' home on the Isle of Palms, a small beach community not too far from Charleston. She had one present already for Alex, but she still needed another before they left tomorrow.

"My earrings are so sparkly." Clare held up her new purchase. "They look at least five carats. Martha Beaumont is going to think these things are real and just flip. Lucy, dear, is this what you kids call bling?"

Julian stared longingly toward J. Crew. "It's called poor taste."

"Let's have a bite of lunch, shall we?" Clare looked toward the food court. "I've always wanted to try a Happy Meal. It's on my bucket list. Item number twelve."

Ten minutes later Lucy sat in a chair next to Julian and watched

Clare's cheeks sink in as she drank her shake from the straw. Her lips squeaked with the effort.

"That's the sound of your arteries clogging." Julian squeezed out some dressing on his salad and threw up a wave at their posse of body-guards at the table beside them.

"Shall we pick up our lesson on the history of Carolina politics?" Clare swirled her fry in a small mountain of ketchup.

"My brain is overloaded from last night," Lucy said.

"You're doing really well, hon." Julian patted her hand. "Today's paper showed Alex finally beating Robertson by a hair."

She had been so excited for Alex. They had celebrated over break-fast in a local café, but instead of being thrilled with the tide change, he wanted more. He wouldn't be satisfied until it was a large margin of victory. And somewhere along the way, Lucy had begun to want the win just as much as Alex. While he got frustrated with all the pomp and circumstance, he genuinely enjoyed the time he spent with his voters one-on-one. And though he still denied it, last week Alex had spent an entire morning listening to a trio of out-of-work shrimp boat workers, only to mail them each anonymous cashier's checks a few days later. It was the action he enjoyed over the policy. He had more in common with Will than he could see.

Lucy rested her chin in her hand and sighed like Clare.

As the election drew closer, Alex just worked harder. He was los-ing sleep, forgetting to eat, and growing more distracted by the day.

He had holed himself in his office for the last three days, and aside from the quick breakfast this morning, they had barely spoken. She wondered if this concentration on a new campaign strategy was sim-ply an excuse to get out of memorial preparations for his brother. The family had decided to wait until after the Fourth to honor the life of Will Sinclair. While Alex might have given her a glimpse of his hurt-ing heart a week ago, he had shut the door on it ever since. She worried about him. Prayed for him.

Lucy tuned back in just as Clare was gaining steam about the all-important topic of hemlines. "It can't be too short, but you've got good legs—much like I did—so no sense in hiding them. You can't go wrong with a sweater set, but ..."

The fashion droning just kept going, so when Lucy's phone's rang in her purse, she couldn't answer it fast enough.

A deep voice greeted her, sending a tingle down her spine. "What are you doing?"

"Listening to Clare's dissertation on how much leg I should show."

"Finally a topic I know something about." She could hear the classic rock in the background and she knew Alex was in his car. "Can you tear yourself away?"

"Only if you have something less painful in mind. Like Chinese water torture."

"Go pick up Marinell and her mom." He read off an address, and she hurriedly scribbled it on a napkin. "I'll be waiting."

◇

The Disney Channel played on the TV as Lucy walked into Carlos's room. Marinell and Mrs. Hernandez sat in hard blue chairs against a window and watched him sleep. He had been placed on a kidney donor list, and the doctors were still awaiting test results to see if Marinell or her mom were a match.

Lucy spoke in hushed tones. "Alex called and would like us to meet him. I think he's found you a place to stay."

Marinell repeated the message in Spanish, and Mrs. Hernandez cast an anxious look at her son.

"We won't be gone long," Lucy said. "He's just a few streets away."

After some prompting from her daughter, Mrs. Hernandez nodded. She gathered her faded leather purse, then leaned down and kissed Carlos's pale cheek.

It was a short car ride to Warren Street, and Lucy pulled the Honda into an uneven driveway next to Alex's Mercedes. The home looked like it was from the last part of the nineteenth century, and its clapboard siding had hung on through every decade.

The door opened and Alex stepped onto the porch. "It's not much to look at," he said. "But it's the best I could do on such short notice."

The floorboards groaned as the women stepped past Alex into the open living room.

"I can have someone here within the hour to clean it, and it probably needs a few pictures on the wall." Alex shoved his hands in the pockets of his gray slacks. "But it's within walking distance of Carlos, and it's yours if you're interested."

"How much?" Marinell asked as family spokesperson.

"Free."

Marinell didn't know what to make of that. "But why?"

"Because I want to." Alex turned those chocolate eyes on his fiancée. "And because it makes Lucy smile."

It did more than that. It made her heart twirl until she could hardly catch her breath. Alex could buy and sell the whole street, but did he have any idea what a priceless gift he had just offered this family?

As Marinell and her mom conferred, Lucy crossed the worn floor and stood before Alex. A million words pranced on her tongue, but none seemed to do the moment justice. Simple honesty was all she could manage. "You make my head spin, Alex Sinclair."

He brushed a stray tendril from her face, then rested his hand on the side of her neck. "You say that like it's a bad thing."

But wasn't it? She couldn't afford to fall in love with this man. When the election was over, he would walk away. And she would be alone. Again.

"What you've done . . . it's incredible."

Her insides melted as he looked at her. "I couldn't stand to see you upset."

"That's not the only reason you did this." She pointed her finger and tapped his oxford shirt. "You have a big heart in that brawny chest of yours."

He laughed and linked his fingers through hers. "Don't tell any of my old teammates. I have a vicious image to protect."

"My lips are sealed."

He bent his head and placed a kiss on her smiling mouth. "So they are."

In the corner of the room, Esther Hernandez fired off something in Spanish, then nodded her head. A decision had been made.

Lucy moved to Alex's side as the woman walked toward them. Mrs. Hernandez stared up at the chiseled quarterback who towered over her at least a foot, then threw her arms around his waist and squeezed with all she had.

Marinell grinned as she joined them. "My mother says she'll take it."

Chapter Thirty-two

"Could this SUV be any more of a cliché?"

Alex drove his black Escalade past a gas station offering discount cigarettes and neon water noodles. "It's a perfectly *nice* vehicle."

"All you need is to roll down the windows and blast some Snoop Dog."

His smile just made it worse. "Somebody is cranky."

The leather seats did cradle Lucy's back nicely, but she would just be keeping that to herself. "I didn't notice the rims, but I'm sure they're silver and obnoxious."

"We have the whole weekend for you to check out my rims."

Lucy gave a half-hearted glare and took a bite of one of Julian's homemade cookies. At the back of the Escalade, Julian and Clare sat watching a movie on her new iPad.

"I still don't see why we had to bring her."

Alex stopped at a red light. "Because she was going to be alone for the Fourth and you would've felt bad."

"It wouldn't have lasted long." Clare was growing on her like mold, yet Lucy had been looking forward to a weekend without her. Clare was anxious for Lucy to welcome her into her life as more than a mentor, but she just wasn't there yet.

Beside her Alex downed a package of peanuts and took a swig of

Gatorade. He tapped the steering wheel to "Born in the U.S.A." and sang off-key with the Boss. From his navy Polo T-shirt to his leather flip-flops, he was the picture of summer relaxation. And it was a lie.

The tension rolled off him so strongly, it was giving *her* a splitting headache. With the excuse of meetings and conference calls, their ten a.m. departure time had turned into three p.m. Then five.

Alex's messenger bag sat at Lucy's feet, and she bent down to find a magazine. "*The Wall Street Journal.* You know there are big words in that, right?"

He cranked up the air and slid her a look. "You pick fights when you get nervous."

"No, I don't." This was a man trained to read signals. It was completely obnoxious.

He leaned into her space and nudged her. "Are you seriously that anxious about this trip?"

"Maybe. But why would that make today different from any other day?" Her every moment in this fake relationship had made her queasy and anxious. It was a wonder she hadn't taken up smoking and street drugs.

His voice was pure Barry White. "Do I make you nervous?"

"Only when you talk yardages and goalies."

He closed his eyes in pain. "Forgive her, Lord. She knows not what she says."

Lucy smiled and ran her fingers along the leather of her armrest. It was like sitting in a recliner and just another reminder that girls like her didn't belong in his million-dollar world.

He threaded his fingers through hers and settled their hands on the console. It would be moments like this she would remember most when their engagement ended. The feel of his strong hand, the unexpected touch to her face at just the right time. The silent way he communicated his support, even his care. And he did care about her. She just didn't know how deep it ran.

"So you were telling me why you're nervous."

Because you're too near. Because I think about you all the time. Because

I don't want to get my heart broken into so many pieces it can't ever be glued back together.

She decided to change the subject. "Alex . . ." Her finger itched to trace that arrogant smile on his face. "Who's Kat?"

Amber sparks flashed in his eyes and the easygoing grin disappeared. "No one."

"She calls." She thought of that night in the ER. And all those messages when she'd had his phone. "A lot."

The cornered look was gone, and the Playboy sauntered back to the ten-yard line. "Are you jealous?" He picked up her hand and skimmed his thumb over her palm, which had healed quite nicely.

"Are you kidding?" What were they talking about? It was hard to maintain a conversation while trying to keep from purring out loud. "I, um, hope she makes you deliriously happy."

"That's your job."

"It's just the day CNN broke the story—"

"I have a whole arsenal of people who work for me." Now his fingers were making figure-eights along her wrist. "She's just one of them. Nobody to be concerned with."

"Hey, Alex?"

His brow slowly raised. "Yes, Luce?"

She leaned over the wood-grained console. "Cheat on me, and I'll rip your arms off and feed them to Squid and Lou for dinner."

His laughter filled the front seat. "Duly noted."

❧

"Nice little place you have here," Julian said from the backseat.

Little was laughable. A large iron gate greeted them, and Alex reached out his window and punched in a number. Swaying palms and tropical greenery lined the driveway that led to the mint-green three story. Behind three large columns it seemed to be all windows and doors, set off by black shutters that hung like welcome-to-the-beach signs.

Alex grabbed their bags, and Lucy walked behind him, gaping at

the porches that jutted out from all three levels and the ocean backyard. He had told her it was a simple place, but as she walked across the
marble floor, she doubted anything this family did was on a small scale.
Though monstrously large, it was cabana chic. Seashell–colored walls.
Paddled fans that hung from tall ceilings. Creamy slip-covered couches
in the living room accented with faded floral pillows.

"Come in! Come in!" Donna Sinclair bustled in to greet them.
The smidge of flour on her cheek made Lucy feel somewhat better.
"Marcus, bring the lemonade," she called behind her. "I just made some
fresh." She wrapped her son in a hug any defensive tackle would be
proud of, then turned her sights on Lucy. "I'm so glad you decided to
join us. It will give us a chance to get to know one another better . . . and
talk wedding plans."

"Right." Lucy struggled to find her voice. "Wedding plans."

"Alex said you set a date."

"He did, did he?" She shot Alex a surprised glance. "I didn't know
we were sharing that yet." Alex just smiled.

"October fifteenth will be here before we know it. It's been such a
hard year for the family, so it's nice to have something fun to focus on."
Donna pulled Lucy in for a quick hug of her own.

"Let's not overwhelm her, Mom. We both want something small
and simple, so there's not much planning to discuss."

Clare sashayed inside, with Julian right behind her, juggling her
collection of Louis Vuitton luggage. Despite the fact that this was a
weekend trip, Clare had packed enough to clothe half of Charleston.

"Did someone say small wedding?" Clare *tsked* and waved her finger. "Not on my watch."

Lucy tried to think of a safer topic to discuss. Like nuclear weap-
ons. "You have a beautiful home, Mr. and Mrs.—"

"I was thinking St. Luke's Chapel or—"

"No." Clare interrupted Donna. "It has to be big. Maybe outside
at the Middleton Plantation. Susan Jiminez's granddaughter held her
wedding there this spring and it was lovely under the mossy trees
and—"

"Ladies!" Alex's voice boomed as he rested his hand at Lucy's hip. "No wedding talk tonight. Every time Lucy sticks a *Brides* magazine in my face, I get that much closer to dragging her to Vegas."

Bridal magazines? Oh, two could play at this game. "Sweetie, you're the one who asked me to see if Michael Bolton was available for our reception."

His grip tightened as his dangerous smile deepened. "I think you meant Bono."

"No, it was Mr. Bolton." She slid her arm around his waist and gave it a little pinch. "I remember because your first choice had been Donnie and Marie Osmond, but I put my foot down on that one." She winked at the ladies and laughed. "He does love that wholesome retro music."

Alex's counterattack was foiled as his sister came stomping through the room toward the stairs. "It's so unfair!" She spun around and focused those fiery eyes on her mother. "Dad took my phone away. He has no right!"

Donna excused herself and walked to her erupting daughter. "He pays the bill, so he has every right. We are going to spend this weekend together as a family and actually talk to one another. If I get another text from you while you're sitting right next to me, I will take care of that phone permanently."

"But how am I supposed to talk to Kyle?" Finley had the teenage whine down to an art.

"You're not," her father said as he joined them. "And no computer either."

Finley's mouth dropped in outrage. "Nobody else's parents treat them like this. You guys are so out of it."

Donna slanted her husband a look. "You are pretty old."

He nodded solemnly. "If only we could be cooler. Maybe if I bought some of those skinny jeans . . ."

Donna patted her husband's chest. "You can just borrow mine."

Finley huffed, rolled those Sinclair heartbreaker eyes, and stormed up the stairs.

Marcus and Donna passed a look that could only be shared among those brave souls raising teenagers. Or wolves. "Welcome to our happy home," Donna said on a sigh. "I used to be a cheery, confident mother."

"Then Finley turned seventeen." Marcus held out a tray of lemonade, serving Clare first.

"You would've tossed Will and me from the second story window if we had acted like that." Alex took a glass and handed it to Lucy.

"She's going through a hard time," Marcus said. "So we're trying to give her a little space."

"She's taken the news about Will really hard," Donna said. "We want to make this Fourth of July as special for her as possible."

Marcus nodded. "Then when we get home we'll move to plan B."

"What's plan B?" Julian asked.

Donna gave a small laugh. "At the moment I'm considering a taser." Her husband smiled. "Or a convent."

⌒

Alex played host and got everyone settled into rooms. Lucy's was across from his on the second floor, and while she unloaded her suitcase on the bed, he dropped his own down beside it.

"I prefer the right side of the bed," he said.

With a laugh, she shoved him out the door. But he ended up coming right back in, where they'd sat in her room for an hour and just talked.

It had been awhile since they'd had time with no distractions, and he wanted Lucy to relax. If she didn't, they'd never pull this off. It was clear his parents were suspicious of the fast-moving relationship, and it pained him to think of what a broken engagement would do to them. And he had no idea what was in Finley's head. Right now the teenager was unhappy with everything. Hadn't it been only yesterday she was playing hopscotch in the driveway with her lopsided pigtails and Kool-Aid mustache? Now she was just a raging commercial for Midol.

His phone rang and he pulled it from his pocket.

Kat.

He stared at her name on the display a moment before finally powering it off. Not tonight. He wanted to find Lucy and spend some time with her. On the drive to the beach, he'd discovered she was a walking cinema historian. They had gotten into a heated debate over Hitchcock's greatest flick, with Lucy arguing that her choice was the best simply because it starred Cary Grant.

After making a few necessary calls to his campaign manager, Alex went in search of his fiancée.

Following the blast of music and giggles, he found her in the media room. Leaning a hip against the doorframe, he took in the scene before him. On the giant screen were animated rock stars wailing for a screaming audience. Finley and Clare stood side by side with their guitars strapped on. His sister danced in place as Steven Tyler belted out an old hit. Clare fumbled with her instrument while Lucy and Julian sat behind her and coached the older woman's every move.

Just looking at Lucy made him smile. She had changed into yoga pants and a Wonder Woman T-shirt. He'd dated a lot of models, spent time with some of the world's most exotic beauties. But when he saw Lucy like this, in her comfort zone, he was in the presence of one of the most gorgeous women God had ever put together. Her blonde curls flew in a wild ruckus as she showed Clare the art of head banging. He wondered if Lucy even realized she'd let her grandmother into her heart. The girl couldn't do hostile and angry—it just wasn't in her. He liked that about her. Even his sister had fallen under Lucy's spell and had temporarily put aside her valiant fight against the world and all its cruel parental forces.

"Game over, my little estrogen muffins," Julian said. "It's daddy's turn to rock."

Clare clutched her guitar. "I called two turns."

Julian rolled his eyes. "You can't do that."

"It's on my bucket list."

He wasn't the least bit intimidated by the former first lady. "So is kissing Pierce Brosnan, but that's not going to happen either."

"It's already pushing midnight." Lucy got between them. "Clare, you can play again tomorrow."

"I'm elderly." She was haughty as a queen. "Who knows if I'll wake up tomorrow?"

"I'm willing to tempt fate." Julian made a grab for the guitar.

Lucy's head tilted as she laughed. And her eyes landed on Alex.

"Oh." He knew she would blush just like that. "How long have you been standing there?"

He moved into the room. "Long enough to see Clare's attempt at the splits."

Clare pointed at the girls. "They told me every rocker did it."

He gathered Lucy to him, giving in to the urge to place a smacking kiss on her cheek. "They lied."

"I'm played out," Lucy said. "I'm going to bed."

Clare only spared her a quick glance. "Rematch tomorrow?"

He walked with Lucy up the stairs to the bedrooms. The past few days had all but sucked the life out of Alex. He had dreaded this trip. Dreaded being shut in the house with his family, people he loved dearly but didn't know how to please anymore. Everywhere he turned, he saw Will. His favorite game of horseshoes in the closet. His favorite kind of cereal in the pantry. Photos on the mantel.

He reached for Lucy's hand. It was soft, it was strong, and it was her. She lifted those big blue eyes to his as she stopped at her door.

"Thanks for coming with me." He was a master of cheap conversation, and this was the best he could come up with? "I mean, I'm . . ." It was the fatigue. His eighteen-hour days. The absence of his brother. "I'm glad you're here."

Her smile was hesitant. "It hasn't been horrible. Yet."

"Tomorrow is day two of Finley without her phone. It's probably going to make doomsday look like Disneyland."

"Alex"—she brushed the hair from his forehead.—"it's okay to miss your brother."

Lightning aimed straight for his chest. He let his hand slide out of hers as he took a step back. "I'm fine."

"You've barely spoken to your family."

"So I'm distracted. I can't just take off for a few days and kick back."

"I'm pretty sure you can."

He couldn't catch a break with this girl. All the other women he'd dated had made him feel like he was the human form of perfection. He could use a little sympathy and adoration about now, but that wasn't going to happen with Judge Judy in the superhero T-shirt.

"I just meant that the campaign doesn't stop for a holiday. Our time is ticking, and there's still a lot of ground to cover." They were just now pulling ahead.

"You could hang out with your sister for a while."

"And interrupt her witching hour?"

"She watches you when you're not looking. When you talk, she hangs on to every syllable."

"At least someone does," he mumbled.

"Finley needs her big brother. And your parents—they just want to spend some time with their son."

He reached into his pocket for his phone. He'd just take a peek at his messages.

Lucy's tug on his hand stopped him. "Can you just be here?" The liquid fire in those eyes had his breath going shallow. "This is about more than getting a checkmark for attendance. They want to spend time with *you*."

The guilt whispered taunts in his head. Even if he won the election, he still wouldn't be half the man Will had been. Alex had been bulking up his portfolio while Will had been saving children. He just wanted something to show his parents—the world—something besides his face on *People*.

"Goodnight, Lucy." He was tired of thinking, and his body ached for rest.

She shook her head and gave that know-it-all smile. "You're afraid."

Did she know he could bench press her with one hand? "Yeah, okay. See you in the morning."

"Those people love you."

"They also have high expectations I can't meet."

"Such as?"

"Forget it." He raked his fingers through his hair. This conversation was over.

"The world doesn't revolve around you." Her voice sliced with a razor's edge. "Why don't you man up and be the son and brother they need?"

Not one supermodel had ever griped him out. Not one.

"You're lucky to have a family to spend holidays with, and instead of being grateful, all you can think about is yourself and your stupid election and how inconvenienced you are."

"That's not what I—"

"Guess where your voters are, Mr. Arrogant? They're at home. Spending time with their families. And guess who they're *not* thinking about?" She looked at him like he had just committed the cheapest of fouls. "You."

She was so out of line. She was supposed to be on his side, the little traitor.

"You told me once you always brought your A-game." Her hair bounced with every bob of her head. "Well, you know what, hotshot? All I'm seeing is one sorry performance."

"You don't understand." He leaned into her doorway, his hand a fist on the wall. "I can't do this right now."

"Sure you can. You pretend you love me." Her smile chilled him. "What's one more thing to fake?"

The door slammed in his face.

He turned, only to find Julian, wide-eyed, standing at the end of the hall, an entire game system in his arms.

"Women," he said. "Can't live with them. Can't let them hog your guitar."

Chapter Thirty-three

*F*ollowing the scent of bacon, Alex opened his bedroom door, the tips of his hair still wet from a shower. He bent down to slip on his shoe when Lucy's doorknob turned, and there she stood. He'd seen New York Warriors dissolve into tears from less intimidating looks than the one she was shooting his way.

He pulled himself upright, using his full height to tower over her. She had her hair pulled into a stub of a ponytail, and yellow tendrils framed that mad face.

"Happy birthday," she mumbled.

She was going to have to do a lot better than that. "I realize you're still mad at me, but I have a family downstairs who thinks we're engaged, and you giving me the stink eye all day doesn't exactly say I'm the air you breathe."

With that deadly look, she'd spit on his birthday cake if she got the chance. "Engaged people fight."

"Not us. You're too crazy about me." There was no way he was going to let his family see them at anything less than their perfectly adoring selves. "So we're going to go down there, listen to my dad try not to talk business, eat my mom's breakfast, ignore Finley's eye rolls, and gaze adoringly at one another until we make everyone sick."

"Fine." Her snarl made it hard to ignore those pink lips, but if he kissed her right now, she'd probably put her fist straight through his nose. "But don't even think about touching me."

Looking at that set jaw of hers only turned up the burner on his own temper. She'd crossed a line last night—telling him he was selfish and giving his family the cold shoulder. She had no idea. Thanks to her, he had tossed and turned all night, her biting words racing through his head like a rookie running drills. So if Lucy thought she was the victim here and could set the rules, she was sorely mistaken.

"If you check our engagement contract, page seven specifically states that we are to act blissfully in love at all times." His head throbbed beneath his temples, but ruffling her feathers was just as good as any bottle of Excedrin. "And that would include a little personal affection."

"Yeah, well, page twelve states that when you act like a complete idiot, I'm exempt from any groping overtures."

"Pretty sure it doesn't." He'd made the stupid thing up.

"It was in the revised copy. Didn't my attorney send that to you?"

His fingers snaked around her wrist as he took a step toward her. She smelled like apple shampoo and angry woman. "Cross me on this, and I'll inform Clare you want to go to her next Junior League meeting."

Her heard her low gasp and tried not to smile. "You are low down, Alex Sinclair."

"You know what occurred to me last night?" As he was lying awake and reciting career stats in his head. Anything to avoid thoughts of Will. Or the woman in bed across the hall.

"You realized you know every word I said was right?"

"I finally figured out your little secret—you're getting attached to me."

"What?" She tried to retreat, but he wouldn't let her.

Lucy suddenly seemed to be having a great deal of trouble looking him in the eye. Very interesting. The playbook in his mind began to rewrite itself. "Are you starting to resent this arrangement?"

"I'm starting to resent your ego."

Something inside him wouldn't let it go. He wanted her to admit she was just a tiny bit interested in him—something that went beyond two signatures on a contract and lots of acting. He was mature enough to confess he was attracted to her. Only a comatose gay man wouldn't be. And he knew, if she'd get honest with herself, she was hot for him too.

"You know what?" He moved in until her back was against the wall. "I think by the end of the day you'll be begging me to kiss you." His finger smoothed a trail across her cheek and down the delicate skin of her neck. "I've got plans for those lips of yours, Lucy. But before I give in to your runaway lust, I'm going to have to hear an apology."

"Apology?" Man, she was sexy when she was mad. Eyes blazing, skin flushed. "From me?"

He gave a lazy smile. "Glad you understand."

She stood frozen to the spot in anger. Speechless.

Taking advantage of the moment, he patted her on the butt. And walked on by.

Downstairs, Alex found Clare already at the table with Finley. Lucy's grandmother sipped tea while Finley practiced variations on her pout.

What he needed was some coffee. That would clear his head and give him a much-needed jolt to get through the rest of this day.

He passed a window on his way to the kitchen.

And stopped.

Beyond the walkway, past the dunes, and across the sand was the very same ocean he and Will had grown up in. It rolled in and out, flowing in the same rhythm of their childhood. But life didn't stay the same. The waves would always be there, a living testimony to two boys who lived for weekends at the beach. But Will was gone. Alex felt him all over the house and knew if he walked onto the shore, Will would be there too.

"Morning." He reached for a mug in the cabinet next to where his mother stood at the stove.

"Happy birthday, sweetie." She kissed his cheek and smiled, but the sadness lurked beneath. "It's a beautiful day outside."

"Yeah, it's . . . nice."

His mom held out the coffee and poured some in his cup as the bacon sizzled on the stove. "We haven't really had a chance to talk lately." The kindness and concern on her face was more than he wanted to deal with this morning. "Alex . . . how are you really doing?"

That should be the question he was asking her, but he just hadn't been able to form the words. "I'm fine." He took a sip, not minding the burn of the liquid all the way down. "Keeping busy. Trying not to think about it."

His mom pressed her lips together and nodded. "You know, it's not just the news of Will's death we're talking about here. You've been distant for a while now."

"It's nothing." Just a daily war in his head. "The campaign requires a lot of time. It will be winding down soon."

"And then?" She tilted her head and studied her son. "I'm proud of you. Your father and I both are. But you haven't been happy in years."

"I'm completely content." He had houses, cars, friends in every state. An election that had totally turned around and was looking more like a sure thing every day.

"Your dad was shocked that you and Lucy got engaged so fast." Laugh lines fanned as she smiled. "But I reminded him that he and I only dated three months before we got married. And a year later we had you two." She reached for a fork and turned the bacon. "We like her, Alex. You should bring her around more."

He knew that translated into *you* should come around more.

"Finley's convinced you're mad at us. I don't know where that girl gets her ideas lately." Hands that had fixed many a family breakfast turned down the burner. "You're not mad, are you?"

"Of course not." How could he tell her? That something had been chasing him for a year. That every night he went to bed with guilt and a restlessness that wouldn't leave him in peace.

"*Are* you happy? That's all we care about."

The tightness expanded in his chest. "Yes. Of course."

"Busy and happy are two different things."

She sounded just like his dad. They couldn't see that he was out there trying to find that happiness every day. Will had made it look so easy. But the more Alex tried to create a life, the more that empty hole widened.

"I love you." His mom put down her fork and cupped his face in her hands, just like she had done when he was young. "You could sell peaches on the side of the road, and we'd still be proud of you. But sometimes I wonder if . . ." She stopped and shook her head. "I lost one son . . . and some days I feel like I'm losing another."

⸎

The family sat down at the table in the pale-blue dining room, and Lucy fluffed her napkin into her lap just as Clare had taught her. She was rewarded with a small nod from her grandmother, who sat across from her. Next to Lucy, of course, was her devoted fiancé. Alex looked tired, and she hoped he had slept as miserably as she had. Probably hadn't given their conversation from last night another thought. If he'd lain awake, it was probably due to hours of sweet talk on the phone with the mysterious Kat.

With the waves crashing in the distance, Marcus led the family in prayer. When he offered up his thanks for Will's life, it was everything Lucy could do not to steal a look at Alex. She could feel his tension radiating like a sunburn.

At the word *amen*, Alex passed Lucy a bowl of mixed fruit, brushing his arm against hers. Did he have to sit so close?

"Sleep well, hon?" He plopped a waffle on her plate.

She batted her eyelashes and turned up the amps on her smile. "Best rest I've had in months, *sweetie*."

"Is that so?"

"Not a care on my mind."

"Well, I didn't get much sleep." Clare poured dainty stripes of syrup. "Whoever hid the controllers to the Wii had better cough them up or I'm not giving Alex his birthday gift."

Julian sniffed. "I'm sure he'll be so sad not to get his cheese-of-the-month subscription."

Donna pulled the butter away from her husband and set it out of reach. "Lucy, Alex has been telling us more about Saving Grace. What incredible work you do there."

"God's really blessed us," Lucy said.

Clare beamed like a proud grandmother. "Some of the girls are quite a handful. Lucy has a kind but firm hand."

"They just need someone in their corner." Lucy brushed a crumb off the corner of her mouth. "We know if they have a support system, their chances for success are significantly higher."

"I like to see someone passionate about her work," Marcus said. "What inspired you?"

"It's a long story." Lucy cut her waffle into tiny bites, knowing carbs and bathing suits did not mix. "But it's definitely what I'm put on this earth to do."

"Lucy does an incredible job," Alex said. "Her girls love her."

She wouldn't let herself be lulled by his flattering words. "So many of them have been abandoned, rejected, and they've been raised to think the worst about themselves." A movie reel of memories played in Lucy's mind, but she willed the dark thoughts away. "They just need to accept that God sees them as beautiful, talented, worthy women."

Alex's eyes lingered on hers. "Sounds like someone I know."

"Speaking of rejection," Finley said. "Alex, how old were you when Mom and Dad left you alone overnight?"

Marcus gave his son a sharp look.

"Um." Alex took a long drink of juice. "Twenty-eight?"

"We're not leaving you alone for a week by yourself," Marcus said. "That's final."

"They're honoring Will at the CNN headquarters next month, and Finley really can't afford to be gone," Donna explained. "She has the SAT and cheerleading camp."

"I'm old enough to take care of myself."

"It's that boyfriend we're worried about." Marcus eyed his daughter. "After the behavior we've seen lately, there's no way we're trusting you to stay home *or* with friends, so you're going with us."

"Come on, Dad," Alex said. "Give her a little credit."

"I found her sneaking out of the house three weeks ago."

Marcus might be as wealthy as Donald Trump, but he was a hands-on parent. Lucy admired him for that. If Steven Deveraux had had that kind of integrity, what would her life be like now?

Then an idea popped into her head.

But she couldn't . . . he would kill her.

"She could stay with Alex."

A trickle of fear crawled across Lucy's skin as his dark eyes slowly turned to hers. "I'm a little busy," he said. "I'm running for this thing. You might have heard of it—Congress?"

Crossing her arms over her chest, Finley assumed the universal pose of indifference. "Like he'd do that."

Lucy was not going to let this go. Alex needed to spend some time with his sister. Plus it would be a nice little piece of revenge for last night. "He would do that. In fact, Alex was just telling me the other day how he didn't get to see you enough. He said he wished there were more opportunities to hang out." She removed the hand he had clamped over her knee. "Didn't you say that?"

Paybacks were going to be brutal. "I'm not sure if I recall my exact words—like you apparently do."

"It's obviously meant to be." Lucy smiled at Finley. "He can get in that sister-time he's been wanting, and you don't have to miss your events while your parents are gone."

His mother didn't look convinced. "Are you sure?"

"He's positive." Lucy leaned against him, bravely resting her head against his shoulder. "Maybe you can both go get your nails done."

"Mani-pedis?" Julian nudged an attentive Clare. "Count us in!"

Chapter Thirty-four

*L*ucy was sun-kissed, frizz-haired, and convinced the sand in her bikini bottom was sent straight from Satan.

The luxurious day had been filled with swimming, bike riding, games, and food. They'd all watched the island's fireworks show from lawn chairs on the beach, then lingered under the moonlight as Donna and Marcus reminisced about past birthdays with Alex and Will. Alex had sat there in stony silence, staring at the ocean. The only sign he'd shown of listening was the grip he'd held on Lucy's hand. She was still mad at him, but she wouldn't have let go for anything.

Despite their desire to make everything festive for Finley, sorrow intruded every chance it got. At one point, as Marcus talked about past holidays, Donna had gotten up and rushed back into the house. She gave the excuse she was checking on the coffeepot, but there had been tears slipping down her cheeks as she walked past Lucy. Her mother's heart was breaking.

Now, worn out and ready to crash, Lucy went into her bedroom after their return from the beach. She dug into her suitcase and pulled out one more wrapped gift. After birthday cake at lunch, Alex had opened all his presents. Lucy had given him a new golf bag, but that wasn't exactly the most personal of tokens.

Clutching the package, she crossed the hall and stood before his door. Though this wasn't a peace offering, she was about to be the big one and step over enemy lines.

She knocked softly, and when he didn't answer after a moment, she pushed the door open.

His room was empty. Looking out his terrace, a light shone below on the beach. He must've gone down there to get some alone time. And she was about to interrupt it.

Lucy's feet sank into the cool sand as she stepped off the narrow wooden boardwalk. The grass in the dunes whispered in the warm breeze as she headed toward Alex.

Chair slung back low, his hands rested on his stomach as he stared at the crackling fire in front of him. Her heart folded in half.

Alex spoke before she did. "My dad gave me Will's Bible."

Her toes dug into the sand as she settled into the seat beside him. "I can't think of a more perfect gift." The flames flickered, giving her a darkened view of his somber profile. The novelty of looking at him would never wear off. Years from now she'd see him on the cover of a magazine in the grocery checkout line and still think he was the most beautiful man she'd ever met. He was more elegant, even now in his khaki shorts and Warriors T-shirt, than she was in her best dress.

Lucy forced herself to focus on the job at hand. "I'm not here to apologize."

His eyes fell on the blue-and-white package in her arms. "If that's an explosive device, I'd ask that you'd at least spare the others."

"You're safe. For now." She held it out, growing more uncertain with each passing second. "I didn't want to give this to you in front of everyone. It's nothing big. I mean, it's just a little something I made, so it's not some major thing or—"

"Lucy"—he took the gift from her bumbling hands—"you're doing that thing again."

"What?"

"That thing where you wave your inferiority complex around like an Olympic flag."

Why had she come down here again? She should've just gone with instinct number two and headed straight to bed.

His fingers traveled under the seam and tape as he peeled open the layers of the package, taking special care as if it were a precious treasure. Wrapping paper removed, he lifted the lid of the box and looked inside.

Alex ran his hand over the raised letters of the photo album. *The Life of Will Sinclair*. His eyes lifted.

"Open it," she whispered.

He stared at her a moment longer as if he might refuse. Finally, he flipped to the first page and then another. There was a picture of him and Will, toddlers on the beach. Will hanging from a tree as seven-year-old Alex stood below and laughed. The two boys in their blue high school graduation gowns.

He was only a quarter of the way through when he shut the book. Leaning his head back against the chair, his gaze searched hers. "I . . . I don't know what to say."

She shrugged. "It's too dark to really see. I know it's nothing, really. Just something—"

"Don't—don't do that." He set the album in his chair and dropped to his knees in front of her. "It *is* something. You did this for me." His voice was rough, questioning as his hands held hers. "How?"

The waves charged the beach only to slide back out again, and though the moon shone overhead, the warmth of the long-gone sun still heated Lucy's skin. "Your mom helped me. I got her to e-mail me a ton of pictures. I'm sure it took her forever, so it's a wonder she still likes me."

"She adores you." His gaze on hers was so intense, she wanted to look away. "How could anyone not?" And then he kissed her.

His lips touched hers with an urgency that threatened to swallow her whole. Lucy tasted salt as she wrapped her arms around his neck. He held on to her like a lifeline, as if she were a balm for his fractured heart. She was drowning in him and helpless to stop it. Didn't even know if she wanted to.

Alex lifted his head.

Their eyes met. Breath's mingled.

His thumb swept across her bottom lip.

His heart beat beneath her palm.

Lucy's pulse whipped wildly as he slid his hands down her arms and joined their hands. "Thank you, Lucy Wiltshire."

"You're welcome."

"No one's ever done something like that for me."

The lantern cast shadows across his face, but she knew it was nothing compared to the ones draped over his soul. "Maybe in the next few days you can look at the rest of it." She squeezed his hands. "You have an amazing family, Alex. They love you. And I know your brother did too. It's so obvious in those pictures."

He slowly nodded. "It's hard to be around them right now."

"Nobody's asking you to earn your time here. Your brother wouldn't want you to live your life like you're being pursued by the hounds of hell."

"I failed him, Lucy."

"No, you didn't. You're your own person. You don't have to save children and dodge mortar fire like him."

"I just want to be more. I want my life to stand for something."

"It does." Releasing his hand, she trailed her fingers through the dark hair and cupped his face. "You're a good man who's doing good things. At what point are you going to be satisfied with that and give yourself permission to slow down?"

"I don't know." He shook his head. "I just know I can't right now."

There was nothing else she could say. Somehow his hurt had become hers, but he would have to be the one to accept the truth. *God, open his eyes.*

Alex cleared his throat as he moved away from her. "I have something for you too. Don't go anywhere." He jogged back to the house, leaving Lucy alone on the beach with her racing thoughts and the lulling waves.

A few minutes later he returned, his feet heavy on the sand. He carried a pink gift bag, stuffed at the top with plumes of tissue paper that shimmied in the wind.

Happiness was a fine wine, and Lucy drank it in. She made quick work of removing the paper and what she saw had tears brimming in her eyes.

Star Trek
Season Two: Episode 19
A Private Little War

"Oh." It was an original script from the show. "Oh my."

He tapped his finger on the cover page. "That right there is—"

"William Shatner's signature!" She couldn't catch her breath.

"You're not going to pass out again, are you?"

She couldn't stop looking at Alex. At the script. And back to Alex. "Where did you find this?"

"I have my ways." His smile was lopsided as he shoved his hands into his pockets. "I tracked it down when your Leonard Nimoy picture got trashed."

She sniffed the ocean air. "I love it."

"Hey, none of that." He brushed a tear away from her cheek. "You know I can't stand that stuff."

"This is . . . amazing. It's Captain Kirk. It's—"

Love.

It was love.

The words opened in her heart like a rusty trap.

Alex had become her friend, her champion. In some ways, he knew her better than Morgan. Certainly better than Matt. He had seen her at her best and worst. He made her laugh. Made her think.

But Alex was sports riddles and tuxedos. Designer suits and homes on the coast.

And she was none of those things.

Closing her eyes, Lucy cursed her stupidity. She adored a man who would never love her back. One who had an agenda that didn't include a wife and family.

"Is something wrong?"

Yes, she thought miserably as Alex pulled her close. Something was wrong.

She had gone and fallen in love with her fiancé.

Chapter Thirty-five

*I*t was week-old meat loaf. A cloud of old lady perfume. Bug guts on the windshield. Love . . . was nauseating.

"For the second time, Lucy, I'm holding up two pictures. Which one is Representative Shively's wife?"

Clare sat beside Lucy at the breakfast table, clutching her beloved flash cards. In a matter of minutes Alex would pick her up for church. Instead of the regular service, they were going to help with Chuck's youth group. Alex had warned that the closer they got to the election, the less they'd see each other. It had been a week since they had left the beach. Enough time to dislodge this ridiculous notion that she was in love with him. She'd held this wild hope that the miserable thing she felt for Alex was nothing but a crush. Perhaps one could even label it an addiction. But no.

It was the big fat L word. And it hadn't gone away.

"Lucy—"

"The one on the right." She sighed and picked up her coffee mug.

"You may think this is juvenile, my dear, but these women are connected to very important allies for your intended."

Well, she wasn't going to marry him, so what was the point? Society functions had gotten much easier, though they still wore her down. This week she had even attended some with Clare, though it was pure drudgery when Alex wasn't there. She just didn't fit in with the political elite and wealthy highbrows of South Carolina. She was never going to be a sparkle.

"You did an excellent job at Tuesday's fund-raiser." Clare returned the pictures to the bottom of the stack on her lap. She'd been quizzing Lucy since Julian had served them pancakes and bacon. Forty-five minutes ago. "Except for mistaking Mrs. Peabody for her mother, you had an almost flawless night. Much improved." Her hand reached out to pat Lucy's. "Much improved."

Lucy checked her watch. Alex wouldn't arrive for another ten minutes. He was ever prompt, but never early. She missed his face. That scent that was his alone. And his laugh. He had called her every day, but instead of rushing to grab her phone like usual, she had often let it go to voice mail. The election was coming up, and they would soon part ways. He would ride off into the Congressional sunset, and she would go back to being a nonprofit worker and social misfit. It was time to put some boundaries between them and wean herself from the drug known as Alex Sinclair.

"Would you like to discuss your father?"

Lucy's head lifted at Clare's random question. She still resented the term *father*. It was a title that needed to be earned, and supplying the other half of her genes did not count for anything in her way of thinking.

"No." Lucy's tone was clipped. "I know all I need to."

"I know you don't owe me anything." Clare's face may have been retouched with a surgeon's fairy wand, but right now she looked every bit of her seventy-six years. "But you owe it to yourself to forgive him. To let the bitterness go. And maybe . . . forgive me as well."

There was too much in Lucy's head screaming for attention.

"All I ask is that you don't hate him," Clare said. "He led a very spoiled, indulged life. I'm to blame for that."

"No." Lucy stood in her black heels. "You're a wonderful person, Clare." There. She'd said it. "You may not have let him fall on his face enough growing up, but at a certain point he had to take responsibility. He had many chances to reach out to me. But he didn't. And it's not your fault."

"Do you really think I'm . . . wonderful?"

Lucy couldn't bring herself to elaborate and give Clare the words she knew she needed to hear. "You are much improved." Her lips curved in a small smile. "Much improved."

"One day . . . I do hope you will forgive me."

Lucy didn't know what to say. In her head she had forgiven her, but there was such lingering bitterness in her heart. She and Clare had forged an unlikely alliance—lived together, worked together—but never quite crossed over into friendship.

Sniffing her regal nose, her grandmother brushed away the moment with a sweep of her hand. "Anyway, on to new business."

"I know." Lucy mentally pulled up her social calendar as she lifted her mug. "I have the literacy council tea on Tuesday and the rural cooperative event on Wednesday night."

"That's not what I want to discuss," Clare said. "I want to talk about you and Alex. I've noticed some troubling developments this week."

The coffee tasted bitter on her tongue. "There's no trouble. No developments. No troubling developments."

Clare's thin eyebrow arched. "No matter what you think of me, I'm not blind. I've noticed that you've spent the majority of the week moping about. At first I thought you were missing your groom-to-be." Her hawk-eyes pinned Lucy in place. "But then a little birdie informed me you weren't taking Alex's calls."

"A little bird?" Lucy asked. "Or a snitch named Julian?" He could forget further invitations to the Hobbits' meetings.

"I believe we covered the importance of discretion in week two," Clare said. "I don't reveal my sources."

"There's nothing wrong between me and Alex."

"Something is amiss. Was there a fight? A misunderstanding? I only ask because it's important that you two present a united, happy front. You may think you can fool the world, but you cannot."

Actually, she thought they were doing a pretty good job.

"Has he hurt you?" Clare's face was full of concern, and guilt squeezed Lucy's conscience. "Because I simply won't have it. He's lucky to have you. You're a diamond among gems, and any man should thank his lucky stars for you in his life."

Now Lucy was the one taken aback. The look in Clare's blue eyes was nothing less than fierce.

"I am not one to exaggerate," she continued. "You are smart, kind-hearted, and wonderful to those girls. Even though I don't always approve of your reading material or lack of updos, I do believe Alex has the better end of the bargain."

Lucy could hear the grandfather clock in the sitting room *dong* the half hour. "Don't be silly." The words wove through her heart, bringing as much ache as joy. She wanted to believe the picture Clare had painted.

"I do not jest. You are worthy of the finest man. Your mother raised a wonderful young woman, and it pains me to see you reject my praise."

And Lucy realized Clare was right. The girls at Saving Grace didn't even have one decent parent, but she had been blessed with a wonderful mother. Her mom had withheld a life-changing secret, but Lucy couldn't hold that against her any longer. She would cherish the memory of her mom, who had done all she could to provide for Lucy—and protect her.

The doorbell rang, interrupting the conversation and announcing the arrival of her fiancé.

There were things still left to be said to Clare, and they hung in the room like the crystals from the chandelier, just waiting to fall. But Julian's blond head peeped into the room as he announced the arrival of Alex.

"Your betrothed is here." Julian waved his hand with a flourish as Alex appeared behind him.

Smiling as he saw her, Alex looked particularly fetching in a dark suit and lime-green tie. "Ready to go?"

Surely there were pills to take to rid her of these bungee-jumping butterflies in her stomach. A magic elixir? Some of Clare's secret stash of Metamucil?

Holding her hand, Alex walked Lucy to the car, shutting her door after she got in. Once inside, he turned the key and fastened his seat belt.

Then leaned over and kissed her.

She sighed as her traitorous hands moved around his wide shoulders, pressing her lips closer to his. She had missed him. He had taken her thoughts hostage this week, and now that he was here, she couldn't let go. He conquered her lips, just as he had conquered her heart. Slowly lifting his head, Alex brushed his knuckles across her cheekbone and caressed her with his simmering gaze.

"Now that we have that out of our systems." He skimmed his finger down her nose. "You want to tell me why you've been ignoring me all week?" Like someone had flipped a switch, he moved away from her and straightened in his seat. With something less than a careful hand, he reached for the gearshift and threw the car in reverse. "I'm waiting, Lucy."

She pressed a hand to her stomach, still waiting for the knots to untie.

The sun flitted through the palmettos lining the street. "I've had six hours of sleep in three days, I've talked policy until I want to gouge out my eyeballs, and my fiancée has decided to give me the silent treatment." With one finger he whirled the car into a left turn. "My patience ran out yesterday, so start talking."

I love you. I hate you. I don't want this to end.

"I've been busy."

"Busy," he repeated with a laugh. "That's good. That's real original."

She'd thought it was pretty good. "It's a hectic time at Saving Grace right now. And I've been checking on Marinell and her family." It had been up and down. They had received word just days ago that neither Marinell nor her mother were a match for Carlos's kidney. But, thanks to Alex, Mrs. Hernandez had a place to live and food was delivered to the house twice a week.

"And Squid said you keep sending them home. I pay them to watch you and keep you safe. It's hard to focus on welfare reform when I'm worried about rogue photographers climbing in your office window."

"I don't need anyone looking out for me. I took care of myself before you came along, and I will take care of myself after."

He shot her a look that could melt Astroturf. "And I thought I was the immature one."

"I haven't robbed you of your title, if that's what you're worried about." She wanted to reel the words back as soon as she cast them out. But what was he so angry about? She was the one who had done the stupid thing of falling for him. What did she care if his little ego got bruised?

"Have I done something to tick you off?" he asked.

"No." Just asked her to marry him.

"Is there something you want?"

She wanted him to care about her. To tell her he couldn't live without her.

"Part of the deal was that you make yourself available," he said. "Our contract states that . . ."

That contract. She'd like to nuke it right off the planet.

"If you're angry about something, have the guts to come out and say it."

"I don't jump on command. Sorry I'm not like all the other girls who drop everything for the honor of your call." Alex was never going to admit deeper feelings for her. Because he didn't have them. She was just a game-winning play.

"Obviously you and your insecurity have had a tough week." He sped through a yellow light, catching red at the tail end. "But you'd better brace yourself because we have a full schedule ahead of us. I hope you can suffer through it."

His phone buzzed in the cup holder, and they both made a grab for it. Lucy was quicker.

Kat.

"Your girlfriend's calling." She slapped the phone into his hand. "Maybe that will bandage your bloated ego."

"Lucy—"

"Take the call. Because this conversation"—she turned toward the window—"is over."

Chapter Thirty-six

*I*t happened in the third game of Alex's first pro season. Thirty seconds left in the fourth. Lewis Simpson was wide open and the end zone in sight. But Alex had misinterpreted the coach's signal. He'd run one play, his receivers another. When he'd thrown the ball, his man hadn't even been open. The Warriors lost that game. A stupid rookie mistake by a young, punk kid. One he'd never forgotten.

Operating on little sleep and a mind full of stress, he had let Lucy's glib response get to him, and he'd fumbled. He'd basically poured out his heart to her at the beach like he was trying to get in touch with his inner Dr. Phil, and then *she* shut down.

And he'd missed her. He'd just wanted her to pick up the phone so he could hear her voice, her laugh. To tell her about the headway he had made in Lincolnville and Ravenel, the endorsement he'd received from the state's previous governor, and about the people he'd met. What kind of friend just ignored you? Didn't she get that he cared about all her fiery opinions? Nobody put him in his place like Lucy.

But he'd blown it. Now she sat fuming beside him in church, legs angled away, and her hands gripping the Bible in her lap.

Like he needed something else to worry about. The time away from her had made one thing perfectly clear. Lucy was a brat.

And he didn't want to let her go.

She was important to him, and they made a good team. Not to

mention every time he touched her it was like flame to dynamite. She felt it too—he'd like to see her try and deny it. They could push out the engagement date and just see where it went. Continue as they were. There was no need to rush things once he secured his seat in Congress. She could still wear his ring for the sake of maintaining the story, but obviously he wasn't going to marry her in October. Marriage wasn't in his plan right now. He had a new career to establish. Surely she could understand that.

"Hey, guys." Chuck stuck out his hand and Alex shook it. "Glad you're here. Lucy, I'm gonna need some help with decision time at the end of the service."

She still wouldn't look at Alex. "Sure."

"Ready for the wedding?" Alex knew Chuck had not been the most hands-on groom.

"One more week." Chuck's smile pushed his round cheeks upward. "I really think I'm ready now." He flipped through his Bible and pulled out some notes. "I woke up at two this morning and had to change my message. Say a prayer for me." Chuck walked away, climbed the stairs to the stage, and joined his worship band.

Alex led Lucy to a seat and, risking possible dismemberment, stretched his arm across the back of her chair, his hand grazing her shoulder. It was a move worthy of any teen boy in the room. "How long are you going to be mad at me?"

"Next century sounds good."

"I brought you a souvenir from my trip to Mount Pleasant yesterday."

She flashed him a look from the corner of her eye. "Give it to Kat."

After a few worship songs, Chuck grabbed a mic and his Bible and reappeared front and center. Funky urban art hung on mocha-colored walls, and fat candles glowed in glass hurricanes on stage. If it weren't for the big cross in the middle of the stage, it could almost be a Starbucks. The wooden prop seemed a bit dramatic and out of place with the acoustic guitars and dimmed lighting.

The room went hush-quiet as Chuck grabbed his duct tape–covered Bible and read from Luke. In a storyteller's voice, he brought the passages of Jesus's temptation to life.

"Jesus had been fasting forty days. Satan knew right when to visit Christ for a little chat—when he was at his weakest. Jesus was worn down with hunger and loneliness, so guess what areas the Big Deceiver targeted?"

Chuck stepped off the stage and stood in the middle of the aisle. His gaze swept every row. "Today I want to inform you, just in case anyone else hasn't, that Satan is a liar. Right now? He's lying to you. And the scary thing is, these lies usually make sense. Do you believe you're ugly? Think you're a loser?" Chuck paused. "Lies. All of it. My friends, Satan is a terrorist. He's a gang leader. The Bible says he is a thief who wants to steal, kill, and destroy you. And you know what? He's succeeding with a lot of you."

Alex's hand slipped from Lucy's chair to rest on her neck, kneading the tight cords of muscle. How easy it would be to just lean into him. She was tired and weary of the fight raging in her heart. Everywhere she looked people wanted things from her. Some too much—others not enough.

Chuck's Converse sneakers scuffed as he walked the floor. "That guy doesn't come out at you like a horned monster. No, he's one smooth dude. You afraid of rejection? He's gonna use it. You afraid of what others think? He's all over that."

Chills pebbled across Lucy's skin. *God, are you talking to me—in a high school service?*

The youth pastor held up his tattered Bible. "This is your armor." He rushed back to the stage and pointed to the crude wooden cross. "And this is the *only* place you surrender. Tell the devil you're through listening. It's time to tell yourself, 'I'm good enough.' It's time to claim the verse in the Bible that says you are a dearly loved child of God. You are adored. And you deserve love."

You deserve love.

"When that voice sneaks into your head with lies, you claim the opposite. Say, 'I'm beautiful. I'm a success. I'm going places.' God doesn't care about your money, your background, what kind of clothes you wear." Chuck's voice rose with passion. "Stop looking in the mirror for your truth. Stop listening to your friends. Don't read that magazine and think that's your reality. They're *lying* to you. Because you are *dearly loved.*" He looked to the left. "Isn't it time we started acting like it?"

Chuck wiped his brow with a handkerchief and stepped up to the stage again. "You want to know what's holding you back? It's not what is or isn't in your wallet. It's not your folks or your face. It's lies." He slowly walked to the cross and touched its rough surface. "Here is where truth begins. Jesus died for you. He died for this moment."

Lucy couldn't breathe. The sound of her pulse pounded in her head.

"You know what lie I've been buying?" Chuck gave a mirthless laugh. "I'm getting married soon. And since day one of meeting my amazing girl, Satan's been telling me, 'You're not good enough. You're too poor. Too fat. Too boring.'" His eyes sought out Morgan in the front row. "'You're way out of her league, and it's only a matter of time before she wakes up and realizes it.' On July seventeenth, I'm going to become one supremely hot chick's husband. And I'm gonna say 'I do' without those lies in my head." Chuck went to the podium, held up a pad of Post-its and a pen, then began to write. Lucy leaned forward to get a better view. "On these three scraps of paper, I've written the lies that I'm not gonna accept from this day forward. I'm taking it to the cross—where it belongs."

He picked up a hammer. Pulled a nail from the pocket of his jeans. And nailed the first lie to the cross. The sound reverberated through the room as the hammer met the metal, and the nail pierced the solid wood.

"Standing up to Satan's lies takes guts." Chuck's forehead wrinkled as the hammer rested in his hands. "I want to live that peace God promises. And I think there are some of you here today who feel the same. You're sick of the lies stealing your joy. They sound like truth. They make sense. Satan plants questions in your mind and says, 'Answer this with logic.' But God says, 'No, answer with faith.'

"Who's going to fight back today? There's paper under your chair. Are you going to be brave enough to surrender that burden and nail it to the cross?" He held out the silver hammer, his fingers tight on the handle. "Who's ready to live like you're dearly loved?"

The keyboardist began to play, but it couldn't cover up the noise of teenagers reaching beneath their seats and grabbing their Post-its. Pens were dug out. Shared and passed around. There was a sniffing behind Lucy. A crying girl to her left.

She hadn't known Chuck had been so insecure. He was the fun, easygoing one who acted like nothing bothered him. Yet all this time he had looked at Morgan and seen his own imagined failures reflected back.

Beside her Alex stared straight ahead, his eyes on the cross. She wondered what was running through his mind. Did he see himself here? He was a prisoner of the lies he had bought into.

Yet so was she. And she wasn't going to live that way any more.

Clare's words came back to her. *You are smart, kindhearted, and wonderful.*

With a trembling hand, Lucy scribbled on one Post-it, then two.

Unlovable.

Unworthy.

Alone.

She watched kid after kid go up to the stage and nail their lies, ridding themselves of the deceptive words that had been stuck to their own hearts, but now were being taken by the two beams of the cross.

Lucy flinched with each strike of the hammer, and she imagined the lies dying and breaths of freedom taking their place.

She wanted that.

God, I'm listening. Everything's been so screwed up. I want it to be simple. I want to see the truth. Take this weight from me now.

"I'll be right back." Fighting embarrassment, she stood up and sidestepped past Alex, her knees brushing his. When he grabbed her hand, she stopped.

Looking down, she studied those eyes so focused on hers.

She thought he would say something, but he only squeezed her fingers. Then let her go.

Heart galloping, Lucy walked down the aisle.

Help me to truly give these things up to you. Replace my lies with truth.

And Lucy swung the hammer.

Until the cross held it all.

Chapter Thirty-seven

*T*hursday brought cooler temperatures and skies drippy with rain. It did nothing but fuel Lucy's blue mood. Last night's event with local farmers' representatives had gone well. Alex had played the part of the doting fiancé as he'd mixed and mingled, chatting it up about government subsidies and regulations. Over the last few months he had transitioned from untouchable athlete and cover model to a voice of the average Joe. He had worn them down with his charismatic personality, while his opponent, a man with an impressive political résumé, trailed behind.

All week Lucy had spent her lunch hour at the campaign office, making calls to potential voters and asking for their support. The election was all over the national news, and Americans watched to see if their favorite quarterback could make the ultimate touchdown.

She parked her car in the front of Clare's house and scurried inside, holding an umbrella over her head. She could smell dinner cooking as she entered the foyer. The scent hinted at roast, but knowing Julian, it wasn't just any traditional recipe. She had gained five pounds since moving in with Clare. Her landlord had informed her it would be at least another week until her apartment was ready. If Lucy didn't get back to her apartment soon, she would have to buy a whole new wardrobe. With elastic waistbands.

"In here, sweetness!"

Lucy followed Julian's voice to the living room, stopping in the doorway. He and Clare sat hip to hip on one of the overstuffed couches. Clare, barefoot, with her bifocals perched on the end of her nose. And Julian, his face covered in a mud mask and a Bible in his lap. Just like Clare. Further proof that parallel universes did exist.

"You're home late." Clare pulled off her red frames. "Working late—again?"

The implication shone in the room like the French bronze lamps on either side of the couch. She knew what they thought—that Lucy had been avoiding them. Avoiding Alex unless duty called. "I was at the hospital with Marinell."

"How is Carlos?" Julian asked.

"Worse. They're running out of time, and so far, no matching donor."

Marinell now stayed full-time in her mother's house, as the two women kept constant vigils at Carlos's bedside. Though her grades had been abysmal, Marinell had passed summer school and could now give her brother all of her attention.

"What are you guys doing?" Lucy moved farther into the room and sat in a gold-striped chair.

"We're trying to read our Bibles." Julian slanted Clare a frustrated look. "But *she* keeps stopping and asking a million questions."

"We're going to read through this whole book this year," Clare said.

Julian rolled his eyes. "We've been stuck in Genesis for three months."

"It's rather confusing," Clare said. "And I keep thinking of all these questions I want to ask Jesus when I arrive in heaven."

"If that occurs *after* you finish the Bible, you won't get there 'til next century."

Lucy smiled at Julian. She would miss seeing him every day when she moved out. "What parts don't you understand?" she asked.

"Here we go." Julian leaned back and waved his hands over his goop-covered face.

"Like this Eve woman." Clare tapped her burgundy fingernail

on a page. "She always gets the blame, but from what I can tell, she was wronged and deceived. If you had been in her shoes, it would've sounded so logical, it had to be right."

Echoes of Chuck's Sunday lesson waltzed through Lucy's head.

"But God told her and Adam not to eat from the tree," Lucy said. "He was pretty clear on that one."

"But he didn't tell her that Satan would come and try to convince her to do otherwise. The Devil made her believe his lies. Don't you get it?" Clare scooted to the edge of the couch and locked her eyes on Lucy. "I'm Eve."

Julian snorted. "I think you mean Methuselah."

Clare shook her white head. "I believed lies too. I thought my image was everything. The devil had me convinced that your mother wanted our name, our money."

Lucy's fingers curled into the fabric on the armrests.

"I only saw the worst in her." Clare paused to make sure Lucy was listening. "And the best in my son. Sure, it sounds ridiculous now—especially from your point of view. But it was as true to me as knowing roses are red and snow is cold."

The days had been leading to this moment. God had been gently nudging Lucy toward this time, this conversation. And now that she was here, she didn't know what to say.

"Lucy, haven't you ever believed things about others or yourself that weren't true?"

Julian nodded. "I once thought I looked good in paisley."

"Have you?" Clare was a woman used to commanding a room, and today was no exception.

"Yes." The past pushed to the forefront, screaming for retribution, but Lucy had nailed those words to the cross. Left them there so mercy could take their place.

"I thought I was protecting my family," Clare said. "That's what I believed. What about the lies you're believing?"

Lucy didn't want her to say anything more. She felt open, as exposed as the night of the Sinclair gala when her dress had fallen apart.

"There's nothing wrong with you, Lucy. You're just as good as anyone else. You think I don't see the way you cower at social events? How you avoid certain people?" Clare set her Bible aside on the couch. "You were rejected as a child, and I'd give up all my Sinclair stock to go back and change it. But you've lived your life anticipating the cold shoulder from everyone ever since, and you can't go on that way."

Tears dampened Lucy's lashes as she once again heard the hammer striking the nails.

"Do you forgive her?" Julian asked, impatient with the whole thing. "Clare needs the words."

Lucy's mind tried to conjure up just the right thing to say.

Julian stood up. "I think there's something you should see."

"I'm hungry," Clare said in a rush. "Maybe we should eat first and—"

"No." He braced his hands on his hips and stared both women down like he was Spartacus come to deliver his people. "We're settling this tonight. There are things she needs to know."

Lucy didn't need any more family revelations, but she got up and followed Julian down the hall.

He walked into the study, went to a gilded cabinet, and pulled out the deep middle drawer. His fingers dug through the contents until he found what he wanted.

"Here." Julian grabbed a book and rested it on a desk with a plop. "Look at this."

Lucy heard Clare come into the room, but she didn't even spare her a glance. She was pulled to the book like a magnet on steel. It was a photo album. There was an oval cutout on the cover, and the picture peeking through was one of her. At the age of three.

"You're not the only one who can make a scrapbook." Julian had helped her put together the one she had created for Alex. And he had known Clare had kept this all along.

Lucy sat down in the office chair and opened to the first page. Lucy's birth announcement was pasted in the center, a yellowed newspaper clipping that announced her arrival. Her father's name wasn't mentioned.

She continued to leaf through the pages, her heart filling with every picture. One of her in the first grade at a dance recital. Her ponytail was crooked and her front two teeth were missing. Lucy remembered when the performance was over, her mother had met her backstage, bearing a single rose for the star.

On page five there was a copy of her eighth-grade report card. She had made the honor roll. She lifted her head in question. How had Clare gotten that?

"You thought you were on scholarship at that snooty school." He cocked his head toward Clare. "Here's your benefactor."

"Why?" Lucy asked.

Clare fingered the gold chain at her throat. "I wanted your mother to have every penny for taking care of you. I knew she wouldn't send you to some place like Montrose Academy. But I thought you needed to go. And maybe you were miserable there, but I believe it made you who you are today—strong and independent."

Lucy continued to turn the pages, overwhelmed by every one. There was a small blurb from a wrinkled newspaper, describing Lucy's acceptance into the University of Florida, and her resulting scholarship. Her eyes lifted again. "You?"

"You got in all on your own," Clare said quietly. "But I might've chipped in a bit on the tuition."

"How much?"

Julian answered for Lucy's grandmother. "All of it."

It took a moment for the lump in her throat to go down. "And my mother knew this?"

"Not that I'm aware of. I made it all look very official and convincing."

The room was silent, save for the small thud of Lucy shutting the book. She pushed it aside, got up from the chair, and went to Clare. The woman's face was a canvas of uncertainty and fear.

Lucy enfolded her grandmother in her arms and pulled her to her. "I love you, Clare." The hurt was an old Band-Aid that had become fused to her heart, and it was time to rip it away. "I didn't expect to love you and didn't want to, but I do." It was the new theme of Lucy's life these days, but it felt good to let the words run free.

The dignified woman broke into a sob on Lucy's shoulder. "Tell me you forgive me. Please—I've waited so long to hear the words."

Bitterness over her grandmother would die in this room and never rear its ugly head again. "I forgive you."

Clare shut her eyes against the tears rolling down her cheeks. "Thank you," she said. "You have no idea what those words do to me— how long I've waited to hear them." She pulled a tissue from her pants pocket and daubed at her face.

"But I'm through wearing your clothes. I have to be me."

"No more pantsuits?"

"I don't know that I love anyone that much."

Julian grinned. "I'll help you burn them."

"I do have one last thing to share with you." Clare took a weary breath. "Two weeks after I handed your mother that check, I received one of my own—from her." She walked to an imposing wooden file cabinet and retrieved a folder. "Anna returned all the money. I never heard from her after that. If she ever caught a glimpse of me at any of your school events, she never said a word. On the very day I got that check in the mail, I took it to my financial advisor. And invested it." She handed Lucy the folder. "It's yours. All of it."

A chill enveloped Lucy, and her hands shook as she opened up the portfolio. The latest statement rested on top, and Lucy read over the numbers. Once. Twice. It was an astronomical amount of money.

"My advisor is quite good," Clare said. "Your money has done very well."

She shook her head. "I can't"—she couldn't get the air into her lungs—"I can't accept this. It's not mine."

"You can and you will." Clare lifted her aristocratic nose. "I've been burdened with that money for years. It's hung over my head like a curse. I was just waiting for the right time to give it to you—when I knew you would be ready to accept it."

"But I'm not ready."

"This isn't about you," Clare said. "It's about me—finally letting the last piece of this go. You have no choice but to claim it."

The zeroes on the page ran together until Lucy had to look away. It was more money than she could spend in a lifetime. More than enough to refuse Alex's payment and fund Saving Grace on her own.

"I hate to break it to you, dear." Clare rested a gentle hand on Lucy's shoulder. "But you are rich."

Oh, the irony was too much. All those years Lucy had been made to feel like the poor girl from the wrong side of town. Not good enough. Different. Uncultured. And now this. God must surely be laughing.

Clare ran her hand over Lucy's unruly curls. "You have given me a gift—more than I ever thought I deserved."

"Ohhh, group hug!" Julian gathered the two women to his chest and squeezed them tight.

"Julian," came Clare's muffled voice. "You're getting that brown junk all over my cheek."

"Girl"—he reached around and tweaked Clare on the nose—"ain't nobody ever died from extra moisturizer."

Chapter Thirty-eight

*L*ucy sat at the dinner table the next evening and wondered where the last hour had gone. At some point she had eaten a few bites.

"I'm gonna try and not take this personal," Julian said as he carried her untouched piece of pie into the kitchen.

Her brain was filled with fog, rolling mists of thoughts and apprehensions that wouldn't leave her alone. If she had been given Clare's money months ago, she'd never have agreed to Alex's wild scheme. Never have fallen head-over-discount-heels in love with him.

But she wouldn't have touched a dime of Clare's money even a few short weeks ago. She still wasn't completely sure she could now.

Julian returned to the dining room, holding out a phone. "One dreamboat holding for Lucy Wiltshire," he said, then went back to the kitchen.

As if her very thoughts had conjured him, Alex spoke into her ear. "I know you're still mad at me—"

"I'm not mad." She was a million different things, but not that.

"I'm begging for help here." His voice sounded exasperated, strained. "I've had Finley for three days, and I'm about to lose my mind."

Her lips shifted into a smile. "It can't be that bad."

"She just asked me to pick her up some tampons and a Yoo-Hoo."

"I think I have a coupon for at least one of those."

"Lucy, I'll do anything—name your price. If you want to see a grown man beg, I'll give you a front-row ticket. But please, *please* come over and help me with this girl."

"Can I bring my camera and sell the pictures to the best paying tabloid?"

"I'll even pose shirtless."

"See you in thirty."

❧

Alex opened the door before Lucy could knock.

She was whipped into a tight embrace, his arms tying a bow around her. "Don't leave. Whatever you do, just please don't leave."

Lucy laughed and reveled in the feeling of being blanketed in his strength. His very desperate strength.

Alex took a step backward, his hands on her shoulders. His brown eyes looked their fill, until she felt her cheeks stain with a blush. "I've missed you." There was no teasing in his voice now.

"I've missed you too." More than she even wanted to think about. Because no matter the outcome of the election, he would be leaving her behind.

She recognized that look, and so it was no surprise when he leaned in to kiss her. His lips aligned with hers—

"Ew, seriously?"

Finley shook her head as she cruised through the foyer and bopped her way down the hall, chatting on the phone.

"See what I mean?" A muscle ticked in Alex's jaw as he regarded his sister like an unidentified species. "She's been like this all week."

"Interrupting you when you were about to lip-lock with a female?"

"Exactly." His smile was rueful as he shut the door. "We were just eating dinner. Want some?"

She followed him in the direction his sister had pursued, Alex muttering under his breath the whole way.

Chinese takeout boxes littered the granite counters in Alex's industrial kitchen. "Are the Warriors stopping by?" There was enough there to feed the entire neighborhood.

"Finley couldn't make up her mind what she wanted. Some things have too much fat. Some things have too many calories. And she now thinks she might be coming down with a bean sprout allergy, so most of the menu will be thrown in the trash."

Finley poured herself a glass of Dr Pepper and hoisted herself onto a bar stool. "I told you last week I totally broke out in a zit after eating bean sprouts. And what does he do?" Finley turned to Lucy for some girl sympathy. "He orders Cantonese Chicken with—"

"With bean sprouts—yes, we got it. I'm the most thoughtless brother in the world."

"I wouldn't go that far," she said. "But I doubt Mom and Dad will let me stay with you again."

"I'm holding back the tears." Alex looked like he had stepped into a lion's den and barely made it out. "Do you see what I have to put up with?"

Smiling, Lucy joined Finley at the bar. "What do we have here?" She lifted up a piece of paper filled with instructions for the week.

"My prison rules," Finley said.

Alex took the stool next to Lucy, swiveling until his knee rested against her thigh. "Directions for the care and feeding of tyrannical sisters."

"Like you've even been home to notice I'm here."

"I said I was sorry for having to work so late this week."

Lucy read from the list. "Homework must be done by seven o'clock."

"AP summer reading," Finley said. "Lame."

"Can't stay out past curfew."

"Like he's let me out of the house."

Number three looked interesting. "No contact with Kyle?"

"That's her boyfriend." Alex scrubbed a hand over the light stubble on his face. "Dad's rule."

"It's a stupid one," Finley mumbled.

"Not if you got caught sneaking out of the house," Alex said. "The boy is a menace. You don't need to be hanging out with a guy like that."

"Like you care." Seeing her brother's face, Finley softened her tone.

"It's Friday night. I just want to hang out with my friends. What's wrong with that? I won't be anywhere near Kyle."

Alex shook his head. "We've got one more day together. I want to deliver you to Mom and Dad in one piece."

"I'm bored, Alex. I promise I won't drive all over town or be somewhere I'm not supposed to. Maybe just a movie with the girls?"

"I'll take you to a movie." He was trying, but it was a little too late.

Instead of spouting her special brand of teen venom, Finley quietly shook her head and returned to eating.

Music blasted from a purple phone, and Finley grabbed it. "Hey, Rebecca," she said. "Uh-huh." Her face fell even more. "No, I can't. I know it's for cheer camp, but my brother won't let me." She lowered her voice to a whisper. "Because I just can't. I promise I'll get my part done, and we can practice Monday morning. Yes, it will be enough time. It'll work out. No, I said I wouldn't let you down and—" Finley stared at her phone before setting it back down on the counter.

"Did she hang up on you?" Alex asked.

"Yeah." She pushed some noodles around on her plate. "Rebecca will get over it. We have a competition next week, and she's just stressed. Nothing new."

Alex opened up a carton of rice. "What kind of competition are we talking here?"

"It's the county cheerleading championship. I haven't gotten to work with my team much this week, and they're meeting tonight. Again."

"Finley—"

"No, don't worry about it." She took her plate to the sink and washed it out. "I'm going up to bed to watch some TV." She walked past them and through the door.

Alex sighed like a resigned parent. "Okay."

She did an about-face and leaned back into the kitchen. "Did you just say something?"

"I said you can go to Rebecca's."

"No, don't worry about it. I'll just get with them on Monday before practice."

"I'm not here to be the bad guy, Finley. And I'm certainly not going to be the one to take away your championship title." Alex stood and aimed a finger toward his sister. "Be back before eleven or I call the National Guard."

"Wow." She just stood there. "Thanks."

"Don't make me regret it."

❧

"Finley left her phone," Alex said as he and Lucy retired to the living room. "She'll probably go into withdrawal before she even gets to Rebecca's." He sat down on the couch and tugged her down beside him, loving the warmth of her hand in his. "What's that look for?"

"I can't believe you just fell for that."

"What?" Lucy Wiltshire was a sight for sore eyes. They'd seen little of each other lately. When they'd been together, Lucy had kept it all business, and he hadn't pushed. But now they were going to sit down and have a real conversation. Then make out like teenagers.

"Your sister totally just played you."

"She did not. If anyone is familiar with teenage hijinks, I'm pretty sure it's me. My sister is on her way to Rebecca's to save the world with their cheerleading."

"She's going to Kyle's."

Alex blinked. "She wouldn't do that to me. No way."

"She's been ticked at you for months. Of course she would."

His sister had been playing the ice queen all week. He knew she was upset with him. Ever since Will's disappearance, she had treated Alex like he wasn't cool enough to share the same last name. But he couldn't believe she would sneak out. She respected him more than that.

Lucy snaked her hand around him, reached into his back pocket, and pulled out his phone. "You're a man with resources. Make some calls and find out where this Kyle lives."

"I know I'm right, Lucy."

"Fine. Then let's prove it."

Chapter Thirty-nine

I feel like a perv."

How had he let Lucy talk him into staking out Kyle's house? Only idiots and creeps did stuff like this, and yet here Alex sat. If Finley hadn't left her phone, this could've been taken care of with a quick call. His legs ached to be stretched after two hours in the confines of his car.

Lucy stared out the window, still and silent. And he didn't like it. Somewhere they had derailed a little. Gone in reverse.

"I don't stalk people." He was getting grumpy and restless in this car. She could at least talk to him. "Especially my little sister."

Drumming his hands on the tops of his thighs, he let her know he was bored. And bored men had few thoughts other than—

"You want to hop in the back seat?"

In the dark of his Mercedes, Lucy finally smiled. "I would, but I already have a crick in my neck."

His frazzled sigh filled the car. They sat there a few more moments, four vehicles down from Kyle Mulroney's two-story home. The rain had started up again, and it tapped lightly on the windows.

Alex picked up her hand from her lap and toyed with her fingers, enjoying the contrast of her soft skin against his. "Lucy?"

"Yes?"

He kissed her knuckles then stared at her over the top of her hand. "I'm sorry for our fight on the Fourth."

"That was two weeks ago."

He nodded, feeling a little off-balance. "And you haven't been the same since."

"Of course I have. I've just been—"

"Making excuses," he said. "Finding reasons to stay out of my way. Reasons not to talk to me unless it's about the campaign." He leaned closer and his senses filled with her. "Call me crazy, but I thought we were better friends than that."

"Friends." She paused just long enough to make him wary. "Yes, we are."

"Then you could at least pick up the phone occasionally. Or man up and tell me why you're still mad." He glanced away at the expectation in her eyes. He wasn't used to explaining himself to anyone. But this was Lucy. His Lucy. And she wanted answers. "Kat . . . is a private detective," he finally said. "She works for the top firm in the country. I hired her a week after Will disappeared, when the government's search for him didn't progress as fast as I thought it should."

Her face softened. "Why didn't you tell me?"

"Because it all sounded so hopeless. The chances of Will being alive were slim, and then when the news broke that he was dead—I knew you'd think I was crazy."

"I don't think you're crazy." She was looking at him with those sympathetic eyes again. "I think you're a man who loves your brother."

"I just"—he took a shuddering breath—"couldn't give up." Organizing his own search had made him feel less helpless, but now it just seemed pathetic.

"He's gone, Alex."

He nodded as the words barreled through him. "I know." And it made Alex's resolve to win the election stronger than ever. He would win this. For Will. He would build a life his brother would've been proud of. Carry on his work.

"I need you in my life, Lucy." His fingers trailed along the line of her jaw. One side then to the other, a lazy caress of the skin. She leaned toward his hand, kissed his palm. Tipping her chin up, he pressed his lips to hers.

He had a plan, but it could be altered a bit. Marriage was still light-years away, but he didn't see why they had to break up when the election was over. He could be flexible.

Lucy pulled away. "So what are you saying?"

Something dangerous glinted in her eyes, and it set him on edge. "I'm saying I like what we have here."

"And what is that?"

"I just think—"

"I don't care what you think," she said. "What do you *feel* for me?"

He was standing over the edge of a canyon, held by nothing but balance. To love Lucy would be to give up his timeline, his plans. She hated everything about his political life. She'd never make it. He could never marry someone like that, a woman who couldn't fit into his dream.

"Never mind." Her voice was a whisper in the darkness.

And he had just fumbled. "Lucy—"

Lights illuminated the car as a truck drove down the street and wheeled into the driveway of Kyle Mulroney's house.

"We're not done with this conversation." Alex straightened in his seat and stared down his new target. "Not by a long shot." He switched on his windshield wipers to clear the view as a lanky teen boy stepped out of the Ford and opened the passenger door.

Out climbed his sister.

"I'm gonna kill that kid." Alex reached for the handle. "I'm going to rip him apart. And then I'm going to feed my sister bean sprouts until she breaks out in zits all over that lying face." His door bounced on its hinges as he swung it wide. "Finley!" he yelled. The rain pelted his skin, but he didn't even notice through the red haze of anger.

She turned, holding an umbrella over her head. "What are you doing here?"

He closed in on the sneaking couple. "I thought you might need help with your cheer routine." He took in the boy beside her. "You must be Rebecca."

"Leave him alone," Finley said.

"Dude, we weren't doing anything wrong."

Alex looked at Kyle like he was standing in the way of him and the end zone. "*Dude*, your breathing right now is all wrong to me. I suggest you take your little Abercrombie-wearing self into your house and lock your door. Because after I get through talking to my sister, I'm liable to come after you. And I'll be all done with talking."

Kyle leaned toward Finley.

"Kiss her." Alex said. "I dare you."

Looking at a force he couldn't contend with, Kyle mumbled an apology to Finley, then ran into his house.

"You are *such* a jerk."

"Call me whatever you want." The rain seeped into Alex's clothes, but he hardly felt it. "You lied to me."

"Who cares!" she cried.

"I do!" he shouted back. "You're my baby sister."

"Don't stand there and pretend like you give a crap. You haven't said five words to me in the last year."

"We talk all the time."

"Yeah, a text here. An e-mail there. You didn't even show up for my birthday last month."

"I was busy." He raised his voice over the growing wind. "I sent you a big gift card to the mall."

She tossed her hands in the air. "I don't want your money. I want my brother back!"

That stopped him. "Get in the car, Finley. We'll talk about this at home."

"No."

He groaned as he saw her lips tremble. A woman's tears were going to be the death of him. "Get in the car."

"No!" The wind howled over them, knocking the umbrella right out of her hand. She spun on her brother. "I hate you! Do you get that? I despise you."

"Don't say that." Rain dripped in his eyes, and he dug in the pocket of his jacket for a tissue. Anything. His hands closed over something, and he pulled it out.

The pieces of paper he had scribbled on during Chuck's sermon.

Failure.

Guilty.

He felt all of those things tonight. While Lucy had nailed hers to the cross, Alex had stuffed his in his coat like the weak man he was. "I'm sorry, Finley," he said. "For whatever I've done."

"You don't even know, do you?"

This was pretty much how his life went anymore. "Tell me." So they could get out of the rain. So he could just fix it. And fix whatever Lucy's problem was. He wanted to see his sister look at him like he was her hero again. And not her biggest disappointment.

"Will died."

The words ripped into his flesh and bone. "I know."

"He died, and you didn't even care."

"Of course I did." He was eaten up with it. It was a consuming plague on his spirit. "I loved him too."

"I needed you." Her hair clung to her face. "One of us is gone, and you couldn't be bothered with it. I was all by myself. I lost two brothers."

"That's not true."

"You were too busy with football. Then when you quit, you just went on to something else. I didn't have anyone to talk to. Nobody to share Will stories with. He's gone." Her body shook with sobs as she sunk to the pavement, her hands covering her face. "Will is gone."

"Hey." Alex dropped down beside her. He peeled the hair from her eyes and pulled her to his drenched chest. Lucy still sat in his passenger seat, and he wondered what she would tell Finley right now. *God, give me the words. I'm a desperate man.*

"You left me." She curled into him, jerking with the force of her tears. "How could you do that?"

"I don't know."

Failure.

Guilty.

Lies he hadn't been strong enough to leave behind.

God, just take them. I can't live under this anymore. I'm giving them to you.

"I was hurting too." The truth peeled from his lips, stinging like a scab ripped away. "I felt guilty, okay?" How could he possibly make this seventeen-year-old girl understand? "Like I should've been the one taken. Instead of Will."

"Neither one of you should have been."

"I know. And it's not fair. And the worst thing is that I bailed when you needed me most." Money had been the cruelest of tormenters. He'd never been more useless in his entire life. "I just wanted to fix it for you, and there was nothing I could do."

Eyes so much like his stared back at him. "I wanted my family around me. Someone to listen to me—who understood what I'd lost."

He had been such an idiot. His family had never done anything but love him. And he had pushed them away, pouring salt on their gaping wounds. "I want to be your brother again." His fingers held tight to her arms. "A real one. It's not too late."

"Are you going to visit more?"

"Yes."

"You'll come over for Sunday dinner?"

He hated his mother's meatloaf. "I'll make it a priority."

The rain couldn't wash away the hope on her face. "I've missed you, big brother."

He crushed her to him. "I'm not going anywhere again. I promise." He was leaving the guilt there in the driveway. It was time he rejoined the family. People who would take him just as he was—if he would only let them.

"Are you still going to beat up Kyle?"

There was only so much giving a man could do. "No, of course not." With his arm wrapped around her, Alex led Finley to the car. "I wouldn't dream of taking away Dad's fun."

Chapter Forty

*T*he harpist played "Yoda's Theme" from *Empire Strikes Back.* From the changing room in the chapel, Lucy could hear the rumble of wedding guests, the three-string band, and her friend Sanjay ordering guests to sign the book.

"Can you just go check on Chuck?" Morgan said. "I know he's nervous, and I need to see if he's okay."

"He loves you." Lucy smiled at her friend. Chuck wasn't the only one nervous. "He's fine."

The bride planted a fist on her hip and pointed to the door. "I'm about three seconds away from going Bridezilla on you."

"On my way."

Lucy crossed the hall, knocked, and slipped into the small room where Chuck waited.

"I'm here to make sure you're not crawling out the window and making your escape."

Chuck glanced to the tiny porthole in the wall behind him. "Not much chance of that."

"You look quite dapper." Lucy reached out and brushed some lint from his jacket.

He smiled. "You look all right yourself."

Lucy looked more than all right. She was radiant in a red chiffon dress with a ruched bodice and a skirt that grazed the bottom of her knee. Clare would be proud of Lucy's updo, though the twin roses pinned at the side gave it the sass that was all her own.

Concealer hid the dark circles under her eyes. She had lain awake all night. Thinking. Praying. And eating Julian's mocha chocolate cheesecake. Today was the day she saw her best friends get married. And a day of decisions for her.

"Those people are totally going rogue on the guest book," Sanjay said as he stepped inside. "Their failure to comply with protocol makes me question the fate of our world."

Chuck checked himself out in the mirror. "Just like it warns in Revelation."

Lucy watched Sanjay pull out his iPhone.

"What are you doing?" Chuck asked. "Did you just get footage of me smelling my pits? Cause if you post that, I will take that feathered pen outside and stick it so far up your nose—"

Lucy laughed and stepped between them. "You're not nervous, are you, Chuck?"

"About the wedding? Yes," Chuck said. "About the next fifty years? No. It was like my sermon last week was for me as much as it was for anybody else. I hadn't realized how much I had let all those negative thoughts take over. I was dreading today, wondering if I had what it takes to make Morgan happy. I'm glad I can go through this ceremony with a clear conscience." He watched her in the mirror as he checked his hair. "When it's right, it's right. You know?"

"Yeah." How about when it was semi-right? Or had potential to be something eventually? She hadn't lingered at Alex's place last night. She had given Alex and Finley their time, but today, there was no escaping the conversation she needed to finish with her fiancé.

"Well, I guess my work is done here," Lucy said. "I'll see you at the altar."

"Hey, Luce?"

She stopped at the door and turned.

"The real deal is worth waiting for. Anything else just looks good, but won't keep you going for the long haul. Kind of like that banana split I had for lunch." His hands rested on her shoulders. "I'm proud of you. You have your girls' home. You're changing lives. And you've finally let the old hang-ups die and given Alex a chance." He glanced at her sparkling engagement ring and smiled. "And just look where it's gotten you."

~

Lucy stood behind her friend at the altar. Holding hands with Chuck, Morgan could've been a model for a bride magazine in her strapless white dress and her delicate tulle veil. Wearing a silly grin, Chuck couldn't take his eyes off her. That's what it was supposed to look like. And feel like. Not the miserable sensation of a derailed roller coaster.

At the pastor's prompting, the couple faced one another to recite their vows. They had written their promises themselves, and when it was Chuck's turn, he stood before his bride, a man confident in who he was.

"Morgan, the day I met you, my life changed."

Lucy let her eyes skim over the church pews and found Alex's steady gaze on her. He smiled and sent her a slow wink. He was easily the most handsome man in the church in his dark suit, with the lights through the stained glass bringing out the auburn highlights in his hair.

" . . . and I stopped settling. It didn't matter that you're hot and I'm bigger than Chewbacca." Chuck never took his eyes off of Morgan, even as the audience laughed. "It didn't matter that you're all refined, and I typically eat dinner with a spork. Because you loved me. For who I am. And I promise you, Morgan Cramer, that I will always put your needs before mine. Always make you feel like you are more than enough for me."

Sweat broke out along Lucy's hairline, yet her skin felt like winter had just swept through the room.

God was talking to her.

Again.

She knew what she needed to do. She just hadn't. Clare was right, she was good enough. She wasn't second-rate, and it was time she started living like it.

There Alex sat. On the fifth row. Waiting for her. Because he knew she would come to him after the service. They simply existed in this twisted holding pattern. Well, Lucy Wiltshire wasn't going to let the game clock keep running. It was time to reclaim her backbone. She was through not being enough—to herself and everyone else.

"You may kiss your bride."

The wedding guests clapped and hooted. Some teens stood and high-fived. There was nothing elegant about Morgan's Chuck. Or the people he hung out with. Herself included.

Guests made their way to the reception hall while the wedding party took pictures. Lucy struggled to focus on the camera as the church emptied out and Alex sat alone in his pew.

The last picture snapped, and the remaining group answered the siren's call of cake and watered-down punch. Except Lucy.

Her peep-toe heels clicked on the floor as she walked to where Alex sat, hands folded over the seat in front of him, looking like a fallen angel just stopping by.

He took her hand, kissed her fingers, and pulled her closer. "I can't stop looking at you."

"Thanks."

Head angled, he leaned toward her.

She halted him with a hand.

"Afraid I'll mess up your lipstick?"

She simply looked at him. The pull to him was so tangible she wondered that there weren't cords tethered between them. "Did I ever tell you about my senior year?"

His eyes studied her, and she knew he was trying to figure out her play. "No."

"My mom and I had moved to Florida to live with her fiancé, Robert," she said. "I had this whole life in front of me. A new school. College." Even after all these years, the memories still had the power to suffocate. "Then the car wreck, and . . . she was gone. And my dream of a home and family died with her." Lucy inhaled and pushed through, because if she didn't, she'd falter and hand Alex her soul. "Suddenly Robert was a single parent, and he couldn't handle it. I went to a few foster homes, but nothing worked out. By the time I left the last one, I still had months to go before I could move to my dorm at the university. So . . . I lived in my car."

"Babe—" He reached for her, but she shrugged his hand away.

"I know what Marinell's life is like. I know what it's like to love your family so much it doesn't matter if you eat or have a place to sleep. And I know what it's like to be so utterly alone you don't know how you're going to get through the day. How you're going to survive in a world that suddenly considers you an adult. I was lucky—many of these kids *don't* survive it."

There was such a look of hurt on Alex's face, she had to close her eyes. He cared, but it couldn't be enough. Not this time. "God pulled me out of that. And for years I let Satan use it to keep me down. But I'm through being the girl who was left behind."

"Luce." He ran his hand down her arm. "I had no idea."

She met his gaze, dared him to look away. "Do you love me?"

His eyebrows slammed together as he frowned. "I know last night was crazy. Maybe I didn't make much sense," he said. "After the election—"

"Don't spin this, Congressman Sinclair." The politeness dissolved from her tone. "What exactly is it you feel for me?"

"I . . ." He was caged. Trapped. They both knew it. "I think you're an amazing person. I love spending time with you."

So that was it. She was still just an expensive prop. Nothing more than a political chess piece and a fun friend. "You know, I thought becoming your fiancée would go down as the biggest mistake of my life." The sanctuary walls closed in on her with each word. "But I seem to have topped that—by falling in love with you."

"Lucy, I—"

"Don't say it." She jerked away from his reach, facing the altar. Retreating within. "Just tell me." She wiped away tears, angry at herself that she couldn't command them to stop. "Do you feel anything for me? Or am I strictly just a means to an end? Was this part of the plan? Make me fall for you so I'd play a more convincing fiancée?"

"I care about you." He leaned forward, forcing her to look at him. "And there's no reason why we shouldn't continue seeing each other after the election. You're an important part of my life."

"How important?"

He said nothing.

"What's going to happen on October fifteenth?"

Alex took a steadying breath. "We tell people we're busy and need more time to plan the wedding. It doesn't have to be a problem."

"Oh, it's a problem." Her laugh was bitter. "Don't you get it? I'm no better than all those stupid girls in *People*. I went and fell for you and thought I was different. Because that's what unites all of us ladies, Alex. We all thought we were the exception."

"You are." His raised voice bounced off the cathedral ceiling. He stood and towered over her. "I have never let someone in the way I have you. You and I are good together—you can't deny that. Are you just going to throw that away because I'm not ready to book the chapel?"

"And where exactly do you see us headed?"

"I still want us to be together. Why do we have to talk future right now? You don't even *want* to be a politician's wife."

No, but she wanted to be Alex's.

"Marriage isn't in my plans," he said, his frustration building. "I've been honest about that. And you also know politics is a team sport. Can you honestly tell me you're up for a lifetime of black-tie dinners and seeing your picture in the press? Do you want to marry that?"

"You say you don't know what's going to happen to us after the election, but I do. Anyone who's ever read one article on your personal life could guess this ending. You'll keep me around a few weeks, but then when you're all secure in Congress, you'll look at me and try to remember why you'd needed me in the first place. You'll have things to do and people to see. And I won't fit into that agenda."

"That's real fair."

"And as history repeats itself, you'll grow bored, and you'll kindly let me go. I'm sure you'll be all charming about it—make me feel like it's the best thing for me. That you're doing me a favor."

He didn't even try to argue. His playbook was no secret.

"So you're just going to walk away?" Anger thrummed in his voice. "Break the engagement?"

"I'll honor our agreement. But on election night, I'm done. You can twist that story however you like for the press. And you can even keep your money. It turns out, I'm a little bit rich." She slipped the diamond ring off her finger. It was one more lie she couldn't stand to look at. "And you can keep this as well."

He held it between two fingers, his eyes fierce. "Fine." Lucy had cut his pride, hit him where no woman had dared. "Walk away. So I get my votes and you get what?"

"Hopefully," she said, "what's left of my dignity."

"I've never lied to you about where we were headed."

"No. But I've been lying to myself." Her heart was a piece of glass, shattered in his warrior's hands. "And this time, I'm not going to be the one left behind."

❧

Alone, Lucy joined the wedding party in the reception hall of the church. She had to pull it together, because this was Morgan's day, and she didn't want to ruin it.

Cake. She needed cake.

Lucy exchanged pleasantries with a few friends as she made her way to the table that held a giant cake in the shape of the Millennium Falcon, the aircraft Han Solo had used to storm the galaxy.

"Hello, Lucy."

She slid her fork into fluffy icing and turned at the voice.

"Hello, Matt."

She waited for the onslaught of feelings, the attack of memories. But it didn't come.

"Nice wedding," he said.

"Yes." The cake tasted like dust in her mouth. She simply couldn't eat. "I didn't know you were here." She'd had eyes for only one man in that chapel.

Dressed in a charcoal-gray suit, Matt presented a dashing picture. Yet her heart didn't give the slightest flutter.

"I wondered if maybe you and I could meet sometime," he said. "Talk."

She shook her head. "I don't think so."

He took a step closer, and she inhaled his familiar cologne. "I can't let this go," he whispered roughly. "I know I hurt you. But I also know we belong together."

She set her cake down, brushed some crumbs from her fingertips. "On paper, yes. We do. But in reality? Matt, you like me because I'm comfortable. Familiar. You were forced out of your routine in Dallas." Lucy gave a small smile. "And for a long time I adored the thought of you—your stability. I loved knowing you'd go to work every day, keep a roof over my head, and return in time for dinner. I could trust your kindness. Your predictability." How had she ever thought she could spend the rest of her life with Matt? "I loved you. But I loved your safety even more."

His eyes pierced hers. "And Sinclair's what you want?"

"Love is what I want." Her ring finger looked empty on her hand. "And this time, I'm not settling." She leaned on tiptoe and kissed him on the cheek. "And neither should you."

Chapter Forty-one

*A*lex sat in his office at the campaign headquarters and twirled a Montblanc in his fingers. He had given everyone the night off, and the place was empty.

Like him.

He threw his pen across the desk where it bounced off a phone, rolling off the edge and onto the floor.

I love you.

Lucy's words played on repeat in his brain. The image of her face when she'd said it—it wouldn't leave him alone. The way he'd brushed her off. The things he couldn't give. It wasn't in the plan. Besides being the antidote to his reputation woes, Alex had picked her because she was safe. Someone he didn't have to worry about falling for.

But then he'd gotten to know her. She had stood up to him. Made him laugh. She wasn't impressed with his face, his physique, his Sinclair name, or his million-dollar passing arm. When Lucy looked at him, she saw the *real* him.

The last thing he wanted anyone to see.

The election was in two weeks. Alex didn't know if Lucy would make good on her promise to stand by him, but he couldn't imagine her not being there. He still needed her. She just didn't need him—not with her money and her demands.

He looked at the latest poll numbers on his phone. His lead was small but steady. The thought of losing had Alex waking up in a cold sweat every night. This bid for Congress was all he had. He hadn't even thought beyond that. If he didn't win, he would be just another sad retired ballplayer. That stupid *Dancing with the Stars* would probably call. Alex didn't *paso doble* for anyone. And what about ESPN? He didn't want to sit next to Troy Aikman and talk about games he wasn't playing and no longer cared about.

God, what am I supposed to do here?

His brother was gone. Now Lucy. Maybe even his career.

And just where did that leave him?

⁓

Lucy walked into Clare's house and shut the door behind her. She would pack up her things and leave tomorrow, whether the apartment was ready or not. It was past time she got back to the real world.

"There you are!" Julian intercepted her in the hall. "Come, come." With sweeping hands he beckoned. "Join us in the living room."

She was too exhausted to protest, so she just followed doggedly behind.

"Where've you been?" Sanjay stood next to Larry, one of the original Hobbits, who was cutting into what looked like a wing of the wedding cake. "Chuck and Morgan gave us the leftover cake, so Julian and Clare invited us over." He reached for a plate balanced on the Ming vase and grabbed her a fork.

"I'm not really hungry," Lucy said.

"Did all that wedding stuff stress you out?" Julian sidestepped two more Hobbits, reeling her in for a side-hug. "Don't worry. I'm going to help you out with your big day." His face pulled into a pout. "Though with only three months left, if anyone has reason to stress, it's your wedding coordinator. These things don't come together overnight, you know."

Clare walked into the room, in deep conversation with one of Sanjay's newest recruits. "But I don't understand why you'd *want* to teleport." She took a bite of cake. "What if you zapped yourself to New

York City and your cells got messed up and your nose was stuck to your—" Clare's mouth clamped shut as she got one look at Lucy and lowered her fork. "My dear, your makeup is all melted and your hair— completely mussed! We've gone over this. See me in my office at once." She charged out before Lucy could argue. Not that she felt like it.

With a resigned sigh, Lucy followed her down the hall and into the study. "I'm too tired for this right now. I know I totally messed up my updo but—"

"Enough!" Clare shut the door behind them and turned to face Lucy, arms crossed over her chest. "I don't care about your appearance."

Lucy blinked. "Do you have a fever?"

"Lucy, what in the *world* happened tonight?" Clare's face softened, and it proved Lucy's undoing. Tears sprang to the surface and flowed freely down her cheeks. "There, there." Clare reached out her arms, and Lucy went right to them. "Tell me all about it."

Heaving breaths kept Lucy from choking out the words.

"Did Alex hurt you?"

Lucy shook her head, then erased that answer with a nod.

"I can take care of that." Her fingers caressed Lucy's hair. "I know people."

Lucy sniffed, wiped her nose, then raised her aching head. "I broke up with Alex."

Her grandmother's eyes widened. "Why?"

One more step into the abyss wouldn't sink her any more than she already was. "Alex and I"—it shamed her to even put the thoughts to words—"we've been faking the engagement."

Clare said nothing.

Maybe she didn't understand. "We made a deal—I would pose as his wife-to-be until the election, and he would give me the funds for Saving Grace." The woman was clearly in shock. Offended to the tips of her pedicured toes. Lucy spoke slower this time. "I'm not really engaged to Alex—we staged the whole thing."

"Well, I know that."

Now it was Lucy's turn to go still. "What did you say?"

Clare *pffftd* and flopped her hand. "Please, I wasn't born yesterday. I've been in this business a long time, and I've seen it all. I could smell the deceit like stale Chanel."

"So . . . we haven't been convincing?"

"On the contrary, you've done a wonderful job." Her eyes shimmered with perception. "So good, you bought into it yourself, didn't you? You're in love with him."

Lucy wanted to curl in bed, pull the covers over her head, and never leave. "Maybe."

"And by maybe you mean—"

"That my heart stopped beating today, and I'm pretty sure it's going to rot and decay right in my chest." She was a rambling idiot. Nothing made sense right now. It was supposed to—she had done all the right things. Shaken off the lies and stepped into the woman God wanted her to be. And she just felt . . . empty.

"You get a good night's rest, and then in the morning I have a feeling your Alex will be here before Julian can flop the pancakes, begging to have you back."

No, she didn't get it. "He doesn't love me."

"Nonsense! How could he not?" Clare's outrage almost made Lucy smile. "You are charming, beautiful, intelligent, and you have a heart of gold—though sometimes your head for historical facts can be a bit lacking. But—I've seen the way he looks at you." She patted Lucy's cheek. "That boy loves you. Maybe he just doesn't know it yet."

"He's a smart guy. I think he's pretty clear on how he feels." And he had shared that insight with Lucy word by heart-wrenching word.

Clare gasped with a new idea. "We should pray!"

Lucy just wanted to collapse into bed.

"My pastor told me I'd be faced with moments like these." Clare's face filled with steely resolve. "My first chance to pray for someone in need. I can't wait to tell Julian. Let us go to the Lord. "

Lucy hoped it wouldn't be one of Clare's long-winded entreaties.

"Jesus, Alex is an imbecile, and you need to fix it." Clare nodded once. "Amen."

Chapter Forty-two

*H*e was nineteen again.

Alex drove toward his parents' house, remembering the time in college when the offensive coordinator had suddenly died. Dropped dead of a heart attack, completely rocking the young team. While the players had gathered at Joe's Bar and Grill, a favorite hangout of Coach Reilly's, Alex had driven eighteen grueling hours to Charleston, wanting the comfort only his family could provide.

Pulling into the driveway, Alex turned off the car, staring at the home of his youth. He missed them—his folks, Finley. And Will. Man, he missed Will.

Would they think it was strange he had shown up on their doorstep two hours before his final debate with Robertson? Would they think he was erratic? Immature? Addled?

He was all that. And he didn't know what to do.

But home was where things had always made sense. Filled with people he could count on. Who loved him. Who didn't just up and leave him when he needed them most.

Like Lucy. It had been two weeks since Morgan and Chuck's wedding. She had said she'd continue to hold up her end of the deal, but she'd missed almost every event since giving back his ring. Marinell's brother had taken another bad turn, and Lucy spent all her free time with the family at the hospital. Only a total pig would fault her for that.

And some days, he did consider reminding her of her contractual obligations—just to pick a fight. To see her again. Laugh with her. Argue. Tell her the election was coming down to the nose, and he was scared to lose. It all hinged on this last debate. But he and his team had worked hard, and Alex knew that smell in the air was victory.

Which still didn't explain why he was at his parents' home instead of reviewing his notes.

Marcus Sinclair answered the knock on his door. He took one look at Alex's face and shook his head. "I'll get the coffee. Meet you in the living room."

Alex paced along the hardwood floor as his mother walked in the room. "Alex." Those gentle eyes took quick inventory. "We were just getting ready to go to the university for the debate. Is everything all right?"

His father came back in, carrying two mugs. Glancing at his wife, he gave a small shake of his gray head. Donna Sinclair walked to her son and kissed him on the cheek. "I'll talk to you later."

Marcus handed Alex his cup of coffee and sat down on the loveseat. "Polls are looking good. I'll come down to the office this week and help make some calls. Your mom and I cleared a few days so we can join your door-to-door campaign. Gotta make the next seven days count."

Alex sat down on the adjacent couch and just stared at his hands. "Do you ever look at your life and wonder if any of it's worth it? If you even know what you're doing?"

Marcus took a slow sip and swallowed. "Well, now, I guess we all think about that. But normally I just look at your mother, at you kids, and then I know what it's all about."

"And your job," Alex said.

Marcus shook his head. "No. Maybe in the early days when I was obsessed with building the company. But what's the purpose of having all we do—of having any success—if you don't have people to share it with? If I didn't have your mother cheering me on, it would be meaningless."

"Will got that." Bitterness burned the back of Alex's throat. "He was just born with a sense of purpose."

Marcus studied his son. "Doesn't mean you weren't. Life took you in a different direction. You've been living your Hollywood life, then God got a hold of you and brought you back down to reality. Of course it's going to take some time to adjust."

"Lucy left me." He couldn't tell his dad about the engagement. It was too much. It was humiliating and so far beyond what a child of Marcus Sinclair would ever do. "Two weeks ago. Said I couldn't commit."

"I'd say the ring on her hand is a pretty good commitment."

Alex left that alone. "I couldn't tell her I loved her."

"Do you?"

Leaning into the couch, Alex let his head loll back and covered his eyes with his arm. "Since I was in high school, it's been all about football. About being the best. And I didn't have to work at relationships. They were always just . . . there."

"But Lucy's different."

In so many ways. And he missed every one of them. "She's the last person I would've picked for myself. She's independent. She's smart and she—"

"Doesn't worship you?"

Alex peered at his father. "No."

"And I'm guessing she doesn't care about all the things the other women did—your money, your looks, your fame." Marcus smiled and ran a hand over his stubbly face, a habit passed down to his son. "And that scares you."

"She's so . . ." He couldn't even put it into words. "She's just so good."

"And how is it a son of mine thinks he's not worthy?"

"It's not that."

"Isn't it?" His father's voice was stern, like he was warming up to ground him. "You look at Lucy and see all that you're not."

The truth settled in, and Alex let it spin in his head. "She and Will would've made quite a pair."

"No," Marcus said. "She chose you. Because she sees what the rest of us see."

And even though they had staged an engagement, Lucy *had* chosen him. And he'd thrown it right back in her face.

"Life is fleeting, Alex." His father's tone darkened. "Look at Will's life—cut so short. If you died today, would you go happy? Without regrets?"

He could fill a football stadium with his should-haves. Was Lucy one of them?

"When I look at you, I still see the son I love more than my own life. But I also see a man who has become so far removed from what matters that his perception is skewed. Family is real, son. A home to settle into—that's real. People who love you and care about you. You've had a phenomenal career, and I'm proud of you. But it's time to stop basing your worth on championships and endorsement deals. You can't buy happiness. You can't earn it. God isn't counting all the deals you're racking up—and neither is your family." He lifted his brow. "And neither is Lucy. For the first time someone's looking at the person inside—and you have to decide if you're going to let her in and be the man she needs you to be." His father turned his head toward a family picture on the mantel. "It's a risk. But one I've never regretted."

But he had goals. A timeline. "This doesn't fit with my plan."

His dad laughed. "I love it when God takes a big stirring spoon to plans. That's when life gets good."

Alex could hear his mother in the kitchen. She would be rummaging through her cookbooks like she always did when she worried. "I'm sorry I haven't been around, Dad."

He smiled. "We're all going to be okay. As long as we hold on to the things that really matter. And you're going to have to decide what that is."

Alex glanced at his watch. "I should go."

"We'll be in the audience. Praying for you. Cheering for you." His father stood up and clasped him on the shoulder. "Believing in you."

Alex's pocket buzzed, a small sound magnified in the quiet of the room.

"Better get that," Marcus said. "Might be your girl."

And what would he do if it was? Alex lifted his phone from his pocket and checked the display.

Clare.

If she was calling him to get another box of Sinclair for Congress pens, she was fresh out of luck. "Yes?"

"It's Lucy," Clare said. "She's gone."

"What do you mean?"

"Marinell took a bus to Tennessee to find her dad. Carlos is fading fast, and his father is a donor match—"

"What does this have to do with Lucy?"

"She's trying to intercept Marinell. But it's dangerous, Alex. Mrs. Hernandez is frightened at what could be waiting for them if they go looking for her husband."

"When did they leave?"

"Marinell caught the four o'clock bus. Lucy must've left about an hour later. Julian just found her note."

"I'm on my way."

Alex headed for the door. He would have to stop by the hospital and get the location from Mrs. Hernandez. Corral his security team. Call his campaign managers.

"Alex?" His dad followed him to the porch. "Where are you going? The debate starts in an hour."

"It's Lucy." Alex said. "She needs me."

And God couldn't make it any more plain that he needed her.

Alex didn't explain. Didn't say good-bye.

Just ran out like a man possessed.

A man in love.

Chapter Forty-three

Nashville. Who hid out from Mexican drug lords in Music City?

It had taken Alex half an hour to get the address out of a hysterical Esther Hernandez. Another hour to charter a private jet for him and his five-man security team to Nashville International. The pilot had robbed him blind, but Alex would've handed over every cent he had. Whatever it took to get Lucy and Marinell safely back home. And with any luck, he'd bring back Mr. Hernandez as well.

"This is career suicide," David Spear had said.

Lauren, his other campaign manager had agreed, going so far as to threaten to quit. "You won't recover from this, Alex."

They were both right. But it was a chance he had to take. Carlos's nurse had painted a grim picture. If Jose Hernandez could save the boy, then Alex had to get the man to Charleston.

While the security team conferred in the back of the plane, Alex sat up front, watching the clouds go by. The debate would be in progress right now. His opponent would be using the time to rehash all the reasons why he was the man for the job. And why Alex wasn't. David was standing in for Alex, and he would do a good job. But he wasn't Alex. And unless the Lord blessed the local TV network with a power outage, the viewing audience would definitely notice the substitution.

The campaign was over.

Alex took a sip of water from his bottle and then dug into his messenger bag. He bypassed his *Sports Illustrated*, his *New York Times*, and even his laptop. His fingers closed around familiar leather binding, and he pulled out Will's worn Bible.

He flipped through the filmy pages, his eyes drifting over the verses his brother had highlighted, written next to. Alex could almost feel Will. Sense him near.

He came to the pages marked by a frayed blue ribbon and stopped. The book of Luke, written by a healer. His brother had touched these pages. Underlined them. Committed them to memory.

For where your treasure is, there your heart will be also.

Words written in red, circled by Will. And lived.

Jesus, I've listened to the lies too long. They've filled my head and led me on a long chase of things that don't matter. I bought into what Satan was feeding me until I barely recognized my own face in the mirror. It took Will's death and Lucy's leaving to show me where my priorities should be.

I want to live for you.

I just . . . want to live.

"Buckle up," the pilot said. "We're ready for takeoff."

∽

Nine hours in a car.

Lucy's nerves were completely shredded, and her butt was numb. In the dark of the early morning, she pulled into the bus depot, a prayer on her lips. She picked up her phone and tried to call Marinell again. Still no answer. She supposed that's how Alex probably felt about now. According to her display, he had called over twenty times. And she hadn't answered once.

It had been tempting, though. To pick up the phone, tell him what was going on. Hear his calm voice tell her he was going to fix it.

But she couldn't do that. Couldn't run to him just because she was scared and needed someone to make the trouble go away.

Her flats slapped on the pavement as she ran toward the Greyhound station. Though it was a warm eighty-two degrees, Lucy's flesh crawled with chill bumps as she tried not to look at her surroundings. The old buildings seemed to lean in and stare at her from the darkness.

She swung open the entrance door.

And found Alex Sinclair.

Lucy blinked twice to be sure. But there he sat, lounged back in a ripped blue seat, his elbows resting on his knees. And those brown eyes trained right on her.

Relief swooshed through her every cell. Safety was just a few feet away.

But so was heartache.

It hurt just to look at him.

"What are you doing here?" She tried to keep her voice even.

He pushed to his feet, drawing himself up tall. "Waiting for you."

Fatigue made her thoughts thick. "Why?"

"Just decided to take a little evening flight."

"Clare called you." Piece by piece, the shapes began to fit together. "Alex, the debate—"

"Did you honestly think I wouldn't come after you?"

She looked at the clock on the wall. After all they'd been through, he'd *skipped* the main event? "What are you thinking—just walking away like that? After everything you've put into that campaign? After all *I* put into that campaign!" She drilled her finger into his chest. "I wore coordinating pantsuits for you."

"If anyone has any explaining to do, it's you." Alex didn't even try to lower his voice among the handful of people. "You're going to help Marinell hunt down a man with a death sentence on his head? You thought it would be okay to intercept an eighteen-year-old kid, then go visit a guy who's basically a walking time bomb?"

Lucy blinked twice. "Did you get the part where I said I made bad clothing choices for your campaign?"

"I love you, Lucy."

Her eyes widened, and she took a step back. "Don't do this, Alex."

"I know this isn't the time or the place, but you have to know I am crazy about you. I was wrong. This whole time I've been wrong, and I'm sorry it took me so long to figure it out."

The words somersaulted through her heart but crashed in her head. "But I think you were right," she said in a hush. "We'd never work. I'm never going to be that perfect woman you think you need."

"What I *need* is you."

A small crowd had gathered behind them. "You tell her, Playboy."

"I want you," he said. "Just the way you are. With your crazy dresses and hot pink shoes. Your weird sci-fi books. And your laugh. And that hideous car." Alex reached out that strong hand and cupped her cheek. "I love your heart for your girls."

"Stop," she said, finding her voice. "I can't do this."

"I need you to understand—"

"What I know is that we're over. I was stupid to tell you I loved you. Out of my mind to think we had a future."

"You love me, Lucy Wiltshire."

"Yes." Hope pushed to the surface, but she shoved it right back down. "But what you feel for me isn't love. You just can't stand to lose—with me *or* the election."

"There's a very good chance I lost that Congressional seat tonight. And I don't think I even care." His voice was a balm to all the rough places in her heart. "Because it's nothing without you. All this time, I've had it so wrong. I've been trying to measure up, prove myself to the world." His hands moved to clasp her shoulders, draw her closer. "All I want to do is spend the rest of my life proving myself to you."

Between the smell of the man two rows over and Alex's early morning confession, Lucy's eyes stung with tears. "I don't even know what to say," she whispered. "I'm afraid you're going to keep talking until you hear yourself. And then you're going to realize you're making a huge mistake."

His eyes never leaving hers, Alex pushed aside a McDonald's wrapper with his foot.

Then went down on one knee.

His hand reached for hers, held it tight. "Lucy," he said in the middle of the Greyhound bus station. "In front of Lou, Squid, ten travelers, and one hobo, I'm asking you to become my wife." His smile dimpled his cheek. "A few months ago we crossed a line, went too far. And somehow God still used it for our good. I can't do this life without you. Please," he said. "Please marry me."

There was love reflected in his face. And it was all for her.

"Let me be your family."

Lucy Wiltshire had finally found home.

"Yes." She struggled to breathe. "Yes."

He reached into the pocket of his black blazer and pulled out her ring. The very same one that had started it all. Slipping it on her hand, he kissed her finger.

A scattering of people clapped as Alex stood up, picked Lucy up off her feet, and crushed his mouth to hers.

"Tell me you love me," he said. "I need to hear it again."

"I love you, Alex."

"I've been miserable without you."

"I'm so glad." Lucy held tight until her pulse slowed to only a gallop. "So . . . besides stopping in Greyhound bus stations in the middle of the night and proposing to women, what are you doing here?"

Alex held her hand and looked at the ring back in its rightful place. "We're going to get Marinell." He jerked his chin toward the brute squad of men behind them. Lou wiggled his fingers in greeting. "Then we go get Jose Hernandez."

"Any exposure could endanger the Hernandez family," Lucy said. "You'll never be able to tell the media where you were tonight."

"I knew that before I even stepped on the plane."

"I don't care what Eli Manning and Tony Romo say." She ran her finger down his jaw. "You, Alex Sinclair, are a wonderful man."

❦

An hour later Lucy walked out of the bus station with Marinell. She knew before Alex said a word the rented black Escalade in the lot was theirs.

"Will Tupac be joining us?" Lucy climbed in the back beside Marinell.

Alex's mouth curled in a smile as he squeezed in beside his fiancée. "Now you're just trying to hurt my feelings." He leaned back in the seat and rested his arm on her shoulder.

"Are you sure these guys know what they're doing?" Marinell pointed to the two giants in the front seat. One more car drove a few minutes ahead of them, carrying even more men who seemed to value large muscles, bald heads, and indecipherable tattoos.

"We're going to get your father back," Alex said. "I have a team in place at his house, and they've already made contact with your dad." His casual tone was meant to comfort and put Marinell at ease. "As long as he follows Squid's directions, it will be a piece of cake."

Lucy wished she could climb inside Alex's mind and see if he was telling the truth. She had no idea what they were getting into, and her fear coiled like a spring.

Alex's hand settled over Lucy's clutched fist. "I'm asking you to trust me. I'm not going to let anything happen to you or Marinell."

Half an hour stretched into an eternity, until the car finally stopped. The headlights went off, and Squid bailed out of the passenger side. The doors locked with a loud click as the Escalade sat there on the deserted dirt road. A line of telephone poles the only sign of civilization.

"I hope he's okay," Marinell whispered in the quiet.

"He will be," Lucy said with more conviction than she felt. "Did I mention I'm grounding you for life when we get back home?"

Marinell's long ponytail bobbed as she nodded. "Toilet scrubbing duty?"

Lucy patted her knee. "With your toothbrush."

The next hour was spent alternating between praying, reminding Marinell they would all be fine, and wanting to pinch herself that Alex was beside her.

The man in the driver's seat touched his earpiece. He spoke in hushed tones before turning to Alex. "The area is secure. Target is safe and en route."

Lucy released the breath caught in her lungs and hugged Marinell to her. Alex just smiled.

Within minutes the other black SUV crawled down the road. The vehicle stopped beside them, and the back door opened.

"Papi!"

With a nod from Alex, Marinell flung open her door and ran into her father's waiting arms.

Lucy watched the scene for a moment before turning her gaze to Alex. "Thank you," she said. "The things you've done for this family—"

"It was worth it."

"Tonight," she said. "But will it be next week? A year from now?"

"Everything has led me to this moment, Luce. You, me, helping Carlos. That's all that counts." He tucked her to his side as they both watched Jose hold his daughter. "Do you have any idea how much you've changed my life?"

"You have a new appreciation for *Star Trek*?" Lucy nestled into the comfort of his arm and reached for the hand she would hold for the rest of her life. They had traveled in the wrong direction, two wandering souls, not knowing where they fit in the world. But God had drawn them together, despite it all.

Alex was her heart, her life, her white picket fence.

"We have to call Clare when we get back," Alex said. "Tell her she has a wedding to plan."

Lucy could see it now. Her new family. Friends. Marinell and the rest of her girls. With Alex at her side, they would start a new chapter. She would become his bride. And it would be the most perfect day.

Just as long as Clare didn't pick out her dress.

Epilogue

Three Years Later

The sun shone down, filtering through the palmetto leaves and bathing Charleston in a hug of steamy heat. The clouds bloomed white in the sky, and the birds sang lilting songs from the trees. It was a beautiful day for a celebration.

Lucy stood by her husband as they cut the oversized red ribbon. The gathering crowd assembled in the yard and clapped as a photographer from the *Gazette* snapped their picture.

The small ceremony over, Esther Hernandez stepped out of the house and onto the wraparound porch. "You come in now," she said. "We eat cake."

"I do love the way that woman thinks," Julian said, speed-walking past Lucy and heading straight inside.

As family and friends made their way into the house for a private celebration, Lucy lagged behind. She stopped in the middle of the yard and just took it all in. It was a two-story home with white shutters and pink clapboard siding that stood out like a smile for the entire street.

Alex stood beside her and slipped his arm over her shoulders. "It never gets old, does it?"

Lucy leaned her head against him, her heart full. "It just never does."

It was the seventh home for young adults they had opened, each one just as special as the last. Many years ago Lucy's mother had cleaned in this house. On hands and knees, she had scrubbed until her daughter lacked for almost nothing. Anna Wiltshire had sacrificed for her, loved her. Her mother had made some wrong decisions, but the ring on Lucy's hand was a testimony that God still moved in those as well.

Holding open the door, Alex led Lucy inside to the dining room where everyone gathered. It was a noisy affair, full of loud voices, laughter, and faces Lucy loved.

"Sit," Esther said, pushing Lucy toward a chair. "Eat. I save corner piece just for you."

Lucy slid in beside Marinell, who was pouring Carlos a glass of punch. The Hernandez family had moved in, with Esther taking over as house mom. It was the perfect fit. She could watch Carlos grow strong, be near Marinell as she went to college, and still have plenty of time to cluck and fuss over the new girls who would fill all the bedrooms upstairs. Jose Hernandez remained a man in hiding, but thanks to Alex's access to security and Julian's knack for designing disguises, Jose had been able to move closer and be a more active part of his family's lives.

A familiar squeal brought a smile to Lucy's face as Clare came down the hall, a curly-headed one-year-old in her arms.

"Come here, Will." Alex reached for his son. "Did that mean old lady scare you?"

"He's just hungry," Clare said.

"And desperate to get away from you." Julian rolled his big blue eyes. "Grammy's got the flash cards out again."

Clare raised her patrician nose. "It's never too early to learn about our past presidents. I hope to see Will's beautiful face on these cards one day."

Donna and Finley Sinclair helped serve cake and ice cream to all of Lucy's girls, including her first graduates. The moment filled her, until she thought she would explode into a thousand pieces of happiness.

Marcus Sinclair stood and raised his Dixie cup high. "To the Anna Wiltshire Home for Girls!"

Lucy clinked her glass to Alex's and blinked back the tears.

"When does the next boys' home open?" Finley asked, looking a little too interested.

"Next month." Alex handed the chubby baby to Lucy. Their third boys' home was one of three slated to open over the next two years, with Alex at the helm. He already had some close friends lined up to mentor the young men. Like Chuck. And Sanjay. And some Warriors, Panthers, and Cowboys. When Alex wasn't overseeing their new foundation for the advancement of graduated foster children, he was storming Capitol Hill, speaking to Congress about foster care reform. Her husband had become a champion for the rights of young adults, and a handful of states had started similar programs.

Lucy kissed Will's little fist as he waved it in the air.

"Working on that arm already," Alex said. "I see a Heisman Trophy in his future."

Lucy laughed and ran a hand over their son's white curls. "He can be anything he wants to be. Athlete, humanitarian, scientist. We're not going to pressure him."

"Don't think I didn't hear you reading him your *Star Wars* book last night."

Lucy frowned. "Puts him right to sleep."

"Don't let it get you down, babe."

"You've spoiled him with SportsCenter. It's all he wants."

"Because my kid's a genius."

Lucy smiled as Alex sat down beside her, and Will gave a toothy grin. "Do you ever wonder what if?" She watched Clare make peek-a-boo faces across the table. "What if you'd gone to that debate, won the election?"

Alex leaned over and pressed his smiling lips to hers. "Then we wouldn't have all this."

And this was more than Lucy could have ever dreamed. Sweeter than Southern iced tea. Bigger than Dixie. And blessed beyond the Charleston treetops.

Tonight she would put down the book and tell her son a story instead. How once upon a time a handsome football star had walked into her office and asked her to marry him. How a first lady had invited Lucy into her aristocratic family. And God had told her to just let the past go.

And they all lived happily ever after.

Because Lucy Wiltshire . . . had said yes.

Acknowledgments

The author is just one of many involved in creating a book. I am very grateful to the following people:

The entire Thomas Nelson fiction team, for being a wonderful home for me and this book.

Natalie Hanemann, for hanging in there and pushing me to kick it up a notch. Or ten notches.

Becky Monds, for your help and input, as well as your brilliant reflections on YA lit and the WWE.

Jamie Chavez, for talking me off a few ledges, for your brain, your creativity, your encouragement, and for always being willing to brainstorm and help me make the books better. Even when I say things like, "I need an entire plot. Any suggestions?"

Chip MacGregor, for giving great award acceptance speeches and for thinking I'm a better person and writer than I am. Praying you continue to stay unenlightened . . .

Jen Deshler, for laughs. Also for laughs. And don't forget giggles.

Katie Bond, for all your generous help in setting research. And for helping me plan a little vay-kay. You are one gracious Southern belle.

Ashley Schneider, for all you do and for being one of the funniest gals I know.

Erin Valentine, for reading every page. A million times. And not barfing.

U. S. Senator John Boozman, for taking time out of your busy schedule to talk to me about the intense, demanding life of a politician. I so respect your values, your heart, and your generosity. You are a good, good man. Any errors in political facts can only be attributed to my gift for mistakes.

Jody McAnally, for going out of your way to help me research and talk to a real live politician. You are awesome.

Laura Jones, for loving foster children and providing me with much-needed information. And for always bringing cheesy potatoes to family dinners. And for helping me reign in Mother and Aunt Judy at concerts.

My mother, for being a good parent. It matters. It makes a difference. And I'm grateful and blessed.

Cara Putman, for being *THE* best prayer warrior, encourager, and friend. By praying over me many months ago, the theme for *Save the Date* was born. Your friendship blesses me beyond measure, and I am humbly grateful.

Writer Sisters, for brainstorming, praying, and listening to me whine. You ladies are ridiculously inspiring. And make me look like a total slacker. (But I'm still gonna be your friend anyway.)

Rachel Hauck, for your writing help and encouragement when this book was just a handful of pages. I appreciate your time and giving spirit.

Becky Schaffer, creator and mama of the real Saving Grace, for reaching out to young women without parents, without homes, without hope. You're changing lives, hearts, and family trees, and I stand in awe of all you've come through and all you give back.

Tiffany Savage, for introducing me to Saving Grace. I would thank you for more, but I'm still mad at you for leaving the state of Arkansas. What some girls will do for an IKEA.

Kent Hughes, for calling and checking on me during deadlines to see if I was still alive. And for providing the occasional meal during those times when I couldn't even dredge up the energy to wash my hair or prepare anything any more involved than a Lunchable.

Natalie Lloyd, for being an awesome writer, inspiration, and friend. I'm so grateful for your kind heart, sense of humor, listening ear, and mutual appreciation for things of high class. Like YouTube clips and inappropriate typos.

Leslie Sheridan, for your friendship and your football help. For answering all those questions that began, "Please don't laugh . . ." and "I know I'm a sports idiot, but . . ."

Reading Group Guide

1. Sometimes we think we've moved on from things, but God puts us in situations to show us otherwise. What "baggage" did God bring back to Lucy?

2. Has there been a time when you've had to revisit an old wound from the past? How did God use that in your life?

3. Describe the difference between Matthew and Alex. Do you believe what Lucy felt for Matthew was truly love? Explain.

4. Describe Lucy's motivation for the fake engagement. Describe some sacrifices you've made—as a mom, wife, daughter, employee, or Christian.

5. In what ways were Marinell and Lucy similar?

6. Imagine yourself in the shoes of one of the young women at Saving Grace. Describe what challenges these women face.

7. How can communities, churches, families, or individuals help kids who are in or have graduated from the foster care system?

8. How was Clare Deveraux blind to the truth of her son? Can you think of a time when you couldn't recognize an obvious truth?

9. Describe the fears that were holding Alex back. How did he finally push through them?

10. As a teen, Lucy was greatly impacted by the opinions of others—so much so that she carried that trauma into adulthood. Why do women have such a hard time with this? Why do we need the approval of others? If God were sitting down to tea with you, what do you think he'd tell you?

11. If you could go back and talk to your teen self, what would you say?

12. In the end, Lucy surrenders it all to God. What did she gain?

13. Where do you see Alex and Lucy twenty years from now?

The only thing scarier than living
on the edge is stepping off it.

A NOVEL OF LOSING FEAR
AND FINDING GOD

*Just Between
You and Me*

JENNY B. JONES

A Carol Award-winning novel

THOMAS NELSON
Since 1798

New York's social darling just woke up in a nightmare:
Oklahoma.

Problem is, it's right where God wants her.

About the Author

 *Jenny B. Jones* writes Christian Fiction with equal parts wit, sass, and untamed hilarity. When she's not writing, she's living it up as a high school teacher in Arkansas. Since she has very little free time, she believes in spending her spare hours in meaningful, intellectual pursuits, such as watching *E!*, going to the movies and inhaling large buckets of popcorn, and writing her name in the dust on her furniture. She is the four-time Carol Award-winning author of *Just Between You and Me* and the Charmed Life series for young adults.